Dancing Prophet

By Glynn Young

Permission to quote in critical reviews with citation:

Dancing Prophet

By Glynn Young

Print ISBN 978-1-949718-00-3

www.dunrobin.us

Dedicated to the blessings who are my three grandsons:

Cameron, Caden, and Jacob

The match that ignited the reformation of the Church of England was lit by three teenagers.

Chapter 1: The Agnostic

On a lightly rainy Friday in mid-September, Trevor Barry watched his two children, feeling the tube car rocking gently back and forth as they traveled toward central London. This was the journey they made together most weekdays from their home in Watford. Both Jane, 16, and Andrew, 12, attended the International Christian School in Notting Hill. He could see Jane was absorbed in *The Return of the Native* by Thomas Hardy, an assignment for her literature class. Andrew, judging by the scribbles he was making in a notebook, was working on maths.

Five mornings a week, their schedule called for Trevor's wife Liz to drive him and the children to Watford Junction to catch the overground train. The three of them would change to the tube at Queen's Park and then ride three or four stations to Paddington. There they'd change to a District or Circle Line train. Jane and Andrew would give him a quick kiss as they exited at Notting Hill Gate. Usually he'd continue on until Temple Station, a short two-block walk from his law chambers.

Today was different. Today he would exit at St. James's Park, for the three-block walk to Buckingham Palace, something he was now doing regularly once or twice a week.

Trevor loved his children dearly, even if he had trouble at times showing affection. He wanted to show affection; the problem had always been with the "how." Jane, a natural blond, had turned into what he considered a beauty. She had her mother's eyes and her father's narrow face and high cheekbones. She was a serious girl and a serious student, and he had worried about her seriousness until just the last few months. Then she had met a boy she truly seemed to like and suddenly blossomed.

Andrew looked like a smaller, younger version of his father, the same thoughtful eyes and narrow face, the same light brown hair, and likely the same six-foot height as he grew older. He had his mother's outgoing personality – gregarious, friendly, always ready with a joke. He also had a surprising tenderness, which Trevor recognized in himself from a long time ago, if not now. Andrew wasn't quite yet interested in girls but judging by the number of girls who called on the phone asking for help with homework, they were certainly interested in him.

When he thought back to when he was Andrew's age, all he could see was a dark, impenetrable wall. The wall frightened him; he didn't like to think about what was behind it. The wall also caused him to struggle with a natural tendency to be over-protective of his son.

Trevor knew he himself had built that wall. It kept the demons at bay. Most of the time.

He looked out of the window into the darkness of the underground. Almost ten months earlier, Trevor's life had changed with a single phone call from Josh Gittings, once the prime minister's political assistant but better known as the PM's hatchet man. Now chief of staff to King Michael, he'd contacted Trevor, asking him to meet with the king. Initially, it wasn't about legal advice. Instead, somehow Gittings had ferreted out Trevor's hobby and avocation – monarchial law and history. The new king, coming to the throne after the assassination of the royal family and what was called The Violence, was a young Anglican priest, raised in Scotland in a middle- to upper-middle-class family, and married to an American wife. The king, Gittings had said, needed help understanding the history, role, and legal considerations for being the monarch.

Trevor had been as stunned as his wife and his colleagues in chambers. He was known for his expertise in parliamentary law, with a secondary specialty in corporate law. He was frequently called upon by large corporations, government ministries, political parties, and others involved in the nation's lawmaking procedures. But never before had he been called upon to advise a king, and on a subject his colleagues often snickered at, thinking he wasn't aware of their jokes. Who cared about a subject as antiquated as the monarchy? He also knew that, behind his back, they called him "the Monarchist." He didn't mind.

As it turned out, someone did care, and care very much, about what Trevor knew: the new monarch, Michael Kent-Hughes. Word had quickly circulated in chambers; the snickers were soon silenced. Instead, his colleagues watched almost in awe as, within a few short months, Trevor's own practice grew and spilled over to their practices as well. No one joked about the Monarchist any more. Now they called him the "Rain Man," just not to his face.

Trevor had been utterly unprepared for Michael Kent-Hughes. Young, handsome, outgoing, and a priest, the man seemed full of life and possibility. He learned quickly, and Trevor had discovered how much he listened to and relied upon Gittings, his communications man Jay Lanham, and Queen Sarah.

And now upon Trevor Barry.

A series of reputation and political attacks before the coronation had had Trevor called to the palace on a regular basis. Most of their conversations focused on Michael's statutory authority with both the Church of England and Government. Trevor had also become a member of the Coronation Committee, advising the members on history, protocol, and procedure. He had brought in legal experts when needed; he himself had prepped the king for a meeting with Muslim protestors, who had made a number of demands upon Michael and Government.

He had watched the televised meeting with his colleagues in chambers. When it was over, he had stood and smiled. "The king did very well," he said. People in the room stared at Trevor almost with reverence. They knew who had advised the king; the chambers manager had told them about the training session.

Trevor and Liz had attended the coronation in May. Their status with the king and queen was signified by where they sat with Andrew – right behind Josh Gittings and his fiancée in the third row. Liz had been nearly beside herself – worrying endlessly about a dress and hat for the coronation and a dress for the ball at Buckingham Palace. Trevor's position with the king had been made plainly obvious by the fact that the Barry family had been given a large bedroom at the palace for their use during the day of the coronation festivities.

Jane had been an official guest of Jason Kent-Hughes, Michael and Sarah's adopted son who also attended International Christian School. He was a year older than Jane, but they shared several classes.

Trevor didn't fully know how Jason and his younger brother Jim had come to be adopted by Michael and Sarah, but both boys were Americans and from the San Francisco area. Trevor knew there had been a period of homelessness for Jason, but he really knew little beyond that.

Trevor had met Liz, a born-and-raised-in-London girl, at the University of London. He had just begun law studies; she was an undergraduate in economics. She had gone to the law library for a research project, and they'd literally run into each other when she rounded a book stack just as he walked up carrying an armful of case studies. Books and papers had gone flying. They had looked at one another with anger and surprise, and then both had burst out laughing, earning them more than one nasty look from students trying to study nearby.

They had begun to date and found themselves falling in love. As they dated, Liz introduced him to Christianity, but it was one very different from his own upbringing. Trevor had been raised Church of England but had left the church as a young teenager and not returned, to it or any other church, much to his parents' sorrow. Liz had been raised an Evangelical Presbyterian, and she had gradually and finally successfully coaxed Trevor to church. They dated for three years before Liz had finally asked him if he was going to marry her or not. They'd been married in the church Liz attended with her family in London. His own parents had been wild about their new daughter-in-law, amazed that Trevor had married a believing Christian. Before children came, Liz had worked in an investment bank in the City while Trevor had joined the same law chambers he worked with now.

When Jane arrived two years later, and Andrew four years after that, it had seemed natural to raise the children in Liz's church, even though Trevor had never formally joined and had never made any kind of formal or informal commitment to faith. He said her church was fine; what he seemed to have a problem with was with C of E churches, saying he didn't like all the liturgical trappings. But Liz's church was "low church," and liturgy was not an emphasis. Liz often worried about his lack of religious commitment, and would talk with him about it, but Trevor seemed almost determined to avoid it. He attended worship service with the family every Sunday, and Liz knew he did it more to please her than to learn or understand anything himself. When the time came for the children to start their education, Trevor had agreed with Liz to send the children to ICS.

Jane had not initially surprised them last March when she rather shyly told them that she had been invited to the coronation of

Michael and Sarah Kent-Hughes as king and queen. They knew that the two adopted sons of Michael and Sarah attended ICS, and that Jason Kent-Hughes was in her year. They assumed this was a school thing for the coronation.

"Is the whole class invited, Jane?" Liz had asked.

"Well, not exactly, Mother." She hesitated as she looked from her father to her mother. "Actually, Jason invited me, and Chris and Laura, too. He has three guest tickets for the coronation ceremony."

Trevor had arched his eyebrows. Jane had been on a few dates with various boys before, but this was the first mention of a connection to Jason Kent-Hughes. He and Liz had been given tickets to the ceremony and the formal ball, but this was the first he realized that his daughter might have a boyfriend, one who was a member of the royal family.

"That must be a great thrill, Jane," he'd said, smiling. "People rarely get an opportunity to actually attend the crowning of a king and queen."

She'd smiled and nodded at her father. "Oh, Dad, it's for the whole thing," she said excitedly, her eyes shining. "It's the coronation at Westminster Abbey, we get to ride with Jason in a carriage in the procession to the palace, and then the coronation ball and the big bash at Wembley Stadium. Jason said that you and Mother would have invitations to Wembley, too, if you were interested."

Liz stared at her daughter. "Jane, we had no idea you knew Jason this well." Trevor thought that was something of an understatement; he could see Liz was borderline put-out that Jane had never previously mentioned anything about Jason.

"Oh, Mother," she said, "he's wonderful. He's not like anything you'd expect, even from all the photos and stories in the newspaper. He's quiet and rather serious, but he's got the most beautiful eyes and smile. And you should see his paintings, they're just incredible for someone so young. He has some rough edges sometimes, I think it has to do with his background, but he's kind and considerate. And he's great fun. We met in the library, and then started studying together, and we've seen each other at parties and friends' houses. He's just wonderful."

As Jane went on about Jason, Trevor could see that his daughter had developed what was certainly her first major crush. And he reminded himself that this was the young man who had risked his own life to disarm the assailant of Sarah Kent-Hughes in the park in San Francisco the previous October.

"Jane," her mother asked, "has he said what his background is, or how he came to be adopted by the king? Michael's not that much older than Jason is." She looked at Trevor, who shook his head. He didn't know, either.

"He hasn't said much, Mother," Jane said. "I have an impression that his parents had given him up for adoption when he was much younger. He said he came to live with the Kent-Hughes not long after they were married in San Francisco."

What had surprised, and favorably impressed, both Trevor and Liz was that Jason had personally delivered the engraved coronation invitation for Jane, introduced himself, and very formally asked Trevor if he could take Jane to the coronation events, explaining exactly where they would be, who they would be with, and what time he would have her home. And he had been true to his word on all counts. Trevor had been impressed, and Liz had been wowed.

Trevor and Liz had gone to the coronation ball but decided that Wembley might be a bit beyond their age bracket. They had been at Westminster Abbey for the coronation, but were later surprised to see Jane, Chris and Laura on the balcony with the royal family, waving to the tens of thousands in front of the palace and identified by name by the newscasters as friends of Jason Kent-Hughes. Trevor had explained to Michael that the balcony tradition was for royals only, but Michael must have decided to break with tradition.

They'd watched Jason and Jane at the ball and had smiled at the thrilled look on Jane's face when King Michael had asked her to dance. ("That's a story she can tell her grandchildren and great-grandchildren," Liz told Trevor. "She danced with a king at his coronation ball.") They had later watched the celebration at Wembley Stadium on television with Andrew at home. When Jason delivered Jane home in a car driven by palace security at 2 a.m., right at the promised time, she and Liz had stayed up until dawn talking about all of what had transpired and reliving the entire day. Liz told Trevor later that of all the events and experiences their daughter had had, the one that had left the greatest impression was Jason's gentle kiss goodnight at the door, their daughter's first kiss by a boy.

Since the coronation in early May, Jason had become something of a fixture at the Barrys' home in The Ridgeway in Watford, an upper middle-class neighborhood of four-bedroom homes. Trevor could see that Jason was as taken with his daughter as she seemed to be with him. Jane's visits to the palace had initially worried Trevor that she might have her head turned by being around Michael and Sarah. But it simply hadn't happened. She seemed to take Jason's family in stride, and it likely helped that Michael and Sarah seemed to have gone out of their way to create something as close to a normal family life as possible.

"Sarah makes the king stay out of the kitchen when she's cooking dinner," Jane said, reporting on a dinner she shared with the family. "He's apparently hopeless when it comes to cooking. Jim tells wild stories of what it was like eating with his father before he and Sarah married. The king minds Hank, changes his diaper, and feeds him while she's doing a meal. And then he and Jason do the cleanup, with Jim required to clear the table."

Trevor didn't know what he was more impressed with – the queen cooking the family's dinner, the king changing a diaper, or the king and Jason cleaning up the dirty dishes. "It seems they're determined to have as normal a family life as possible in that fishbowl of a place," he said to Liz.

He found himself truly liking Jason. He could see what Jane had meant about "a bit rough around the edges," as if there had been gaps in his education or at least in some aspects of his social development, but the young man was both polite and could carry on a conversation incredibly well for what one normally expected from teenaged boys, especially when the conversation was with the parents of the girlfriend. And Jason told him a little about his background, confirming what Jane had said about being given up for adoption at an earlier age ("My mother had remarried, and my stepfather didn't want me"). Trevor assumed that he had been in some kind of foster care situation until adopted by Michael and Sarah. Liz really liked the boy as well, but Trevor felt a strong connection with the young man, as if the two of them were on a deeper level of communication than their surface conversation would indicate. And he had seen something of a similar response in Jason. For all the differences in our backgrounds, it was almost as if they could read each other's minds.

Their home was not far from the London Northwest Trail, which Trevor cycled as much as he could. He was something beyond being a cycle enthusiast; Liz often referred to him as the bike fanatic, which he himself admitted was closer to the truth. She often suggested that he find a friend to cycle with, and while he agreed that was a good idea, the fact was that Trevor had few if any male friends, and none who cycled.

He could feel the tube train slowing as they approached Notting Hill Gate Station. Jane stood and smiled as she leaned over and kissed Trevor's cheek, followed by Andrew doing the same.

13

"Have a good day, you two," Trevor said, smiling at his children. He watched them as they exited the car, quickly blending into the crowd.

He had to remind himself to exit at St. James's Park. The habit of exiting at Temple Station was sometimes too strong, and he needed to arrive at the palace early. Michael wanted to talk with him privately before the advisory meeting started. It was a meeting unlike any Trevor had ever considered attending – a small group of church and lay people quietly drawn together to begin discussions of what a reformed Church of England might look like.

Michael had been giving sermons at various churches in the London area since he had arrived the previous December. He was drawing increasingly large crowds to hear his message on reforming and rebuilding the church. His sermon at Southwark Cathedral had remarkably started something of a revival in the diocese, to the point where the newspapers even published stories about it. And Michael's speech at a bishops' conference two weeks before the coronation had rocked the Anglican world, inspiring both a backlash from the church hierarchy, widespread support from Anglican churches in Africa and Asia, and the introduction of several proposals in Parliament, mostly as amendments to previously introduced legislation. But parliamentary progress had slowed; the proposals seemed to have become bottled up in committee hearings.

Trevor recognized the irony of him, an agnostic on a good day and essentially nothing on most days, being relied upon for advice and counsel by a deeply Christian king. Michael knew where Trevor stood spiritually, which was anywhere except belief, but that hadn't stopped Michael from relying upon him and fully trusting him. At first surprised, Trevor had come to appreciate how much the king's trust meant.

He had also begun to understand how much the king was part of something larger than himself, and it had begun to unsettle Trevor's decades-old comfort with agnosticism. Liz carried the spiritual leadership in their home, and he was content with that. But he had never made any kind of personal decision or commitment.

And he knew Liz often wondered why; he had overheard her quietly talking with his parents when they visited from his hometown in Yorkshire. She knew Trevor had been raised an Anglican; his father had told her that after age 12 or 13, Trevor had adamantly refused to attend church.

"He'd been so involved before that," Trevor's mother had said to Liz. "But then he just refused to go anymore."

Trevor knew his unsettled feelings had begun in a conversation he'd had with Josh Gittings. Trevor had been surprised that someone with Gittings' reputation had thrown over politics to work with the King. He was equally surprised that someone with Michael's reputation had hired Gittings as his chief of staff. Gittings himself had been completely candid about it, acknowledging what was on Trevor's mind the first time the two men met, and openly discussing his reputation as something of a political shark. And then, later, a second conversation had left Trevor with a strong sense of personal disquiet.

After a meeting with Michael, Gittings and Trevor had walked together to the palace's security entrance and then to the St. James's Park tube station. Trevor headed east to return to his offices in the Temple and Gittings headed west for lunch with Zina Chatwick, his fiancée, in Chelsea near Sloane Square.

"In a way," Trevor had said as they walked, "well, perhaps more than one way, it's rather an odd thing that Michael finds himself on the throne."

"What do you mean?" said Josh.

"Well, the fact that he was a priest, for starters," Trevor said. "Britain's royals have always had either direct military experience or some strong tie to the military. Even Queen Elizabeth was in the military in World War II, and King James had done his obligatory duty at Sandhurst. But Michael is the first ordained priest ever to become king, without any military experience whatsoever."

"I had this very conversation with Father John Stevens in San Francisco," Gittings said. "He was the senior minister at St. Anselm's."

"I met him and his wife at the coronation," Trevor said. "Delightfully charming gentleman."

Gittings nodded. "He'd worked very closely with Michael for two years, and he had some solid insights into both Michael's ministry and Michael as a man. When I made that same observation about Michael being a priest who became king, Father John just chuckled. 'Why do you think that might be?' he asked. I said I had no idea other than coincidence, and he said God doesn't work in coincidences."

"What did he say?" Trevor said.

"He said that God picks the man needed for the job at hand. And wasn't it fascinating that Michael had essentially been exiled to the hinterlands as a child, reared completely away from anything even remotely royal, felt called into the priesthood when he was relatively young, and was then sent to what he called the outer edges of the Anglican world, away from the center and all that the center implied.

'God was preparing Michael,' Father John said, 'as surely as you and I are sitting here. And He was less interested in military and palace experience and far more interested in raising up a man after His own heart.' A man after His own heart, Father John said, would spend a lot of his time in prayer, seeking to do God's will rather than his own. Military experience, or years spent in the palace environment, or even understanding the political world paled in comparison to what God was doing."

Trevor had been quiet for a time, taking in what Gittings had said, and then spoke. "It does look like too many coincidences for there not to be a plan."

Gittings had laughed. "Oh, I think there's a plan, all right. The trick is finding out what it is. God didn't conveniently write it all down, unfortunately. And it keeps Michael on his knees."

This morning, following a short conference with Michael, Trevor would help open the advisory group's first meeting and lead the discussions. Michael had asked him to make a presentation on monarchial law as it related to the Church of England, with a good dollop of royal and church history thrown in. Trevor had spent weeks preparing, amusing Liz no end by burying himself in his study with tomes like *The History of Ecclesiastical Law in England* and

Contemporary Church Law in Britain, Fifth Edition. He saw the irony,
but he knew she hoped that his association with the king would lead
him to question his own lack of faith. So far, that hadn't directly
happened. But Trevor felt the unraveling at the edges, and he didn't
know where it would lead.

As long as it didn't lead behind the dark wall.

Chapter 2: A Tale of Two Speeches

Promptly at 11:30 a.m., the car carrying Sarah Kent-Hughes pulled up in front of the Marriott Grand Hotel in the City of Westminster in central London. She was there to speak at a luncheon meeting of the British-American Chamber of Commerce. The chamber had donated more than a million pounds to the fund for rebuilding after The Violence, a fund created by Sarah and her husband Michael. She was there to thank the chamber for its support; proceeds from paid attendance at the luncheon speech would also be contributed.

The ballroom seated 2,000 people. At 150 pounds per person, it would gross 300,000 pounds, or about 420,000 American dollars. Half of that would go to the fund, the other half to expenses.

The event had been sold out for weeks, a not entirely unexpected event for the young American Queen of Britain.

"Are you ready, your majesty?" said Meredith Hamilton, Sarah's communications lead accompanying her along with two palace security officers.

Sarah nodded. "No matter how many times I give a speech, I always get butterflies in my stomach."

"You'll do fine, ma'am," said Meredith. "You're prepared and it's a good talk."

They stepped out of the car and were greeted by officials from the chamber.

"Your majesty," said Home Secretary Thomas Hawksworth, "this is unprecedented."

"I know, Thomas," said Michael Kent-Hughes, "but it is my speech and I'm giving it on behalf of my Government."

At a 7 a.m. breakfast meeting, the two were sitting at a table in the library of Buckingham Palace. The Home Secretary was accompanied by an assistant to Prime Minster Peter Bolting and two members of Bolting's communications staff. The two staffers had been assigned the normally perfunctory duty of writing the King's speech for the opening of Parliament, less than two weeks away. With King Michael were Josh Gittings, the King's chief of staff; Jay Lanham, the king's communications director; and Jonathan Crowe, the king's new speechwriter who had joined Lanham's communications staff in June. The breakfast had been amicable enough, until they began discussing the purpose of the meeting.

"We understand that, sir," said Hawksworth, "but traditionally Government provides the speech and the monarch reads it at the opening of Parliament."

"Thomas," said Michael, "I know that. I understand Government's plans and priorities. But I asked for this meeting because I've already received three drafts which were not acceptable. I've asked for changes, especially regarding the discussion of the Church of England, and what comes back are a few minor word changes. I asked for this meeting to make sure what I'm saying here is absolutely clear."

Gittings and Lanham exchanged brief glances. They both recognized the tone in Michael's voice. Usually he was the most gentle and reasonable of men. But when his back was up, and he knew he was being deliberately ignored or misheard, a steely note of firmness would creep into his voice.

They both knew that Hawksworth did not share their experience with the king and did not understand what the change in his voice meant. And they knew that Hawksworth had likely carried an instruction from the Prime Minister to obtain the King's approval on what Bolting viewed as the final speech text, without any additional changes.

Hawksworth reddened and then calmed himself. "Your majesty, the Prime Minister is quite satisfied with the speech as it now stands," he said.

"Here's what I'd like you to do," Michael said. "Mr. Crowe here has taken your latest draft and reworked it. I'd like you to take it back to the Prime Minister and then you, Peter, and I can talk. I think you'll see that we've included every single plan and proposal that's in your draft, and that we've added detail for the Church of England section. We have not committed Government to endorse what I've proposed for the church. The other differences are style; Mr. Crowe has cast the text into the words and language that sound like me.

"My words are very important to me, Thomas. And they need to be my words."

Sarah took the arm of the president of the chamber and they walked through the large hotel lobby.

The hotel was almost brand new; it had opened a month after The Violence of the previous October, a civil unrest that started with the assassination of Britain's royal family, jihadist attacks and riots in Britain, and attacks on Michael and then-pregnant Sarah in San Francisco. The attack on Sarah had failed; Michael had nearly died from gunshot wounds. Michael's older half-brother, Duke Henry of Kent, had been murdered in a parking garage near his office in the City of London. More than 2,000 people had died during the insurrection.

23

"Should I be talking publicly about more substantive things?" she had said to Michael that morning as they were dressing for the day.

"Sarah, my bride," he'd said, "what you're doing is likely more important than you might think. You're publicly representing the familiar side of the monarchy, and the people need to hear and see that familiarity. The British people will tolerate what I'm saying about the reformation of the church as long as they know I'm not advocating revolution. And that's why thanking people for their generosity, for their contributions, talking about the family and children is so important. You're explaining that we're actually normal people, with the same cares and concerns." He smiled. "I'd gladly trade places with you this morning. I have another round with the Home Secretary over the speech to open Parliament, and it hasn't been going at all well."

"So, I should see what I'm doing as providing air cover?" she'd said, grinning.

Michael had laughed. "It's more than that, and you know it. And it's important, and not only for you to be seen and heard. You're learning, too, I bet. You've toured mental health hospitals, you spoke at the Royal Academy, you've been to schools, and a bunch of other things. I suspect you're learning more about Britain than you would just living with a Brit." And Michael knew what Sarah herself didn't yet know: she added more than a touch of glamour to the royal family with her beauty, her poise, and her clothes. She might be an American by birth, but the British people had embraced her as one of their own.

Sarah had given what seemed dozens of speeches and talks; this one at the Marriott would be the largest audience yet. She always worried about having something original to say, and Meredith had proven herself useful over and over again with helping develop each new speech. Sarah's self-confidence was growing; she still might get butterflies each time, but she was learning to anticipate and enjoy the occasions.

As Meredith had explained, this would be mostly an American audience, and 100 percent friendly, although Sarah couldn't say that she had actually encountered any unfriendly audiences or even unfriendly members of audiences. While she knew there were people opposed to the monarchy, and critics of her husband's stand on reforming the Church, she also knew that she and Michael were atop a mountain of support and admiration in Britain as well as the United States.

And instead of taking it for granted, she and Michael thanked God daily for the people of Britain and their support.

Wearing a soft blue, ankle-length dress and matching hat with a broad brim, Sarah entered the large ballroom, packed with luncheon tables and people.

Already seated, a couple in their mid- to late-50s watched the Queen as she entered the room. The man worked in the London office of a New York investment bank; he had extensive experience in managing venture capital projects. His wife, also an American, did volunteer and fundraising work for the Friends of the National Gallery and a children's hospital in Chelsea.

They'd lived in a London townhouse for five years. During The Violence the previous October, they had stayed in their home in South Kensington while most of their neighbors had fled. They'd heard gunfire from time to time, and an occasional explosion, and had lost their electrical power for more than a day, but they hadn't had any direct personal experience with rioters or looters, who'd been drawn to the attractions of nearby Knightsbridge.

They'd first seen Sarah Kent-Hughes during her famous televised press conference broadcast from the San Francisco hospital, where she had just given birth and her husband lay near death. Both the man and his wife had been shocked, recognizing her immediately by the name they knew her by – Sarah Hughes. Like millions of others, they had been overwhelmed by her plea for The Violence to stop, a plea that had been successful.

The last they had seen her in person was the beginning of her senior year in high school. She was now 26.

When the invitation arrived to hear her speak at the chamber luncheon, the man had convinced his wife to go with him, that the crowd would be so large that there would be no chance of her seeing them.

He turned out to be mistaken.

Josh Gittings escorted the Home Secretary and his group from the library to the car waiting in the courtyard. In the library, Jonathan Crowe followed his boss's lead and said nothing. They both waited for Michael to speak.

"Am I being unreasonable?" Michael said. "Should I just read what they provide?"

"Well, sir," said Lanham, who was two years older than Michael's 27. "It seems to me that if you want people to listen and to read it, then you need to stand your ground."

"The last version was only slightly less boring than the original," said Crowe.

Michael and Jay both laughed. "That is a spot-on analysis, Jonathan," the King said.

Lanham had searched for months to find a speechwriter for Michael. Up until June, Lanham himself had worked with the King on his speeches, and especially the speech given at the bishops' conference in Birmingham in April, two weeks before the coronation. Michael had rocked the conference and rocked the church in his condemnation of Government's report blaming The Violence on institutional racism and his call for broad and deep reformation of the church.

Michael had finally insisted that Lanham hire a full-time speechwriter. Jay's communications duties had become more than a single job, even with additional staff for digital media and media relations. Almost from his first day, Lanham had had his hands full with a series of crises orchestrated, as it had turned out, by the Archbishop of Canterbury Sebastian Rowland and his PR operative, Geoffrey Venneman of Fanning, Bullard & Lord, or FBL, the largest public relations firm in Britain.

Venneman and the archbishop were now undertaking a different strategy. Rowland had himself been speaking publicly and giving interviews, quietly suggesting, but not for attribution, that the throne had been taken over by a religious zealot whose only hallmark was intolerance. Several friendly bishops had joined with Rowland in speaking and interviews. Venneman was also overseeing a quiet but intense lobbying effort in both the Commons and the Lords, with the result that Michael's proposals for the church were being slowly strangled in meetings, study committees, and special projects, and obliquely criticized in newspaper columns and editorials.

Lanham had not advertised for a speechwriter. Instead, he had put a quiet word out among friends and started following reports of well-received speeches. And it was a friend who had suggested he check into Jonathan Crowe.

Crowe, 27, was a graduate of the University of London. He had attended on full scholarship after his school English literature teacher had pushed him, convinced his parents, wrote recommendations, and personally delivered him for his entrance exams.

Crowe's family, who had emigrated from Jamaica, lived in Brixton in south London. Jonathan had been born and raised in the Brixton area, and attended schools there. His father was a janitor and his mother worked in a laundry and dry cleaners. The Crowes had sacrificed much to provide a better life for Jonathan and his younger sister Amelia and had made sure their children were anchored in their evangelical church in Brixton. It had been no easy task; the area they lived in could only be called tough, and that was on a good day.

The English teacher had spotted what few others had seen in the boy: Jonathan had a remarkable gift for language and a love for British literature. And with the teacher as a mentor, Jonathan had flourished, eventually graduating from university with honours. He had been hired by *The Guardian* as a reporter. While his salary was good, it was nowhere near what was needed to live even modestly in London, and so he had remained with his parents in Brixton, paying them room and board in their flat.

The friend who suggested Lanham take a look at him had said it was only a matter of time before the *London Review of Books* pinched him from *The Guardian*. "I know Jonathan," the friend had said, "and he would do well but likely become increasingly unhappy. He has a strong Christian faith that ultimately won't sit well with a newspaper or the LRB."

Jonathan was the sixth person Jay interviewed, and the only one he scheduled to have a conversation with the King. Michael had been thoroughly impressed with Jonathan's credentials, and more than thrilled with his faith.

After accepting the job, Jonathan went home and told his parents he was leaving *The Guardian*, and that he had a new job, chief (and only) speechwriter for King Michael. As proud as they were of their son and his abilities, his parents had been shocked by the news. When he told his former English teacher, the man had gotten tears in his eyes and hugged him.

On the arm of the chamber president, an executive vice president of Microsoft UK, Sarah walked through the tables toward the dais, where she would be seated for the luncheon. The American couple, with rising anxiety, watched her as she moved closer and closer to their table. She was smiling and greeting people she recognized as she walked forward. Meredith was following directly behind her.

As Sarah walked by the couple's table, a banker seated with them accidentally knocked his water glass into his wife's lap. The stricken woman jumped up, drawing attention to herself and the people seated at her table.

Sarah and the chamber president stopped, as he leaned toward the woman to offer assistance. Sarah smiled sympathetically at the woman and then looked at the people sitting with her. She stared at the

American couple, not losing her smile, but stared nonetheless, focusing on the woman. And then she and the chamber president turned to move on toward the dais.

The man leaned over to his wife. "I don't think she recognized us," he said, whispering.

At that moment, while walking forward, Sarah turned her head back toward the couple.

"I think you're wrong," the woman said.

As Sarah was seated on the dais, she wrote a note on the provided pad. She signaled to Meredith, seated at a table nearby, who came forward to receive it. She read it and nodded. Sarah watched her walk to one of the chamber officials. Several minutes later, Meredith handed Sarah the note and returned to her table, to watch for any further instructions.

Mr. and Mrs. Tyler Zimmer. They're Americans. He's an investment banker; she does volunteer work for the National Gallery and a hospital. Do you want me to arrange an introduction after the luncheon?

Sarah looked at Meredith and nodded. She then continued her conversation with the chamber president.

The speech went better than she could have hoped. After she and Meredith had wrestled several ideas to death, Meredith finally suggested that, for this audience, Sarah keep the serious part short and instead focus on what she could do easily – tell stories about Michael and the children. But this wasn't to be just a disconnected series of funny stories and jokes, but a weaving of specific stories that centered on the importance of family – and ultimately the importance of the British-American family.

It was different, it spoke directly to the audience, and it had elements of hilarity. The audience loved it.

When she finished and was congratulated and thanked by the various chamber officials, her security officers escorted her and Meredith to a small waiting area adjacent to the ballroom.

Mr. and Mrs. Tyler Zimmer were waiting.

"I suppose the only thing we can do at this point is wait," Michael said to Jay and Jonathan. "I don't know when we'll hear back, but they can't take forever since the opening of Parliament is in 10 days."

Michael stood, causing Jay and Jonathan to jump to their feet as well.

"I have a meeting with Trevor Barry and then my church advisory committee," Michael said, "but after that I'm giving myself the afternoon off. Sarah and I are going to play tourist and take Hank with us to the British Museum. Jason is staying this weekend with his friend Chris, and Jim is spending the night with his school chum Dhruv George. So, we thought we'd take a few hours and see how long we can go incognito." He smiled. "Not long, I expect. Anyway, Jonathan, thank you for the work you've put in on fixing that terrible speech. It's actually readable and interesting, and I love the funny bits. Jay, thank you for your work as well. If the Home Secretary or the PM comes back with another round, we'll just have to deal with it. I'm not ready to cause a government crisis over this, but if I'm supposed to open Parliament then I want to use my own words to do it. Do you think I'm being arrogant?"

Jay answered for them both. "No, sir," he said. "You're being firm. The Home Secretary is right that it's unprecedented. But I don't think that it's sufficient reason for resisting the change."

Michael nodded and left the room, heading to his meeting with Trevor Barry.

Jay and Jonathan stood for a moment in the library.

"This is a side of his majesty I have not seen before," Jonathan said. "I'll be surprised if he goes along with Government on this."

"It seems a small thing," Jay said, "but it's actually not. Like the Archbishop and the other church officials, the Government actually serves at the King's pleasure. No one has tested that to see exactly what it means. And I don't think the King is trying to test Government and the PM. He's telling the PM that he won't be a Government robot and merely repeat whatever they hand him. He'll present Government's plans, but he'll do it in his own way and his own words. And he's not happy with the weasel words they wanted him to say about the church. You figured out a way around it in your draft. So, we'll see."

In the car back to Downing Street and Whitehall, Hawksworth fumed but said little in front of the others. Traffic was moving slowly, and he was just about ready to jump out and walk the rest of the way when one of the communications people chuckled.

"What is it?" Hawksworth said, clearly irritated.

"It's this speech of the King's," the young woman said, "the new version they gave us. It's actually quite good. And it's funny."

"I don't think the PM will find the humor in this at all," Hawksworth said.

"Perhaps he should, sir," the woman said. "Here, read it for yourself. Perhaps you should tell the PM to go with the King on this. It's an excellent speech. And it's far better than what we sent the King. It ticks off everything that's needed to be included and it handles the church thing rather adroitly."

Chapter 3: How a Reformation Begins

The church advisory meeting had gone well. As Michael had expected, Trevor had prepared an excellent presentation, framing the discussion precisely the way it needed to be framed. And then he had moderated the meeting incredibly well. Michael continued to be impressed with his legal counselor.

He was in what the family called the loft, the part of the palace that had been the old nursery but which they had had reconstructed into an extensive loft-like living space. Hank was in his high chair; Michael had given the governess, Joan Plunkett, the afternoon off. He'd fixed himself a sandwich and a glass of milk and had just taken the first bite when he heard the loft door open.

"Sarah?"

She stood at the door of the kitchen. Michael could see she was upset.

"What happened?" he said. "Did something happen at the speech?"

She shook her head. "The speech went fantastic," she said.

And then she burst into tears.

"I was rude, Mike," Sarah said through her tears. "I told my mother and biological father I'd have my secretary call to make an appointment."

They were sitting in the loft's living area, with Michael's left arm around Sarah and his right holding on to Hank on his lap.

"You were trying to grapple with the shock of seeing them, Sarah," he said. "Rudeness, if that's what it was, can be forgiven in the circumstances."

"What do I do?" she said. "I need to call my brothers. And what about Dad? How is he supposed to respond when I tell him his ex-wife and the real father of what he had believed were his own children showed up?"

"First," Michael said, "your father can handle this. He'll know you won't shut him out. Seth tried to blot everything out once before and it didn't work, remember?"

"Only because you talked sense into him."

"He was angry," Michael said, "but he came around. And he loves your nephews Scottie and Gavin and he loves Hank here. Second, you can call David and Scott this weekend, and you'll see David next week in Edinburgh. You don't have to do anything right at this moment."

38

Sarah slowly nodded.

"And third," he said, "you and I and the prince here have a date for the British Museum, and we are not going to give up what we planned so carefully just so we can hang around here and stew. So, your majesty, it's time to change and head for the museum. It's high time you see the Elgin Marbles and the Rosetta Stone."

The British Museum was crowded with tourists and students. For a long time, it had been the most visited tourist site in the United Kingdom. Michael had been here a few times when Ian and Iris McLaren, his guardians in Edinburgh, had come to London for a holiday. There for an hour, Michael and Sarah had already seen the Rosetta Stone, and Sarah had been overwhelmed by the beauty of the Elgin Marbles from the Parthenon. Michael pointed out that Greece and the United Kingdom were still arguing over ownership.

They stood before the display case in the semi-darkened gallery and stared at the game pieces, some 82 in all. To see better, both Michael and Sarah had removed their sunglasses. Michael was holding Hank, while Sarah was pushing the collapsible stroller. The two security agents with them were standing nearby, dressed in casual clothes.

So far, no one had noticed them. They looked like any other young couple with a baby, gawking at the museum's phenomenal exhibits.

"These chess pieces are wonderful," Sarah said.

Michael was looking at the exhibit card. "It says they were likely made between 1000 and 1150 A.D., most likely in Norway. And discovered in the first part of the 19th century on the Isle of Lewis. Eleven pieces are in Edinburgh."

"They're a thousand years old," said Sarah.

"They would have been made after the Viking invasions of Britain had ended," Michael said. "Things were settling down, trade was well developed, and the Normans were beginning to stir across the channel. Of course, the Normans were descended from Vikings as well. And for some reason, someone buried these chessmen in a remote area, probably hoping to return and dig them up one day."

"I'm so glad we came," she said. "I would have been moaning and groaning if we had stayed home."

"We need to get to the main exhibition hall," Michael said. "It's just about the time on our tickets."

They arrived on the main floor and joined the line for the 4 p.m. entrance to the special exhibition of Rodin and the art of ancient

Greece. The exhibition was the story of how the sculptor had visited the museum to see the Elgin Marbles, and how his art had changed as a result.

An older American couple stood in line ahead of them. The lady turned and smiled.

"You have such a beautiful child," she said. "I was watching you as you came to the line. He's really beautiful."

Sarah smiled back. "Thank you. Right now, I'm thankful that he's chosen to cooperate today and stare at all the exhibits rather than make a fuss."

The lady laughed, and then looked at Michael. "I suppose people have told you how much you look like King Michael," she said.

Michael laughed. "I think I've heard that a few times."

The line started moving forward, and soon they were inside the exhibit, which featured some of Rodin's most famous works.

Sarah was mesmerized. She soon became lost in the exhibit, reading every display card and listening to her audio guide. Michael found the exhibit interesting, but he was fascinated watching how it was affecting his wife. He had watched her paint, and the effect was something similar, almost seeming to take her out of time. She was in a place he almost couldn't touch.

They reached the exhibition exit, which led them directly into the sales shop. Sarah walked to the table containing the exhibition catalogs.

"I'd like to get this," she said.

Michael laughed. "Why am I not surprised?"

Sarah paid in cash. As they walked toward the entrance to leave for home, they suddenly heard a voice shouting "Your Majesties! Your Majesties!" They turned and saw a woman rushing toward them, followed by several museum staffers.

"Oh, Your Majesties," she said, slightly out of breath, after curtsying. "I'm Dr. Margaret Burris, director of the museum. We had no idea that you were visiting. One of our security guards sighted you and rushed to tell me."

A crowd started gathering. People began pointing to Michael and Sarah. Their two security guards moved closer.

"Dr. Burris," Michael said. "We wanted to visit the museum without a lot of fanfare. We've had a lovely time this afternoon, and Sarah here adores the Rodin exhibit. But we didn't call ahead because we were hoping to avoid disrupting the museum with a formal visit." He paused. "And perhaps see what it used to feel like to be just tourists."

The director was suddenly aware that she had created a crowd, one that was growing larger by the second.

"Oh, I am sorry," she said. "I didn't know. I –." She stopped, completely flustered.

"It's fine," Michael said, smiling. "This museum is a treasure filled with treasures. And we were able to experience it like everyone else. That meant a lot to both of us. There's nothing to apologize for, really." He saw one of the security men signaling. "We will make arrangements to come back for a formal visit, if that's all right with you. And now, I'm afraid we must go. Please thank your staff for the wonderful exhibits."

They hurried toward the entrance, smiling to people as they walked. Mobile phones were flashing all around them.

Their car was waiting on Russell Street in front of the museum. The driver took side streets to reach Shaftesbury Avenue and then Piccadilly. They drove down Constitution Hill and turned into the palace.

The following Tuesday morning, as Sarah's secretary was contacting Tyler and Marie Zimmer to set a date for a meeting, Sarah was on her way to Edinburgh for a speech and a visit to a hospital in

Leith. She would be spending the night with Ian and Iris McLaren, the couple who had served as Michael's guardians from the time he was almost six and whom he called Da and Ma. Iris was preparing dinner for Sarah, her brother David, and David's wife Betsey. They were bringing their son Gavin, now two years old. David was working as a lecturer and tutor at St. Andrew's University, the start of what looked to be a promising academic career.

Michael was preparing for a luncheon speech of his own to a group of businessmen meeting at the Guildhall in the City, sponsored by the Lord Mayor of London. The car would be leaving the palace at 11, and both Josh Gittings and Jay Lanham were accompanying him. He had been contacted earlier that morning by the PM's office, to let him know that the PM found the speech text for the opening of Parliament, now six days away, to be eminently satisfactory and that the PM was greatly looking forward to it.

"I'm glad that's settled," Michael said to Josh and Jay as they walked to the car.

As they drove, Michael looked through his notes for the speech. He'd been invited to speak on the status of the rebuilding efforts undertaken through the donations to the royal fund, and he hoped that the speech might further loosen some executive purse strings.

The damage in London from The Violence had been extensive. In little more than two days, riots, fire bombings, and street battles had caused an estimated 200 billion pounds in property damage alone; the cost of looted and burned goods was at least that much. Deemed a civil insurrection, the damage was not covered by insurance companies. Michael and Sarah had themselves made a 10-billion-pound donation to the rebuilding fund, and Michael had singlehandedly helped raise the funds needed to restore St. Martin-in-the-Fields Church on Trafalgar Square. Churches and mosques had been damaged all over the city; shops in Knightsbridge, Mayfair, and Belgravia had been looted and burned. Most of the speeches being given by Michael and Sarah were aimed at raising funds for rebuilding.

Just as Michael's car entered the large Guildhall courtyard, driving right past St. Lawrence Jewry Church, deputy security chief Paula Abbott turned from the front passenger seat and handed her mobile to Michael.

"It's Mitchell, sir, at the palace," she said.

"Mr. Mitchell?" Michael said.

"I'm sorry to disturb you, sir," Mitchell said, "and I know you have your speech, but the school just called. Jason is missing."

Michael felt his heart skip a beat. "Do you have any details?" he said.

"I'm leaving for the school now," Mitchell said. "Apparently there was some problem yesterday having to do with a prayer group, and that continued over into today. It wasn't exactly a fight, but there seems to have been some kind of altercation. The boys' security man was checking on Jim in his classroom when the head's office buzzed him on his mobile."

"Is Jim accounted for?" Michael asked. Jim was in fourth grade in the ICS lower school.

"Yes, sir, he's in his class," Mitchell said.

"Jason was very quiet at dinner last night," Michael said. "I asked him if something had happened at school, and he said that there had been a problem, but he was taking care of it." He paused. "I'd the impression it had to do with his girlfriend, but it looks now like my assumption was wrong."

"Jason's friend Chris seems to know what happened, sir," Mitchell said, "but he said he can't say anything except directly to you. This has something to do with the rules of their prayer group. The school also said that there were news media at the gate who'd picked up the report on the police radio."

"We'll leave for the school immediately," Michael said, and rang off. "Jason's missing from school. Josh, I need you to give the speech. Do you think you can do it in my place?"

"I can, sir, but everyone will understand if we have to reschedule," Josh said.

"If you can explain that an unexpected family issue has arisen, I think we can do this as planned," Michael said.

He handed Josh his typed text. "Jay, I'll need you to come with me to the school. We apparently already have the media there. And can you text Meredith in Edinburgh and tell her to let Sarah know once she's finished her speech and to sit tight until we know more. Ms. Abbott, can you arrange for a car to pick up Josh when he's finished here?"

When the family had arrived in London the previous December, both Jason and Jim had been enrolled at International Christian School, or ICS for short. Josh Gittings had investigated several schools and knowing Michael and Sarah's preference for a classical Christian education for their adopted sons, had recommended

ICS. Its student body pulled from both native British and the large number of international families in London. Jim's classmate Dhruv George had family roots in India; Jason's friend Chris Whitney was an American born in Texas whose father worked for the Royal Dutch / Shell Group.

As they drove to ICS in the Notting Hill area, Michael at first said nothing, and simply stared out of the window. At one point, Jay saw that he'd closed his eyes, and he knew that Michael was praying. When Michael opened his eyes, he spoke.

"Something was troubling him last night," Michael said. "Sarah and I both saw it. And I asked him if he needed to talk, but he said he needed to wait to see how things went. But what the things were, he didn't say."

Arriving at the school, they found three police cars in front, with a BBC truck already setting up for broadcast. Reporters from several newspapers were at the gate, held back by a policeman.

As Michael, Jay, and Paula Abbott hurried from the car, reporters started shouting questions.

Jay Lanham held up his hand. "We know less than you do right now. We'll have a statement later." And they walked quickly into the building.

Reginald Owens, head of the school, met them at the door, and took them to a conference room within the administrative offices. Ryan Mitchell and his agents were there, as were two police officers. They were taking a statement from Colin Slattery. Everyone stood as Michael entered the room.

"So, what do we know?" Michael said.

Slattery explained what had happened that morning. "When the students were arriving at school, they discovered some vandalism in the hallway in the junior class wing. Words had been spray-painted on three lockers – Jason's, Chris Whitney's, and a student named Robert Hood. All three are in the prayer group that I sponsor. One of our students, Elton Jenner, who's also in the prayer group, eventually confessed to spraying the paint. There was apparently some altercation yesterday, but Elton won't say much if anything. It happened in their prayer group, and they're not supposed to talk about what they pray for, unless there's an emergency of some type. Chris Whitney knows, but he's refused to say anything to anyone except you, your majesty."

"Where's Chris?" Michael said.

"He's in my office with another teacher," Owens said. "I'll take you there." Mitchell, Abbott and the two policemen followed them to the office. Chris was sitting next to the teacher in a chair in front of the desk and looked up as they entered.

"Hello, Chris," Michael said. "You have something to tell me about Jason?"

Chris stood and shook Michael's hand. He nodded and then looked at the others crowding into the office.

Michael turned to them. "I'd like to speak to Chris alone, if I may. I know it's important for everyone to hear, but I'd like to speak to him alone." Mitchell and one of the policemen started to protest and then stopped and nodded. The rest quickly left the room and closed the door.

Michael sat in the chair next to Chris. "Chris, what can you tell me?"

"It started with our prayer group yesterday, sir," Chris said.

During their prayer time on Monday afternoon, each boy was sharing a specific prayer request. Chris asked for the focus and personal commitment to maintain a daily regimen of personal Bible study and prayer. Another boy asked to do well on a math test. Elton Jenner asked for a victory in the upcoming soccer match with archrival

Central London School on Friday. Jason asked for continued prayer for his parents and for Michael's struggles with the church.

When it was Robert's turn to share a request, which he declined to do at previous prayer times, the boy looked down for several moments, as if gathering up courage to say something.

"Come on, Hood," Jenner said, "we don't have all day."

Robert nodded. "I'm sorry, Elton. It's just this is hard."

"Take your time, Robert," Chris said gently, giving Jenner a "back-off" glance.

Robert nodded, then spoke. "There's this man."

The other boys waited expectantly.

"There's this man I know," Robert repeated. Jason could see that it was taking a tremendous effort for Robert to say anything.

"He makes me do things."

Jason looked at Chris, who had a look on his face of "What's going to happen here?" Robert was still looking down at the floor.

"He makes me, he makes me," Robert was stammering, and then started to cry. "He makes me sleep with him and do things."

Jason and Chris looked stunned, unsure how to respond. Jenner saved them the trouble.

"Oh, gee, you're a faggot," Elton said. "I can't believe this. I can't believe they let you into ICS. Read your Bible. Faggots go to hell."

Robert gave a strangled cry and ran out of the room.

Jason looked furiously at Elton. "And you're a total ass!" he shouted. He rushed out of the room after Robert.

Robert had vanished. There was no sign of him in the hallways.

Jason, almost uncontrollably angry, ran back to the group's room. The girls had heard the commotion from their room across the hall and were standing in the doorway. Chris, Elton, and the other boys had stepped into the hallway as well.

"You don't know!" Jason yelled at Elton. "You don't know what it's like!"

"And I suppose you do?" Elton said, sneering.

Chris and the girls could hear the anger in Jason's voice. "I was 11 years old when my mother put me in a home for adoption, because my stepfather didn't want me. I wasn't there a week when four older boys caught me and held me down while they raped me. And then they came back, again and again and again. I went to the house father, begging for help, and he called me a liar. And he told them, and they came back, and he was with them. Again and again and again. And I ran away. I lived on the streets for four years, and I did what I had to do. I sold drugs, I stole, I broke into cars, and I sold myself. You don't know what that is. You don't know what he's gone through. You just sit there like some stupid self-righteous hypocrite and tell him he's going to hell. He needs help!"

Jason saw the look of shock on Chris' face, and then turned and saw the girls. Jane Barry looked horrified.

"I have to find him," Jason said and ran down the hall.

"Jason was crying, sir," Chris said. "We were shocked, even Elton, who can usually be counted on to act the bully. I went looking for Jason but didn't see him, until I saw him getting in the car with Jim to leave."

"Chris," Michael said, "we knew part of Jason's story, but we didn't know the details. I knew he hated that home, but he would never talk about it." Michael shuddered. "My poor boy."

"I should have called him or texted him or something last night," Chris said, "but I didn't. I didn't know how to deal with what he said, and what Robert said. When I got to school this morning, I decided that, no matter what, Jason was my best friend, and I just couldn't turn my back. So, I waited for him at the school door."

"I've looked for Robert, but I haven't seen him yet," Chris said to Jason. "Did you find him yesterday?"

Jason shook his head. "I looked but he was gone."

"Well, we've got 10 minutes before class starts. Why don't we see if we can find him?"

Jason felt enormously encouraged. Chris wasn't turning away from him. *Maybe this will go okay.* The security officer behind him moved toward the office, where he stayed in a small cubicle each day except for periodic checks on Jason and Jim.

The two boys walked into the junior class hallway to their lockers. A huge crowd of kids packed the area, listening to Colin Slattery yelling. Other teachers were standing there as well.

Slattery was shouting. "Who did this?"

Jason and Chris looked. Jason's locker, and Robert's nearby, had been spray painted in a dark pink with the word FAGGOT in capital letters. Across the hall, Chris' locker had been spray painted with the words FAGGOT LOVER.

Jason stared. And then he saw Jane, who looked at him and then turned away, making her way toward the back of the crowd. The kids standing nearest to him and Chris saw him, and stepped back, as if wanting to avoid contamination.

"Chris! Jason!" Slattery yelled. "Do you know who did this?"

"You could start by asking him," Chris said, pointing at a smirking Elton Jenner.

Jason turned around and pushed his way through the students. He disappeared down the hall.

"I wouldn't say anything except to you, sir," Chris said. "I didn't think it was right for me to tell anyone about what Jason said, although all of us in the Bible study group heard it, including the girls. We're not supposed to repeat what we pray about, about our individual requests. But he said this in the hallway."

"Thank you, Chris," Michael said. "Thank you for being his friend. I didn't know what had happened at the home in San Francisco. He never said anything other than he would never go back there." Michael looked down. *Jason's hurting and I want to hold him.*

He looked up at Chris. "Do you have any idea where he might have gone?"

"I think he went to Robert's house, sir," Chris said. "We didn't find him this morning. Jason tried to find him yesterday."

Michael walked to and opened the door. He looked at Reginald Owens. "Is Robert Hood in school today?"

"I'll check, your majesty." He walked over to where the office staff were waiting.

Michael turned to Chris, standing next to him. "Did Jason say anything to you about yesterday? I mean, did he refer to it this morning?"

"No, sir," Chris said. "Only about looking for Robert. We'd just started to do that when we walked into the junior hallway and saw the lockers."

Owens walked in, followed by the others. "Robert's not here," he said, "and there's no excused absence call from his mother. The assistant had put in a call at her office this morning, but they said she was on an assignment and wouldn't be back until Friday. We've told them to get hold of her as soon as possible."

"Jason may have gone to Robert's house," Michael said. "Can we drive there without the media in full cry behind us?"

"I can drive you," Slattery said. "I don't have another class today until 2:30. My car's parked in the faculty carpark behind the school. I live not too far from them, and I've visited Robert and his mother."

"Thank you," Michael said. "Jay, I need you to stay here in case the media get unruly." Jay nodded, and Michael, Mitchell, and a policeman followed the teacher to his car.

As they started out, Michael's mobile rang.

"It's Sarah," he said, looking at the caller identification. He answered, and quickly outlined the basics of what they knew, leaving out most of what Chris told him.

"I'm coming home now," Sarah said.

"Just wait a bit," Michael said. "If he's not at Robert's, I'll let you know. But I'm hoping this will turn out okay. You can always make the decision to fly back in an hour." Sarah had traveled to Edinburgh on the royal airplane.

"Okay, Mike," she said, "but you are to call me as soon you set eyes on him. And if I don't hear something from you within an hour, I'm coming back."

"I'll call, my love, I'll call." He powered off the phone.

Slattery was driving north.

"How long?" Mitchell asked.

"About 15 minutes," Slattery said.

"How would Jason have known how to get to Robert's house?" Mitchell asked. "Were they friends?"

"I don't know," Michael said. He paused while he punched in numbers on his phone. "I keep trying to reach him on his mobile, but he must have it turned off."

"Jason's been reaching out to Robert," Slattery said. "I think he sensed a need in Robert. Jason was the one, in fact, who got Robert to join the prayer group." He paused. "It might help to know some of Robert's background. He's one of our scholarship students, on full tuition. His parents are divorced, and he hasn't seen his father in years. The vicar at their church has been a kind of mentor and helped him get the scholarship. He's a very introverted boy, very much a loner, and not much for sports. He does well in academics, though."

After a few more minutes, they arrived at a block of extremely modest attached row houses. Slattery stopped in front of No. 24. "They have a two-bedroom flat on the ground floor," he said.

Michael walked up the short flight of steps to the door and rang the bell marked "Hood." There was no answer.

"No one's home," said an elderly woman standing on the porch next door. "She left early this morning for work with a suitcase, so she must have been going out of town. She does that sometimes. Robert and his chum left a little while ago. I'm not sure what they're doing; they should be in school at this time of day."

Michael said a short prayer of thanks for busybodies. "Did you see which way they went?"

The woman nodded. "That way. To your right. Probably heading for the square at the end of the block and across the street." She peered more closely. "Do I know you? You sound familiar, but my eyesight isn't the best."

"I don't think we've ever met but thank you for your help." They returned to the car and drove to the end of the street. They could see a small park across the street.

"Mr. Mitchell," Michael said, "I'm going to walk into the park alone. You and the policeman can follow, but I need you to stay well behind me. I know it's not regulation, but I need you to do this."

Mitchell looked at the king. "All right sir, but I'm not going to be more than 40 feet away."

"That's fine. But if they're there, I need you to stay out of earshot while I talk with them."

"Yes, sir," Mitchell said.

Michael got out of the car, crossed the street, with Mitchell and the policeman well behind him.

The park wasn't large, and more of neighborhood green space or square than an actual park. It had a children's playground and a paved walk through to the other side.

Jason and Robert were sitting on a bench, talking. Michael stopped, realizing for the first time how frightened he'd been. He then walked to the two boys.

"Jason?"

Jason saw him and jumped up. "Dad!"

Robert jumped up as well.

Michael put his arms around Jason and hugged him.

"I know I shouldn't have left," Jason said, "but I had to find Robert."

"Hold up," Michael said. "I promised your mother I'd call as soon as we found you." He punched in Sarah's number on his mobile.

"I'm with him now," Michael said. "He's fine. No, you can stay with Ma and Da as planned. We'll call tonight and explain. Right. I love you, too."

He looked at Jason. "Your mother's going to have your hide when she gets home, if there's any left over after I'm finished." Michael then looked at Robert. "You're Robert Hood?"

The boy nodded. "Yes, sir."

Michael motioned them both to sit on the bench and then sat between them. "You've given us all a great scare. I've talked with Chris, and I understand what's happened." He looked at Robert. "Robert, your mother is out of town?"

"Yes, sir," he said. "She's working a trade show booth for her company. She's in Leeds."

"When is she due back?" Michael asked.

"On Friday."

"Where are you supposed to be sleeping? At home by yourself?"

Robert shook his head, tears forming in his eyes. "With him."

"Dad," said Jason, "he can't. We can't let him."

Openly crying, Robert looked at Michael. "I'm supposed to stay with him. But I can't. I can't go back to the church."

Mitchell and the police officer watched the three talking on the bench. At one point, they saw Michael put his arm around the Hood boy's shoulders, while the boy seemed to sob and then bury his head on the king's shoulder. After a good 20 minutes, Michael stood up and motioned to them. He also signaled to Slattery, who'd been waiting near the car farther away.

"Mr. Mitchell, we need to stop at Robert's house and pick up some clothes. He's going to stay with us at the palace for at least tonight, possibly tomorrow night as well. To be on the safe side, let's get clothes for several days. After we get his things, we'll go back to the school. I'll need you to take the boys to the palace and let me and Jay deal with the media." He looked at the policeman. "We're also going to need the Metropolitan Police, probably an inspector-level type, someone familiar with abuse cases, to come to the palace as soon as possible to talk with Robert. Can you call now and arrange for that?"

The policeman nodded and pulled out his mobile.

"I'll have a security car waiting on the faculty parking lot when we arrive back at the school," Mitchell said. "And I'll alert the palace that a policeman is coming."

"That will work," Michael said. "You take the boys with you, and Jay and I will ride back from the school with Ms. Abbott. Somehow, we'll need to contact Robert's mother, who's in Leeds at a trade show. The police can probably do that best. If she calls, we need her to talk with Robert, and I'll talk with her as well."

"Yes, sir."

Back at the school, Michael and Jay, followed by Abbott, walked to the news media at the front gate. Their numbers had now grown to several television stations and more than 20 newspaper and radio reporters.

"Thank you for being patient," Michael said. "Jason is fine. He'd left school to find a friend who was distressed. Both boys are okay. He should have had permission from us or the school, or at least told someone, but when you're 17 years old you often act before you think, and he wanted to help his friend."

The reporters, looking almost disappointed with how things had turned out, asked a few perfunctory questions. Jay then ended the press conference and they walked back inside the school.

"Headmaster," Michael said to Reginald Owens, "can we talk in your office? Jay, I need you with us."

In Owens' office, Michael explained. "This is about sexual abuse. It's not connected to any of your staff at the school, but rather to Robert's church. From what I've understood from Robert, there may be other children involved, and some of them may be students here. He doesn't know of anyone specifically, but the circumstances are such that it may be likely."

Owens nodded, white-faced.

"I need to get Jim," Michael said. "I know it's a bit early, but I need to bring him home with us now. Robert's coming home with us, and I'm going to keep Jim and Jason home for the rest of the week. We'll check for any of their assignments on the website. I expect all three boys to be back at school on Monday. And if Robert's mother calls, please have her call me at the palace. This is the number – she'll get security first and then they'll put her through to me." He handed a card to the headmaster.

"Your majesty, is there anything else we can do? I deeply apologize for what's happened," Owen said.

"Headmaster, this isn't your fault or the school's fault," Michael said. "I'm sorry for all the trouble that's been caused. But I don't think this is the end of this, and it may well be only the beginning. The school, simply because it is a Christian school, drawing students from all over London, may be particularly vulnerable. When I get a better understanding of what's happened, I'd like to talk with you about what we might do. I'll call by tomorrow, and we'll likely need to stay closely connected over the next week." He paused. "I'm keeping Jim and Jason at home because, if this breaks in the news, as will likely happen, we'll attract hordes of journalists just by showing up in the morning, and it may reduce the pressure here."

"You're expecting more problems or reports?" Owens said.

"I don't know for sure, but if there are, they will likely be horrible," Michael said. "As a precaution, I'll have Jay here find some communications help for you, and I will cover the expense. Jay will also be available to talk with you or whomever you might designate, to provide counsel and advice."

Returning to the palace, Michael and Jay met with Josh. Michael explained what he knew and what he thought might happen, going into far more detail than he had with the headmaster. "I'm hoping that the school will escape attention, but that's probably unlikely," he said.

"An arrest, sir," Jay said, "will create a media storm."

Michael nodded. "And the connection to the boy and the school will eventually be made, even if they're blameless. That's why they'll need communications help."

"I'll do it now, sir," Jay said, and left for his office in the administrative wing of the palace.

"Michael," Josh said, "the fact that you're a C of E priest may be a liability here. People may think, or even be led to believe, that your involvement may smack of cover-up."

"I know, Josh, and we'll just have to deal with it when and if it happens." Michael smiled. "How did the speech go?"

"There was some disappointment that it was me and not you," Josh said, "but they seemed to understand. And pledges were made of some 100,000 pounds."

"Maybe you should do this full-time."

An hour later, Inspector Detective Roger Frees of the Metropolitan Police, Sexual Abuse Unit, sat in the library at Buckingham Palace, interviewing Robert. The boy had asked that Michael be there as well. They'd been talking for 10 minutes.

"And you say, Robert, that this started several years ago?" the policeman gently said.

"When I was 10, sir," Robert said. "It was right after my scholarship was approved by the school."

"And Rev. Wickham had helped with the application?"

"Yes, sir. And then he said he knew I wanted to do something special for him, because of the scholarship."

"Robert, how long did this go on?" Frees asked.

The boy hesitated. "It hasn't stopped, sir."

"How often does this happen?"

"Two or three times a month. Sometimes my mother has to travel with her job, and she has me stay with him because he's a close family friend. Usually it's just a day or two. One time it was for a whole week."

"And you say it was generally the same kind of activity or behavior each time."

"Yes, sir, usually. Except when there were others."

Michael saw the policeman's hand clench. "Others?"

"Yes, sir. Sometimes there were other priests."

Michael saw the policeman pale. "Was this one or two others?"

"Usually, sir, it was just one or two." He looked down. "A few times it was six or seven." The boy seemed to falter. "And sometimes…"

"Yes, Robert?"

"There were other boys. They made us do things to each other. I never saw them, because they'd cover our heads with a cloth bag, except when, except when, when we had to be what they called the doer." Robert began to quietly cry. "It was for the film."

"The film?" Frees said.

Robert nodded. "They filmed it. Every time."

The policeman looked down at his notes for what seemed a very long time. When he looked up, Michael could see that Frees could barely control his emotions. Michael himself had tears on his cheeks, and he'd already heard the story once in the park.

"Robert, we're finished here for the moment. You've been incredibly brave in answering these questions, and I know it's very hard to talk about these things. At some point, we may need to talk with you again. Do you think you'd be up to that?"

"Yes, sir."

"It's likely that you'll have to have a physical examination by a doctor, and they may do blood tests."

"Yes, sir."

"Is the Rev. Wickham expecting you to be at the church tonight?" Frees said.

"He was," Robert said. "My mother arranged it with him. But Jason had me call him and leave a message that I was staying with a friend from school tonight."

"Excellent," Frees said. "Robert, I'll need to tell your mother about what we've talked about."

"I told her some of this before, sir," Robert said. "But she didn't believe me."

Brent Epworth, Master of the Household for Buckingham Palace, escorted Robert upstairs to the family loft. Frees called his supervisor at the Met, and then stood talking with Michael.

"The boy's telling the truth, sir," Frees said. "I've investigated too many of these cases to know when the child is being truthful and when there's exaggeration or outright falsehood. And Robert's telling us the truth."

"Even about his mother knowing?"

Frees nodded. "Even that. A lot of parents think the child is making the stuff up, or they go to the other extreme and think everything and anything is true. If the individual is a close friend of the family and one that's particularly trusted, like an authority figure, it makes it harder for them to believe the child." He paused. "Like if it's your priest." He paused again. "But this, this is monstrous."

"Robert's staying with us right now, Detective Inspector," Michael said. "We think it will be for one or two nights, until his mother comes home."

"It could be longer, sir. We're going to move to arrest Wickham by tomorrow. The warrants are being readied but they take time. Once we move, the media will be close behind. And we're calling the Leeds police to get to the mother at the trade show. We're waiting right now on a search warrant for the church as well; we'll need to check files and what computers may be around. If this is what it looks like it is, what Robert's been going through may be only the tip of the iceberg."

"What do you think you have here, Detective Inspector?" Michael said.

"It sounds to me that we have a ring of child molesters," Frees said, "and most likely pornographers, embedded right in the middle of the Church of England. Robert's specifically cited seven or eight priests, as least by presence. And we'll have to try to find the other children."

"Should I inform the Archbishop of Canterbury?" Michael said.

Frees shook his head. "No, sir. It might compromise the investigation. We don't know the extent of involvement by anyone associated with the church, or if others outside the church are involved. So, I need you to hold your counsel for a time."

"Well," Michael said, "it would be hard for me to believe that the archbishop knows anything about this, but given that he hasn't spoken to me since I arrived last December, it's likely not a problem anyway."

Chapter 4: Dinner in Scotland

After her luncheon speech and tour in Leith, Sarah was driven to the McLaren farm, some 40 miles outside of Edinburgh. The farm itself was comprised of about 80 acres, including a barn where Ian McLaren housed his veterinary practice and the horses he was treating, and extended grounds where Iris McLaren had used to develop a series of gardens for her garden consultancy. Iris's garden designs could be found on properties all over Scotland and northern England.

This was the home where Michael had been brought at six years old, sent away from his home in Kent by his then-21-year-old half-brother Henry after the deaths of the Duke and Duchess of Kent in an automobile accident. And this was the place the Kent-Hughes family loved best in Britain, and the place Michael called home.

Meredith Hamilton had flown commercial back to London. Two security officers were sharing one of the McLarens' guest bedrooms. Michael had purchased an adjacent farm with a small farmhouse and renovations were underway to use it as a security base whenever the family visited.

Sarah changed into jeans and a blouse and joined Iris in the kitchen to help prepare dinner.

"Is the Queen of Great Britain supposed to be working in the kitchen?" Iris said, grinning.

"The Queen of Great Britain wants to earn her keep," Sarah said, "and we usually fix our own meals in London, unless some big to-do is scheduled. It's a blessing to be doing normal things."

Iris, Ian, and Sarah all insisted that the two security officers join the family for dinner. They were joined by David and Betsey Hughes with 2-year-old Gavin. The dinner took on the air of a small family reunion; Sarah hadn't seen her twin brother and his wife Betsey since the coronation in May. When they finished eating, the two security officers excused themselves, leaving the family to talk around the table.

"David," Sarah said, "this might not be the time or place to talk about this, but last week in London, Mother and Ty Zimmer showed up at one of my speeches."

David looked stunned. "Mother?" he finally said.

Sarah nodded. "They've lived in London for the last five years. They have a place in South Kensington. He's an investment banker with some firm and she's doing volunteer work for the National Gallery and a hospital in Chelsea." She explained the meeting after the speech.

"When did you last see her?" Betsey said.

"About eight years ago," David said. "Right at the beginning of our senior year in high school."

The McLarens listened, saying nothing. Ian seemed to be paying closer attention to David's and Betsey's son Gavin, who was sitting on his knee.

"She asked about you and Scott," Sarah said. "And we're arranging a time to talk further." She paused. "I don't know if this is a good thing or not. And I haven't said anything to Dad. I don't know how he'll react."

"I remember that first Christmas," Iris said, smiling. "Michael brought you both here."

David nodded. "We, and Dad, had just learned that he wasn't our real father. He walked away from us for more than a year. Until Michael showed up at his office in Los Angeles and yelled some sense into him."

"I remember when he came to Edinburgh," said Betsey. "You can't imagine the shock when I opened the door with Gavin on my hip and there was a man saying he was David's dad from Los Angeles. And then David came home and, well, it was a bit tense for a time."

"It was a lot tense for a time," David said. "But we worked it out. And Scott and Barb somehow managed to hold us together as a family long-distance until Dad came around."

"What should I do about Mother?" Sarah said.

"I suppose you should meet with her," David said. "Do you know if she wants anything or does she simply want to hang around the Queen?"

"David," Betsey said, "that's a bit harsh."

"I know,' he said. "I'm sorry. It's just you think some scars have healed over and something happens to rip open the scar again."

"It was hard," Sarah said. "When we came home from school that day in Denver and found the note saying she'd left, it was a shock. And then Dad came home, and he had his own shock." She reached and touched David's hand. "The smarter and more organized of the Hughes twins held us together, until Scott flew in a few days later. Dad wasn't in good shape. His wife had just left him for his business partner and best friend. His personal life and his business life had turned upside down."

"Then when we were here at university, he finds out that none of us were his biological children," David said. He glanced at Iris and

Ian. "And it was the McLarens who took in the two American orphans for Christmas."

"And look where that eventually led," Ian said, nodding at Gavin.

They all laughed.

"So, when I get back," Sarah said, "I'll find out when we have a meeting scheduled. Do you want to be there?"

David shook his head. "I have lectures and tutorials. You'll have to let me know how it goes."

Chapter 5: What's Not in the Red Box

After breakfast the next morning in London, the boys were in the loft, ostensibly doing assignments from school, and Mrs. Plunkett was managing Hank. Michael was in the palace library, which he'd been using as an office while renovations were made to the room that would become his office on the ground floor. He was reviewing the daily red box of communications from the PM's office.

Jay Lanham knocked and entered with Brent Epworth, the master of the House, and Josh Gittings. "We're sorry to disturb you, sir," Josh said, "but has the PM said anything about the situation with the Greater London Authority?"

Michael shook his head. "No, there's been nothing in the red box, and I've just finished reviewing today's briefs. But I did see short items in *The Times* and *The Guardian* about some ruckus at their meeting yesterday."

"I'll send more detailed information from some of the other media," Jay said. "Apparently, partisanship has been tearing the Authority apart, the mayor has sided with one faction, and now the annual budget approval is stopped dead with arguments over numerous revenue proposals."

"What does this mean?" Michael said. "Obviously, you think it means something or you wouldn't be telling me about it."

"We think, sir," said Gittings, "that they may not be able to agree on the budget. There's a good possibility that the government of Greater London will shut down, with no sanitation, transportation, and other essential services."

"Surely, they'll work this out," Michael said. "We're talking a city of nine million people and more if you count commuters and the tourists on any given day. Why hasn't this received more media coverage?"

"It's been bogged down in subcommittees, scheduling interminable meetings at all hours of the day and night," Jay said. "Yesterday, it surfaced at the Authority meeting, and enough members walked out to shut the meeting down. That finally caught everyone's attention. The budget has to be approved by Friday or the city will start hitting operational funding issues. First to go would likely be rubbish collection, followed by the buses and the underground. Transport for London may find themselves without funds to operate or pay their employees."

"What do you think will happen?" Michael said. "Parliament is supposed to open on Monday."

"I think we're headed for problems," Gittings said. "The factions are at daggers points, and it's about five different groups, none of whom wants to cooperate with anyone else. The regular coalitions have broken down. I've talked with several of my contacts there and they're saying every proposal for compromise immediately hits a brick wall."

"Does Parliament have any authority to maintain services in London?" Michael said.

"After 30 days," Gittings said, "Parliament can declare an emergency and step in. A two-thirds vote is needed, however, and that may be difficult. Unless MPs decide that walking to work through mounds of garbage is too much of a nuisance and decide to do something."

"Assume things stop," Michael said, looking at Brent Epworth. "What happens here at the palace?"

"Sir," Epworth said, "I've already been stockpiling basic food and other supplies for the family, staff, and scheduled functions. If it looks like the city will shut down, I'll order as much as I can as fast as I can. We'll also need to consider the staff, sir, and getting to and from home to work. I've written a plan for essential workers, but it's by far the vast majority; the staff is lean and we have virtually no one we could do without beyond just a few days. I'd suggest we have them prepare to sleep here. That may mean taking over some of the guest bedrooms and other areas, and making provision for beds, linens, and other materials."

"Sarah will be home later this morning," Michael said. "We'll need to look at our schedules and see what we may need to adjust for next week, perhaps longer." He paused. "What about our staff who have children in school or daycare, or elderly parents to care for? We can't ask them to stay here for a few days if they have family to take care of."

"I'll do the check today, sir," Epworth said, "a quick survey. And find out."

At lunchtime, Michael was with the boys in the loft, waiting for Sarah's return. He had talked privately with Jason about what he had said during the prayer meeting at school.

"Had you been to Robert's house before?" Michael asked.

Jason shook his head. "I looked his address up in the school directory last night. I didn't think he'd come to school today. And then I mapped it on the internet and figured out which buses would get me there."

"It took great courage to do what you did, Jason," Michael said. "And I know this hurts. But you saved that young man."

"I couldn't let him go back, Dad. I knew what it was like."

"You never said what had happened at the home," Michael said. "We knew there was this almost irrational fear of, how did you say it, going back to Juvenile, but I'd no idea of what you'd gone through. Why didn't you tell us?"

"I was afraid, Dad," Jason said. "I was afraid if I said what had happened then you and no one else would have wanted to adopt me." The church in San Francisco had decided to provide for Jason and several other teenagers living on the streets. That had included adoption, and Michael and Sarah had adopted Jason.

"My son," Michael said, "that was an awfully heavy load for you to carry by yourself. And while it might have shocked us to know, I don't think it would have changed our minds."

"I think I know that now, Dad," Jason said, "but I didn't back then. I was afraid if I told you you'd make me leave." He paused. "I dream about it sometimes, like it's happening all over again."

"Do you want me to arrange for counseling?" Michael said. "It may help to talk it out with someone."

"I've got you, Dad. If I need someone else, I'll tell you." Jason paused. "Last night, Robert said that talking with you made him feel safe. He said he didn't think he could trust any man, but you made him feel safe. And you do. Sometimes I can't believe that I have you and Mom. I feel like I don't deserve you."

"Jason," Michael said, "God granted us a great blessing when he brought you into our lives." He kissed Jason's head and held him.

While Michael and the boys had been eating dinner at the palace, the Metropolitan Police descended upon St. Mark's Parish. Entering the church during the mid-week service, they had walked down the main aisle, surprising both Rev. Wickham and the 20 or so mostly elderly parishioners sitting in the pews. Wickham, who'd been giving a short homily on climate change and global warming, stopped in mid-sentence.

As two policemen handcuffed him, Detective Inspector Frees told him he was under arrest for child molestation, and then began to read him his rights. Wickham burst into tears.

With a search warrant in hand, a team of 12 policeman and forensic specialists entered the church's offices, Rev. Wickham's living quarters at the church, and a large basement room that the reverend always kept locked.

Samantha Hood had finally been reached in Leeds and had traveled back to London by the early train on Thursday. She was met by a security agent at the station, and driven to Buckingham Palace, arriving almost exactly at 10 a.m.

Meeting with Michael, Josh Gittings and Detective-Inspector Frees at the palace, and feeling more than a little bit intimidated and overwhelmed by the surroundings and the presence of the king, Samantha tried to explain that Robert had an active, and what she believed was an overactive, imagination.

"He's made these claims before," she said. "And it just can't be true. The Rev. Wickham is a godly man, and he's been wonderful to me and Robert. I just can't believe this. There must be some mistake, or Robert totally misunderstood something."

"Did you ever ask Rev. Wickham about what Robert said?" the detective said.

"Of course not," she said. "I would never embarrass him like that. I'm afraid you've all gone to a great deal of trouble over nothing more than my son's overactive imagination. And I don't understand how you're involved in this, your majesty."

Michael explained what had happened with Jason and Robert in the prayer group.

"It's terrible that he's now saying these things to other students," she said. "I just don't know what to do."

Extracting several photographs from the folder he had with him, Frees handed them to Samantha.

She stared.

"These were among some 150 photos on Rev. Wickham's computer, many far worse than what you're looking at. There are additional ones on CDs that we're checking now. There are also videos we found in the basement room at the church where most of this happened. There was a fairly elaborate film system set up."

She kept staring at the photographs. White-faced, she looked at Michael. "Where's Robert?" she asked.

"He's upstairs with my sons in our family quarters," Michael said. "Mrs. Hood, your son has shown tremendous courage in telling this story. What he's been going through for six years is unimaginable. He's going to need your support, and he's going to need a lot of counseling. But he's a courageous young man."

She looked at him with tears in her eyes. "I can't afford counseling. What am I going to do? How can I face him? How could they do that to him? He's just a boy. I wouldn't listen to him and I condemned him to that," she said, gesturing with the photographs, which Frees gently retrieved from her. "I'm responsible for what he's gone through. I wouldn't listen to him." She began to sob.

"Mrs. Hood," Michael said, "I will arrange for counseling for both Robert and you. Josh here has been checking on who the best counselors might be in working with abused children, and we have several possibilities."

"Why are you doing this?" she asked. "You don't even know us."

"My Jason knows what Robert has gone through," Michael said, "because he went through something like it a number of years ago. We're in a position to help, and we want to do that."

They heard a knock at the door. Jay stuck his head in. "I apologize, your majesty, but the news is breaking on television. I've alerted the communications firm for the school."

Michael looked at Josh. "Josh, get to Dr. Owens at the school immediately. The media may start making the connections and if it does the school will be blitzed. I'll talk with him as well." Josh nodded as he left with Jay.

"Detective-Inspector," Michael said, "will Robert's name be kept confidential?"

"In theory, yes," Frees said. "That's what's supposed to happen. But depending upon how big this becomes, all bets may be off. And he's now 16, which is the age of consent in Britain, although the fact that most of this happened before should cover confidentiality. We'll do everything we can to keep his name out of it, but I can't guarantee it won't happen."

Frees stood to leave. "I'll have to get to the station. If you need anything else, here's my card with my cell phone number. Call at any time, day or night." He turned to Samantha and gave her his card as well. "Mrs. Hood, you need to love that boy like you've never loved him before. The worst of the nightmare is behind him now. But there's a different kind of nightmare ahead – the media, the courts and what he'll need to heal. So, love that boy." She looked at him and nodded.

"Thank you, detective," Michael said, as Frees left the room.

Michael walked around the library table and sat next to Samantha. He put his hand on hers.

"I can try to imagine what you're feeling personally right now, Mrs. Hood, and I know it's awful. But the policeman is right. The most critical thing right now for you to focus on is Robert. I know you have your own issues to deal with, but you need to set them aside for the moment. There's a 16-year-old boy who's going to need all the love you can give him."

She looked at Michael, her tears continuing.

"Robert will need to be examined by a doctor," Michael said. "We don't know the extent of what he may have suffered. They'll need to examine him and take blood tests. He could have serious health issues. Robert already knows this."

Still weeping, she nodded.

"By tonight, returning home may be impossible. The news media will be everywhere, and if they get hold of Robert's name, it's going to be a circus. Eventually you'll have to deal with it, but I think a few days in seclusion will help you and Robert. So, I'm inviting you both to stay here. Security controls access to the palace, and if and when they trace you here, we can handle the media."

Samantha looked at him. "Thank you, your majesty, thank you. I don't know what to say. Can I see Robert now? Can I see my boy?"

Michael walked Samantha to the elevator, and then to the loft on the back side of the palace's west wing. Jason, Jim and Robert were in the living room, staring at the television. A news reporter was standing in front of St. Mark's Church.

"Robert?" Michael said softly.

The boys looked up, and Robert saw his mother. He leaped over the sofa to run to her.

Michael led them both to Sarah's art studio in the loft. "I'll leave you here for a bit. We'll be in the living room if you need us."

Michael sat with Jason and Jim and watched the news reports. The arrest charge against Wickham had cited an unnamed teenaged boy, and that the abuse had gone on for years.

As Jason flipped through the news channels, they could see that the story was everywhere. In the middle of one report, the reporter broke in with breaking news, that three other C of E priests in London had been arrested on the same charge involving the same victim, and that more arrests were expected.

"It's Robert, isn't it?" Jim asked.

Michael and Jason nodded.

"What did they do to him?" Jim said.

Michael looked at his 9- almost-10-year-old son, realizing that Robert had been the same age when it had all started, and he shuddered. "They did bad things, Jim," Michael said. He motioned to Jason to turn the television off. "I hate to tell you this, because it's all about sin. And like all sin it's ugly, and this is cruel and evil. But you need to know what to do if you have to confront something like this. Before I say anything else, I want you to know that this was not Robert's fault. What these men did is their sin, not Robert's." And he proceeded to describe what had happened as carefully as he could.

When Michael finished, Jim just stared at him. "That's horrible," he said.

"Aye, Young Jim, it is indeed horrible," said Michael. "And Robert needs help, including our help. They did this to him, Jim. And it will take a long time for him to heal."

"A long time ago, Jim, it happened to me," Jason said.

Jim stared at his brother. "Did it hurt?" he finally said.

Jason nodded.

Jim leaned over and hugged his brother. Jason looked at Michael with tears in his eyes.

"I'm unbelievably blessed with my two sons here, and that little one in the nursery, the one I think I hear stirring right now,"

Michael said, glancing at the baby monitor on the table in front of them. He smiled. "You're both a special blessing."

Henry Ian Kent-Hughes had been born in San Francisco the night of the attack on Michael and Sarah. Tommy MacFarland, Michael's best friend since childhood, had been flown by a U.S. military jet from an architects' conference in Chicago to San Francisco, and had coached Sarah through childbirth while Michael had been in surgery. Tommy, with a gift for nicknames, had anointed the baby as Hank the Yank. And it was by Hank that he was called by his family and indeed the British nation.

As Sarah had begun to see the day after his birth, Hank bore a striking resemblance to his father, a resemblance that had continued to grow through his first year. While Hank still had the chubbiness of a baby, his black hair, facial features and sky-blue eyes marked him as Michael's son. The unusual blue color of his eyes was a trademark of Britain's royal family.

Both Jason and Jim doted on him. It had taken months for Jim to get used to having a baby in the family, especially with some of the less attractive sights and smells associated with having an infant around. But when Hank was six months old, he'd grabbed Jim's nose when Jim was holding him, which Jim found totally hilarious, and something in the action resulted in Jim bonding with his little brother.

Jason had taken to Hank immediately, and would change his diapers and bathe him, and play with him for hours on end, loving every minute. Michael and Sarah had seen Hank peel back Jason's tough exterior to expose a core gentleness.

As much as Hank responded to both boys, Sarah could see the even stronger bond the baby had formed with his father. His eyes followed Michael around the room, and he seemed most content when his father held him. At nine months, Hank had surprised all of them by reaching his arms toward Michael with a "Da!" gurgling from his lips. It was still the only word he spoke, and Sarah was waiting patiently for a "Ma." And three weeks before, Hank had taken his first unassisted steps. He was now maneuvering himself with increasing agility each day.

Hearing the baby stirring, Michael walked into the nursery as Joan Plunkett was preparing to change his diaper.

"Mrs. Plunkett," Michael said, "why don't I take over? With all the uproar we've been in, you've had him for more than your fair share."

"He's an easy baby, your majesty," she said. "Like all of them, he's a lot of work, but he has just the sweetest disposition. But I think I may take you up on your offer and get my soup and sandwich and have a little rest, if that's agreeable."

"You do that, Mrs. Plunkett," Michael said, "and I'll take over the Prince here."

Hank, standing up in his crib, cooed in glee when he saw Michael come for him. "Da!"

"Okay, big guy," Michael said, smiling, "let's get that soggy nappy taken care of."

With a freshly powdered and diapered Hank in his arms, Michael walked into the living area. Samantha and Robert had joined Jason and Jim at the television, and Michael noticed that Jim was holding Robert's hand. *Young Jim has a big heart*, Michael thought to himself.

On the television, a news reporter was standing in front of Lambeth Palace, the formal residence of Sebastian Rowland, the Archbishop of Canterbury. The reporter was saying that the Church of England was officially not commenting on the arrests of four of its priests, other than to ask that the law be allowed to take its course and the rights of both victim and accused be honored.

"I think it would be a good idea if we turn the television off for a bit," Michael said. "Mr. Malone will be having lunch brought up soon, and Sarah is due in here at any moment." As Jason powered off the television, they heard the door to the loft opening. As if on cue, Sarah walked into the room.

Michael's heart melted when he saw her. He had fallen in love with her from the first moment he had seen her in a class on medieval church art slightly more than four years before, and he felt like he fell in love with her all over again every time he saw her. She stood 5 foot 7 in her stocking feet, with golden brown hair, high cheekbones and what he called her "beautifully soft" brown eyes. And while it had taken her only slightly longer to fall in love with him, and considerably longer to embrace his Christian faith, she had ultimately done so, and found herself falling more in love with him with each passing day.

It was to Michael that her eyes went first. And she walked straight to him and kissed him, and then Hank, who laughed to see her.

Turning, she saw Samantha and Robert, and walked to them, introducing herself. As she shook Robert's hand, she saw the mixture of pain, relief and fear in his eyes, and she hugged him.

"We're glad you're with us, Robert," she said.

She hugged and kissed Jim, and then looked at Jason. Jason shared her talent for art, and the two of them had spent considerable time painting together and talking about art in general and their art in particular. While Jim would have preferred walking on nails, Jason eagerly accompanied her to all of the art museums London had to offer.

Jason, expecting a reprimand for his leaving school without permission but knowing it would be made with love, looked at Sarah. "Hi, Mom," he said.

She walked to him and hugged him. "I want to strangle you and hug you at the same time," she whispered. "But you're my hero." Jason smiled.

"So, have I missed lunch?" she asked the group.

They heard the knock on the door, indicating the arrival of Davy Malone, the palace's chef.

"It sounds like it's arriving as we speak," Michael said.

"Ma!" Hank said, holding his arms toward Sarah.

Absolutely thrilled, Sarah reached for her son.

"I'm not sure where our Hank gets his sense of timing from," Michael said, laughing as he handed the baby to his mother, "but it is uncanny."

Chapter 6: Ripples Become a Wave

Through Thursday afternoon and evening, the news coverage continued unabated. Most of the afternoon reports were repetitious. In one 6 p.m. television report, however, the reporter had asked a parishioner at St. Mark's who the teenagers at the church were, and the woman replied there was only one, and mentioned Robert's name.

Michael and the boys had been watching the report, while Sarah and Samantha had been getting dinner together in the loft's kitchen.

"Mother!" Robert cried.

Samantha, with Sarah in her wake, walked quickly into the living area to see reporters standing in front of their home. Mrs. Binch, the next-door neighbor who had told Michael where to look for the boys, was being interviewed.

"They're such a nice family," she was saying. "This is just terrible for them and for the neighborhood. Robert often helps me with odd jobs."

"When did you last see him, Mrs. Binch?" the reporter asked.

"It was yesterday. His mother left for work with a suitcase, she often has to travel with her job, and he usually leaves for the bus stop right after. I didn't see him, but I assumed he'd left. An hour or so

later, another boy was knocking at their front door, and then I saw
Robert let him in."

Jason and Michael exchanged glances.

"They were inside for only a few minutes," Mrs. Binch said,
"and then I saw them leave and start walking toward the park. I called
to Robert and told him he should be in school. He goes to that nice
Christian school near Notting Hill. Well, anyway, he nodded at me and
the two boys continued toward the park."

"What happened next, Mrs. Binch?" the reporter said.

"Well, it couldn't have been 15 or 20 minutes later, a car pulls
up in front, and four men get out and knock at the Hoods' door. I told
them no one was at home, of course. I only talked with one of the men,
and he sounded familiar but my eyesight being what it is, I couldn't
recognize him, and he didn't identify himself, only thanked me for
telling him to look in the park. But one of them was a policeman, I'm
sure of that, I could see the uniform. But not the man I talked with."

"And then?"

"Well, it must have been a good 30 or 40 minutes later, the car
came back, and Robert got out with the policeman, and they went
inside. I could see the other young man in the car, sitting in the back, I
believe. And then Robert and the policeman came out, Robert with his

backpack and a suitcase, and they drove off. But it wasn't a police car they were in."

As the reporter then moved into speculation as to what have might happened next, Michael dialed Jay on his cell phone.

"Jay. You've seen the report."

"Yes, sir, and I've got Dr. Owens and the communications team on my land line. They're at the school, and they say television trucks are setting up in front. I'll work with them to handle it, sir."

"Thanks, Jay," Michael said, and rang off.

"They call this journalism," Michael said. "They take irresponsibility and cruelty to the next higher level and call it journalism and the public's right to know."

"What do we do?" Samantha Hood asked, her voice catching. She was holding tightly to Robert, who looked terrified.

"We're going to pray," Michael said, "and then I'll talk with Detective-Inspector Frees. But we need to pray first."

Ben Hurst, a reporter for the London Record, and no friend to the Church of England or King Michael and his evangelical Christianity, watched the report on Channel 6, and wondered. He had been at the school on Wednesday to cover the report of the king's son going missing and had heard Michael's reference to Jason helping a friend in distress. What if that friend were Robert Hood? And what if the man looking for the boys was the King? And what might one conclude if a Church of England priest, even if he were the king, had inserted himself into a child molesting case involving four C of E priests? Might that suggest some kind of cover-up?

At Lambeth Palace, the Archbishop of Canterbury and his chief of staff, sitting with their FBL consultant Geoffrey Venneman, had watched the Channel 6 report.

"If I am to help you," Venneman said, "I need to know everything that's known about the priests involved." He looked at Canon Martin Land, the archbishop's chief of staff and the churchman they all knew might have the greatest influence over Rowland. "You said there were complicating issues. I need to know what those are."

After clearing his throat, Canon Land began to speak.

At the police station, Frees talked with Michael by phone.

"I've scheduled a press briefing in 15 minutes, sir, right at 6:30," Frees said. "Mostly to castigate Channel 6 for its totally unethical report. But it's getting out of control, and the rumors are becoming a tidal wave." He paused. "One reporter has asked if there's any connection between the case against Wickham and Jason's disappearing from school yesterday."

"If you're asked that question, Detective Inspector," Michael said, "you should tell them the truth. There'll be some questions, I imagine, about the king's involvement, given the fact that king is, after all, an ordained C of E priest. What's behind the question is most likely the thought, possibly the hope, of a possible cover-up for the church, so that they can catch me and the church at the same time."

"I will tell them exactly what happened, sir," Frees said.

The 6:30 p.m. press briefing at the police station was broadcast live on all London television stations. Frees began with a short update of progress in the case, saying that one of the arrested priests was cooperating with the investigation by providing additional details and information.

When the reporter for Channel 6 raised her hand to be recognized, Frees stared at her. "Concerning your report tonight, I have seen unethical actions from the news media over the years, but your performance is the capstone. And don't hand me your rubbish about the public's right to know when we all know this is about your station's right to profit." He then nodded at Ben Hurst of the *Record*.

"Detective-Inspector," Hurst said, "yesterday, King Michael's son Jason disappeared for a time from the International Christian School. The king told us in a press briefing that his son had left without anyone's permission to help a fellow student in distress. This evening we learn that the victim in this case is a student at ICS. Was Robert Hood the student in distress? And just how much is the King involved in this, given that he is an ordained priest of the church?"

Frees considered for a moment before answering. "What you're asking me, Mr. Hurst, is a speculative shot-in-the-dark question that you want to use to impugn the king's character, suggesting that as a priest the king is engaging in a cover-up for the church. I will answer your question, but let's make sure we all know why you're asking it, and I suspect it has nothing to do with the case at hand."

Hurst turned red with embarrassment.

"Yesterday," Frees said, "Jason Kent-Hughes left ICS to find a student who was indeed in great distress. Jason left the school property without permission from his parents or the school."

At the palace, watching the press briefing on television, Jason looked at Michael and Sarah.

"And the student he was trying to help was Robert Hood," Frees said. "And I will say nothing else about the young man, so don't ask me to confirm or deny anything about him. The school notified the king that his son was missing, and the king came immediately to the school. And while a teenager suddenly disappearing from school or home may not necessarily be unusual, the king's family has different concerns than you or I. Don't forget that all of their lives were endangered just a short year ago.

"One student knew what had happened and would give his information only to the king. Assisted by the school and the police, the king went to the Hood home, and eventually found both boys in a nearby park, as you heard on the report. The king talked with the boys, and then had my office immediately contacted on an emergency basis. I was interviewing the young man within an hour of his meeting with the king. So far from trying to cover anything up, Mr. Hurst, King Michael did exactly what any responsible citizen would do, and got the police involved immediately. He's done far more, in fact, than anyone might reasonably expect. And I have nothing but praise and admiration for the man and how he's conducted himself."

Canon Land had watched the press conference by himself in his office. He powered on his mobile, punching in a number he knew by heart.

"It's Martin," he said. "I was watching the press conference."

"I saw it as well."

"The king's involved," Land said. "He could use this to further his reform cause."

"You don't know Michael. He will not use something like this. But if he thinks there is something bigger here, something worse than one boy at a London church, he will not let go."

"Can you talk with him?" Land said. "Can you tell him to let the investigation take its course and to stay out of it?"

"I don't have that kind of influence over Michael. I will see what I can do. At a minimum, I may learn something."

"Let me know," Land said, and powered off.

Watching the briefing on her television, Mrs. Binch suddenly realized why the man she had talked with on Wednesday had sounded so familiar. Stunned, she sat staring at the television. *Well, I would have done a curtsy if he'd told me!*

Trevor Barry used the remote to turn the television off. He and his wife Liz had heard the early report connecting the abuse case to a student at ICS. Jane and Andrew had watched the police's press briefing with them.

"We need to get dinner on the table," Liz said, patting Trevor on his leg as she stood up. With her eyes, she signaled to Jane and Andrew to help with setting the table and serving the food. Trevor glanced over at Jane and could see she was unusually subdued. She and Andrew followed their mother to the kitchen.

As the Barry family sat at dinner, Trevor watched Jane pick at her food. Liz seemed more engrossed with Andrew's account of his day at school than with noticing Jane.

After cleaning up in the kitchen, Trevor walked to Jane's room. Lying on the floor, she had a school book, maths he thought, open in front of her, but she was staring at the wall.

"You didn't seem hungry at dinner," he said, and she nodded.

"Is it a fight with Jason? I notice he hasn't called. Is it about what happened with Robert Hood yesterday?"

She shook her head.

"And I'm butting in your business," he said, smiling.

"Dad, we haven't had a fight, but it is about Jason." And then it came spilling out of her, and she told him what had happened in the hallway on Wednesday afternoon, including what Jason had said about his background.

At first Trevor thought he was going to be sick. He immediately understood what the rough edges were about. The boy had lived on the streets, with everything that implied. He looked at her for a long time, fighting his own internal emotion, and then said, "Is this a problem for you?"

She nodded. "It's horrible. I know it's not his fault. It was something that happened to him when he was little, younger than Andrew. But I can't deal with it. I wish I'd never heard it."

Liz was standing in the door and had heard most of the conversation. She knelt on the floor beside Jane. "Oh, Jane," she said, as she put her arms around her daughter, "I know it's a shocking thing. And I know the questions it raises in your mind. I'm so sorry. I know how much you liked him."

Trevor stared at his wife. She's already talking about him in the past tense. "What have you said to him, Jane?" he asked.

She shook her head. "I haven't said anything. I'm avoiding him. He wasn't in school today; they're keeping him and Jim home at the palace right now. He's sent me an email, but I didn't reply." The girl looked down. "I don't know what to do. I can't look at him without thinking about it." She started crying on her mother's shoulder.

"You need to say something to him," Trevor said. "He's probably hurting. He said what he did because he was trying to defend Robert Hood, or make people understand."

"I know, Dad," she said, "but I don't know what to say. I don't want to see him right now. I just want it all to go away."

Later, as they were getting ready for bed, Liz looked at her husband, who was sitting in bed with a book open in front of him but staring off toward the window of their bedroom. "I know you like the boy, Trevor," she said. "I like him as well. And I know whose son he is. But don't be too hard on her. You're right, she does need to say something to him, even if it's to end their relationship. But she's 16 years old. And I know what's running through her mind. She's liked him so much that she naturally thought they'd be together forever and suddenly she has to confront this horrible thing that happened to him. You have to ask yourself what kind of scars it left, if something could happen later, even if he has any diseases that could preclude marriage. You know, the whole range of things, STDs, HIV, AIDS, all of those things. Relationships are difficult enough without having to deal with that as well."

Trevor was quiet for a long time, and then smiled at his wife. "I know, Liz. I know. I don't want to make her struggle any worse. I just feel for the boy." He looked at his wife. "And he's a believer, isn't he? Isn't he what you call a new creature in Christ?"

Liz reddened. Trevor's words stung, made worse by the fact that she deserved the rebuke.

Late that night in their bedroom in the loft, long after the boys and Samantha Hood had gone to bed, Sarah lay quietly in Michael's arms, her head on his shoulder and her hand on his chest.

"I think these are my favorite times of all," she said. "Just lying here with you. I love listening to your heart. And your body's so warm."

"I feel you next to me and I know we're one," Michael said, touching the bare skin of her back, and then pulling the sheet to cover her. "I haven't even asked how your visit with Ma and Da went."

"It was short, but it was so good to see them. They're doing well, Mike, and they've got pictures of the boys all over the place."

"Doting grandparents. No surprise there."

"We need to think about Christmas. Do you want to go back to Scotland?"

"Aye, I do, my love. Maybe we'll stay at Holyrood if Tommy and his architects and construction people have it fixed up by then."

"Maybe they'll be late, and we'll have to stay with Ma and Da."

Michael laughed. "We all love the farm."

"Mike?" she said, as she moved her hand across his chest, feeling the scar from the operation that had saved his life after being shot twice in San Francisco at the start of The Violence.

"Yes, my own self?"

"What's going to happen with Robert? I'm not thinking about the counseling and healing, I know that will be hard and take a long time. I'm thinking about Monday, or whenever it is that he returns to school. How will he face that?"

"Only with God's grace," Michael said. "Sarah, what happened to Robert is far worse than I hope anyone ever knows. But God makes the human spirit to be resilient, and I'm hopeful for that." He paused. "To see Jason reach out to him, and keep reaching out to him, has been an incredible thing. He took a huge personal risk to help Robert, and now he has to face his own personal issues at school, not to mention the possible loss of his girlfriend."

"Did Jane say or do something?"

"I don't know, but he's said very little about her, except that he might not have a girlfriend any more. She heard his outburst against the Jenner boy, and Chris said she looked horrified. But let's not blame her. It must have been a shocking thing for her to hear. We would have been shocked as well."

"Do you think that man is still at the home in San Francisco?" Sarah said. "That was six or seven years ago."

"I don't know, but we should have someone check. I hope he's long gone. But I'll ask Josh to check tomorrow. And now we should get some sleep. We don't know what tomorrow will bring."

"I love you, my big hunk."

Michael smiled in the dark and held her closely, listening to her breathing as she gradually fell asleep in his arms.

Chapter 7: London Calling

On Friday morning after breakfast, Michael sat in the library, talking with Rodgers Clarke. A Tory MP from Dorset, Clarke and his wife Marguerite had been to Buckingham Palace several times for dinners with Michael and Sarah. Sarah had met them when she, Jason, and Jim had attended a Sunday worship service at Westminster Chapel, a short two-block walk from the palace.

Michael had asked Clarke to be part of his church study team, which would be meeting again in 30 minutes. Michael would not be participating in this meeting, but Clarke had asked for a few minutes to "discuss a matter."

"Marguerite's brother Elliot Martin is on the Greater London Authority," Clarke said. "I gather you know that today they're meeting for a last desperate attempt to pass a budget."

Michael nodded. "We've been following this," he said. "The potential disruption to London and even our own day-to-day activities here at the palace is enormous."

"We had dinner with Elliot and his family last night," Clarke said. "Elliot is not at all optimistic about what will happen today."

"Has he said what he thinks might happen?" Michael said.

"Elliot is one of seven Conservative members on the Authority. That's seven out of 25 boroughs, plus the City. After the various minor parties – Greens, Radical Socialists, Liberals, and what-have-you, Labour has 13 seats, a majority of one. Except the majority is itself riddled with factions, and that's the problem. They won't coalesce. The mayor threw his lot in with the largest faction, trying to force resolution, and that ripped it wide open." Clarke paused before going on. "Elliot believes that the Authority will not be able to pass a budget today."

"Our Master of the Household has been stockpiling food and supplies," Michael said. "He's also put together a plan for the staff. Essentially, our people with children or family to care for will do what they can to work from home. Everyone else will temporarily move into the palace. We'll have to cancel or postpone a number of planned functions, but there's nothing critical. But I'm far more concerned about London."

Clarke nodded. "Basic services will continue through Sunday," he said. "Statutory authority for the budget expires Sunday night."

"And we open Parliament on Monday," Michael said.

"It's likely to be chaotic if the buses and underground aren't operating," Clarke said. He cleared his throat. "Elliot asked if I might have a word with you about all this. If it all goes the way it looks like it will go, would you consider an appearance at a meeting of the Authority?"

"For what purpose?" Michael said.

"Elliot thinks, and I agree with him, that a plea from you might convince enough of the Authority members to approve a budget. He could arrange to yield his allotted time for speaking to you, and he's lined up the other conservative members to do the same."

"And what happens if they don't listen?"

"Nothing other than what would happen anyway," Clarke said. "Except there might be some embarrassment for you."

Michael glanced at his watch. "Rodger, you have the study team in two minutes. Let me talk with Josh and Jay about this. I'm inclined toward doing it, but I need to take counsel with them as well. Let's see what happens today, and then we can talk by phone this afternoon. Tuesday is the earliest I could do anything, assuming Parliament is able to open on Monday."

Josh, Jay, Jonathan Crowe, Brent Epworth, Sarah, Ryan Mitchell, and Trevor Barry joined Michael for lunch. The purpose had been a final review of the procedure and timing for the opening of

Parliament. Each of them had an identical notebook. Trevor led them through the discussion.

"I have a question," Michael said, when they finished. "And Mr. Mitchell, you may be the one with the weightiest answer. What happens Monday if we have no buses and the Underground?"

"On a typical day," Mitchell said, "between 300,000 and 400,000 people commute to work. That doesn't include residents going to medical appointments or shopping, etc. Throw in tourists and that's another 120,000. So, you could have half a million using buses, the Overground, and the Underground on a given day."

"Clearly people couldn't replace that traffic with cars," Michael said. "What about the opening of Parliament? Would you expect to see people in the streets?"

Mitchell nodded. "Normally, there would be anywhere from 100,000 to 200,000 people lining the route you and the Queen would be taking in the carriage from the palace to Parliament. Without public transportation, I would expect considerably fewer. The plan is for The Mall and Birdcage Walk to be closed to traffic at 8 a.m., and Whitehall at 9 a.m. If traffic has already become snarled with automobiles, we'll likely scrap the carriage and take you in an automobile via Petty

France and Broadway down to Parliament. We would plan to return via Victoria and Buckingham Gate."

Michael nodded. "And Tuesday, assuming public transport isn't operating, would there be a way to get me to Greater London Authority?"

Every head at the table looked at Michael.

"And why would you be going to the Authority on Tuesday, my husband?" Sarah said.

"It's another item for discussion with this group," he said. And then he explained what Rodgers Clarke had proposed.

For a short time, there was a silence. Josh spoke first. "I don't think I've heard of a king becoming involved in Greater London politics before, at least openly."

Trevor nodded. "At least, not since Queen Victoria's time. It would certainly signal the gravity of the situation." Under the plan put together by Brent Epworth, Trevor and Josh would both have accommodations at the palace, as would Jay, Jonathan, and most of the communications staffs for Michael and Sarah. They would be alerted on Sunday at 1 p.m. by text message if the plan was to be implemented.

"Joshua," Michael said, "do you see any problems? And Jay, I need you to weigh in here as well. Is there a downside to me doing this? Would it be better for me to stay out of it and let the Authority thrash it all out?"

The conversation went on for some time. The consensus was that, if it looked necessary, Michael should do it.

Then he turned to his security chief. "Mr. Mitchell, how might I physically get there, if traffic is at a standstill?"

Mitchell thought for a moment. "The river, most likely. We could take a water taxi."

Michael laughed. "That's brilliant. Can you make those arrangements?" He then nodded at his speechwriter. "So now, I think I need Jonathan here to come with me to the library to work on what I should say."

With that, the group broke up. Before she left them, Sarah reminded Michael that she was supposed to be having lunch with her mother and Tyler Zimmer on Tuesday.

"Perhaps if public transport has stopped," she said, "I might have an excuse to postpone?"

"Is the lunch here at the palace?" Michael said.

"No," Sarah said. "it's supposed to be at their house in South Kensington."

"Mr. Mitchell will have to figure it out," Michael said. "But why do I suspect that you're hoping everything shuts down?"

"Well," she said, "it would temporarily delay the inevitable, I suppose."

Michael laughed.

The rest of Friday brought no new revelations about the abuse issue, although not for lack of trying by the news media. A brief statement issued by ICS simply asked for prayer, and said the school was cooperating fully with the police and would not potentially jeopardize the ongoing investigation with any additional comments. A similar statement was used by Jay Lanham to news media inquiries at the palace, referring all queries to Detective-Inspector Frees.

Considerable speculation arose about the whereabouts of Robert and his mother, but nothing concrete could be determined.

Frees arranged for a medical team to examine Robert at the palace. The boy bore the examination with a quiet grace.

At 4 p.m., an acrimonious meeting of the Greater London Authority broke up in shouting and a fist fight between two Labour members. No budget was approved, and the members went home, knowing the earliest they would be meeting would be Tuesday. All metropolitan government offices were closed Monday for the opening of Parliament.

Late Saturday afternoon, the police announced the arrest of eight more C of E priests, including three in Manchester, bringing the total to 12, and said that the investigation was continuing, with more arrests anticipated. At a 5 p.m. press conference, Frees said that the investigation had determined that additional children had been victimized, and that numerous witnesses and victims were coming forward with additional information and promising leads.

"Make no mistake," the policeman said. "We will be relentless in hunting these predators down. And this may go back decades."

An hour later, Frees called Security at the palace and asked to speak to Michael. Michael returned the call a few minutes later.

"I'm sorry to bother you, your majesty," Frees said, "but something's come up in the investigation that we're not sure is a lead or not, and I thought you might have an idea. One of the priests arrested, the one who's been cooperating, said something about all this having started at seminary."

"Seminary?" Michael said. He paused. "Was he speaking generically, or did he mention a specific one?"

"Apparently it was the one outside Norfolk," Frees said.

For a moment, when the king didn't respond, Frees thought he had lost the connection.

"Sir, are you there?" he asked.

"Oh, yes, Detective, I'm sorry, I became distracted," Michael said. "The seminary you're referring to is St. Simon's. It's not affiliated with a specific church or cathedral, like many of the theology schools are." He paused. "At one time, I was very keen to do my theological training there. But I ended up at a special program that had been recently organized at the University of Edinburgh. So, I do know a bit about St. Simon's program of study."

"Well, sir," said Frees, "we don't know if it's important or not, and I'm not sure how to go about determining if it is, short of banging on the door and demanding entrance."

"I know a few of the graduates," Michael said. "If you want, I could ask them about their experiences there."

"If you could do that, sir," Frees said, "that would be most helpful."

Michael slowly put down his telephone, staring at the desktop. He actually knew only one graduate of St. Simon's. Andrew Brimley, the vicar at St. Botolph's in a village near the McLaren's farm in Edinburgh, had been the first person to hear Michael, at age 15, say he was being called to the Anglican priesthood. Brimley was a talented vicar, with a gift for preaching and counseling. He had assisted the Archbishop of York at Michael's coronation, and he had been the priest who had baptized Hank in January.

And when Michael had told him of his desire to follow in his footsteps and study at St. Simon's, Brimley had instead suggested a new program just established, one much closer to home, at the University of Edinburgh. Michael had at first been puzzled, but Brimley had ultimately been successful in convincing Michael to attend Edinburgh.

The question in Michael's mind now was, why?

At Lambeth Palace, Geoffrey Venneman looked across a table in the Archbishop's private conference room at Canon Land.

"You said yesterday there were four priests you knew about. Now we have 12. I'm either told the truth now or I walk, and you can handle this yourself. This has the potential to upend everything we've been doing in Parliament and with the news media to stop Michael."

Canon Land's palms were sweating. "I will have to check personnel files," he said, "and our Human Resources people won't be in the office until Monday."

"That's too late," Venneman said. "And we may be facing a suspension of all public transport. You need to get access to those files as soon as possible. We need to know what we're ultimately dealing with and get out ahead of it." He paused. "Is there any possible way to implicate the king?"

Land was shocked. "No! Categorically and absolutely not. He was never assigned to a parish here in Britain and his theological training fell outside the usual seminary process. He has not been involved."

Venneman smiled. "Tis a pity," he said. "But you need to check those files by tomorrow at the latest. And don't be so defensive, Canon Land. You sound rather protective of the king."

Only later, as he took the tube back to his flat in the Docklands, did he realize that Land had included the word "seminary" in what he said. *Where did that come from*, he wondered. He briefly considered resigning the account before things got too mucked up, and then reconsidered. He wasn't quite ready, nor would his bosses at FBL, to forgo that 150,000 pounds a month consulting fee from the Archbishop.

On Sunday, Jonathan Crowe was eating lunch with his parents and sister after church services at the family's favorite restaurant in Vauxhall. He felt his mobile vibrate with a text message.

The text was from Brent Epworth. The plan for the palace staff was being implemented.

"I have to get home and pack," he said to his family. "We're to report to the palace by 4 p.m."

His father gave him a long stare. "The king considers you to be a critical employee," he said.

Jonathan nodded. "Yes, papa, it's part of the plan."

"I hope this will not last long," his father said, "but it is difficult for me not to express the pride I feel for my son right now."

Michael waited until late Sunday afternoon to call Andrew Brimley. He'd been seeing a steady stream of palace staffers arriving with their suitcases and overnight bags. Brent Epworth had set up tables in the palace ballroom for staff to receive their room assignments, meal schedule, and what amenities were available in the palace and nearby.

"Michael! I mean Your Majesty!" said Brimley. "This is a delightful surprise!"

They made small talk for a few minutes, Michael asking about Brimley's wife Susan and their two teenage girls.

"So," Michael said, "I have a question for you, and if you need time to think about it, I can call back later. If you could go back almost 10 years, to that discussion we had about the theology program at the University of Edinburgh."

"I remember it well," Brimley said.

"Can you tell me why you urged Edinburgh and not St. Simon's? I'd been keen on following in your footsteps. I mean, in hindsight, I think Edinburgh was the best choice, particularly with what it led to, with cycling and Sarah. But I've wondered why you weren't enthusiastic about your own school."

For a time, Brinley said nothing. "Well," he said finally, "I suppose I could give you all kinds of platitudes, but I suspect that won't be sufficient. It's a long story, too long for a single phone conversation." He hesitated. "There were problems at St. Simon's, Michael, and I really and truly thought you would do better at

Edinburgh. You needed the space afforded by a larger school. You had talents, like cycling, that St. Simon's couldn't accommodate."

"Was that all, Andrew?" Michael said.

"Obviously," Brimley said, "that you're asking that question suggests you think there was something else. Have you heard something?"

"What I've heard is vague and essentially nothing," Michael said. "There's a suggestion that St. Simon's may be involved in some way in the church abuse scandal that's been unfolding this past week. But it's only that, a suggestion, and a fairly obscure one at that."

Michael could almost hear the St. Botolph's vicar *thinking*.

"Michael," Brimley said, "I'd prefer to talk with you face to face, and then you can decide if what I know is significant. I will say this. It is not outside the realm of possibility that St. Simon's is involved. In fact, it would be surprising to me if it wasn't."

"Andrew, the police may need to hear what you have to say."

"Let me do this," Brimley said. "I will come to London tomorrow. I know you're opening Parliament in the morning, and I won't be arriving until sometime well after lunch. You must have a ferocious schedule, but I would rather talk with you face-to-face."

"London may be in the midst of a city government breakdown tomorrow," Michael said. "You may be able to arrive at King's Cross but getting from there to the palace may be difficult. Let me do this. Let us know your arrival time, and I will get a car to pick you up. You can stay with us in one of bedrooms here in the loft; I'm afraid we have just about every room in the palace occupied by staff riding out the expected transit shutdown tomorrow."

"I can wait a few days," Brimley said.

"Actually," Michael said, "sooner may be better than later. The police may need whatever you know."

"This won't be an easy conversation," Brimley said. "There are things about St. Simon's I would rather forget." He cleared his throat. "Have you ever wondered why I've stayed at St. Botolph's since my ordination?"

"Given your success with growing the congregation there," Michael said, "I think I'm surprised that you weren't moved on to larger parishes or responsibilities."

"It's because of St. Simon's, Michael," Brimley said. "It's because I wasn't what they called a team player. I've paid for that. And I've been content with St. Botolph's. This is where God has had me, so I am content. And while some in the church may have meant to hurt me, what no one, including me, would have dreamed is that I would be the priest who would encourage a teenage boy to follow his calling. Many things were hard, Michael, but I knew what the plan was that day you walked into my office to talk. You were what, all of 14 or 15, and confidently asking how you might become an Anglican priest. I didn't know all of what would happen, but I talked with you, and somehow, I knew that you were the future of the church. I'd an inkling that the possible reformation of the church had just walked through my door. That's gotten me through many a hard time, that, a lot of prayer, and my family."

After they rang off, Michael walked through the palace. People were everywhere, and mostly moving in the direction of finding their scheduled dinner. People smiled and nodded, and a few stopped to talk. His question about the adequacy of the accommodations generally drew an appreciative laugh.

He walked to the large stone patio at the back of the palace, and sat for a time, staring at the lawn and the woods, thinking. And then he began to pray.

As Andrew Brimley and his wife Susan prepared for bed, he could see she was bursting with questions but knew he needed to rest before rising early to catch the train from Waverly Station to King's Cross.

"I don't know where this will lead, Susan," he said. "I don't know if it will lead anywhere."

"But the king knows, or suspects," she said. "They've kept us in near-poverty for 17 years, Andrew, because they wanted you to go away. You knew too much. And so, they throttled your career."

"Susan," he said gently, "you forget that God was also involved. We've never lacked for anything we needed. We have two beautiful daughters. We have a church that's loved us since we came in the door. We've never lacked for anything, including loving support."

"But it still hurts," she said, in tears. "To see someone with your talents not be able to use them, well, it just hurts."

"I know," he said. "But God loves us. He's always loved us. And he is the judge, not us."

Chapter 8: Opening Parliament

For a long time, Parliament had officially opened each new session in late June. This year, Peter Bolting had called a spot national election shortly after the coronation, counting on increasing his Labour majority after the warm national glow of Michael and Sarah being crowned. It had paid off: Labour had picked up 10 seats, mostly at the expense of smaller and fringe parties. The Conservatives had maintained their numbers. Since the election was in June, followed by the period most members devoted to summer holiday, the official opening had been set for the last Monday in September.

Trevor Barry had worked closely with Michael and Sarah, walking them through the entire event, what they would be expected to do, what clothes would be appropriate, and the journey from the palace to Parliament. It had been two years since the last official opening; this would be the first time for Michael and Sarah.

Sarah wore a formal, floor-length white satin dress. Michael, not feeling comfortable in an honorary military uniform ("It suggests I'm a faux soldier, which would be accurate") was wearing a suit. They chose to wear their platinum crowns. Michael's robe of state was waiting at Parliament.

With the Greater London region now budget-less, the expectation had been that bus drivers and tube drivers would not show up for work. On Sunday night, the union had announced that, in recognition of the opening of Parliament by the new king and queen, buses and tube trains would operate normally until 3 p.m., when all drivers would walk off the job if no London budget had been approved.

All London public and private schools, including ICS, were closed for the day.

Promptly at 9 a.m., Michael and Sarah entered the state carriage in the palace courtyard. The household guards, on horseback, preceded and followed them through the palace gates and toward The Mall. Crowds were 15 and 20 deep on both sides of the street. Metropolitan police, MI-5, and Ryan Mitchell's security team walked alongside the procession.

The crowds were wildly enthusiastic. British flags were waving everywhere. More than a few people were holding homemade signs reading "Michael for Mayor of London."

"Where did that come from?" Sarah said. "Are you running for mayor?"

"Absolutely not," Michael said. "I think people are worried about what's happening with London. This may be a very different place after 3 p.m. today. I'm just thankful the transportation drivers essentially volunteered to work today for free." Michael had had Jay Lanham issue a statement thanking the union and the drivers for their decision; there had been no statement or response from Downing Street or Parliament.

The procession traveled The Mall and through Admiralty Arch, skirting Trafalgar Square before turning on Whitehall. The crowds here were just as thick and enthusiastic.

They finally reached Parliament and rode to the Sovereign's entrance. Leaving the carriage, they proceeded to the robing room, where Michael put on the robe of state. They then walked to and entered the House of Lords. After they were seated on the raised platform, the clerk of the Lords sent "Black Rod" from the room. His name taken from the rod he carried, Black Rod walked to the House of Commons, where, following the long tradition to demonstrate an independent Commons, the door was slammed in his face. Black Rod then knocked three times on the door, it was opened, and members of the House of Commons followed Black Rod to Lords to hear the King's speech.

Michael wasn't comfortable giving a speech while sitting, but Trevor Barry had reminded him that if he stood, all members of Parliament and all guests in the galleries would have to stand as well. So, he had practiced the speech while seated in the throne room at the palace.

As the members found seats, Michael looked up at the galleries, smiling when he saw Josh Gittings, Jay Lanham, and Jonathan Crowe. He also noted three people next to Jonathan, and he assumed they must be his parents and sister. He smiled and nodded at them as well, and he saw Jonathan's mother lean to her husband and say something. Jonathan's father looked at the king and simply beamed.

There are some very proud parents, Michael thought. *And they should be.*

When everyone was seated, the clerk introduced Michael with a general shout of "God Save the King," with the members and galleries responding with the same.

Michael began to speak.

The first thing people noticed was that Michael was not reading the speech. He was actually speaking, even without referring to notes, having memorized the text. No one's attention wandered from the king.

Using his own words and his conversational style, Michael walked the members of Parliament through Government's planned program for the session. He used stories and self-deprecating humor. People laughed at the jokes and stared almost in open wonder. The speech was interesting, it was informative, and it was also entertaining. No one could remember a monarch's speech like this one.

And Michael made it clear that he had not asked Bolting's government to endorse his proposals for the church, because he hoped that all parties would find common cause and consensus.

When he finished, MPs and Lords alike were on their feet, applauding and even cheering.

Michael and Sarah left through the Sovereign's entrance, and the carriage, again accompanied by the mounted Household Guards, retraced its journey back to the palace. The crowds were just as thick as earlier, and just as enthusiastic.

"You memorized the speech," Sarah said, as they waved to the people along the way.

"I did," Michael said. "It was actually Trevor's suggestion. We had practiced so many times that I had it just about memorized anyway, and he wondered if I might consider not using notes. I did have the text with me if I needed it, but it worked out fine."

"You stunned Parliament with that," Sarah said. "No one looked at their mobiles, no one looked away. It was almost as if they wanted to see if you would make it to the end." She waved and smiled at a group of what looked to be American tourists, waving the U.S. flag. "To be honest, Mike, you stunned me as well. That was amazing."

"Remind me to thank Trevor Barry for the idea," he said.

The crowds quickly dispersed for the tube stations, train stations, and bus stops. At 3 p.m., just as Andrew Brimley's train arrived at King's Cross Station from Edinburgh, the tube and bus drivers walked off their jobs.

London was without public transportation. An announcement on the Greater London Authority website said that the scheduled meeting for Tuesday morning had been canceled.

Like always, it was busy and crowded inside King's Cross. As Rev. Brimley exited the arrival area and moved into the terminal, he saw a man holding a card with his last name on it. Brimley walked up and introduced himself.

"Reverend Brimley," the man said, introducing himself as Eric Wilson, "if you'll follow me, sir. We have a car waiting by the British Library." He smiled. "It may take us a while to get to the palace; the tube and buses have just closed, and the streets may be a bit chaotic. Here, let me take your bag."

Exiting the station, they walked toward the British Library, a block away and next to St. Pancras Station. He could see crowds milling about the entrances to the King's Cross tube station.

"The taxis and private car services will be doing a bang-up business for the next few days," the security man said. "At least until the London Authority approve a budget."

"Are they meeting to try to work it out?" Brimley said.

"They were supposed to meet tomorrow," Wilson said, "but the meeting's been cancelled. There had been talk of the king speaking at the meeting, but that's been put aside now as well. Here we are, sir."

Wilson opened the rear door of the car for Brimley, and then got into the front seat, next to the driver. "We're going to see what congestion there is, and if we can't get to the palace by the most direct route, we'll try to go around on the north side."

As it turned out, with many offices and all the schools having closed for the opening of Parliament, and the buses not operating, they were able to get to the palace in almost record time.

As they entered the palace's interior courtyard, Brimley could see Michael and Sarah waiting for him at the portico.

After dinner, Brimley and Michael were sitting in the palace library, each with a glass of wine.

"I thought it might be easier to talk here rather than in the loft," Michael said, "with Sarah and the boys plus Robert Hood and his mother. And you've seen the rest of the palace."

"It's like a massive dormitory right now," Brimley said.

"We have about 150 palace staff and security people staying here at the moment," Michael said, "and we don't know how long this will last. Mr. Epworth, our Master of the Household, has had food and supply trucks arriving all day. Some of the staterooms are serving for storage right now, and our Davey Malone, the chief chef, has doubled his kitchen staff."

"I forget that the monarchy is a branch of the government," Brimley said. "And you have to continue to operate, whether you have buses or not. Has Parliament done anything itself to prepare?"

Michael shook his head. "No, and neither have Government ministries. If this continues for any length of time, Government will likely have to shut down."

They both sipped their wine.

"Seeing Robert Hood puts a human face on the scandal," Brimley said.

"And it's worse than it looks," Michael said. "Far worse."

"I suppose it's time for me to get to the point of my visit," Brimley said.

Michael smiled. "I haven't talked with Detective Inspector Frees since Friday," he said. "He's the man in charge of the investigation. Everything I've heard about St. Simon's is what I told you yesterday. As I said, it's vague. Frees said it came up when one of the priests charged was being questioned, something about St. Simon's being involved."

Brimley nodded. "I was 23 when I entered St. Simon's," he said. "I'd graduated from the University of London, and Susan and I had just been married. I knew I was being called into the ministry. I talked with my vicar and several others, and all suggested that St. Simon's was one of the best theological training schools in the country. I applied and was accepted."

"We lived in married housing with several other couples. Generally, the wives would be working in the area or even Norfolk; it was only 15 miles away. Susan secured a position at a local school; it was a temporary job for one of the teachers on extended maternity leave." Brimley took another sip of wine.

"At first, things went incredibly well. I loved my classes, my teachers were mostly first-rate, and we made friends, primarily with the students in my class, and their wives, too, if they were married. The head of the school was always very visible, introducing himself, inviting new students to dinner with him and his wife, sitting in on classes, very much a hands-on type of leader. He was a rather handsome man, tall, broad-shouldered, with an almost military bearing." He paused and looked away. "It turned out that he was a bit too hands-on."

"I'm not sure how or when I heard the first rumor, I think it might have been three or four months after I started. And it was really an odd kind of friendly warning from a second-year student, kind of mentioned with a laugh. 'Don't let yourself get caught alone with the head.' I asked for an explanation, but he just laughed and said I would likely find out sooner rather than later, and maybe never, if I was lucky."

"It was that first January, late one Friday afternoon. Susan had had to stay late at the school, and I was struggling with Greek verbs, so I was using the quiet of the library. It's a beautiful place. The late winter sun was setting, catching the glass and filling the place with an almost ethereal light. Suddenly I felt a hand on my shoulder, and I almost jumped. I hadn't heard anyone coming in. It was the head. He sat next to me, and asked how I was doing, how my studies were going, and so forth. It was a normal conversation, except he let his hand rest on top of mine. And then he asked me to come to his office; he wanted to have a talk."

"I gathered up my books and papers and followed him to his office. The school was almost completely empty; our footsteps were echoing down the corridor." He looked down and shook his head. "When we got to his office, he shut the door, locked it, and then turned to me." Brimley visibly shuddered. "He pinned me against the door and started groping me. I pushed him away, but he was rather strong, certainly stronger and bigger than I was. He came back at me. As you might imagine, it was rather horrible."

"I finally shouted at him and shoved, and he fell away. He was suddenly furious. He said some pretty awful things about me and Susan, and then he said I could be a team player or not. Good things happened to team players, he said. And difficult things happened to those who were not. I told him to leave me alone. And somehow I got through the door and ran from the building." He smiled. "When I was outside, I discovered it was snowing, a light snow. Why I remember that, I don't know."

"What happened next?" said Michael.

"I didn't say anything to anyone," Brimley said. "At least at first. I was a bit in shock, and it was hard for me to believe that it had actually happened. I even wondered if I'd imagined it. But a few days later, I passed him in a hallway. When I saw him stare at me, I knew it was real, that it had happened."

"Somehow, I managed to finish the first year without anything else happening. The head left me alone. Nothing was said. I hadn't said anything to anyone, including Susan. And perhaps especially Susan. She would have been outraged and confronted the head, his wife, and anyone else."

"So, I pretended to myself that it was some anomaly. He hadn't made any other moves on me or anyone else I knew of. And I thought that perhaps it had just been a lapse, a momentary weakness. As it turned out, I was wrong."

"I was three months into my second year when one of the first-year students killed himself. He'd hung himself in his room. It was his roommate who found him, and he was quite sure he had seen an envelope on the desk. But he rushed out of the room to give the alarm, the teachers and the head came running, and the police eventually called. No one found an envelope or any kind of note."

"A suicide had never happened at St. Simon's before. It shook students and faculty alike and cast a pall over the entire school."

"We were friends with another student and his wife, another second-year student like myself who had become a kind of mentor. He was about five years older than I was. And the two of us were having coffee one day, and we started talking about Jerry, the young man who killed himself. And my friend said, 'I suppose he had trouble becoming a team player.'"

"I was stunned, and I probably looked it, with my mouth hanging open. I asked him what he meant, and he laughed. 'If we're to get anywhere after graduation, we have to be team players,' he said. 'It's distasteful, but it's reality at St. Simon's. You know what I mean.'"

"I told him I had no idea of what he was talking about. And he laughed, rather bitterly, and said, 'Andrew, you never would have made it to second year if you hadn't slept with the head.'"

"I was too shocked to reply. And finally, I told him that I wasn't a team player, I had never slept with the head, and somehow, here I was, in my second year. And how could he say such things?"

"He became visibly upset, told me I was lying, and rushed away." Brimley shook his head. "I didn't know what to do. I knew what happened my first year, I knew my friend was deadly serious, and I didn't know what I had stumbled into. And I didn't know why I'd been left alone. I went to a professor I trusted implicitly, a man who was a fine priest and an excellent teacher. And I poured all of this out to him."

"And what he told me was this. Keep your head down. Finish your studies. You never heard any of this. Ignore rumors about the head and any connection to the suicide. He told me that, in student review meetings by the faculty and staff, I was viewed as dependable and solid but not quite outstanding, and that I would be eventually recommended for a position with a small parish, without much hope for advancement. And then he told me it was the best I could hope for, because I wasn't a team player. And he said there was no evidence, none, and if I went to the authorities the worst they could prove was activities between consenting adults."

"I was devastated. The seminary considered one of the best in the Anglican world was engulfed in darkness. I felt helpless. And to be honest, Michael, I also felt caught. What if this did go public? Every student, every graduate, hundreds and hundreds of priests, would be smeared, simply by association. Including me. And so, I did the cowardly thing, and I said nothing. The fact that I had no evidence was beside the point."

"Why do you think you were left alone?" Michael said. "Do you think God protected you?"

"He did, Michael," Brimley said, "and he did it by making me a black man at birth. The head normally left black students alone; my one incident was something out of the ordinary."

Brimley stood up and paced. "There's more, of course," he said. "There's always more. I was sent to St. Botolph's in Scotland because they believed I would be a failure. A dying church, mostly older members, in a mostly rural area, with a new priest who happened to be black. They thought it would be a perfect recipe for failure, my failure."

"But God had other plans," Michael said.

"Yes, Michael, he did," Brimley said. "He blessed my ministry, and he blessed me personally with Susan and my girls. And then you walked in the door one day, seemingly out of nowhere. The minute I saw you, it was almost as if God was telling me that the future of the church, the reformation of the church, was standing in front of me.

"And I knew you couldn't go to St. Simon's. I was flattered that you wanted to attend my school, but I knew what would happen. The head wouldn't have been able to stay away from you, and when you resisted him he would destroy your calling. It was fortunate that the University of Edinburgh had started their program a few years before. They had good teachers, and good priests."

"But it was just one man, Andrew," Michael said, "even if he was the head. Just the one."

For a moment, Brimley didn't speak, but poured himself another glass of wine. "Michael," he said finally, "it was the head, but he had already been at St. Simon's for 20 years when I arrived. He's affected hundreds if not thousands of priests. He actively recruited young men of like mind. He trained priests of God to be predators. St. Simon's is still the most prestigious seminary in the Anglican world. What church wouldn't want a St. Simon's graduate to be their priest? And, Michael, he's still the head of school."

"Michael, if you have doubts, the friend I told you about, the one whom I considered a mentor and then told me I had to be a 'team player' to make it into my second year?"

"Yes?" said Michael.

"He's now the bishop of Bristol, and he's on the short list to become the next archbishop whenever a vacancy arises. Do you know how many in the church hierarchy have cycled through St. Simon's as students and faculty? Even if they are not predators of children themselves, they can be made to make way for priests in their parishes who are, or who have been caught in other parishes and need a haven. All it takes is a phone call from the old head of the school, your old headmaster, who can remind you what you did when you were a student."

The two men sat in silence for several minutes, Brimley with his head down and tears on his cheeks.

Michael was the one to break the silence. "Andrew," he said, "you need to tell this story to Detective Inspector Frees. Perhaps I can arrange something for tomorrow morning. But first, right now, could we pray together? And if you need me to, I'll say the prayer."

Brimley nodded.

"Do you think you can tell Frees your story, like you told me?" Michael said.

"Yes, Michael," Brimley said. "I believe I can. Somehow this has to be stopped."

After they prayed, they walked back to the family loft. Michael hugged Brimley, who then went to his room. Michael went to his study and called Frees.

"Detective Frees," he said, "would it be possible for you to come to the palace tomorrow? I know we have the transportation and congestion problems, but there's someone here you need to talk with."

"I can, your majesty," Frees said. "You'll probably be reading about it tomorrow, but we have more arrests. We have another 10 in London, six in Kent, and five in the Bristol area."

"Bristol?" Michael said. "Detective, from what I've heard tonight, Bristol is not a surprise. And this may be just the tip of the iceberg." He paused. "I looked into what you said about St. Simon's. It may be important to your investigation."

After he rang off, he saw he had a voicemail from Josh Gittings.

"Your majesty, Rodgers Clarke called this evening. He said that the Greater London Authority cobbled together enough votes to hold a meeting on Thursday. And he hoped that you'd be able to attend. I told him I'd talk with you and get back to him. I've taken some soundings, and it looks like you may be the one person who could get the Authority to agree. I've heard that the mayor has drafted his resignation but will wait to see what the outcome is on Thursday."

Michael called Josh back.

"Josh," he said when Gittings answered, "what happens if the Authority can't reach agreement and the mayor resigns?"

"Normally," Gittings said, "the mayor's resignation would lead to the council electing an interim mayor, until the next scheduled election. It's doubtful, though, whether they could settle on a candidate. They do have the emergency option; they can declare an emergency and appoint what we would have to call a tsar to run the city for up to six months. The tsar's powers would include dissolving the council and calling for new elections."

"We're talking here about the equivalent of a dictator to run the city?" Michael said. "This happens only with totalitarian regimes, not democracies."

"Michael," Gittings said, "it took me to step away from the PM's office and parliamentary politics to see something that I couldn't see when I was in the thick of it. Our democracy is increasingly fragile. We may have already sucked the life out of it. And I'm talking the country, not only London."

"We should talk tomorrow," Michael said. "By the way, where are you?"

Gittings laughed. "I'm in the front wing of the palace, on the first floor. Brent found me a rather decent bedroom not far from the balcony room. Jay and Jonathan are nearby. How did your meeting with Rev. Brimley go?"

Michael didn't immediately answer. "I think I would have to say, Josh, that we're now beginning to watch a slow-motion implosion of the Church of England. And perhaps something faster than slow motion."

Chapter 9: Walking into the Past

On a normal Tuesday, with a heavy schedule for Michael and Sarah, Davey Malone would have breakfast brought to the loft. Today, Michael had told the family, the Hoods, and Andrew Brimley that they would all join the staff for the breakfast buffet set up in the ballroom.

"The kitchen staff is stretched thin," Michael said, "and we need to help wherever we can. And it will be important for the staff to see us doing exactly what they're doing for meals." Because of the transportation shutdown, schools were closed. ICS had sent emails informing school families that teachers would be working from home, developing televised lessons.

The family created something of a stir when they arrived in the ballroom at 7 a.m. Everyone stood, and then bowed or curtsied.

"Please," Michael said, as loudly as he could and motioning with his hands, "please continue to eat."

Davey Malone had reserved a table for the family and the guests, and soon they were eating and talking.

"Do you have a busy schedule this morning, Sarah?" Michael said.

She nodded. "It's been revamped and kept fairly close to the palace. At 10, I'm at the Tate Britain to open a new art exhibition.

From there I go to the Zimmers in South Kensington for lunch." She gave Michael a knowing look but offered no comment. "And then, at 2:30, I'm at the military hospital in Chelsea. Mr. Epworth is joining me there."

"I'd expected to be at the London Authority this morning, but they cancelled their meeting. Mr. Frees is now coming by at 8:30, and then I'm open until 11, but I have to talk with Josh about the London Authority meeting on Thursday. I have lunch here with the dean of Southwark and some of his staff." He glanced at Jason, who was working his mobile. "Are there any reports on London traffic this morning?"

"I'll check," Jason said. "I just need to tell Chris goodbye." He pulled up a live traffic map, and then held his phone so they could see. All the major thoroughfares were glowing red, indicating heavy congestion.

"Well," Sarah said, "maybe I won't be leaving the palace after all."

"It's playing havoc with everyone's schedules," Michael said, "so we'll just have to be as flexible as we can." He leaned over to Hank, seated in a high chair next to Michael, and caught his hand as he prepared to hurl a slice of banana.

Meredith Hamilton accompanied Sarah to the Tate Britain in Pimlico. Sarah had not become an official royal patron of the art museum, but she and Jason had visited several times, and she'd been on an official tour with the director and several of his staff. When she received the invitation to open the exhibition on John Constable, she had quickly accepted.

By taking back streets from the palace, they were able to avoid most of the traffic jams. The biggest problem had been getting across Victoria, where traffic was moving at the pace of a parking lot. Policemen were able to keep the intersection at Buckingham Gate open, and the queen's car finally made it through. The driver avoided the most direct route, which was Millbank along the Thames, because it, too, was crowded with slow-moving traffic.

They came up from behind the museum, and turned down Atterbury Street, which provided the most direct access to the museum and the quickest walk to the exhibition hall. The director and his staff were standing outside and welcomed Sarah. A few reporters and photographers were there as well.

A ribbon had been stretched across the entrance, and the crowd was surprisingly large, given the traffic issues in London. The director opened the ceremony by speaking to the importance of Constable, spoke briefly of the exhibition, and then introduced the Queen.

Sarah didn't speak long, perhaps five or six minutes. But she spoke of how she was introduced to Constable by a professor in Edinburgh, who taught a course on the artist and J.M.W. Turner. "Of course, a course on two English artists at a university in Scotland didn't make for a packed lecture hall," she said, drawing laughter from the crowd. "But for the ten of us who were there, it was a remarkable experience." And then she spoke on Constable's art, its themes and the techniques he used.

The crowd could hear the interest, knowledge, and passion in her voice. It was the queen speaking, but it was also Sarah Kent-Hughes, the artist.

The ribbon was officially cut, and the director escorted Sarah into the exhibition itself.

Some 75 paintings comprised the show, and Sarah could only spend a few seconds in front of each. She wanted to spend hours.

When they reached the end, she touched the director on his arm.

"I want to come back," she said, "perhaps in a few weeks when I can give the exhibition the attention it deserves. We'll set something up, if that's all right."

"Of course, your majesty," the man said, smiling. "Whatever you'd like to do."

At the palace, Detective Frees arrived at 8:30. Traffic had been snarled on Whitehall, and he decided to walk. It was a fine morning, and a walk on Birdcage Walk along St. James Park turned out to be exactly the soul-quieting experience he needed, despite the slow-moving traffic. He was accompanied by a junior-level detective, Siobhan MacRae, a young woman recently assigned to his unit whom, he was told, was very bright and needed mentoring. So far, he'd been impressed by her desire to learn.

They said little as they walked; he was turning over the case in his mind, while she was trying to absorb the facts on the case in hers.

Arriving at the security entrance, they were soon taken to the king in the palace library.

The man with the king, Frees thought, must be Andrew Brimley. And he remembered Brimley from the coronation service, the priest assisting the Archbishop of York whom the commentators had said had first heard a young Michael describe his calling to the priesthood. Frees could also see Detective Sergeant MacRae was a bit overwhelmed to be in the presence of the king.

The king saw the same thing. "I'm going to leave you with Andrew," Michael said, after introductions. "I think it will be easier without me in the room, and I have no first-hand information to offer anyway. Perhaps, afterward, we can have coffee or tea." He smiled and left the room.

"So, I need to tell you my story," Rev. Brimley said.

From the Tate Britain, Sarah's driver maneuvered the car through back streets in Chelsea and eventually reached South Kensington. They'd been receiving reports via text from the palace about street congestion; they continued to avoid the major thoroughfares. Soon, almost right on time, they reached The Boltons, the residences grouped around an oval with St. Mary The Boltons church in the middle. Many of the townhomes dated from the late 18th century; a few had been divided into flats.

The Zimmers lived in one of the smaller three-story townhouses. The property and the area had been checked thoroughly by palace security. A security man was already in place at the rear of the property and another would be stationed with the car in front. A third would accompany Sarah and Meredith inside.

Sarah knew that Meredith was uncomfortable with how the luncheon conversation might turn and had asked Sarah if she shouldn't return to the palace. Sarah had pointed out that she'd need to return for the 2:30 tour anyway.

"And I think it would be helpful, Meredith," she'd said, "if a non-family face was present to help keep the conversation on an even keel." Meredith still felt apprehensive, but she knew the queen felt even more apprehensive.

As they left the car, Marie and Tyler Zimmer walked out the front door onto the porch. Both were smiling.

"We're glad to see you made it through the traffic," Tyler said.

Sarah smiled. "It was back streets all the way, but we missed most of the congestion. You remember Meredith, of course, my communications lead, and this is Stephen O'Nan, one of our security officers."

The Zimmers led the way inside and up the stairs to what the British would call the first floor and the Americans the second. Sarah looked around. It was a beautiful home, mostly done in muted light browns set off by splashes of blue in seat cushions, draperies, and even a few abstract paintings.

"We'll have lunch in the dining room," Marie said, "but perhaps you'd like some tea. We could sit here in the living room before we eat." She walked to a tasseled pull and rang the kitchen. "Please have a seat."

Marie sat in a chair nearby, while Sarah and Tyler sat on the sofa. Meredith and O'Nan sat on another sofa across from Sarah and Tyler.

"How is David?" Marie said.

"I saw him last week in Edinburgh," Sarah said. "He's well. He's been married for three years now and he and Betsey have a little boy, Gavin, who's two. He's just about finished a doctorate and has started to tutor at St. Andrew's, with even a few lectures on the side. He'll be defending his thesis in early December, but it's already been accepted by a publisher here in London."

"And Scott?" Marie said.

"He's doing well," Sarah said. "He and Barb really love San Francisco. Scottie's going on 11, and they adopted another boy. His name is Eduardo but we all call him Hondo."

"Hondo?" Tyler said.

Sarah smiled. "It's a long story."

"And, of course, we know you have the three boys," Tyler said.

Sarah nodded. "Jason's 17 and Jim turns 10 in November. We adopted them two years ago. They're both attending International Christian School in Notting Hill. And Hank turns one next month." She smiled. "He just started walking. And until last week he said only one word, and that was Da. He just added 'Ma,' so that was a great thrill. But he's definitely a daddy's boy."

"And Seth?" Marie asked.

"Dad's doing well," Sarah said. "He was here last month with his fiancée; they stayed with us at the palace. And Gran is just as feisty as ever. She turned 76 this year."

"Seth's engaged?" said Tyler.

Sarah nodded. "Her name is Catharine Lewis. She's a few years younger than Dad. They met in January at a golfing fundraiser for a charity. We met her when they came for the coronation in May."

"I'm surprised," Marie said. "I never expected that Seth might be interested in remarrying."

"Well," Sarah said, "it's been eight years."

In the silence that followed, Meredith noticed Marie Zimmer's cheeks redden.

"Yes," Marie said, "I suppose it has been a long time."

A woman brought tea service into the room.

"Thank you, Amah," Marie said. She looked at the others. "Amah has been with us for three years. Amah, this is Sarah Kent-Hughes."

Amah looked down and curtsied.

"It's nice to meet you, Amah," Sarah said. And she introduced Meredith and Stephen. The woman nodded and smiled and then left the room. Marie poured the tea.

"Tell me about this boy you call Hondo," Marie said.

"He was born in the U.S., but his parents were illegal immigrants from Guatemala," Sarah said. "After his parents died, he came to live with a group of other children led by Jason. They were in an old warehouse not far from the church. They all ended up becoming Christians, and various church families adopted them. It's an incredible story that's best told by my incredible husband, who had a lot to do with it. Jason ended up with us."

"Was Jim part of that group?" Marie asked.

"No," Sarah said. "Jim and his mother attended St. Anselm's Church, and she died right at Christmas time three years ago. She'd named Michael his guardian, so Jim came to live with him about nine months before we were married." Sarah opened the briefcase she'd brought with her. "I brought some photos you might be interested in." She handed a small album to Marie.

"David's boy looks just like him as a child," Marie said, pointing to a photo of David, Betsey and Gavin.

"I saw them at dinner last week at the McLaren's," Sarah said. "They were Michael's guardians, although he thinks of them as his parents."

"So many mixed and matched families here," Marie said, as she looked through the photographs.

"Yes," Sarah said. "I would agree. In all kinds of ways." She paused before continuing. "There are so many things I want to say and ask. But I'm not sure where to begin. We often wondered what had happened to you." She looked at Marie and then turned to Tyler.

Marie looked at Sarah but didn't respond.

"Gran told me that she thought you had stayed in Denver for a while," Sarah said, "and then left. But she didn't really know, and Dad said very little, as you might imagine. At least, after the initial shock was over and we moved to L.A. after David and I graduated high school."

"Where did you stay in L.A.?" Tyler said.

"David and I were getting ready for UCLA," Sarah said, "and we ended up staying with Gran for the summer in Santa Barbara. Dad bought a condominium in Beverly Hills. Then we lived on campus, and after our freshman year stayed with Gran again. Then it was back to UCLA, and back to Gran, and then we were in Edinburgh for our junior year abroad."

"Sarah," said Tyler, "when did you learn that Seth wasn't your biological father?"

At that, Meredith noticed Stephen shift next to her. She realized that he might not know the story, which Meredith herself only heard after the first meeting following the speech at the Marriott.

Sarah looked at Marie before responding and then turned back to Tyler. "While we were in Edinburgh, Dad went up to San Francisco to see Scott and Barb for Thanksgiving, and Scott talked Dad into giving blood for a drive they were having at the hospital. Dad told Scott his blood type was AB, and Scott told him he had to be mistaken, because Scott was Type O and so were David and I." She looked down as she sipped her tea. "He immediately understood the implications, and he took the news pretty badly. He put money in an account to cover us for the rest of college and he walked away. He wouldn't see us or talk to us for a year and a half."

She set her cup down. "And then Mike came back into my life, not that he ever really left it, but we met in San Francisco after being separated for almost a year, we got engaged, and unknown to any of us he went down to L.A. to talk to Dad. It was a pretty stormy scene, but in the end, Dad came back. He walked me down the aisle at our wedding."

She looked from Tyler to Marie. "I wish you could have been there, but we had no idea where you were. I often wondered why you didn't try to contact us or get word to us."

"It's a long story, Sarah," said Tyler. "And it's complicated."

"I understand a marriage breaking up," Sarah said, "but you can't just walk away from your children and grandson, can you? But you did. And Dad was destroyed. Couldn't you have at least told him, and told us? For the longest time David and I felt like it was our fault."

At this point, Amah returned to the room and said that luncheon was ready. Marie and Tyler led the way to the dining room.

After they were seated and eating, Marie resumed the conversation. "I'd like to explain what happened," she said. "And I don't expect forgiveness, Sarah. I know there's a lot here that you and your brothers would have to forgive."

"The three of us met in college. Seth and Ty pledged together in the same fraternity and became good friends. They had a lot of the same classes as well, because they were both studying finance. I was majoring in education. A friend fixed me up on a blind date with Ty."

"It was a football game," Ty said. "Fraternities would sit together and then go back to the house after the game for a party, often with a band."

"And, of course, we would sit with Seth and his date," Marie said. "And I found myself really liking Ty and spending lots of time with Seth and whomever on double dates. I'm afraid I don't remember too many of them; Seth always dated shy, quiet girls, which I clearly was not. Our double dates were always interesting, because Seth and I played one-upmanship at every opportunity, keeping all of us entertained. And we'd usually battle to a draw.

"Ty and I got engaged at the beginning of our junior year." Marie looked at Tyler. "He was the kindest, gentlest boy I'd ever met, and I believed that the rest of my life was going to be spent with him.

"Then, during the summer between our junior and senior years, a sorority sister was getting married, and I was in the wedding. Ty was interning in Chicago, and I flew into Denver from Tampa for the wedding. Tampa was where I was from. Seth was interning with a bank in Denver, so he was staying for the summer instead of going home to Santa Barbara. He picked me up at the airport to take me to a friend's house where I was staying for the wedding."

She looked at Ty. "This is still hurtful for me to talk about." He smiled and nodded.

"Well," Marie said, "like I said, Seth picked me up at the airport, and we hadn't gone 10 feet when we started the one-upmanship again. By the time we were on the freeway into town, we were arguing. He pulled off the road at some exit and stopped the car, we were that angry with each other. We were yelling at each other, and I don't even remember what it was about. I suppose it doesn't matter; the point for both of us was to win the argument, no matter what the cost. And then he leaned over and kissed me, and I kissed him back. And then things progressed rapidly from there."

"Except for the rehearsal, and the wedding and reception, I spent the entire five days I was in Denver with Seth." She paused and took a deep breath. "The one decent thing I did was to call Ty and break off the engagement."

"Did you tell him why?" Sarah said.

"I told him I had fallen in love with Seth," Marie said. "The problem was that Ty loved us both. And while he was angry and hurt, he also hoped we'd be happy, because we were the two people he loved most in the world."

Sarah, feeling the tears in her eyes, looked across at Ty. He was watching Marie, and Sarah could see the tears in his eyes.

"It was true," Tyler said. "I felt crushed and betrayed by both of them, but I still loved them. My best girl and my best friend."

"Seth and Ty stayed friends," Marie said. "We stopped the double dating, but they remained good friends. Seth and I married right after graduation, and Ty was the best man. For a couple of years, they worked for different investment firms, and then decided to go into business together.

"Seth wanted children from day one. And we tried. He was so desperate, and I was so desperate to please him that we both finally were tested. I was at home when the call from the doctor came, and he told me that Seth was sterile."

Sarah nodded. "Gran said he had mumps when he was 15, but that Granddad refused to have him tested."

"After hearing the doctor's news, I sat there for the longest time. I decided I had a choice. I could tell Seth, or I could do something else. I decided that Seth would be personally devastated by the news, and I called Ty."

"I never stopped loving her," Ty said. "I generally avoided being alone with her, but I knew that she was the one that was meant for me. I'd been content just to be Seth's partner and the good family friend. And then she called me."

"I got pregnant almost immediately," Marie said. "And we had Scott. For a long time, I worried, because it was obvious to me whom Scott looked like, but Seth and his parents never raised a question. And Sarah, as serious as it was, that was all that happened between us for almost 12 years. But Seth wanted more children, even though I kept trying to dissuade him. His persistence finally wore me down, and I turned to Ty again." She hesitated. "Except something happened this time. This time I fell in love with Ty. I found myself in love with two men at the same time. Can you understand that?"

Sarah shook her head. "I'm sorry, but I can't. I love my husband so much I can't imagine loving anyone else."

"You're fortunate, then," Marie said. "But I loved them both, and I realized that I loved Ty more. I think I knew when you and David were born that my marriage to Seth was over. But it took almost 17 years for me to do anything about it, and when I finally did, I hurt everyone in sight."

"We decided to just slip away," Ty said. "We acted more like two immature teenagers, I suppose. But we both wanted to avoid a confrontation with Seth, and we worried about the effects of a confrontation on you and David. Or that's how we convinced ourselves. This sounds so lame in hindsight, but that's what it was. It was cowardly and not what Seth or his children, our children, deserved. But that's what we did. We disappeared, and let our attorneys deal with Seth. Although we did attend your high school graduation. We sat in the upper balcony of the auditorium and used opera glasses to see you and David receive your diplomas."

"Seth's attorneys drove a hard bargain," Marie said. "While it was almost moot at your age, Seth insisted that I cede all parental rights over you and agree not to see any of you, including Scott and Scottie, for seven years."

"He was crushed," Sarah said. "David and I came home from school that afternoon and found the note you'd left. It was a total shock. We called him at work. For hours, he just wandered around the house, drinking and crying. We were terrified. David finally got him to bed. The next morning when we got up, he was in the kitchen, making breakfast for us. And then a day or so after that, he got the note from Ty. That's when he told us he was moving to L.A. when we graduated,

164

and since we were starting at UCLA in late August, we went, too, and stayed with Gran."

"We knew you'd left Denver," Marie said, "and figured it was for L.A. There wasn't much point in staying in Denver ourselves. I couldn't see you and David, and too many friends knew what had happened. So, Ty and I left for New York. That's where we got married, once the divorce with Seth was final."

"We wondered about you, David, and Scott as much as you wondered about us," Tyler said. "We knew Scott had ended up in San Francisco. But we didn't know about you and David until we saw you on television at your press conference at the hospital. And it was a total surprise to find that you were in San Francisco and married to the next king of Britain."

Sarah smiled. "It was a total surprise for all of us," she said. "I didn't know Mike's connection to the royal family until just before our wedding."

She looked at the Zimmers. "So, what do we do next? Where do we go from here? Assuming you want to go somewhere from here?"

"I'd like to know my daughter again, Sarah," Marie said.

"It's why we went to the speech," Tyler said. "It's hard to live in London these days and not be reminded of who the king and queen are. And I think we've both felt a need, and a desire, to meet you again and explain. Like Marie said, Sarah, we're not expecting forgiveness. There's almost too much to be forgiven. We're both terribly sorry that all of you were essentially abandoned without a word, even a simple goodbye."

"I don't know how we might go about doing this," Sarah said. "There's so much to work through for all of us. But perhaps we could start slowly and see what happens? And there's also David and Scott to consider."

Sarah glanced at her watch. "It's five after 2," she said. "I need to be at the Chelsea Military Hospital at 2:30, so I'm afraid we need to leave." She stood, as did everyone else at the table. "I'll talk with David and Scott, and I think we need to talk with Dad as well. So, we'll talk again?"

"Of course," Tyler said.

Simultaneously, Stephen O'Nan's mobile buzzed with a text and the doorbell rang.

"Were we expecting anyone?" Tyler said to Marie.

"Three women are at the front door," Stephen said, reading the text.

"It's probably just some friends stopping by," Marie said, as she hurried downstairs to the door.

Amah had reached it first and opened it. Three women, dressed as if they were attending a cocktail party, burst through the hallway just as Marie reached the ground floor with her guests and Tyler right behind.

"We know we're a little early, Marie dear," said one of the women in an American accent, "but we just couldn't stand the suspense. Has the queen agreed to attend the gallery opening?" She looked up and behind Marie and saw Sarah.

"Oh, my, it's her, it's Sarah," the woman said. "She's really here." And the woman did what Meredith thought had to be the most awkward curtsy she'd ever seen. "We are just thrilled to meet you, Sarah. When Marie invited us to meet you for early cocktails, we were just beside ourselves. It's just wonderful to actually meet you." The two other women kept nodding in agreement.

Marie attempted to halt the social damage. "Cathy, dear, I'm afraid we're not quite at the point of talking about –"

"Oh, please," the woman said to Sarah, "please say you'll come to the opening. It's in Mayfair next month, and it will be such a huge boost for Harry's business."

At that point, Stephen O'Nan inserted himself between the three women and Sarah.

"I'm sorry," he said, "but her majesty must leave for another engagement."

"Oh, no," said the first woman. "We hoped for a commitment today so we could get the announcement and invitations printed. And, Marie, we talked about a royal warrant for the window? You said it wouldn't be a problem?"

"Well," said Marie, "we haven't had a chance to discuss it, but, Sarah, if you let me explain –"

At that, Sarah pushed past Marie. "I'm sorry, but I must leave." Meredith hurried after her through the door and O'Nan almost walked out backwards to make sure they weren't followed.

Sarah stopped on the sidewalk, and then she turned back toward Marie, standing on the porch. "So," Sarah said, "is it because you wanted to see me, or is it you think I can do something to help your friends?" She turned and got into the car. Meredith followed her.

The security officers quickly closed the doors and they sped off.

Tyler stood on the porch, watching the car depart. He turned to his wife.

"Marie," he said, "what have you done?"

Detective Inspector Frees and Detective Sergeant MacRae talked with Andrew Brimley for an hour. When they finished, Brimley agreed to accompany them back to Scotland Yard, and said he didn't mind walking. While he went to the loft to get his briefcase, Frees and MacRae stood talking with Michael. Michael could see that both detectives were shaken.

"It's a difficult story to hear," Michael said.

"Your majesty," Frees said, "what's becoming clear is that this isn't simply a case of a child pedophile ring being run across parishes all over the country. We'll now have to look at a facilitator network, the people who provided cover and safe havens with no questions asked." He paused. "It means they're accessories before, during, and after the fact. We could be talking scores of people, or hundreds."

"I've been going round to churches, Detective," Michael said, "talking about reformation. It was something I felt called to do, even before we left San Francisco. It was as if God was telling me that reformation of the church was imperative." He looked away for a moment. "Now I wonder if I misheard what I thought God was saying. What if He was telling me to help people prepare, not for a reformation, but for the destruction and recreation? He knew what was happening. He knew the evil that had to be stopped."

"They're going to hate you for it, sir," said MacRae. She colored slightly, as if speaking out of turn. "I mean, people doing evil like to keep it hidden. When the cover's ripped away, they'll hate you because of the stand you've taken."

Frees looked from MacRae to the king, and he realized that the two them were speaking on a wavelength of faith that he could see but not completely grasp. But he saw the truth in what she was saying.

"You'll need to talk with your security people," Frees said to the king, "and anyone else involved in your protection. The detective-sergeant here is right; they'll see you as the figurehead. You're going to have to be very careful. If you'd like, I'll talk with your security people."

Michael felt a sudden chill. "Yes, Mr. Frees," he said. "I would appreciate that. And for the family as well."

With an open morning before his luncheon, Michael walked to the administrative wing and was glad to see Josh Gittings in his office. Gittings was on his mobile, but waved Michael in as soon as he saw him.

"I have to go," he said to whomever it was he was speaking to on his mobile. "We should continue to talk." He rang off. "How did Frees and Rev. Brimley get along?"

"He's going back to Scotland Yard for more interviews and to get him officially on the record," Michael said, sitting down in one of the wing chairs facing Gittings at his desk. "Their conversation apparently went well. Frees started doing what I did last night – and that's the math. Joshua, there will be far more people involved in this than we can imagine right now. The church will only survive this with God's grace. But I'm not sure it should. Anyway, I wanted to talk with you about what you said on the phone last night, about the fragility of our democracy."

Josh nodded. "I've been reading, but I've mostly been talking with people. Let me rephrase that. I've been listening to people, like on the phone just now, a conservative MP from Durham. What I'm hearing and seeing is a kind of political exhaustion. People are tired of the constant fighting and bickering, tired of the endless arguments that never seem to end, tired of power plays and sacrificing principle for power. And it's not only the Greater London Authority. I'm hearing this in Parliament as well. This goes beyond mistrust. There seems to be a growing loss of faith in government institutions. And I have to say, Michael, that I helped contribute to that. I just wish I knew what I could do about it."

"Probably nothing," Michael said, "except to pray. We're both feeling heavy burdens right now, my friend. Each day they seem heavier, and that's because they are. And the best thing for both us is to give them up to God. We can't solve these problems ourselves. We may be used as tools or instruments for solutions, but we can't solve the problems we're facing. So, we pray, encourage one another, love one another, and we trust God."

"I talked with two members of the Greater London Authority," Gittings said. "Both are Labour, but they're in different factions. As you might expect, the closer you are in party, the more intense the factional differences become. Neither believes that the Authority will muster the votes needed Thursday to pass a budget. I didn't say anything about a possible appearance by you, but they both asked me if you might consider working behind the scenes. Of course, what they want is for you to work on the other factions, not their own. I told them I would mention it, but this wasn't something that fell within the king's normal duties."

"I will pray, Joshua." Michael said. "I don't know enough about London politics to be able to tell anyone what they should definitively do. I'm a voice among a lot of voices. But I will pray."

The afternoon traffic in central London was becoming slower and more congested. Fortunately, the Zimmers' home in The Boltons was less than two miles from the military hospital in Chelsea. Sarah listened to Meredith as hard as she could for a final briefing before they arrived. But she was inwardly reeling. She was also thankful for the slow traffic; it gave her time to try to calm herself.

"Mr. O'Nan," Sarah said to the security officer riding in the front seat, "I didn't thank you for extricating me from that mess. I didn't know what to do, and I was afraid I was about to start screaming at everyone. Thank you for getting me out of there. And I apologize both to you and to Meredith for involving you in something that was so unbelievably crass."

"Yes, ma'am," O'Nan said, smiling. "The security men with the car and in the back were particularly helpful, sending that text when they did. We didn't have much time to react, but at least we had an idea of what to expect."

"Ma'am," said Meredith, "just as a reminder, you don't have any speeches or even short remarks at the hospital. You're going to visit the ward they reserve for recently injured soldiers who have been transferred from Iraq, and then the ward where soldiers who have lost limbs and had other serious injuries are housed, for physical therapy and related recovery programs. Just briefly talking with them and encouraging them will be sufficient."

"As upset as I feel right now," Sarah said, "my problems are miniscule compared to what they're facing and what they've experienced. I need to keep that front and center. Do I look okay? I mean, I hope I don't look like what I should look like, like I just barreled through a gaggle of howling people?"

Meredith, O'Nan, and the chauffeur all laughed.

"You look fine, ma'am," Meredith said. "Not a hair out of place."

They finally reached the hospital. Brent Epworth was waiting along with the commander in charge, the head nurse, and several others.

The Royal Military Hospital was a newer complex built on the grounds of the Royal Hospital Chelsea. The older hospital had been established in 1682 by Charles II as a retreat for army veterans. It had eventually become a retirement home for veterans with no families. The "Chelsea Pensioners" were a familiar group in this part of London.

The new complex had been built to allow for both military governance and access to London's broader medical facilities if needed. This had been the complex that friends had spirited Brent Epworth to, after he'd been found in a Brixton squat. In detox recovery, he'd met Henry Kent, Michael's half-brother, during a visit to the hospital complex and was eventually hired as the Duke's "man" to run his household.

Sarah shook hands with the staff and then followed the commander to the wards as he explained how they operated, what she might expect to see.

"I should mention, your majesty," he said, "that the wards are full at the moment. That most recent action near Baghdad resulted in quite a few casualties. We have some fairly serious cases in a smaller ward; those are not on your itinerary today."

"Are the men in those rooms conscious?" Sarah said.

"Some are," he said. "Some are in induced comas. A few are in a very bad way and are not likely to survive."

"To the extent it's possible, sir, I'd like to see those soldiers as well," Sarah said.

"Of course," he said. "You just need to be prepared for some horrific injuries."

They entered the first ward, where injured soldiers were recovering. These men had been shot during engagements and had been sent home to recover. A few had wives or other family members sitting with them in the large ward.

Sarah made a point of introducing herself and greeting each one, thanking them for their service and in some cases sacrifice. With one man, who was bandaged for the loss of his left eye, she sat for a few minutes and held his hand, letting him tell her of his experience.

They then moved to the next ward, on the floor above. This was where soldiers who had lost limbs, usually from land and road mines, were housed. Sarah remembered the visit to a room just like this in Basra, right after the coronation. She, Mike, the boys, and Brent Epworth had visited Basra and then the American air base outside Baghdad. And they had been in a ward just like this one.

The ward included an adjacent area for therapy and exercise, with an array of machines used to help the men build strength and learn how to walk again or used prosthetic limbs. The men in this area were in gym shorts, and mostly shirtless. There was some mild panic when they saw the queen and tried to race for t-shirts and pullovers.

"It's okay," she called out. "I've seen bare chests before. I have a husband and three sons, so there isn't much that can surprise me."

Amid the laughter, she began introducing herself. From the exercise area, she went into the sleeping area of the ward, where some men were sitting on their beds and others propped up with pillows. She talked and even laughed with a few who had ready jokes. She asked about their families, how they were doing, and then asked Brent Epworth to describe his own experiences and injuries.

Meredith marveled at how natural Sarah seemed, even talking with men with some disfiguring injuries. She offered empathy without pity, and she offered encouragement. Sarah made a point of thanking each soldier by name.

When they finished and left the ward, the commander noted that Sarah had already gone past the scheduled two hours and they would understand if she didn't have time for the final visits.

"No, I'm fine, sir," she said. "I have time, and I want to meet these men. It's important."

The small room had two men who were conscious and a third who wasn't. Because of the intensive care-like conditions, only Sarah was allowed in with the commander. One man was recovering from severe burns over a third of his body, but he maintained a good humor and was genuinely surprised to see the queen.

"We're not exactly fit for royal eyes," he said.

"You are exactly fit for royal eyes," Sarah said, holding his hand while they talked.

The second man had had horrible scarring on the left side of his face, the result of a bomb explosion in a Basra café when he was off-duty. Two members of his unit had been killed, he said. "I have nightmares, your majesty," he said. "I don't know how else to answer how I'm doing. They were my mates, and they were splattered all over me."

The commander almost intervened at that point, but Sarah held her hand against him.

"What do you do to cope with the nightmares?" she said.

"I pray, ma'am," he said. "I'm a Christian, and I pray. But it's hard."

"Would you mind if I prayed for you, right now?" she said.

The soldier looked completely taken aback. "Yes, ma'am, that would be fine."

She took the hand of the burned soldier and the hand of the disfigured one, and she prayed for both of them, for their encouragement, for the recovery road ahead, and for their families.

When she finished, still holding the soldiers' hands, she asked them if it would be all right for the commander to keep her informed of their progress. "And when you're able," she said, "I'd like you to talk with Mr. Epworth, our Master of the Household. He's here today, and he's lived his own serious war injury. And he can speak to you in ways that I can't." She kissed them both on their foreheads before she walked to the unconscious man.

Without anyone having to tell her, she could see he was in a bad way. From the position of the sheets covering him, she could tell that he was missing both legs. Only one arm was visible, with an empty place for where the other arm should have been. He was also on oxygen and had several drips attached to his arm and hand.

Tears in her eyes, she touched his forehead. She sat quietly praying, and when she finished, she stood and kissed him.

Back in the hallway, she stood for a moment to collect herself.

"Thank you, your majesty," the commander said. "Thank you for visiting our men. All of them."

"What's the prognosis for the last man?" she said.

The commander shook his head. "Not good, I'm afraid. It's unlikely that he'll regain consciousness. The doctors think it could be any time now."

"Does he have family?" she said.

"His wife is here," the commander said. "I think she's likely in the small waiting room at the end of the hall. They weren't married long before he shipped out. School sweethearts, originally from Belfast. She lives near the army base in Sussex."

"I'd like to meet her," Sarah said.

The commander walked her to the waiting room, and there Sarah saw a young woman, probably around 20, with red hair and what Michael would call a beautiful Irish face. And she looked about eight months pregnant.

Recognizing Sarah, the woman struggled to her feet, almost in alarm.

"It's okay," Sarah said, motioning her to sit, and then sitting next to her. "How are you coping?"

"Not well, I'm afraid," she said, tears forming in her eyes. "I can't stop crying. I don't want Pete to hear me, so I come in here."

"Are you by yourself?" Sarah said.

The young woman nodded. "My name is Mandy, Mandy Flaherty. The staff here have been great. They found me a kind of bedsit that's only a couple blocks away. The military own it, otherwise I never could afford it."

"Is there family nearby?" Sarah said.

Mandy shook her head. "Our parents are in Belfast. Neither side can afford the trip, and Pete's not going to make it. It's days, the doctors say, maybe less." She began to cry. "I'm sorry, I don't mean to dump this on you."

"You're not dumping anything on me, Mandy," Sarah said. "Commander, can you ask Mr. Epworth to come here?"

When Epworth arrived, Sarah introduced him to Mandy. "Mr. Epworth, can you call the pilots at Luton and find out if they can arrange to fly to Belfast and then back tonight?"

"We're on it," Epworth said, as he flipped open his mobile and made the call. He spoke for a few minutes. And then rang off. "They have to file a flight plan, but they should be ready to leave in an hour.

It will take another hour for the flight. Say three hours at most, but shorter on the way back. I told them to land at Belfast City Airport."

Sarah turned to the young woman. "Mandy, can you call your parents and your in-laws and have them go to Belfast City Airport?"

Almost in shock, Mandy nodded.

"And commander," Sarah said, "can you arrange accommodations for them? If not, we'll arrange something. If there's any cost involved, I'll cover it."

The commander, tears in his own eyes, nodded. "Yes, ma'am."

"Mandy," Sarah said, "there's one more thing. Can you keep us informed of Pete's condition?" Sarah looked at Meredith, who handed Mandy her business card.

"Just call, any time," Meredith said. "It has my office phone and my mobile."

The usual way to the palace from the Royal Hospital was simple – Pimlico Road to Buckingham Palace Road. But at 5:30, traffic on Pimlico Road was nearly at a standstill, so the driver diverted up Ebury Street and followed it all the way to the Royal Mews. Rather than drive to the front of the palace, Sarah told the driver to drive directly into the Mews. From a back gate, she,

Meredith, Brent Epworth and the security men walked through the garden to the rear of the palace.

"I'm glad we did the hospital," Sarah said, as they walked along. "I needed to see those soldiers."

"I believe they appreciated the visit, ma'am," Meredith said.

"Not half as much as I did," Sarah said. "I feel like I was the one being ministered to."

"It's amazing how that works, ma'am," Epworth said.

Chapter 10: Reverberations

On Wednesday morning, the royal family was sitting at breakfast in the ballroom.

"Mr. Epworth tells me," Michael said, "that, so far, we're managing here at the palace. Our food bill's gone up a wee bit, as you might expect, and there are some other expenses that we're incurring with utilities, but so far, the palace is functioning close to normal. And we're still able to get deliveries of food and other supplies, so that's a blessing."

"The garbage and trash are beginning to pile up," Sarah said. "I mean, on the streets. We saw it yesterday coming back from the hospital,"

Michael nodded. "The last trash pickup was Saturday," he said. "I certainly hope that the pressure is mounting on the council to break the logjam and get the city funded again." He looked at Robert Hood, Jason and Jim. "And you three are all caught up with your school lessons via the website?"

Both Jason and Robert nodded. Jim squirmed.

"Jim, my son, are you caught up as well?" Michael said.

"Almost," Jim said.

"And almost means what?" Michael said.

"I got my maths and grammar done," Jim said, turning slightly red in the face.

"And your four other subjects?" Michael said.

"I'll do them now," Jim said.

"Then you need to do today's assignments, too, so you don't fall behind," Michael said. "And I know you'll do it, even though they may seem boring and there are more exciting things to do."

"Yes, Dad," the boy said.

Michael glanced at Sarah, his eyes smiling if not his mouth. Jim was not the academic scholar in the family, and there were many things he found more interesting than his school subjects.

As they finished eating and Jim left to return to the loft, Meredith Hamilton came up to Sarah.

"Meredith?" Sarah said.

"I'm sorry to disturb you, ma'am, but you asked me to let you know if we heard anything," Meredith said. "Mandy Flaherty called a few minutes ago." She paused, tears in her eyes. "Peter Flaherty died this morning about six. His parents and hers arrived at the hospital last night about midnight, and he'd been moved to a private room. They stayed with him, and about 5:30 he regained consciousness. Mandy said he asked who the beautiful lady was who kissed him on the forehead. He thought she was an angel."

Sarah's own tears started.

"His vital signs were flagging," Meredith said, "but they all did have those final few hours before he died. Mandy said to tell you that they plan to bury him in a family plot in Belfast."

Michael took his wife's hand. "I take it you were the angel who kissed him on the forehead," he said.

Sarah nodded. "I thought he was unconscious." She turned to Meredith. "Can you find out from Mandy or the hospital what the funeral arrangements are when they have them?"

"Yes, ma'am," Meredith said, "I'll check now."

"And can you ask Mr. Epworth to make the arrangements for flying the family and Mandy back to Belfast?" Sarah said. And then she looked at Michael. "We don't need the plane for anything coming up, do we?"

Michael shook his head.

"And it's OK to fly the family home?" she said.

"Of course," said Michael. "It's a splendid thing to do."

They left the table and were leaving the ballroom when Michael saw Jay Lanham motioning to catch his attention.

"What is it, Jay?"

"The newspapers this morning," Lanham said. "Fourteen more priests have been arrested, all in different parts of England."

"There's no reference to Rev. Brimley?" Michael said. Brimley, after meeting with the detectives at Scotland Yard, had taken a late train to return to Edinburgh.

"No, sir," Lanham said. "But *The Times* is reporting that four bishops are 'helping the police with their inquiries.'"

"Do they say which ones, like Bristol?" Michael said.

Lanham looked surprised as he nodded. "Did you know about this?"

"I knew the Bishop of Bristol might be questioned, but not from Detective Frees," Michael said.

"The other three are Rochester, Birmingham, and Plymouth," Lanham said.

"Jay," Michael said, "can you find Trevor, he's somewhere here this morning, and find out how hard it might be to arrange a meeting of our study committee? If the transportation is still messed up, perhaps we can do a video or phone conference?"

"I'll check with him, sir," Lanham said.

"I think," Michael said, "that we have to consider developing a crisis plan."

"To handle the priest abuse issues?" Lanham said. "Isn't that the Archbishop of Canterbury's responsibility?"

Michael shook his head. "No, not the abuse issues. To handle the implosion of the church. No one is seeing it this way yet, largely because they don't know the extent of what's happening. The archbishops and especially Canterbury will only be looking at the crisis at hand. They won't be looking at the disintegration of the church as we know it. And I think we need to start preparing for it."

If Lanham was surprised, he didn't show it. And he now knew Michael well enough to know that he, as young as he was, had insights that few others had.

"Yes, sir, I'll find him and ask," Lanham said. "As a reminder, sir, you have Jonathan at 8:30 to talk about what you might say tomorrow at the Authority meeting. And we'll need to work out a communication strategy, to explain why you're speaking. I expect the press will have questions."

"Right," said Michael, glancing at his watch. "I should have just enough time to get through the PM's red box. I'll be in the library. Have Jonathan meet me there, and then you join us 30 minutes later."

Geoffrey Venneman had walked from his flat in the Docklands to his office at FBL in the City. The streets were a mess, and the only way to get to the office was by foot. And he didn't mind the walk, really; walking was something he was used to since childhood, when he had walked the hills of Cumbria, mostly to get away from his parents.

At the office, he sent a text to Canon Land at Lambeth Palace, asking for a 9 a.m. videoconference. This was another reason for walking to the office; he didn't have the equipment for video at his flat and he needed to see the faces of Land and the Archbishop.

He assembled three of the younger members of staff to join him. And promptly at 9, the conference started. Lambeth Palace also had videoconference facilities; Venneman had checked.

"Good morning, Archbishop," Venneman said, "and Canon Land. We're meeting by video this morning because traffic congestion makes a face-to-face impossible. I believe we've all seen the morning papers, with the story about the new arrests. One thing I found surprising was the reference to four bishops helping the police with their inquiries. Do you have any insight into that?" He spoke evenly and straightforwardly, but inwardly he was seething; he was getting tired of this client giving him information only when they were forced to.

"This was surprising to us as well, Mr. Venneman," Archbishop Rowland said, "and completely unexpected."

"When Canon Land checked the HR records and we talked Sunday night," Venneman said, "he said it looked like up to 30 priests might be involved. We're now right at that number, plus those bishops. And a source I have at Scotland Yard, who's not involved in the investigation, says that it's continuing to expand, with 10 members of the Met already assigned plus police detectives in the various cities."

"This is all very distressing, Mr. Venneman," the archbishop said, "but I'm not sure how to find what other information might be available. For that, I would have to have first-hand knowledge of this priest problem, and I don't, of course. I'm learning as much as you are with the news reports."

Venneman had seen Land turn to the Archbishop as he was speaking. *I didn't ask him anything about his own involvement,* Venneman thought, *but that's what he jumped to. And Land obviously knows more than he's telling, and he knows the archbishop just lied.*

"Of course, Archbishop," Venneman said. "No one is suggesting otherwise. My concern here is both tactical and strategic.

On the tactical side, each time there's a new arrest or new development, we have to revamp our plans completely and almost start over. Strategically, we're becoming hostage to the news reports and whatever information Scotland Yard chooses to announce each day. It is very difficult to see a report, work out a plan with appropriate messaging, get that to Lambeth Palace, make sure Canon Land and other spokespersons are solid with handling the media, before the next round erupts. We're finding ourselves constantly behind the eight ball. Is there anyone at all who might have an overall understanding?"

Venneman caught Rowland's hesitation before answering. "I don't believe so, Mr. Venneman," Rowland said. "From what I can see, the problem goes back decades at least, even before I joined the priesthood."

There's that personal concern again, Venneman thought. *He may be more involved in this than he's letting on. I've got to toss a grenade or two, and there's only one grenade that will suffice.* "Have you heard if the king has said anything?" he said.

He thought for a moment that Rowland would come off his chair.

"No," Rowland said, with barely controlled anger. "I have not. Has he been talking to the media?"

"Not that I'm aware of, Archbishop," Venneman said. "There's been a rumor that the first boy involved, Robert Hood, I believe his name is, is sequestered at Buckingham Palace. But that's not been confirmed. And that detective leading the investigation did say that the king had been involved in uncovering and reporting the abuse case involving the boy." He paused. "But I understand the king had lunch with the Bishop of Southwark and some of his staff yesterday?"

"Yes," Rowland said, "they did. The bishop told me. I had heard about it and called him. And he said all they talked about were these Bible studies Michael instigated with his sermon last December. I ask him pointedly if Michael talked about the arrests and the news reports, and he said Michael made no reference, directly or indirectly."

Venneman thought for a minute. "Do you find that odd, Archbishop? That the king would say or ask nothing about the biggest story involving the Church of England right now?"

Rowland stared at Venneman via the camera. "Yes, Mr. Venneman, I do. Very odd indeed. Almost as if he knows far more than he's letting on, or he doesn't want to compromise the investigation. Which would suggest that he's being kept abreast of developments."

"I agree, Archbishop," Venneman said. "I agree completely. And it will have to be watched very closely." He paused. "You might check back with the Bishop of Southwark. Michael may have made no reference to the issue, but did the bishop?"

After ending the conference, Venneman turned to the staff.

"We need to be prepared to cut our losses," he said. "They know more than they're saying, and if this thing develops as it looks like it's going to, then we have to be very adroit about when and how we exit. We are in a situation where we can't trust what our client is telling us, and we must avoid being dragged down. My best guess is that we have at most about two weeks before we'll need to resign the account."

At Lambeth Palace, after the videoconference had ended, Rowland told Land to find out anything he could from the Southwark delegation who had visited Michael. "I'm being misled," Rowland said. "Michael had to say something. Find out what it was."

Land knew the Bishop of Southwark and his people would say less than nothing; the bishop and Sebastian Rowland were old theological adversaries. So, he decided to go one better, and made his phone call.

"I need to see if you've heard anything," Land said.

"Michael called me last night."

"He called?" said Land. "What did he say? It's vitally important that we know."

Land could hear hesitation in the response.

"He arranged for someone to meet with that Yard detective leading the investigation. I probed, but Michael wouldn't say who it was. I had the impression it was a priest, or someone low level in the hierarchy. Whoever it was had come from out of town; Michael said something about the individual staying at the palace. It could be anyone."

"Did this person have information?" Land said.

"Michael was vague, and it sounded to me like he was being deliberately vague. The only specific thing I heard was a connection to the seminaries."

Land inwardly shuddered. "We need you to find out more. It's imperative. Offer him some tidbit in return, like the name of someone you've heard who may be involved. We must find out more about this reference to seminaries."

"Canon Land, it's beginning to feel like the net is tightening."

"Can you ask him to stop this as a personal favor?" Land said.

"No. That's equal to waving a red flag. He would rightfully ask why. And then what would I say? That child rapists might be harmed? Be realistic, Land."

"You may have to ask," Land said, repeating himself. "You know where this will lead."

In the palace library, Jonathan and Michael had started working through what the king needed to say at the meeting of the Greater London Authority.

"I've looked at the news coverage," Jonathan said, "and there doesn't seem to be much understanding of exactly what the issues are concerning the budget. I talked with a friend of mine who works for the Authority, and he said it mostly has to do with the funding for the various commissions."

"The commissions?" Michael said.

Jonathan nodded. "The Authority has a penchant for setting up commissions to address whatever the topic of the hour might be. It avoids making an immediate decision, for one thing. But they appoint commission members, give them some funding for staff, and ask them to develop recommendations for policies and, in some cases, to actually implement them."

"What kinds of issues do they address?" Michael said.

"Social justice, diversity, street life, crime, and others; it's a pretty wide assortment," Jonathan said. "The original commission, the one that the others are modeled after, is the London Heritage Commission, which deals with historical celebrations, archaeologist digs, the placing of plaques and monuments, things like that. Because it's the oldest, it's also the largest and best funded. The more progressive Labour members want some of that funding diverted to the issues they are more interested in. The more progressive they are, the more funding they want diverted. That's the ostensible cause of the development of the factions. In some cases, there are some personal animosities involved."

"This sounds like a quagmire," Michael said.

"I think it is, sir," Jonathan said. "But it seems to me to be irresponsible to argue over one commission getting a few thousand more pounds than another while you allow your transportation system to stop and your garbage to pile up."

"That, Jonathan," said Michael, "is the heart of it, and that's what we should build my comments around." There was a knock on the door, and Jay Lanham entered.

"Jay," said Michael, "we've just worked out the central point that I need to make. And it's essentially that, while the commissions may do important work, the citizens of London expect their representatives to make sure the buses and the trains run, the garbage is collected, and order is maintained. It's about priorities. If garbage is piling up in the streets, no one is going to care about a new diversity issue. Does that sound reasonable?"

Lanham nodded. "Yes, sir, that works, I think. I've drafted some very basic ideas for communications, and we'll build those around your message." He paused. "We should likely wait until the Authority members vote or don't vote, and another failure to approve the budget would be the best time for you to speak. My instinct tells me that we're not going to try to make a big splash with this, because the media will do that anyway. Instead, we'll explain, add detail, respond, but we'll go easy on the initiative side of things."

"That sounds excellent, Jay," Michael said.

Jay and Jonathan left to return to their offices, talking about drafting, next steps, and timing.

"There's something about this that leaves me uneasy," Lanham said.

"Uneasy in what way?" Jonathan said.

"Like there's a wild card or two that could be dealt," Lanham said, "like we may get a surprise or two thrown at the king." He was silent for a moment. "After we get the message and the communications plan drafted, let's the two of us talk through the range of possibilities. Like good reactions, bad reactions, unexpected things. Let's just blue-sky it and see if we can think through some basics of what we might do in case of the unexpected."

After lunch, Meredith arrived at Sarah's office to talk through the queen's schedule for the rest of the week, and to bring a piece of news.

"Your majesty," Meredith said, after she was seated, "Tyler Zimmer has called to request a short meeting with you."

"Just him?" Sarah said.

Meredith nodded. "Yes, ma'am, just him."

"All right," Sarah said, "if it's just him. Work with Elizabeth and Carrie to find a spot on the schedule. You can tell them what happened, so they'll know how much time to schedule. But not more than 30 minutes." Carrie Waldman was Sarah's secretary and Elizabeth Wade her administrative chief.

"And Mandy Flaherty called again," Meredith said. "The funeral will be in Belfast next Monday. And she asked me to thank you again for helping them and being at the hospital."

Sarah thought a moment. "Can you check with Carrie to see what my schedule is on Monday? And ask her to see if I can get to Belfast for the funeral."

Chapter 11: The Tsar of London?

On Thursday, the elected representatives of the Greater London Authority, with the Mayor of London presiding, began their meeting at 11. The anger, unease, and mistrust were so thick that they could almost be seen. Even with automobile-clogged streets, businesses and tourism disrupted, schools closed, garbage piling up daily, and their constituents loudly complaining, the members remained in an uncompromising, unrepentant mood.

An official roll call had been taken, and all 32 members were present. The arguments over the first item on the agenda, the old business of the budget, began almost immediately and soon generated into shouting. The galleries were packed with government workers, union representatives, journalists, and the public.

And then King Michael I entered the room.

The plan to travel to the meeting by automobile was abandoned even before it was implemented. Traffic on the streets of Westminster was at almost a standstill. The king's car had traveled from the palace to Victoria Street, normally no more than a three-minute ride. They had been inching their way for 30 minutes until all agreed to find a way to the Thames.

Michael suggested they walk. He donned a pair of sunglasses and, accompanied by a security contingent positioned ahead and behind, Michael, Jonathan Crowe, Jay Lanham, and Josh Gittings crossed Victoria Street by foot and headed toward the river. Ryan Mitchell had arranged for a boat at a small landing at Victoria Tower Gardens, next to Parliament and in between the Westminster and Lambeth bridges. They reached the landing in about 15 minutes.

After boarding the small yacht maintained by the Royal Navy, they sailed east toward the city, their destination City Hall on the South Bank, across from the Tower of London.

"This has to be," Michael said, "one of most spectacular views of London you can get." They passed Parliament and the London Eye, the National Theatre complex, the Tate Modern, Shakespeare's Globe Theatre, numerous office buildings on both sides, Southwark Cathedral and London Bridge, and then the HMS Belfast and Tower Bridge came into view. The Tower of London was on the north bank, and City Hall on the South.

The river had been crowded with boat traffic; others had found this most ancient of London's highways to still work best with the current congested streets and no Underground.

Their pilot docked the boat at the pier used by the Belfast. The few tourists standing in line for the ship were surprised to see a group of security men in dark suits and sunglasses suddenly appear, followed by a smaller group. Even with his sunglasses, Michael was soon recognized. He smiled and nodded, acknowledging the recognition.

A five-minute walk along the embankment brought them to City Hall. It was about 11:10.

They made their way to the Authority meeting hall. The raised voices and arguing continued for a few moments until everyone realized that the king was there. There was a general noise of chairs scraping and seats moving as everyone in the room stood.

Michael motioned with hands for everyone to sit.

"Mr. Mayor," said Elliot Martin, the council member who was the brother-in-law of MP Rodgers Clarke, "a request. I would like to yield my allotted five minutes of speaking time to King Michael, as would the next two scheduled speakers behind me."

"This is highly irregular, Mr. Martin," said the mayor, "but I grant permission."

Nearly every journalist in the room was texting or tweeting, as were most of the people present. Mobiles were suddenly visible everywhere as people sought to record a video.

"Mr. Mayor, members of the Authority," Michael said, "thank you for allowing me to speak. I know this is irregular and unusual, but I also know we are in an irregular and unusual situation. And sometimes, when that happens, the regular fails to work.

"I was born in Kent, and raised in Scotland, but now I live in London. I am a Londoner.

"I am not giving anyone the news that, as a city, as one of the great cities of the world, London is ceasing to function. I was able to travel here this morning only by boat. The streets are clogged; traffic is at a standstill. Businesses and banks are closing. The London Stock Exchange closed this morning. Government ministries have admitted defeat and shut down. Hospitals are unable to send ambulances for emergencies."

"I am not telling you anything you do not already know."

"Buckingham Palace can still manage to function because we took steps to provide for staff and because the world will not come to an end if a state dinner has to be postponed." Some laughter followed that statement. "I can still do my job, because I don't have to catch a bus or the tube to get to my office. Meetings via the internet can still happen, but surgeries can't. Restaurants can't serve food via the internet. Truck deliveries can't be made via the internet. The basics of day-to-day life can't happen only electronically."

"I am a Londoner. I understand the political divisions and disputes. But I shouldn't need to remind you that you were elected to make sure, above and beyond anything else, that Greater London maintains essential public services."

"If the janitorial team can't get to the National Gallery to do its job, then city government has failed."

"If rats begin to take advantage of the piles of garbage mounding up on our streets and sidewalks, then city government has failed."

"If bond traders, bankers, stockbrokers, or loan officers can't get to their jobs, then the national economy is affected, and city government has failed."

"If streets can't be cleaned and maintained, then city government has failed."

"I am a Londoner."

"I do not suggest to you that the various commissions are not important. What I do suggest to you is that you yourselves deny their importance if you allow this great city to shut down, because their work and purpose becomes meaningless unless the trains and buses are running, the garbage is collected, and city offices are open to do their routine business. The very people intended to benefit from the commissions will have no opportunity to do so, if they can't get to work, to school, and to government offices."

"I would submit to you a two-fold suggestion. First, separate funding for the commissions from the rest of the budget. And second, commit to stay in session and not leave this building until that budget is approved. Then deal with funding for the commissions."

"If you want my help in any way, please tell me. I am a Londoner. I believe that the people of London would offer you their help, too, in any way. We are all Londoners here today."

"Please, do not hold our people, the people of London, the people of this great city, hostage to political disagreements."

At that, the galleries erupted in applause, even from the journalists. People stood on their chairs and cheered.

Michael nodded at the Mayor and the Authority members, turned, and left the room.

Jonathan Crowe looked to see how the representatives were reacting. Some were nodding and had joined the applause. Some were red-faced. And others looked ready to explode in anger.

The king's party quickly left the building and walked toward the moored Navy yacht. Michael said nothing until the boat had turned and was heading upstream toward Westminster.

"Jay," Michael said, "is there any reaction online?"

Jay Lanham nodded. "It's all over social media. I've been following the reporter for *The Times* on Twitter and *The Times* website. He was live blogging the meeting, and they've put it right at the top of their main page. He's captured the essence of your speech. And he's saying that the Mayor has called a short adjournment for 15 minutes and then an executive session to discuss the emergency."

Michael looked at Josh Gittings. "Is that a good thing, Josh?"

Gittings didn't respond immediately. "I think so, your majesty," he said finally. "It implies that the mayor recognizes that there is now an emergency. They have two options. Pass the budget, as you suggested, or declare an emergency. The fact that the mayor cited the word 'emergency' suggests which way he may be leaning. It would be simpler and smarter to pass the budget without funding the commissions. But that may not be politically possible."

"Have you talked to the PM about this?" Michael said.

"Last night," Gittings said. "I asked him if he or the Home Secretary could lean on the Labour members of the Authority to enact the budget. He was not optimistic, and he said that he was reluctant to intervene in a city dispute, unless it could be done as an all-Parliament action."

"Which means what?" Michael said. "Is Peter saying he won't intervene at all?"

Gittings nodded. "Your majesty, the PM has the same factions in the national Labour Party that exist in the city government. If he attempts to intervene, he may not be able to hold his ruling majority together. The recent election with the additional 10 Labour seats masked what's really developing. It looks like it's all Labour from the outside, but from the inside, it is centrist Labour, traditional Labour, and radical Labour. Since the elections were only a few months ago, I don't think he wants to test whether he can hold the party together."

"So, then," Michael said, "the best outcome will be that the Authority passes a budget on its own."

"They can't do that in executive session," Jonathan said. "That vote must be held in public, so they will have to come out from executive session."

"And they may not want their votes publicly known," Gittings said.

"Sir," said Lanham, "Jonathan and I did some blue-skying 'what-if' scenarios yesterday, and there's one we think we might need to prepare for."

"And that is?" Michael said.

"What if the Authority declares an emergency, triggering the six-month appointment of a tsar to essentially run the city?" Lanham said. "Trevor Barry had members of his chambers check the law, and the emergency executive can be anyone. There are no restrictions. It wouldn't even have to be a British citizen, as long as the executive was approved by a three-fourths majority."

"I don't understand," Michael said. "Why would we need to prepare for that?"

"What if," Lanham said, "they appointed the king?"

Michael looked puzzled. "Don't you think that's a bit over the top?" he said. "I don't have any experience in running a city government. Can they do that?"

"Their options are wide open," said Lanham. "But could the Authority members agree on anyone else? You're the only person in Britain and London who enjoys widespread support. To reach agreement on anyone else might be impossible."

Now Michael looked stunned. He turned to Josh.

Gittings nodded. "Even if you hadn't spoken this morning, it would be entirely possible. Rodgers Clarke called and asked me yesterday if we knew about the emergency provisions in city law. I said yes, we did, but at the time I didn't think there might be other implications of his question."

"Josh and I talked with Trevor early this morning," Lanham said. "We asked him to fully research those emergency provisions and tell us the full authority an emergency executive might be given. I didn't have to explain it to him, sir; he knew why I was asking. He said he would have a preliminary report waiting when we returned from the Authority." He paused. "Your majesty, I feel like I failed here. I should have said something about this before you spoke to the Authority."

They had reached the mooring at Victoria Tower Gardens.

"Jay, you did not fail me," Michael said. "As upsetting as this is to me personally, I want you all to know that, if I had known about this before I spoke, I would still have gone with what we did as planned and said exactly what I did." He closed his eyes. "But I do need to pray. Right at this moment."

When they arrived back at the palace, having walked from the Thames, Michael found his secretary, Myra Frobisher, waiting for him. Myra had been the secretary to Michael's half-brother Henry and had escaped death at the hands of the jihadists only because she left Henry's office five minutes before he did.

"Sir," she said, "there's some lunch in a warmer in the library. I expected you wouldn't have had time to eat and Mr. Malone was ahead of me; he already had it in preparation when I went to ask him."

"Thanks to you both," Michael said. "I am hungry."

"Detective Frees has called twice," Myra said. "He says it's important that he speak with you."

"I'll call him when I get to the library," Michael said. "Did he give you any specifics?"

"He said something about more arrests," she said.

"And Jay and Josh will have a report from Trevor's chambers," Michael said. "I'll need to discuss it with them as soon as I finish with Frees. Is there anything on the schedule this afternoon?"

"There was," Myra said, "but it had to be postponed because of the traffic situation. So, you're clear."

In the library, Michael began eating as he called Detective Frees, who apologized but said that he had a question.

"Some 40 additional priests have been arrested," Frees said, "including ten here in London. I'm sorry to report two suicides believed to be linked: both were priests, one in a parish near Cambridge and another in Devon."

"Oh, no," said Michael, "this is awful. No one wants suicides. This is terrible, detective."

"Your majesty," Frees said, "police departments all over Britain are receiving reports from likely victims, mostly men but also some women. Do you know how many parishes there are in the country?"

"I don't have an exact tally," Michael said, "but it's something like 16,000. That's parishes, not priests. Some priests cover for multiple parishes. The number of C of E clergy would be about half that number, maybe close to 9,000. You have larger staffs in the cathedral cities and in the administrative centers, like Lambeth Palace. Say, a total of 10,000 or so."

"What about retired priests?" Frees said. "Do you know about how many of those there might be?"

"No," Michael said. "A guess would be about the same number as active priests, but it's perhaps more. Those 16,000 parishes used to have at least one individual priest. But that's no longer the case. There are priests covering multiple parishes, usually because of dwindling numbers of parish members."

"I'm asking these questions," Frees said, "because right now we have about 70 priests who've been arrested, and if the numbers go the way they look they're going, the actual number may get closer to several hundred."

"That would be," Michael said, with an inward shudder, "worse than it sounds, because there will be a considerable number of priests and bishops who weren't directly involved but had to deal with the aftermath, and thus they would have known."

"Accessories after the fact," Frees said. "Yes, it's a felony." Michael could hear Frees shuffling papers. "Rev. Brimley was extraordinarily helpful, by the way. He provided an in-depth overview of the seminary structure and graduates, plus where a lot of people might have been sent or ended up. He left us his seminary yearbook, so we had a head-start with names. You might consider checking in with him, sir; he was quite broken up when he left here yesterday."

"I will do that, detective," Michael said.

"The Bristol police detained the bishop there," Frees said, "and then interviewed him under caution. He had an attorney with him, but he's now being held without bail; the judge there was adamant that bail would not be allowed because he considered the bishop a flight risk. Search warrants have also been executed, and we've been combing through personnel files at the four dioceses. What I'm hearing is that other dioceses are being implicated."

"How many victims do you think there might be?" Michael said.

"Well," Frees said, "it's hard to say at this point, and we may never have a complete total. Simply because many will not come forward. But I would say, sir, that we're probably looking in the thousands, perhaps more, possibly as many as 10,000. I could be wrong, and I hope I am, but that's my educated guess at this point."

They talked for a few more minutes, and then rang off. Michael sat at the table, his head down. His spirit felt heavy, almost weighed down. And he did what he usually did at such times; he prayed.

Trevor Barry, Jay Lanham, and Josh Gittings met in Gittings' office.

"This is a fairly quick review," Barry said. "Fortunately, there was a court case when this was enacted by the Authority six years ago. Several groups sued to have the emergency provisions struck down, but the courts held for the Authority. The arguments were considerable, and a number of people have dissected the decisions, so we have a good overview of the law and its real and potential meanings."

"First, there are a number of conditions and situations that qualify as potential emergencies. A breakdown in essential services – defined to include transportation, police, infrastructure maintenance, trash collections, and several others – is one of the qualifying events, if the Authority recognizes it as such. An inability to enact a budget for whatever reason is also specifically mentioned. A terrorist attack paralyzing services is another area. The judgment of my colleagues who are more expert on this is that our current situation qualifies in several ways. The key is that the Authority has to vote to recognize a situation as an emergency."

"Second, once that happens, the Authority has a free hand in appointing anyone to serve as the emergency executive. One of the legal objections had been that the law was written so broadly that even a non-citizen could be appointed. The courts recognized that, and then they pointed out that this actual discussion had occurred during the legislative process, and that the Authority wanted to have the freedom to choose the best person available."

"Third, the term for the executive can last up to six months, and even longer if the Authority includes that recognition in the appointment. The Authority representatives are free to specify the term in the appointment."

"Fourth, the executive is given all of the powers of the Authority. He or she can write and implement laws, approve budgets, create new programs as needed, and levy taxes. All department heads report to the executive, who can hire and fire any and all personnel."

"Finally, at or before the end of the specified term, the executive must call for elections of a mayor and borough representatives. The election period lasts 30 days, so essentially elections must be called at least one month before the end of the emergency executive's term."

Barry looked down at his notes. "That's it. Admittedly, it's a barebones summary. We've written it up as a short report for you and the king."

For a moment, no one spoke.

"I suppose," Gittings said, "we can always hope the Authority pass the budget and avoid this entirely."

"We can hope," said Lanham, "but it sounds like a very faint hope." He shook his head. "I feel like we've let the king down. We should have worked this out before advising him to accept the invitation to speak."

"Jay," said Gittings, "we don't know if this is a real possibility or not, and we won't find out until the Authority announce something. Trevor, do you or your colleagues have any sense of how this might go?"

"No, I don't," Barry said. "I've not really followed Authority politics and governing very closely. For those of my colleagues who have, they think one of two things will happen. Either public pressure will force a budget approval, or they will activate the emergency law. If it's the second option, they said to expect a term appointment of six months. But some time may be required for the Authority to identify the person, contact them, and have their decision accepted. And the situation is growing worse by the hour." He paused. "If they do declare an emergency, the pressures on the executive will be rather intense. We've all assumed that you asked for this because of the possibility they might name the king? Is he aware of the possibility?"

Both Gittings and Lanham nodded.

"We talked on the boat coming back," Gittings said. "We were all surprised at the idea, and he looked rather shocked, but we all understood the possibility."

"Then," Barry said, "my advice would be to start developing a plan, and right now. Determine what the most critical things would be to do in the first 24 hours. Once the decision is public, call a meeting of all the major departments as soon as possible, like within hours, by videoconference if need be. Transport for London and Environment London would be at the top of the list for action plans, simply because of the transportation and garbage removal crises. Figure out a system quickly for announcements, rules, and changes. The Authority bureaucracy is on the large side, and they tend to move slowly. You may have to prepare for dismissals if they seem reluctant to act."

"We owe it to the king to start on this now," Gittings said. "Can you both stay? Let's start getting this down in writing, with a basic plan with key action steps right up front." He glanced at his watch. "Let's see what we can get down in the next hour. I'll get my admin in to take notes."

"I'll call mine for easel charts," Lanham said. "We'll need to see what we're doing."

Sarah quietly slipped into the palace library. She wanted to talk with Michael about Tyler Zimmer and how the Authority meeting had gone, but as soon as she spotted him, she could see he was praying. So, she waited, and stood in place as she watched him.

Never did her heart feel so full as when she watched him pray. And Michael had been praying a lot lately. She knew that the disclosures of the past week had begun to weigh heavily on her husband; with her alone had he wept as he talked the previous night about the victims like Robert Hood.

"Sarah, they hurt the very people they were supposed to shepherd," Michael said. "The children. And this may have been going on for decades. How could they do this?"

She'd held his hand to her face. "You've said it yourself more than once, my husband. Humanity is fallen and sinful."

He had nodded. "But the church was in effect setting predators loose to prey upon children. This was almost institutionalized at the leading seminary in the country. How could anyone who even suspected ignore an evil like this?"

"I don't know, Mike," she'd said, "but they need prayer, too."

And now he was praying again. *He must have talked with Detective Frees again*, she thought. *More bad news.*

Michael finally finished praying and looked up. "Have you been here long?" he said.

She shook her head. "Just a few minutes. I didn't want to disturb you." She walked over and sat next to him. "How did the Authority meeting go? Meredith showed me some of the news and social media reports."

"It went as well as it could have, I suppose," he said. "Some of them didn't look particularly happy to have the king give them a verbal spanking. But the people in the galleries cheered, including many of the press."

"Do you think they'll pass a budget?" she said.

"I don't know," he said, "but you need to be aware of something that may happen." He explained about the appointment of an emergency executive, and who that person might be.

"You're joking," she said.

"I wish I was," Michael said. "Josh and Jay are meeting with Trevor right now. Trevor's colleagues helped to draw up a summary of the emergency law and the responsibilities of the executive, if one is appointed. They're supposed to be coming here soon with the report."

"Do you need me to leave?" Sarah said.

"No," he said, "I need you to stay. If this plays out like they think it might, you'll be as much affected as me." He started to write on a tablet in front of him, and then stopped. "I'm thinking about something, and I'd like to know what you think. I'm thinking about calling the Archbishop of Canterbury."

"Really?" she said.

He nodded. "Sarah, the way this priest abuse thing is going, and the fact that Canterbury has so far rather bungled its response, suggests to me that the church is in a dire condition, even worse than I thought it was. I'm not sure it can survive what's likely to come out publicly. And Sebastian Rowland has to start making a vigorous response. He's hiding behind legalities and mutterings of honoring due process of law, which is all well and good, but it also delays decision-making by the church. He's simply kicking the can down the road, hoping to buy time."

"What should he be doing?" she said.

"Undertaking his own investigation," Michael said. "Shaking down the hierarchy. Demanding immediate accountability. Asking the dioceses for any and all reports involving abusive priests. I just don't understand why he's sitting in Lambeth Palace seemingly doing nothing."

Sarah was silent for a time before speaking. "Mike, what if he can't?"

"What do you mean?" he said.

"What if he can't because he's involved himself?" she said.

Michael stared at his wife. "I hadn't thought of that," he said.

"It doesn't have to be as a perpetrator," she said. "He could be involved in helping to cover it up. The newspaper reports suggest this has been happening for a long time, and there's simply no way it could have been kept hidden, without the involvement of people in powerful positions."

"I didn't think of that at all," Michael said. "But if it's true, it would explain a lot. Oh, my goodness, Sarah. To have this and the London problems at the same time seems almost overwhelming."

"I could easily be wrong," she said. "And the London problem may not happen at all." She paused. "And I have what will sound like a trivial matter, at least in comparison. Tyler Zimmer contacted Meredith, and he asked if I could talk with him alone. We have him scheduled for next Tuesday, here at the palace."

"I think you should hear what he has to say," Michael said. "Your mother won't be with him?"

She shook her head. "He told Meredith that Mother didn't even know he was asking to talk with me."

Michael put his hand on hers. "This is hard, isn't it? I mean. Not just the church or London or family issues, but all of it, coming like it is. Maybe we should have signed up only for the flower show openings." He smiled. "It was less than a year ago that I was practicing sermons and you were waiting rather impatiently for the arrival of a certain baby. It seems like decades, and another life."

Sarah took Michael's hand in both of hers. "It was another life. Even if we don't know what we're doing, Mike, or what we should do, God does. The stuff that's horrible or appalling or perplexing, he knows it. He has us both here for a reason, if we can't fathom it and even if we want to be anywhere else but here. Mike, he's ripping the lid off the sewer; it's just hard to be one of the workers he sends in to clean out the pipes."

They heard a knock at the door. Josh stuck his head in.

"I'm sorry to disturb you, your majesty," Gittings said, "but I have Trevor and Jay with me. We can come back if this isn't convenient."

"Not at all, Joshua," Michael said. "Come in. I asked Sarah to join us for our talk. Has there been any word from City Hall?"

Gittings shook his head. "No, sir. They're still in closed session. We have an observer in the galleries and we're also following media reports." Trevor and Jay, carrying easels, set them up in front of the library table.

Trevor quickly walked Michael and Sarah through the report from his chambers, and then he and Josh began the discussion of what kind of plan might be needed. The five talked for more than two hours. By the end, the outline of a plan had been hammered out.

When the meeting ended, the others left, and Michael remained in the library. It was hard to believe that his speech to the Greater London Authority had only been a few hours before; it seemed like days.

The clock on a nearby table read 4:30. He decided to make two phone calls.

First, he called Andrew Brimley in Edinburgh. Brimley sounded subdued, but Michael could tell he was processing all that had happened since Sunday and was convinced he had done the right thing.

"Michael," he said, "where is all of this leading, do you think?"

"Andrew," Michael said, "I don't know, but I think the days of the Church of England, at least as we've known known it in our lifetimes, are numbered. I don't think it will be able to withstand what's coming, unless significant changes are made, changes far beyond even I was thinking. I don't think the public will be able to accept what is going to happen; people will demand change, deep and profound change, or they'll simply walk away."

"I suppose I added my own bit of fuel to the fire," Brimley said.

"A better way to say it, Andrew," Michael said, "is that you helped to channel it in a direction it needed to go. The rot and corruption were far beyond even what I had thought. By the way, I believe it's public now, the Bishop of Bristol has been arrested and is being held without bail."

"I hadn't heard," Brinley said. "All of this leaves a terrible ache, a deep and abiding sadness. I suppose the proper thing for me to do is to pray for him."

"And Andrew," Michael said, "I need your prayers as well. In addition to this horror with the church, the situation in London government is coming to a head, and it looks increasingly like I will be involved in what happens afterward. I feel uniquely unqualified."

"Then I will pray for you, too," Brinley said. "But you know as well as I that God calls whom he calls. And what we consider to be impeccable qualifications often mean nothing at all to God."

After ringing off, Michael called Myra and asked her to put any call from the mayor, Elliot Martin, or Rodgers Clarke through immediately. She reminded him she was staying in the palace and that she was planning to work late.

"Can you do one thing now, Myra?" he said.

"Yes, sir?" she said.

"Can you call Lambeth Palace and say that the king needs to speak with the Archbishop of Canterbury?" he said. "If Sebastian isn't available when you call, please have him call back."

If she was surprised, her voice didn't show it. "Of course, sir," she said. "I will call now."

Sebastian Rowland was in his office, talking with Canon Land.

"What records do we have here at the palace?" Rowland said.

"The master records," Land said. "Everything is secured in the vault in archives. There are some 30 boxes of personnel files."

"How many records are we talking about here?" Rowland said.

"The actual number of priests?" Land said. "Some 917 active priests. Included in that number are 12 bishops and two archbishops. Not included is whatever the current situation is at St. Simon's Seminary outside Norfolk, St. Olaf's Seminary in Cardiff, and St. Ignatius Seminary in Glasgow. As far as we know at this point, the other seminaries and colleges are not involved."

Rowland could hear Land's voice, speaking in monotones as if wishing to distance himself from what he was saying. "And what about retired priests? How many of them are potentially involved?"

"Another 430, Archbishop," Land said., "perhaps more. I'm still checking records."

Rowland felt almost immobilized. They had told Geoffrey Venneman that the total number would be about 100 at the very worst. The reality was some 15 times that number, and possibly more.

"If Venneman learns these numbers," Rowland said, "he will cut us adrift like one of those piles of smelly garbage showing up on the sidewalks right now."

Land was no fan of Mr. Venneman. "There are likely worse things to endure, Archbishop."

"Have you looked at any of the records for active priests yourself, Martin?" Rowland said.

Whenever the Archbishop used his Christian name, Land knew that something was whirling inside Rowland's mind.

"Not lately, Archbishop," he said. "Not in the last two years, other than to add additional files to those in the vault."

"Thirty boxes sound like a lot, but they are a finite number," Rowland said. "I think that, for safekeeping purposes, those records should be transferred from Lambeth Palace to more secure accommodations." He paused. "If you get my meaning. It would be terrible if something happened to them. Do you know if anyone has copies of the files?"

"These are master personnel files," Land said. "Many of them are still under seal. Few if any would have copies, except perhaps at the retreat house in Cumbria, where priests are sent for treatment and counseling."

"Is it possible for us to get those records as well?" Rowland asked.

"Theoretically possible but not likely," Land said.

"It would be a terrible thing, Martin," Rowland said, "if the records were destroyed during a warehouse fire, for example. Or if we consolidated all records at Cumbria and there was a fire."

There was a knock at the door, and Rowland's admin stuck her head in.

"I thought I'd said we weren't to be disturbed," Rowland said sharply.

"Yes, sir, you did," the woman said, "and I apologize. But you have a phone call I believe is important. It's Buckingham Palace. King Michael has asked to speak to you."

Rowland was so surprised that, at first, he didn't respond.

"Well," he finally said, "patch him through."

Twenty seconds later, the phone on the archbishop's desk rang.

"Archbishop, it's Michael Kent-Hughes."

"Yes, your majesty," Rowland said. "I have you on speaker phone. With me is Canon Martin Land, my chief of staff. I presume you're calling about the abuse issue."

"Archbishop," Michael said, "I know we have our differences, and that I may be the last person you wish to speak with. But we have to talk about the church. Four bishops have now been arrested and are being held without bail. Were you aware of this?"

Rowland reddened in fury as he looked at Land. Land looked at his mobile, searching for any message or text from Venneman, who was monitoring media and was supposed to alert them of any new developments. There was nothing. Land shook his head.

"No, your majesty," Rowland said, "I was not aware. Have they been charged with abuse?"

"No, Archbishop," Michael said, "they have not. They have been charged with being accessories after the fact and covering up the abuse cases in their dioceses. This is also a felony. The police have executed search warrants of diocesan records and computers."

Both Land and Rowland went white.

"What I need to know, archbishop," Michael said, "is if you believe you have a sufficient plan for dealing with communications, responses, and actions. And it needs to be something more than saying the church is respecting due process and the course of law."

Rowland, whose right hand had started shaking, recovered himself. "Your majesty, we have a complete plan that is being implemented as we speak."

"Do you need help?" Michael said. "I'm asking because the situation has gone beyond critical and is now headed for melt-down. This is only the very tip of the iceberg. And I will be frank, Archbishop. Apart from any criticism I have made these past few months, I have my doubts as to the long-term sustainability of the church, given everything we now know and what we suspect. It is incumbent upon both of us to put personal enmity aside and do what we need to do."

"What else have you heard?" Rowland said.

"Archbishop," Michael said, "I'm not at liberty to say. I can only speak to what is public knowledge."

"We fully intend to defend the church and her priests," Rowland said. "This is being blown completely out of proportion."

At first, all they heard was silence in response.

"I wasn't talking about the priests, Archbishop," Michael said. "I was talking about the victims."

"What are you suggesting here?" Rowland said, clearly growing angry.

"I'm talking about plans for restitution and closure for the victims. What are you considering that addresses that?" Michael said.

"Your majesty," Rowland said, "that will be decided, if it's decided at all, in a court of law. I would like to remind you that I am not personally involved in this; all of this happened on the watch of my predecessors. I will take effective steps to make sure all of these issues are addressed."

"What I hear you saying, Sebastian," Michael said, "is that Lambeth Palace has no plan, Mr. Venneman has no plan, and that no one has even considered what might have to be done. We're not talking a simple court case here. We're talking about tens of thousands of victims and hundreds of priests. Not to mention their enablers and facilitators in the church hierarchy. Sebastian, I think we could be looking at the collapse of the church."

"We are looking at no such thing," Rowland said, the anger finally surfacing. "You want to take advantage of a few problems to force through your reformation. Well, I won't stand for it. You will not destroy the Church of England."

"I'm not trying to destroy the Church of England, Archbishop," Michael said. "It's obviously doing a good enough job of that on its own. I'm trying to make sure there's a Church of England left after all of this blows up. And let me be clear. You know what ecclesiastical authority I have as the head of the church of England. That is not a threat; it is a simple statement of fact."

"You would not dare," Rowland said. "You'll destroy your reign."

"I'm sorry, Archbishop," Michael said. "I had hoped we could lay our differences aside for a time and look to what's needed to be done. If nothing else, I've learned that doesn't appear to be possible. I ask you to consider your words and your plans and examine your heart. If you feel you need us to talk, you can call. I will make sure any call is expedited. Goodbye, archbishop."

With that, Michael hung up.

Rowland look at his chief of staff. "He wouldn't dare remove me. It would cause a firestorm," he said.

Land said nothing. He knew that King Michael had a better understanding of what was unfolding than the archbishop did. And he realized that Rowland was more than blatantly suggesting that the personnel records needed to be destroyed and how to do it.

But Land said nothing. He looked at the Archbishop, and he nodded.

Later, Land made another phone call.

"Michael called the Archbishop," Land said.

"Canon Land, the fact that Michael called the archbishop is unnerving enough. The implications are horrendous. It tells me that the situation may be far worse that we thought."

"Four bishops have been arrested," Land said. "And the head of St. Simon's Seminary is being required to defend his position and why he shouldn't be fired, and then strip searched to make sure he's not hiding documents."

At dinner in the ballroom. Jay Lanham worked his way through the tables to find Michael.

"Sir," Lanham said, "we just received word that the London Authority had adjourned without any announcement except to say that discussions would resume tomorrow morning at 8. Our observer said that the members filed out of their session looking rather tight-lipped, which could mean anything."

"Let's hope," Michael said, "that they're negotiating the budget."

"And I thought you might want to see this," Lanham said, extending two evening newspapers. The banner headline on both was in quotation marks: 'I am a Londoner.'

"Oh, my," said Michael, showing the papers to Sarah. "Well," he said, "it's accurate. I did say that. Several times."

Chapter 12: Yes, the Tsar of London

The morning newspapers repeated the headlines from the night before, which Michael thought would likely rub salt in the Greater London Authority's wounds. Josh Gittings reported that there were large crowds gathering at London City Hall, and police from the Met were on hand to maintain order.

"It's getting ugly," Gittings said. "Several people have been arrested for throwing rocks at the building, and the police are trying to bring water cannons to the scene in case they're needed."

The Guardian had published a story of an elderly woman who lived in Brick Lane in Spitalfields who had had heart trouble and called emergency, but an ambulance had been unable to get to her because of the traffic-congested streets. The woman had died.

"Some of the signs at City Hall this morning," Gittings said, "equated the Authority to murderers." He paused. "And the papers are reporting scores more arrests involving priests and other church officials, with two priests being attacked by angry mobs before the police could get them inside the stations. A vicarage in Surrey was also torched."

"Joshua," Michael said, "do you have a minute? Can you take a short walk with me?" Michael was the only person Gittings knew who used his full Christian name, Joshua. "You know it means 'he saves,' don't you," Michael had once said, playfully. "It's also the name Jesus would have been known by in Israel." Gittings hadn't realized both the meaning and the connection to Jesus.

They eventually found themselves on the palace terrace. Michael continued to walk toward the gardens and the woods on the palace grounds.

"I want to continue that conversation we started the other day," Michael said. "The one about things coming unglued. And I don't want to talk where we might be overheard, which is rather difficult right now with all the staff."

"Have you been thinking more about this?" Gittings said.

"What with the church and the London Authority, it's about all I've been thinking about," Michael said. "In more normal times, if there is such a thing, the church might have provided some cushion for dealing with major local and national issues. But it can no longer do that. Joshua, the church as it's currently constituted will not be able to withstand the storm that's begun to blow." He paused. "I called Archbishop Rowland yesterday."

"You did?" Gittings said, clearly surprised. "What did you say?"

"Our conversation did not go well," Michael said. "I asked him to put aside our differences and try to work to develop an effective response. I came away from the conversation with two things. First, he claims no personal involvement, although I didn't ask about that; he felt compelled to volunteer it, which makes me even more uneasy. And second, he and the church hierarchy, even with Mr. Venneman's help, are woefully unprepared." He looked around at the quiet of the small woods, which made it difficult to imagine he was standing in the middle of a large city. "I may have to remove him as archbishop."

"And not a minute too soon," Gittings said.

"I need a few days to pray and consider," Michael said. "But Rowland is in over his head; all he's thinking about is personal damage control and that I want to take over his job. Perhaps I do, but not for the reasons he thinks. The church is falling into an abyss, and Sebastian doesn't see it."

"Have you talked with York?" Gittings said. "Perhaps Archbishop Johnston might have some counsel or encouragement."

Michael looked away. "Briefly," he said. "But it was very short. As much as I want to, I can't."

"But why not?" Gittings said. "Because of the ongoing investigation? Surely he would understand the –." He suddenly broke off. "Oh, no, Michael," he said. "You can't because –"

"Because he's likely involved, yes," Michael said. "This is another part of the tragedy that's unfolding. You can't be an archbishop or bishop and not know or at least strongly suspect what was happening. Your signature will be on transfer documents. Even if it isn't, there's no way any senior church official couldn't know." He paused. "When the Bishop of Southwark was here for lunch, we talked about it. He said that there had been rumors about the church in general, but Southwark had had a long history of training up its own priests. They have their own theology school. Virtually none of the priests in the diocese came from outside Southwark. While that can lead to theological inbreeding, in this case, it looks like it may have protected the parishes and their people. It also helps explain the reaction to my sermon last December; the church had already been the good kind of salt in the community."

At that moment, both men heard a voice calling out for the king.

"Your majesty! Your majesty!"

Jonathan Crowe was almost breathless, having almost run from the back of the palace.

"I'm sorry, sir," he said, trying to catch his breath. "We've been looking all over. The mayor of London has called and says he needs to speak to you urgently."

Michael looked at Gittings. "And so, the shoe begins to drop?"

They gathered in the library. Trevor, Josh, Jay, and Jonathan were joined by Sarah and Brent Epworth. They all stood as Michael sat at the table he used for a desk.

The telephone rang, and Michael answered.

"Good morning, Mayor," he said. "I take it you have some news."

"I hope you find this good news, your majesty," the mayor said. "While the representatives of the Greater London Authority were unable to reach agreement on a budget, they did unanimously agree to declare an emergency, invoking the Emergency Powers Act. Are you familiar with this act?"

"Yes, I am," said Michael.

"Then you know that, once an emergency is declared," the mayor said, "an emergency executive is appointed. We have taken that step, for a period of six months. And the representatives, after much discussion, decided that the executive should be yourself, as you are the only person who is acceptable to the public, the city government, and the elected representatives."

The group in the library all looked at each other. Sarah placed her hand on Michael's shoulder.

"I know this comes as a surprise, your majesty," the mayor said, "and that you may need a period to consider it. But time is short, as you yourself noted yesterday."

"Can you fax the document or the meeting minutes where it's noted, including the vote?" Michael said.

"Yes, I'll do it now," the mayor said. Jay Lanham introduced himself and gave the mayor the fax number for the machine there in the library. They heard him give the instructions to his admin. A minute later, the fax machine started.

"Your majesty," the mayor said, "the entire council of elected representatives, myself included, are putting ourselves at your disposal, ready to do whatever you tell us, assuming you accept the position."

"I will arrive at City Hall in 30 minutes, Mr. Mayor," Michael said. "I need you to assemble the representatives and all department heads who are available. You may also allow the news media to attend."

"Sir," the mayor said, "you may have heard, but we had some unrest here this morning. Crowds are still milling around on the embankment. There have been several arrests."

"I heard," Michael said. "I will be there in 30 minutes." He ended the call.

"Mr. Epworth," Michael said to his Master of the Household, "is the helicopter on its way?"

"Yes, sir," Epworth said, "it should arrive in 10 minutes."

"Jay and Josh," Michael said, "I need both of you to accompany me, as we planned."

"We already have security people at City Hall," Joshua said, "and two will accompany us on the helicopter."

"We might have just enough time before we leave for a bio break," Michael said.

Epworth had checked: City Hall had no helipad but there was one atop an office building nearby. The flight took 10 minutes and traveling down the elevator and walking to City Hall about the same amount of time. Michael, Josh, Jay, and the two security officers walked through the crowds; Michael was instantly recognized and greeted with cheers and applause.

They made their way to the meeting chamber, and they found it packed with people. The representatives sat in the seats at the table; the department heads were in the front row. Most of the people in the room, including the press and the department heads, expected an announcement about the passage of a budget. Even the king's appearance didn't lead many to suspect a different kind of announcement; he had been there yesterday, and it would be appropriate, they thought, for him to take some credit for breaking the logjam.

No one expected the mayor's announcement, made with Michael standing at his side.

"Yesterday and today," the mayor said, "the Greater London Authority labored mightily to reach agreement on a budget for the city government. Despite our best efforts, we failed."

That reverberated like a cannon firing in the room.

"Instead," the mayor continued, "we did reach unanimous agreement on the declaration of a city-wide emergency, invoking the Emergency Powers Act of the Greater London Authority. For a period of six months, we have appointed an emergency executive, who will exercise the full power of the Authority. Our unanimous choice is His Majesty, Michael Kent-Hughes."

Michael stepped forward. "If there is one thing I've learned since our arrival in London last December, every day is a new day, and a different day, in our city."

The people in the room stared in stunned surprise.

"I have some announcements," Michael said, surprising the mayor and several Authority members.

"First, this council is dissolved," Michael said, "under the provisions of the Emergency Powers Act. That includes the position of the mayor.

"Second, the budget recently expired is now reconstituted, with one exception. The work of all commissions is suspended immediately. Each will be reviewed, and a determination made.

"Third, all staff for Transport for London and waste disposal services are asked to return to work immediately. The transport maintenance staff will work with drivers and other staff to get the Underground and the buses on a normal schedule as soon as tomorrow. Our goal will be a restoration of all transport services by Monday morning. No one will be docked pay for the halt in services this week.

"Fourth, if you do not have the appropriate sticker for operating an automobile in central London, you must remove your automobile by 2 p.m. this afternoon. Trash vehicles from several surrounding counties will be arriving to help clear the sidewalks and streets of garbage, and we need unauthorized automobiles off the streets as soon as possible.

"Fifth, as allowed by the Emergency Powers Act, an election for representatives and mayor will be scheduled for five months from today, with oaths of office being taken six months from today.

"I will have more announcements in the days to come. And now I'd like to meet with the department heads. It's an open meeting, so the public and the press are welcome to stay. Thank you."

The 32 former members of the Greater London Authority, and the mayor, stood, looked around at one another, and then left the room.

Michael turned to the department heads, seated in the front row.

"My admin from the palace will be calling your offices today to set up appointments for next week," Michael said. "These will be simply get-to-know-you meetings, and they'll be here at City Hall. I don't need formal presentations with PowerPoint slides. I just want to talk, hear about your department's strengths and challenges, and what your most pressing problems are. You know your departments, so let's just talk.

"As you know, my experience is not administrative," he said. "The closest I've come to that was running the youth program at my church in San Francisco, which is not quite the same thing as operating the London Underground." Some laughter followed. "At the palace, I've had the great blessing of extremely capable and gifted people serving as administrators. They have their hands full as it is, and they won't be involved here in city administration. I may ask their advice, but they and I won't be second-guessing anyone.

"I'm starting from the assumption that all of you are capable and experienced administrators, who care deeply about making sure you and your staffs serve the people of London. We will have to work closely together for the next six months, and if you have a problem with any decision I make, you must tell me. And our goal will be to hand the responsibility for serving the people of London to a new mayor and a new council of representatives, knowing that we have done a job to be proud of. You should plan on a weekly meeting as a group with me on Mondays at 10 a.m., and our first meeting will be Monday next." He paused. "And thank you for being here this morning."

Michael spent the next two hours talking with the department heads, shaking hands with visitors in the gallery, and talking informally with reporters. The chiefs for Transport for London and waste management both introduced themselves to Michael and then quickly left to manage the resumption of services. Josh and Jay, and several reporters who decided to tag along, went with Michael to the city administration offices. The king offered words of reassurance and encouragement, asking people about their jobs, their work, and their families. They ate lunch in the City Hall cafeteria, where Michael met more people and talked with the cafeteria staff.

By noon, trash trucks began to rumble through London. At 3 p.m., the Circle and District underground lines reopened on a reduced schedule. Alerted by the Transport for London staff, Michael, Josh, Jay, and the two security officers walked to Tower Bridge, crossed the river, and made their way to the Tower Hill tube station, catching one of the first Underground trains to resume operation and traveling to the St. James's Park station. By 5 p.m., several bus lines had resumed operation, also on reduced schedules, including the No. 15 with its trademark Routemaster buses.

Everywhere Michael went, people applauded, cheered, and offered congratulations and thanks. The king's repetitive response:

"Let's thank the people of Transport for London and city government for working hard to get things up and running."

When they returned to the palace, Brent Epworth said that the staff would be spending their final night there and returning home on Saturday. "It might be an idea, sir," he said to Michael, "to turn tonight's dinner into something of a celebration."

"That's a splendid idea," Michael said.

Myra Frobisher told him that the meetings with the city department heads had been scheduled, and she handed him the meeting plan for the next week. The schedule combined both city and palace activities. "We've shuffled and moved a few things," she said, "but I believe it's manageable. Barely. You're going to be kept quite busy. Oh, and sir, Detective Frees called and asked that you call him back."

"I'll call him from the library, Myra," Michael said, "and thank you for your help here. Can you work with Josh to get some help for you for the next six months? Otherwise, I suspect you'll be doing double duty."

Michael spent a few minutes in the library before returning Frees' phone call. He looked through his mail, signed letters left for him by Myra, and checked what phone messages he might need to return.

Then he called Scotland Yard.

"Well, detective," Michael said, "how are you? And I mean that question exactly. I know you're here to talk about the investigation, but I want to know how you're bearing up."

"Thank you for asking, your majesty," Frees said. "Investigations involving child abuse are always difficult. This one is, how should I say, almost overwhelming. It covers an extended period of time, with scores if not hundreds of abusers and thousands of victims."

"And, even if you're not a regular attender or any kind of believer," Michael said, "it involves the church, and whatever image or understanding you had of it."

"There's that, too, sir," Frees said. "I see from the press that you've been keeping yourself rather occupied. I've actually seen a bus or two on Whitehall."

"Yes," Michael said, "we learned this morning that I was appointed the emergency executive."

"Could you have refused?" Frees said.

"I could have," Michael said. "And the chaos would have continued. So, I accepted and told them to expect organized chaos."

The detective laughed. "All the chatter at the Yard is that the king is getting London straightened out," Frees said.

"We'll have to see how true that is," Michael said. "Much of this could have been avoided by simply agreeing to pay people for the work they do."

Frees cleared his throat. "Why I called. We've been looking at church and diocesan personnel records. They're woefully incomplete. While I don't expect churchmen to be excellent record keepers, what we're finding is only the thinnest of files and vaguest of references. We've been looking through the St. Simon Seminary records as well, but all we have there, really, are names and files for students. They provide leads, but they wouldn't have anything after they left and went on to their first church assignments.

"Do you know where more substantive records might be kept, or should I consider the possibility that records have been destroyed or perhaps hidden?"

"Has your investigation or any of the other police departments reached the archbishop level yet?" Michael said.

"Not yet," Frees said. "Do you think they may have more records?"

"It's possible," Michael said, "but not likely. It sounds to me like the records have been moved somewhere. It's only been recently that the church began to computerize personnel files, but that's only the new ones. I don't think anyone has done that with the old files. Are there no indications anywhere in the files?"

"On one file at Bristol," Frees said, "we found a code with some odd numbers and letters on a back page. The file was for a priest who's one of those arrested. We asked the bishop and his secretary, but neither said they knew what it could mean. It's short, if you have a pen, I'll read it to you – B-LP-113-117-2005."

Michael wrote the letters and numbers down and studied them.

"The '2005' is likely the year," Frees said. "It's an older file. And the 'B' could refer to Bristol."

"And the LP could be Lambeth Palace," Michael said. "The notation could indicate that this file, consisting of four folders, was moved from Bristol to Lambeth Palace in 2005."

Frees stared at the page on his desk. "It's almost obvious, once you know it."

"How many times had this priest been moved?" Michael said.

"Four," Frees said.

"And that might account for file numbers 113 to 117," Michael said. He shuddered. "If that's what it is, it could also mean there were 112 previous numbers, representing reports on priests from churches. No other file had a number like that?"

"Just the one," said Frees.

"Let's hope it was the only one and that my suggestions are ridiculous and farfetched," Michael said.

"But if you're right," Frees said, "the trail could lead to Lambeth Palace and the Archbishop of Canterbury."

"I called him yesterday," Michael said, 'and asked him if the church was planning anything related to the victims. He said that the church would defend its priests and that he himself was not personally involved. I did not ask him if he were personally involved or not; he volunteered that information."

"Did he now?" Frees said. "That's interesting."

"Detective," Michael said, "if there are records and they are being kept at Lambeth Palace, they are likely in potential jeopardy."

"You think the Archbishop would destroy them?" Frees said.

"No," Michael said, "but he would possibly get others to do it, through insinuation and suggestion."

"I see I better move quickly if we're to get a search warrant," Frees said. "I may need something more than supposition about a code. Is there someone on the Archbishop's staff that we might interview as part of our investigation?"

"The archbishop's right-hand man is Canon Martin Land," Michael said. "If the archbishop is involved, you can be sure that Land is the key person. Land has been there for years and served the previous two archbishops as well."

Somehow, Brent Epworth had arranged for a disc jockey after dinner in the ballroom. Tables were quickly cleared away, and the staff of Buckingham Palace were able to celebrate the end of the transit shutdown in London and the return to their homes on Saturday.

During a slow dance, Michael and Sarah were finally able to have a brief moment.

"And how is my tsar of London doing?" said Sarah.

"Your tsar," Michael said, "is incredibly grateful that he has a moment with his beautiful tsarina."

Sarah laughed, then turned serious. "You'll have to pace yourself, Mike. You have everything here, the church thing, and now London. Can you manage all of this?"

"Likely not," Michael said. "But I'll rely on the people God's given me and we'll see it through." He paused. "It's the church I'm most concerned about. The storm is still building. We still haven't seen most of what will come out."

She put her fingers to his lips. "That's a worry for tomorrow," she said. "Tonight, we just have fun."

The dance ended, and the next song was "Can't Stop the Feeling." A cheer went up, and soon what seemed a choregraphed dance began.

Michael and Sarah were right in the middle, laughing and leading the crowd. At one point, Sarah touched Michael's arm and pointed. Jason, Robert Hood, and Jim were dancing. Except, Jim wasn't just dancing; he was performing with the natural grace of a professional dancer.

Michael didn't know how it happened, but suddenly he found himself in a line with the three boys, and the four of them danced in syncopation with the music. When it ended, Michael nearly collapsed in laughter. Robert was laughing with him, possibly the first laugh he'd had since leaving school the week before.

"James Zachary Kent-Hughes," he said, gasping in his laughter, "where did you learn to dance like that?"

"My friend Dhruv George," Jim said. "He taught me."

"My perfect Englishman taught you to dance like that?" Michael said.

Jim nodded. "He's a great dancer."

More than one palace staffer filmed the dance with a mobile phone, and soon the video began appearing on YouTube and social media.

Chapter 13: The Flood

Michael awakened early on Saturday. It was a beautiful early autumn morning, with just the first hint of color change in the trees in the palace park. He sat with his coffee on the terrace; one of the kitchen staff had thoughtfully brought a carafe on a tray.

He could think of a hundred things he needed to be doing, but to sit here, in the quiet of the early morning and the silence afforded by the trees and the palace walls, was a luxury he decided to accept as a gift. He could sense the approaching storm of the church clergy crisis; he knew that his schedule on Monday would become crazy busy with the work of London. This moment, for however long it lasted, was something to be savored and thankful for.

His mobile pinged. Two text messages had arrived almost simultaneously. Jay Lanham said the videos of Michael and the boys dancing in the ballroom had gone viral, with a combined total so far of 13 million views on YouTube and posts on social media exceeding the tens of thousands. And the numbers were continuing to grow.

The second message was from Frees. He would shortly be arriving at Lambeth Palace to interview Canon Martin Land.

And then a third message arrived, this one from Joshua. The director of Transport for London was reporting that all buses and underground trains should be back to normal schedule no later than Monday at the morning rush hour.

Suddenly Michael was aware of someone behind him. He turned to see Jason standing tentatively, carrying his own cup of coffee.

"Drag up a chair and join me," Michael said.

For a time, the two just sat, enjoying the morning.

"School's reopening on Monday," Jason said. "Jim and I are going for sure, and I think Robert's decided he's returning as well. His mom isn't sold on the idea, but she's not stopping him."

"Parents are often more fearful than their children," Michael said. "You'll find that out one day."

"I'll likely see Jane," Jason said. "There's still no word from her. I stopped sending emails and texts a few days ago. And she's posted nothing on Facebook or Instagram."

"You're afraid that she's turned her back on you for good?" Michael said.

Jason nodded. "This really hurts. I mean, I really like her. I understand why she's responded the way she has, hearing me say what I did, but I'd hoped we could still be friends, if nothing more. But it hurts, Dad. I didn't know something could hurt like this."

"It's your heart that's hurting," Michael said. "It can feel like a physical pain, but it's your heart. When Sarah and I broke up at the end of university, I felt physically ill at times. It eased, but it took time. Training for Athens helped, and then my job at St. Anselm's. But the hurt lingered."

He glanced at Jason and saw the boy had tears in his eyes. Michael reached over and put his hand on Jason's.

"I suspect, my son," Michael said, "that Jane's struggling every bit as much as you are. And while you want to hear her voice and hold her hand and be close to her, you have to let her struggle through this on her own. You can't answer the questions she has. But if she's indeed the person we've come to know, she'll make the right decision. And that might hurt, too."

"Relationships aren't always wonderful, are they?" Jason said.

Michael smiled. "No. Even the best ones bring hurt. But the ones that last are the ones that know that and make allowances for that and just stick together, because you both come to realize that the other person is more important to you than you are to yourself. Ma and Da have a relationship that we all envy, but they've had their trials, too. Sarah and I do, too. It's how God melds two people into one."

Geoffrey Venneman took a perverse kind of pleasure in irritating Canon Land, and late Saturday morning was going to be one of his better efforts. His social media guru at FBL had called to let Venneman know about the viral video of King Michael and his sons dancing.

"Have you seen the video?" Venneman said, when Land picked up the phone.

"Video?" said Land. "What video?"

"Buckingham Palace threw a staff party last night," Venneman said. "Most of the staff had camped out at the palace this week because of the transport shutdown."

"Why should I look at a video of a party?" Land said, clearly irritated.

"It's a video of King Michael dancing with his sons, Jason and Jim," Venneman said.

"So?" Land said.

Venneman emailed Land the link. "Click on the link in your email."

He waited while Land began watching.

"I still don't get it," Land said.

"Look at the lineup," Land said. "There's King Michael, and Jim next to him, and Jason next to Jim."

"So, who's the boy next to Jason?" Land said. "Is that the question you want me to ask?"

"Canon Land, the boy's name is Robert Hood," Venneman said. "You know, the priest's abuse victim the media is full hue and cry over to find?"

Land was silent.

"This is a party for people staying at the palace," Venneman said. "And Robert Hood is staying at the palace. With the King. Who knows what stories he's been telling? I suggest to you that King Michael may be up to his eyeballs in the police investigation. The police know where Robert Hood is."

"The King called yesterday," Land said.

"What?" Venneman said. "He called? Did you talk with him?"

"No," Land said, "I didn't. He talked with the archbishop. I was in the room and it was on the speaker phone, so I heard the conversation."

"What did he say?" Venneman said. "Did he threaten the archbishop?"

"No," Land said, "he didn't, but the archbishop took the entire call as a threat. Michael asked if the archbishop, you or anyone in the church was planning for how to deal with the abuse victims."

"Me? He called me out by name?" Venneman said.

"Yes," Land said, feeling like for once he'd turned the tables on Venneman. "He did. He specifically asked if you had prepared a plan to help the archbishop deal with the issue." He paused. "And one other thing. Detective-Inspector Roger Frees is coming here at 10 this morning to ask me questions about the abuse issue. It's apparently a prelude to questioning the archbishop, who said that, if that happens, he would like you and the C of E attorney to be present."

For several moments, Venneman said nothing. Then he spoke. "Did the detective say why he was interviewing you?"

"No," said Land. "He said they had some questions related to their investigation that we might be able to help with. 'Strictly routine,' I believe he said."

Venneman had a clear picture in his mind of what was happening. The archbishop's position was beginning to unravel; the police likely knew something that either Rowland and Land hadn't told him or they didn't know themselves. But this interview suggested they were involved in some way. The detective wouldn't show up on the doorstep of the leader of the Anglican world without some solid cause.

This account was quickly turning toxic, more quickly than he had expected. He would talk with his boss on Monday; Cheryl Pinsky was never to be disturbed on the weekend. He would have to maneuver a way to resign the account and separate himself and the firm from what was becoming a mess. Yes, he would talk with Cheryl on Monday. The plan would be to resign the account by Friday at the latest.

"Canon Land," Venneman said, "as soon as your interview is concluded and after you've briefed the archbishop, I need to know what happened. And try to glean what information you can; the police don't show up unless they think they have a reason. I'll ask again, you've told me everything you know that's relevant to this issue, correct?"

"Yes, Mr. Venneman," Land said, "we've told you everything that could possibly be relevant."

Elton Jenner and his family lived in an upscale suburb of north London, several miles to the east of where the Barrys lived. The home was understated in its elegance, the understatement itself emphasizing the family's upper-middle class status, as Elton's father Richard had intended it would.

Richard had been more than a little displeased, and vastly embarrassed, when the school called him and told him that Elton had spray-painted the three boys' lockers. Dr. Owens had informed him that Elton was being suspended from school for three days and was already attempting to clean the offending words from the locker doors. And then the transport shutdown had closed the school.

The suspension meant that Elton missed the football match against Central London that afternoon. Elton was his team's goalkeeper, and he played his position well, helping ICS move into second place in their league. A win against Central London would knock that school from first place and lead to the league championship, with only two other games to play and those against weaker teams.

Because of the suspension, Elton could not play. And ICS had lost 2-1 in overtime.

Richard had been furious with the boy. On Friday night, seated at his study desk, with Elton standing before him, Richard had with devastating effect and in a calm, monotone voice told Elton how he had let his team down and humiliated his family. The boy had stood for an hour in front of his father, not allowed to speak. As he finished, Richard told him he was grounded for a month, and that he was not to speak to his father unless first spoken to for the entire month.

Richard required the entire family to watch the police department's regular daily press conference at 5 p.m. on Saturday. Edith had initially protested that it might be too strong for their daughter Amanda, in her first year of the upper school at ICS, and Nicholas, who was two years behind her and still in the lower school. One look from her husband silenced her. Still not speaking to Elton, he had Nicholas bring his brother from his room to the family room to watch the conference.

"This will be a good example to all of you of what evil there is in the world," Richard told them as they seated themselves. He was particularly thinking of Nicholas, who had developed a more independent and, Richard thought, rebellious streak than either his older brother or sister. Elton, in fact, had always been the most docile of the three Jenner children, which had made this locker incident all the more remarkable in Richard's mind.

As the press conference ended, Richard turned off the television set. "Let this be a lesson to all of you," he said. "Even churches can be filled with evil men. Let us be thankful that we have a godly pastor like Rev. Arnold, who resists the world and fights to keep the world away from his church. His work with Elton has been important, despite this most recent incident at school. I've already talked with Rev. Arnold about it, and Elton will stay after church tomorrow for additional instruction."

Elton was looking down at the floor. He said nothing.

"And, I'm pleased to say," Richard said, "that Rev. Arnold has agreed to begin teaching Nicholas in the same way, and his lessons will start in November."

Elton looked up. He started to speak, hesitated, and then spoke. "Father, I must talk with you."

Richard ignored him. Edith, Nicholas and Amanda were astounded at Elton violating the requirements Richard had set for grounding.

"Edith," Richard said, "we need to get ready. We're supposed to be at the Herringtons at 6:30 for dinner."

Edith Jenner nodded at her husband, and then looked at Elton, who had stood up.

"Father," Elton said, "I have to talk with you."

Richard stood and continued to ignore his son. "So, Edith, let's get ready."

"Father!" Elton said, almost pleading.

At that, Richard exploded. He reached across and slapped Elton so hard that the boy stumbled and fell.

"You will not speak to me unless I speak to you first and ask for a response!" Richard shouted. "You have just extended your grounding by one week!" And with that, Richard turned and began to leave the room.

Edith reached toward Elton.

"Edith!" Richard shouted. "You are to get ready now!"

She pulled back, and quickly followed her husband out of the room. At 6:15, they left the house for their dinner engagement. Richard told Amanda and Nicholas that they would return at 11.

Amanda and Nicholas were in the kitchen, Amanda putting a pizza in the oven and Nicholas setting the table for the three of them. Elton, an ugly red welt on the side of his face, walked in, wearing his jacket and back pack.

"Amanda," he said, "Nick and I have to leave."

They both looked at Elton, amazed.

"Father won't listen to me," Elton said. "We have to go. Nick can't go to Father Arnold."

"Elton," his sister said, "what's wrong? I don't understand."

He swallowed, and she could see the tears in his eyes. "Father Arnold is one of those priests like they've arrested. He and others have done to me the same things those priests did to Robert Hood. And he'll do it to Nick."

Amanda gasped. Nicholas looked at Elton with frightened eyes.

"Father won't believe me," Elton said. "He'll make me go to Father Arnold tomorrow. And Father Arnold will tell me he has to give me his special punishment. He'll do the same to Nick. We have to leave." He looked at his brother. "Nick, get some clothes and put them in your back pack. We have to get out of here."

Nicholas looked at his sister and then back at his brother, and he made his decision. He dashed out of the kitchen in the direction of his room.

"Amanda," Elton said, "you're not in danger. Father Arnold only likes boys. And I have to ask you to do two things."

She nodded, feeling terrified and horrified for her brother.

"I need you to give this envelope to Father when they get home tonight," Elton said. "Don't open it yourself. It's instructions for getting to a website. He'll have to pay with his credit card to get into it, but then he can follow the instructions in the letter. The second thing is I have to ask you not to call them at the Herringtons. Give us a chance to get away. I know Father will punish you, but please don't call them."

Nicholas came into the kitchen with his back pack and jacket. "I left my books from school."

"It's okay," Elton said. "Amanda?"

She looked at her two brothers. And then she hugged Elton.

"Go," she said. "I won't call them." She took the envelope from Elton's hand. "Where will you go?"

"I know where we're going to try to get to," Elton said, "but I'm not going to tell you. That way, you can tell Father the truth and say you don't know. But I'll find a way to get you a message. Check your email later tonight or tomorrow." He looked at his brother. "Nick, let's get our bikes. We have a long ride ahead of us. Are your light and reflector working?"

Nicholas nodded.

Elton hugged his sister. "We'll be okay. Tell Mom I'm sorry. I know she'll worry. But I can't let it happen to Nick. And you don't have to tell them anything I've said. Father should be able to see it all on the website."

The boys got their bikes in the garage, and Amanda watched them pedal down the street, Nicholas following behind his brother.

Because of his father's position with Shell, Chris Whitney's family moved often. They had arrived in London three years before. Chris' older sister Lisa was a sophomore at Rice University in Houston, where the family had lived prior to London. Chris had been born in Houston, in fact, but the family had moved a lot with his father's work – California, Singapore, South Africa, and then back to Houston.

Chris loved London, and he loved his school. He had been elected captain of the football team in his second year and reelected this year. He'd played his heart out and kept rallying the team during the game with Central London. He'd been severely disappointed, but he knew they had all played beyond their best. *If Jenner hadn't been suspended, we might have won.*

He was also a responsible young man and mature beyond his years, perhaps because of adapting to all of the change of his father's nomadic international business life. His parents had known they could leave him by himself when, the transport situation easing, they'd left Saturday morning for a short, two-day visit to Paris.

He was sitting at home, watching television. He usually would have been over at his girlfriend Laura's house, or at the palace with Jason Kent-Hughes. But Laura and her family were out of town visiting relatives in Cornwall, and when he called Jason, Jason told him they had people over and he couldn't do anything.

Chris had been astounded to hear Jason blurt out what he had in the school hallway. His first reaction had been like Jane's, *just get away as fast as possible*. But the more he thought about it, he realized that Jason had done something heroic in defending Robert. And regardless of what had happened to Jason in the past, the fact was that he was Chris' good buddy, and good buddies stick together. He and Jason had hit it off from the day Jason walked into ICS. Chris had been assigned to be his official greeter, kind of a host for the first week to help new students acclimate, and the two Americans had become close friends.

The locker situation had been a jolt. Elton had been smirking so much he might as well have been wearing a sign that said, "I did it." And then Jason disappearing. When Chris had called Jason, all his friend would say was that he had found Robert and then his dad had found the two of them. He didn't expect to be back at school for a few days.

"Is Robert OK?" Chris asked.

"He's okay, Chris," Jason said. "Dad's trying to keep him out of harm's way."

The stuff on television made Chris understand why. The reports about Robert were everywhere. *Poor guy. To go through what he went through, whatever it was. And now the whole world knew.*

A bowl of popcorn in his lap, and tired of watching all the news, he had turned on a British sitcom that had started at 9 p.m. when the phone rang.

"This is Officer Regan at the front gate," the man said. Chris and his family lived in a small gated community in Knightsbridge, which had a security service manning the gate at all hours and which had protected the neighborhood during The Violence. The area had been especially vulnerable to looters, with Harrods within easy walking distance. "I have two boys on bikes here who say they're here to see you. They give their names as Elton and Nicholas Jenner. Are they expected? We didn't have them on our visitor log for tonight."

"No, officer," Chris said, "they weren't expected. But you can let them in."

"Will do. I'll add their names. Will they be staying the night?"

"I'm not sure but I'll let you know," Chris said.

What's this about? Chris walked to the front door and stood on the porch, waiting.

A few moments later, Elton and Nicholas cycled up.

"Chris," Elton said, "we need your help."

"Elton, what happened to your face?" Chris asked.

"It's not important. I have to talk with you."

An hour later, Chris called the security guard. "Elton and Nicholas are staying the night, sir. So, put them on the list."

"Yes, sir. Thank you. I'll do it now."

He looked at Elton. "You and Nick can stay here tonight. Tomorrow we'll go to Jason and his dad. They're taking care of Robert. They'll help us figure out what to do."

After what Richard considered a very successful evening indeed at the dinner with their church friends the Herringtons, he and Edith returned home, right at 11 p.m. As they walked through the kitchen from the garage, he was pleased to see that the children had cleaned up the kitchen after dinner.

Amanda was in the family room watching the news and jumped up when they entered.

"Nicholas is already in bed?" Richard said, smiling.

Amanda looked at her mother, and then back to her father.

"Father," she said. "Elton asked me to give you this." She held out the envelope.

He stared at it. "Amanda, your brother knows he's not to communicate with me right now unless I speak to him first."

Amanda moved around the sofa to stand by her mother.

"Father, Elton's not here. He and Nicholas are gone."

He looked at her. "Where are they?" Richard said quietly.

"I don't know," she said, starting to cry. "He wouldn't say. But he said he had to go and he couldn't let Nicholas go through with what he's had to. He said it's explained in the letter."

Richard snatched the envelope from Amanda's hand.

"When did they leave?" he shouted.

Amanda moved partly behind Edith. "Right after you left for dinner."

"And why didn't you call us immediately?"

The girl was sobbing. "He said Father Arnold had done to him what those priests had done to Robert Hood, and he had to get Nicholas away before he did the same thing to him. So, I told him I wouldn't call you." She cowered behind her mother as Richard raised his hand. "Please don't hit me."

Edith could see the rage on her husband's face and stood directly in front of her daughter. "You'll have to hit me first," she said.

Richard stared at his wife, and then tore open the envelope. He began to read. After a minute, he abruptly turned and walk to his study, slamming the door behind him.

Edith looked at her daughter. "How did they leave?"

"On their bikes. He said they had a long way to go. He said to tell you not to worry, that they'd be okay. Mother, he said Father Arnold and other priests did the same thing to him, and that he'd get a special punishment tomorrow if Father made him stay after church. And he's trying to protect Nicholas." Amanda was crying uncontrollably.

Edith held her, and felt a mother's horror, and terror, in her heart.

In his study, Richard stared at the computer screen. He had had to create a special account and pay a 50-pound access fee. Horrified by the first page he saw appear, he followed the instructions Elton had left. He had to move through a succession of pornographic pages, until he found an obscure link at the bottom of the final page. He clicked on it and entered the user name and password Elton had written in the letter.

Father Arnold gave me the password to see the pictures, so that I would never tell anyone, Elton had written.

He saw the photographs of his son and Father Arnold. Some of the pictures were old; Elton would have been no more than 12 or 13. Others were more recent. All told, there were almost 100 pictures of his son. He realized that someone else would have had to have been there to take the photographs.

There was a special promotional offer for the video, with a free preview.

Sitting on the sofa, Edith held Amanda in her arms. The girl had calmed down but was saying very little. It had been more than an hour since Richard had gone into the study.

She heard the study door open. Richard walked into the family room. Edith and Amanda looked up at him.

Richard seemed to have aged 10 years. His face was gray. He looked at the two of them on the sofa.

"Amanda, you were right not to call us," he said quietly. "My son did what he had to do to protect his brother. He could not depend upon his father for that protection."

"Richard -"

He held up his hand. "Edith, I'm going out. Don't wait up for me. We will not be attending church tomorrow. You and Amanda will need to stay here."

"The boys, Richard. What about Elton and Nicholas? Should we call the police?"

He shook his head. "The police cannot help at this point. It's too late. Elton will take care of his brother. Leave them be for now." He pulled his car keys from his pocket and looked at his wife. "Tell my son, tell my son that I'm proud of him, that he did right."

He walked out of the door. Edith and Amanda heard the garage door open and Richard drive away.

Richard drove to his Lexus dealership. Unlocking the door, he walked to his office, from which he managed all six of his dealerships. He loved the building, having had it designed and constructed to specifications he had worked laboriously over with the architect.

Sitting at his desk, he unlocked the lower left-hand drawer. He picked up the revolver that he had kept there for emergencies and had never used except for target practice at the shooting range. He had impressed his officers in his army unit with his ability to hit virtually any target they practiced on. It had not surprised him. His father had taught him to shoot and hunt, and by 15 he had already surpassed his father's skill level. He'd never been able to interest Elton in hunting.

He checked to make sure the revolver was fully loaded. And then he sat and waited for the clock. Church service would begin at 9 a.m. sharp. The Rev. Arnold was never, never late.

At 7:15 a.m., Chris, Elton and Nicholas were on their bikes, pedaling toward Buckingham Palace. Chris had a road bike and had begun to get serious about biking in the past year, partially inspired by King Michael, who had won three Olympic gold medals for cycling at the games in Athens three years before. Jason had shown him the medals and photos at the palace and explained the four paintings by Sarah that hung on the walls of the loft's living area. "She calls them the 'Michael Cycle,' and she says the Olympics had a lot to do with them," Jason had said. The two boys also watched a DVD about the

Olympics and the famous crash of the cycling peloton, a tragedy that had catapulted Michael to fame in Britain and around the world.

The three boys pedaled in a line, Chris in the lead, Nicholas in the middle and Elton bringing up the rear. Traffic was light, almost non-existent, and the boys made good time in reaching Buckingham Palace.

"They may have gone to church," Chris said, looking at his watch. "It's 7:45. We'll have to convince the guard to call someone inside. If we have a problem, I'll text Jason."

They walked their bikes to the guard station, where the security officer gave them a stern but friendly look.

"Please, sir," Chris said, "I know this is unusual, but my name is Chris Whitney, and this is Elton and Nicholas Jenner. We go to school with Jason and Jim. We have to talk with the king."

The officer smiled at them. "And what may I ask is the subject?"

"It's about the priests, sir," said Chris. "We have to get help for Elton and Nicholas here."

Chapter 14: Seeking Refuge, Seeking Revenge

Michael had made an unusual decision for this Sunday. The entire family would stay home and not go to church, Michael knowing that reporters would be likely to be waiting at St. Edward the Confessor's, where the Kent-Hughes family had been worshipping for the past four months. St. Edward's was conveniently close to the palace, and its pastor was a good friend of Philip Johnston, the Archbishop of York. The archbishop had recommended St. Edward's pastor, the Rev. Brian Ward, as sound in doctrine and conservative in his theology. And Michael and Sarah had found the archbishop's assessment to be accurate. Michael liked the priest immensely, and they had had the priest and his wife Judy to the palace several times.

Michael knew that many in the press were aware of which church the royal family attended. And he simply didn't want to face badgering questions about the clergy abuse issue or London government.

So, at 7 a.m., instead of going to church, the family had gathered together for a time of prayer and family worship. Robert had joined them, but his mother had remained in her room.

They'd just finished when the phone rang.

"It's Farley, sir, in Security. I'm sorry to bother you so early."

"Not a problem, Mr. Farley. We've been up for a while. We just finished devotions and our almost one-year-old alarm clock doesn't allow for much sleeping in as it is."

"Sir, there are three boys at the guard station. One is Chris Whitney, and the others identified themselves as Elton Jenner and Nicholas Jenner. They say they're school mates of Jason and Jim, and they've asked to speak to you."

"Did they say what about?" Michael asked.

"They said it was about the priests," Farley said.

Michael stared out the nearby window. "See them in, Mr. Farley, and have them come to the loft."

"Yes, sir. Right away."

Chris had been at the palace numerous times, having often spent the night with Jason in the family's loft. As they went through the x-ray check and walked toward the elevator, Elton and Nicholas stared wide-eyed. They left their bikes at the Security station for safekeeping.

"Pretty big place," Chris said. The two brothers nodded.

They were accompanied by Mr. Farley. They rode the elevator to the second floor, and then walked down long hallways to reach the family loft. Farley knocked at the door in the center of the wing, and they followed him in.

Coming into the main living area of the loft, they saw Jason and Jim, the king standing nearby, the queen on the sofa holding Hank, and Robert and his mother seated near the queen.

Michael smiled. "Hello, Chris." He shook the boy's hand. "And this must be Elton and Nicholas?" He shook each of the Jenners' hands. "Chris knows just about everyone here, except for Mrs. Hood. Nicholas and Elton, you know my boys, and this is Sarah, my wife, and Hank there on her lap."

Elton nodded, and bowed. Nicholas stared at Robert until his brother nudged him, and he bowed as well.

"I understand from Mr. Farley that you needed to speak with us?" Michael said.

Chris nodded. "Elton and Nicholas need help, your majesty. They left their home last night and biked to my house, and they spent the night with me. Elton can explain what happened." He looked at Elton standing next to him.

Elton looked around at the group, simultaneously frightened and ashamed of what he needed to say.

"Sir," he finally said to Michael, "it's just me. Nick's not involved yet, but I had to get him away." Michael could see the fear on the boy's face.

"Elton," Michael said, "why don't you and I get something to drink? You can get some water or juice and I'll get some coffee, and the two of us can talk in the little study we have here. Mr. Farley, I need you to be available." Farley nodded.

Michael walked the boy to the kitchen, they got their drinks and then Elton followed Michael to his small study. Michael sat down while Elton remained standing.

"You can sit yourself, you know," Michael said with a smile.

Elton sat down and told Michael his story.

In the living area, Chris nodded at Robert. "It's good to see you, Robert."

"Did it happen to Elton, too?" Robert asked.

Chris nodded.

"My dad wouldn't listen to him," Nicholas said. "So, Elton got me out of the house last night. I was supposed to start lessons with Father Arnold in a couple of weeks."

Sitting next to Sarah, Samantha Hood began to cry.

Shortly after 8, Michael and Elton finished talking. Michael held the boy while he cried.

"You've done a brave thing, Elton, to protect your little brother. It would have been easy to let him fall into the clutches of Rev. Arnold. But you did the hard thing and the brave thing."

"I have to apologize to Robert, and to Jason," Elton said through his tears.

"I think they'll understand," Michael said. "I'll have to call the police, and Detective Frees will likely come here to interview you. If you want to be alone with him, you can talk here. If you want me to be with you, I'll do that. It will be your choice."

Elton nodded. They stood and walked back to the living area.

"Mr. Farley," Michael said, "I need you to call Detective-Inspector Frees at Scotland Yard and ask him to come to the palace."

"Yes, sir." Farley started punching the number on his cell phone.

Thirty minutes later, Frees was ushered into the loft. Michael introduced him to Elton and led them to Michael's study. Elton had decided he could talk with the detective alone.

Frees looked at Michael. "When Elton and I have finished, sir, I'll need to talk with you."

Michael nodded and quietly closed the door. He walked back to the others in the living area.

"Is my brother okay?" Nicholas said.

Michael put his arm around Nicholas' shoulders. "Nick," he said, "your brother is a brave young man. He's going to have a lot of rough patches ahead, but always remember that he loved you enough to save you from what happened to him."

He looked at Sarah, who had put Hank to sleep for his morning nap. She could see the tears in his eyes.

Parked across the street from St. Thomas Church, Richard watched parishioners begin to stream into the church for the 9 a.m. service. He had stayed in his office all night, writing separate letters to Edith, Amanda, Nicholas and Elton. Especially Elton, the son he had so miserably failed. He'd left the letters in his safe at the dealership. He knew he was unshaven and mostly unkempt, which he never was in public. But for the first time since he could remember, he didn't care about his appearance. He was still wearing the clothes he wore to the

Herringtons, which now seemed like decades ago, another world and another lifetime.

Richard Jenner's world, so straight and unbending, the world he had so carefully created and protected for most of his 48 years, had cracked and shattered in a matter of minutes.

At 8:48, he got out of his car and walked into the side entrance to the church office, where he knew the Rev. Channing Arnold would be finishing dressing and gathering his notes for the service.

He felt the revolver in his coat pocket.

At 8:50, Frees and Elton emerged from the study. Frees shook Elton's hand, and then hugged the boy.

Elton rejoined the group. Frees nodded at Michael, who joined him in the study. Frees closed the door.

"If I didn't think I was making a difference I couldn't keep listening to this," Frees said.

Michael nodded. "What you're doing, Detective Inspector, is important."

"Elton got everything Robert Hood did and was tortured as a bonus."

Michael nodded.

"Your majesty, I'll need to come back later."

"Yes?"

Frees nodded. "I'll have the doctor with me."

"To examine Elton?"

Frees nodded his head. "Yes, but also for Robert." The policeman looked away, and then at Michael. "He's HIV positive."

Michael closed his eyes.

Amanda had finally nodded off on the sofa about 3 a.m. She was curled up in an almost fetal-like position, and Edith found a blanket to cover her.

She had tried but found herself unable to pray. Richard had not come home. *I should be terrified, but all I feel is numb.* She had dozed off around 6, waking at 8:30. Amanda was still asleep on the sofa next to her. She went into the kitchen and fixed a cup of instant coffee in the microwave.

She looked across the family room to the door to Richard's study. From Amanda, she knew that Elton had placed instructions for a website in the envelope for Richard. At one point last night, she had been tempted to go into the study to see what might be found, but then stopped herself. Whatever it was, it had drained the life out of her husband. She had thought about calling her parents but decided to let events take their course. She'd spent a lifetime allowing others, first her parents and then Richard, to dictate her every action and decision. She didn't have the energy to change. Not yet. Except she wouldn't let Richard hit Amanda. That had shocked her more than it had Richard. It shocked her even more than seeing him raise his hand to his daughter.

Worry finally overcame inertia. She walked to Richard's study, and over to his desk. Propped against the computer screen was an envelope marked "For the Police" in Richard's straight up-and-down handwriting. She looked at her watch. Almost 8:55. She picked up the phone, and then set it back in its cradle. And debated with herself. And then realized with utter clarity what Richard was likely to do. She picked up the phone again and hurriedly called the police. It was 8:58.

At Lambeth Palace, Canon Land, after spending a tortured night in his quarters at the palace, walked to the Archbishop's office. Rowland was scheduled to speak at St. Paul's Cathedral this morning and had in fact already left.

Approaching the Archbishop's desk, Land placed an envelope in the center. Inside the envelope was a summary of the letter that Land had already mailed to the king at Buckingham Palace. He had taped a key to the original. At 2 in the morning, he'd walked to a post box on the Embankment by the Thames and mailed the letter to the king. With a Sunday pickup posted for 11 a.m., the king should receive the letter first thing Monday morning. Assuming his staff was more efficient than the staff at Lambeth Palace, which was highly likely, the king could see the letter as early as lunchtime. He stared at the post box for a long time, and then looked up and across the river to the Houses of Parliament.

He had tried to sleep but couldn't. He'd gone to the 7 a.m. service at the palace, but more out of habit than desire. He remembered little of the service, except that one of the hymns sung was "Jerusalem." At 8:15 a.m., he had placed the envelope on the Archbishop of Canterbury's desk.

He made one final call. As expected, it went to voicemail; the receiver would be at worship service. He left a voice message. "I'm done with this. I can't keep going on. I've sent a letter to the king." He then walked outside.

It was a beautiful fall morning, but Land only passed a few joggers or walkers. People liked to sleep in on Sundays. For a time, he sat on a bench and watched the passing river traffic, light since it was Sunday. He walked to Lambeth Bridge and entered the bridge's pedestrian walkway. Occasional cars drove by. He stopped in the center of the bridge and looked down river. The view was spectacular.

He looked at his watch. It was almost 9 a.m.

Carefully, Land hoisted himself up on the guardrail, and jumped over the side. No one saw him.

He hadn't expected the water to be as cold as it was.

The Rev. Arnold had just finished putting on his robes for the 9 a.m. service when Richard walked into his office.

"Why, Richard -"

Richard punched him in the jaw, spinning Arnold into his bookcase.

"What? What? Richard, stop -" as Richard punched him in the stomach, doubling him over as he sank to his knees.

"You destroyed my son, you pervert," Richard snarled, smashing his fist into Arnold's chest. Arnold heard bone crack. Blood was seeping from the corner of his mouth.

Richard pulled out the revolver. Arnold's eyes became huge with fear.

"Oh," Richard smiled with a murderous edge in his voice, "I'm not going to kill you, reverend. Death is too good for filth like you. I have other plans for you, Vicar."

He jerked the priest to his feet. "It's time to meet your parishioners. Let's give them a real sermon today."

He dragged the priest to the door and out of the office.

Frees left to return to the station, to prepare the warrant for Arnold's arrest. Michael asked the boys if they'd eaten breakfast, and asked Jason and Jim to set the table and get out some cereal, fruit, and juice.

He smiled at Sarah. "I need to be alone for a short bit; I'll be back in a moment." Sarah watched him walk toward their bedroom. *He's collapsing under all of this*, she thought.

Michael closed the door of the bedroom and leaned against it, breathing deeply to hold back the horror he felt. He walked to the bed and knelt beside it. He remained there for several minutes, unable to pray.

Dear Father in heaven, I am devastated. This burden is too much. There is too much sin, too much evil. Father God, these boys. They are victims. They have suffered. You know how they've suffered.

And they will pay more than the sinners who did this. Father, this young man, with his life in front of him, now faces a life of, a life of, a life that may be no life at all. And Elton, Father, this boy, they did horrible things to him, Father.

You ask me to pray for these horrible men, Father. And I must, because your word tells us to pray for them, too. And so, Father, I lift them up to you, as much as I want to make them suffer, and I ask that you bring good out of what they have done and forgive them their sins against these young men.

Michael was crying so uncontrollably that he didn't hear the door quietly open. He prayed on in a choking voice.

Father, all of us need your grace. This burden is too much. Please take it from me. But if not, then give me the strength and courage to go on, give me courage and love for these young men, to help them through this. Help me carry their burden.

Unable to go on, Michael collapsed in sobs. Sarah knelt beside him.

Father God, I lift up my husband to you, I lift up this man who in the depths of his pain and horror reaches out to you. I ask you to hear his prayer and give him strength. I ask you to hear his prayer, and love him, and let him feel your grace. And let him know, Father, that he is carrying these burdens, because he is the one you've chosen to do this, because you know he loves you and will honor and obey you in all things. And give me the strength to support my husband, to love him, to cherish him, and honor him, the father of my children. Let him know, Father, that his wife and his children love him, and we praise you because you've given him to us.

Michael reached to his wife and pulled her to him, his chest heaving with great sobs, as he clung desperately to her.

At 9 a.m., the side door into the altar area opened, and Rev. Arnold, shoved by Richard, stumbled into the altar table, knocking over the bread and the wine set there for communion. The congregation, expecting their normal Sunday worship service, either sat stunned or jumped up.

"Stay where you are!" Richard yelled, pointing the revolver at the congregation. Several women screamed.

"Behold your beloved priest," Richard shouted. "Behold the Rev. Channing Arnold, keeper of the faith, priest of the most high God, rapist of children!"

Richard threw a large envelope down toward the pews. "You! William Whiting, head elder of St. Thomas' Church. Pick it up!"

Whiting, in the front pew with his wife Joyce, stood immobilized.

"Pick it up!" Richard shouted, pointing the gun at him.

Whiting leaned over and picked the envelope up.

"Open it!" Richard shouted.

Whiting opened the envelope and pulled out several dozen sheets of paper.

"Pass them to the congregation! Now!" He aimed at gun at Joyce Whiting, who had moved beyond terror into shock.

Whiting quickly obeyed. He began passing sheets to each row, actually counting the number of people seated in each to get the number of pages right. Two minutes passed.

"There are no more," Whiting said, whimpering

Richard and the congregation began to hear sirens in the distance.

"So, fellow believers, let us study our text for today! The gospel according to the Rev. Arnold! See him rape the 12-year-old boy! See him violate a child for his own pleasures! And if the pictures aren't good enough, go to the website and buy the movie! Watch him torture the boy!" Richard kicked Arnold; the priest screamed in pain. "Watch him rape a child for years!"

Richard spit on the priest.

"And behold the father who trusted this piece of filth with his son, who gave his son over to be brutalized and tortured."

The sirens were much louder. Screeching tires could be heard outside the church.

Richard aimed the revolver at his own temple and pulled the trigger.

He was still an expert shot.

Being driven back to Lambeth Palace after what he considered a successful sermon at St. Paul's Cathedral, Archbishop Rowland began to consider how to keep Geoffrey Venneman and FBL involved in what was happening. The news about the clergy abuse issue and the ongoing investigation, widening to include the entire country, was giving fresh wings to Michael's proposals for reform.

Venneman had managed to bottle the proposals up in parliamentary bureaucracy, but now support seemed to be emerging. The MPs were nervous. No one knew how this was going to shake out, but whatever direction it went, it did not look good for the church.

Fortunately, Canon Land had held on to every email, every calendar entry, and every submitted plan from Venneman. It could well be an insurance policy of sorts.

Arriving at Lambeth Palace, Rowland went directly to his office. On his desk was an envelope. He began to open it, just as he heard a knock on the door. Expecting Canon Land, he was surprised to see one of the junior priests assigned as staff.

"What is it?" Rowland said, a bit abruptly.

"I'm sorry to disturb you, Archbishop," the priest said, "but you need to see the news. There's been a shooting at St. Thomas Church in north London."

In their bathroom, Michael splashed cold water on his face. He finally felt composed enough to rejoin the group. Sarah had stayed with him, holding him until he stopped crying, and then kissed him. She had already returned to the living area.

The boys were talking quietly among themselves. Samantha Hood was staring out of the window at the gardens behind the palace. Michael stood next to her.

"The gardens are beautiful," she said.

"Mr. Albright, our head gardener, has a great gift for growing things," Michael said. "He and his staff worked very hard this spring and early summer, and we're just beginning to see the result."

"How many children have been harmed, your majesty?" Samantha Hood said.

"I don't know, Mrs. Hood. I understand there are more, but the police haven't yet said."

"Why would God let this happen to my son and to Elton? And to others? What is the point?" she said.

"I don't know how to answer your question," Michael said. "It seems monstrous. It seems monstrous to allow this to happen."

She turned to him. "Thank you for your honesty. I was expecting a sermon or a Scripture verse." She paused. "It's easier to think there is no God. I have been faithful to him all of my life, I worshipped him, and tithed, and raised my son the best way I knew how. I raised him in the church, your majesty. I've fought and struggled to make a home and a life for us, and I kept honoring God. And God gives me this. He spits on me."

"Mrs. Hood, God gave you Robert. God did not violate or rape Robert. That was man's doing, not God's. God died for that sin."

She turned back to looking at the garden. "I can't believe in God any more, your majesty." She turned and walked toward her bedroom.

Father, Michael thought, *what happens when she learns Robert is HIV positive?*

Michael walked over to the boys. Sarah was sitting with them.

"Elton," Michael said, "you need to call your parents. If your father is still angry, you can remain here. Or I'll talk with him. But you need to let them know that you and Nick are okay."

"I sent my sister a message from Chris' email last night," Elton said. "I told her to tell them we were okay and had a place to sleep."

"She may not have checked her email," Michael said. "Your mom and dad need to hear your voice, and they need to hear Nick's. If your father has looked at the website, he'll know what you've been dealing with. And he'll want to hear your voice."

Elton stared at Michael, and finally nodded. Chris handed him his cell phone. Elton punched in the number.

"Mom? It's Elton. We're okay. We're with friends right now. Can I talk with Dad?"

He looked at Michael. "He's been gone since last night. Mom doesn't know where he is."

Through the phone, Elton heard his sister scream, and then his mother.

"Mom! Mom! What is it? Mom!"

Elton looked frantically at Michael. "The television!"

Jason rushed to the remote and powered on the TV.

They saw the police cars and ambulances in front of St. Thomas Church.

Five hours and one press conference later, Frees arrived back at the palace. He had the same medical team with him to examine Elton, and a specialist in immune system diseases to talk with Robert and his mother. Frees hoped that Michael would be part of that conversation. The policeman looked devastated and felt worse than he looked.

Elton's mother had been hospitalized in hysterical shock. Her parents had been called to be with her. Farley and Security Officer Paula Abbott had accompanied Sarah and Nick Jenner to pick Amanda up at home and bring her to the palace.

When the team arrived, Elton nodded and walked with the doctor to a bedroom. He had spoken very little since he had seen the television report. Amanda had told them what Richard's last words to the family had been.

Frees asked Robert and Mrs. Hood, along with Michael, to talk with him in Michael's study.

"Mrs. Hood," Frees said, "we have the preliminary results from Robert's physical examination on Friday. There is extensive evidence of repeated abuse."

Samantha Hood closed her eyes.

"Mrs. Hood, Robert, we also have the results from the blood tests," Frees said.

Samantha's eyes remained closed, as if she were expecting the blow.

"Robert," the policeman said, "I…" He faltered and looked down.

Michael took Robert's hand in his. "Robert, the blood tests show that you're HIV positive. It doesn't mean you have AIDS, or that you will ever get AIDS. But it is something that you will have with you the rest of your life. And you can live almost all of a normal life. But you will have to take great care of yourself and take precautions."

The boy began to shake. Michael pulled Robert to him and held him. Robert began to sob. The image of a laughing Robert dancing at Friday night's party started running through Michael's mind.

"Mrs. Hood," Frees said, "Dr. Winters outside is a specialist in this area. And he's here to answer any and all questions you might have. And if today's not good, he can come back when the time is right for you."

Samantha opened her eyes and stood up. "I'm sorry, Detective-Inspector." She left the study.

Frees looked at Michael, and then dashed after her.

"Mrs. Hood!" he said.

She didn't answer as she walked to her bedroom.

Michael walked to the living area, his arms supporting Robert.

Samantha Hood came into the living area with her suitcase. She looked at all of them.

"Mrs. Hood," Michael said gently.

"I'm sorry, your majesty," she said. "I have to leave. I can't deal with this."

"Mrs. Hood," Michael said. "Robert needs you."

She looked at her son, then at the king. "I'm sorry. I have to go." And she walked out of the door. Frees went after her.

Sarah looked at Robert, who was sagging against Michael. "Mike, ease him into a chair."

Michael gently lowered him into the chair next to the sofa.

Jason, Jim, the Jenner children, and Chris looked at Robert and then at Michael.

"Jason," Michael said, "would you lead us all in prayer?" Michael knelt by Robert and held his hands tightly.

Jason began to pray.

"I walked with her all the way to the guard station," Frees said. "She kept saying that she understood, but that she had to go. I begged her to stay. She said she couldn't deal with this. When I asked her how Robert was supposed to deal with this by himself, she said she had signed her son's death warrant, and she had to leave. And then she was gone."

Michael and Sarah were talking with Frees in the hallway outside the entrance to the loft. The medical team had finished its examination of Elton and left, along with Dr. Winters.

"Robert can stay here, Detective-Inspector," Sarah said. "We'll keep him here until we get something figured out. The Jenner children as well."

"So far, we've identified an additional 40 boys here in the London area who've been abused," Frees said. "There are still more. The calls from victims and parents are coming in faster than we have people to handle them." He paused. "Richard Jenner left Elton's instructions at his computer, and from the website we've identified a number of additional priests." He paused and looked at Michael. "And 12 bishops, and two archbishops."

"Dear Father in heaven," Michael said.

"We're not finished, your majesty," Frees said. "There are still more. What I thought was a ring looks more to be a rather extensive network, or a series of rings that operate independently with occasional overlaps. And Rev. Wickham and several others appear to have a pattern of staying at parishes for only two to three years and then being transferred to another parish. St. Mark's is the longest he's been anywhere, and he's been a priest for more than 30 years."

"Which suggests what?" Michael asked.

"Which suggests someone knew about their problems and instead of dealing with it just moved them to another parish," Frees said. "Who would have the authority to do that?"

"Are the parishes within the same diocese?" Michael said.

"There are a few regional concentrations," Frees said, "but generally they look to be all over England."

"Then you'll have to look at Lambeth Palace, Detective-Inspector," Michael said. "Only there could someone move a priest continually between dioceses."

"Sir," Frees said, "which seminary did you attend?"

"I didn't," Michael said. "I took theology instruction in a special program at the University of Edinburgh."

Frees nodded. "That's good."

"Why is that good?" Michael said.

"Three seminaries appear to be involved," Frees said. "St. Simon's, which you know about, and one near Cardiff in Wales and Glasgow in Scotland."

After Frees had left, Michael sat with Sarah in the study. She was holding Hank.

"It's getting worse and worse," Michael said. "I'm afraid to find out where it's going to end."

Sarah hugged him. "You need to eat something and get some rest," she said. "You have to be at City Hall tomorrow morning and I'm flying to Belfast for the funeral."

Michael nodded.

Rowland had been so shocked by the news coverage of what had happened at St. Mark's that he forgot about the envelope on his desk. When he returned from the commons room where the wide-screen TV was, he noticed it again, and then opened it. He stared, and then gripped the chair to steady himself.

He rushed from his office. He grabbed the first priest he found.

"Find someone in security," he said. "Quickly! Have them meet me at the church vault next to the parking lot. Hurry!"

The priest sped off and Rowland almost ran outside, crossed the parking lot, and entered the building containing the vault.

He paced back and forth until a security officer arrived.

"I need the vault opened," he said. "Do you have the key?"

The man nodded, extracted a key on the ring of keys he was carrying, and unlocked the door.

The room was large and looked like what a church attic might be expected to look like – dusty, sheets covering odd shapes, even some old stained-glass windows leaning against a wall. Rowland walked quickly across the room to a door, which opened into a smaller room. The room contained mostly filing cabinets. What he expected to see – some 35 fairly large cardboard boxes – was not there. There was an empty space signifying they had been there. But the boxes were gone.

"Do you know what might have happened to the boxes that were collected here?" Rowland said to the officer.

"Canon Land had them removed yesterday morning," the officer said.

"Do you know where they were taken?" Rowland said.

"No, Archbishop, I don't," the officer said. "Canon Land didn't say. He drove the truck away himself."

"I need access to Land's office," the Archbishop said.

The security officer took him to Land's office and stood there while Rowland searched the desk, filing cabinets, and appointment book.

"There's nothing," Rowland said. "We have to find those boxes."

"Do you want me to call the police?" the officer said.

"No!" Rowland said, almost shouting. "See what you can find here. Call anyone who was here on the grounds yesterday. They may have seen or heard something."

"Archbishop," the officer said, "can't you just ask Canon Land?"

"He's gone," Rowland said. "And I don't know where to find him."

Chapter 15: Behind the Dark Wall

Sunday evening meals at the Barrys' house were informal. Often Trevor and the children would work up fun food, like tacos or a homemade pizza. And even though the children were now getting older, they still seemed to enjoy playing a game with their parents, usually a board game, while they ate. Jason had often been there on Sundays for dinner and the game, and to be with Jane.

This Sunday evening, Liz could see that the family was flagging. Trevor had been totally preoccupied and distracted; she assumed it was something with his work for the king. He had returned Saturday after living for the week at Buckingham Palace with the palace staff. "It worked out well," he'd told Liz on his return. "A good portion of the week was spent sorting this business with the king running London, and it helped to actually be there in the room. I don't know how Michael is going to manage all of what he has on his plate."

Jane was still subdued and saying very little. The news reports on St. Thomas Church had shocked them all, and Trevor had finally said he had to stop watching, shutting himself away in his study. Andrew said that Nicholas Jenner was in his class at ICS and he hoped he was okay. A few reports had said that the Jenner children were in seclusion, but it was not known where.

Liz popped small frozen pizzas in the oven and got out a board game for the dining room table.

"Mother, can we not do the game tonight?" said Jane, standing at the door to the kitchen. "I just don't think I can handle this right now."

"Jane, I know this is hard," Liz said, "but we have to remember that we're a family, and we have to try to retain some normalcy around here or we'll all go insane from watching the news."

Liz dragged Andrew from the television in the family room, and finally rousted Trevor from his study.

As they sat around the table, Trevor's and Jane's pizzas going cold, Liz still attempted to keep up a brave front. She passed out their pieces for the game and rolled the dice to determine positions in the game.

"Okay, Jane," she said, smiling. "Your turn."

"Mother, I can't," she said. "I don't know what to do about Jason. I don't want to break it off with him. I can't. I care for him too much. I've already hurt him. I need to apologize. I feel like what I've done is unforgivable. I don't know what to do." Tears started down her face.

"Jane," Liz began, "we've talked about this. If you think you should break it off -"

Trevor interrupted her. "Rev. Wilfred Frawley," he said.

Liz looked at her husband. "Trevor? What?" The children looked at him as well.

"The Rev. Wilfred Frawley," he said again.

"Trevor, I don't understand. Is this someone you know?" his wife asked.

He shook his head, and then nodded. He looked at his daughter. "Jane," he said. And then he faltered. "What happened to Jason. And Robert. And Elton."

Jane looked at her father and nodded.

"It happened to me."

His family all stared at him without speaking.

"It happened to me," he repeated.

"Trevor?" Liz asked.

"I was 11," Trevor said. "I was an altar boy at our church. He was the new priest."

Jane's and Andrew's eyes had gotten huge. No one said a word.

"He'd been there for three months, when he caught me after choir practice. He liked to practice the service with the choir. And he told me to stay when we finished, because he needed my help."

Trevor was speaking in an almost monotone, but still looking directly at his daughter. He glanced at Liz as he continued.

"He waited until everyone had left. And then he told me to come with him to his office. That's where, that's where," Trevor said, his voice again faltering, "that's where he raped me."

He swallowed and went on.

"He told me that if I said anything, I would be taken away from my parents and sent to reform school, but that no one would talk about it, because this was a secret thing that all little boys were supposed to do, and it was just my turn because I had become old enough."

Liz stared with growing horror on her face.

"He stayed at the church for a year after that. I wanted to quit but my parents made me stay an altar boy. It was a whole year." Trevor looked down at the game board. "A whole year. They didn't know, and I couldn't tell them. I was too ashamed." He paused.

"And then suddenly Father Frawley was gone, almost overnight, and there was a new priest. So, the first night of worship practice with the new minister, I waited until everyone had left, and I followed him to his office. I shut the door and started taking off my clothes."

Liz's hand was at her mouth. Andrew was crying. Jane stayed riveted on her father's face.

"He stopped me and asked what I was doing. And I told him what Rev. Frawley always said, that I was serving God."

A sob broke from Liz. Tears were rolling down Jane's face.

"He hugged me and made me get dressed. And he told me this wouldn't happen anymore. That I was free of Rev. Frawley. And he wouldn't tell anyone." He paused. "But I wasn't free. I've never been able to forget it. I never went back to the church. The new minister was kind. He was a black man from Nigeria. But I never went back. I walled it off and did everything I knew how to forget it, to pretend it never happened. But that was impossible.

"So, what happened to Jason happened to me, too, Jane." He stood. "I'm going for a walk."

"Trevor, wait!" Liz said through her tears. "Wait!"

"I'm just going to walk, Liz. I'm not going to do anything else. I just need to walk." He walked out the side door.

Jane stood and looked at Liz. "I'm going after him," she said, and then hurried out the door after her father.

Liz rose to go after them, but Andrew stopped her. "Mom, let Jane. She knows. Because of Jason."

In the darkness, Trevor walked down the sidewalk, headed in no particular direction, but only to walk. He wanted to feel rage and anger, but all he felt was a numb emptiness. His black wall was down, cracked, and it seemed a vacuum was on the other side. He thought about Jason and knew why he had felt a bond with the boy. He thought about how the boy with the rough edges had so gently treated his daughter, much like Trevor had always tried to treat Liz. *Part of it is fear, because you don't know what to do. You don't feel like a man.* He thought about Robert Hood and Elton Jenner. He thought about the tragedy that had unfolded that morning at St. Thomas Church.

Trevor felt numb. The black wall of his childhood had cracked and shattered, and it was pain that was pouring through, and his guilt and shame and hurt. His pain. He felt tears on his cheeks.

Jane followed him, then caught up to him, and finally walked alongside him. And then she placed her hand in his and squeezed. When he finally squeezed back, she knew her Dad was going to be okay.

Liz sat on the sofa with Andrew. So many things had suddenly become clear, as if a blindfold had been removed and the light was overwhelming. Too much information was rushing into her head. Why he waited so long to propose. Why she had had to take the lead on their wedding night and so often in their lovemaking. Why he never had any close friends, especially male friends. Why he was something of a loner. Why he never talked about the church he grew up in and was unwilling to make any kind of commitment to faith. She held Andrew's hand, realizing that her husband had been younger than their son when it had happened.

They heard the side door open.

That night, Liz lay next to Trevor in bed, his arm around her. He wasn't saying much, but when he and Jane had arrived home, he'd taken Liz into his arms and held her. Like he was doing now.

"This was why you waited so long to propose," she said.

He nodded. "I was scared. I didn't know if I could be a husband. All the memories kept coming into my head. But I loved you. I was terrified on our wedding night."

"I thought you were nervous."

"I was terrified that I couldn't do anything, that I couldn't make love to you. Or that I'd mess it up."

"You were wonderful."

He kissed her forehead. "It's better now, but it still comes back. I still have dreams. I see him coming for me with that horrible smile on his face. And I wake up in a sweat."

"You let me prattle on the other night about AIDS and HIV. You didn't say anything until you rebuked me. It made me angry, but you were right. I was blaming Jason for what had happened to him. I was being stupid and probably sounded like everyone's stereotyped Christian."

"You didn't know, Liz, and I was afraid to say anything," he said, and then paused. "I understand Richard Jenner, the outrage and impotence he felt. And the guilt."

She kissed his chest. "I love you, Trevor Barry. Always and forever."

"Liz, you're the best thing that's ever happened to me," he said. "You've loved me; you gave me those two great kids. You'll never know how much you've saved me."

"Did Jane say anything while you walked?" she said.

"She just held my hand."

On Monday, Robert and the Jenner children remained at the palace. Sarah left for Luton Airport, to fly to Belfast for the Peter Flaherty funeral. Edith Jenner's parents said she remained hospitalized, and policemen had been posted at the hospital to turn the media away. Television, radio and the newspapers from all over the world were mesmerized with the story of Richard Jenner, Rev. Arnold, and what had happened at St. Thomas' Church.

Jason and Jim decided that they would return to ICS, and Michael rode with them and Jay Lanham to the school on Monday morning. Ryan Mitchell sent five security officers with them to run interference if needed. Dr. Owens had called the palace early to warn that the media were still camped out in front of the school.

In the car, Michael cautioned both boys about any specific references to Robert and the Jenners. "If your friends ask where they are, you should tell them the truth. But I'm asking you both not to go into detail. You've heard and seen many things over the past five days, and we have to do whatever we can to protect what little privacy they have left." Both boys nodded their understanding.

In front of the school, it was indeed a media gauntlet that they ran. Officer Abbott led Michael, the boys and Jay, surrounded by the five agents, through a howling horde of reporters, all shouting questions. Michael held up his hand and said he would speak to them when he returned. Chris Whitney was waiting for Jason at the entrance.

"Media are calling from all over the world," Dr. Owens told Michael inside. He looked at Jay gratefully. "Your communications firm is handling everything. We'd be swamped without them. They've taken over the main conference room and set up a special phone bank."

Jay looked at Michael. "I'll stick my head in and see what's up."

Michael nodded and turned to the headmaster as Jay walked to the conference room. "Dr. Owens," Michael said, "Robert and the Jenner children are still with us at the palace. Robert's mother has left; she's unable to deal with all of what there is to deal with right now but I'm hoping she'll return. But she may not. In the meantime, you can contact us if there's anything specific about Robert. You have the palace number and they'll patch you through if I'm at City Hall."

"And the Jenners?" Dr. Owens said.

"While their mother remains hospitalized, you can contact us about them as well, and we'll see what needs to be done," Michael said. "Their grandparents are at the hospital with their mother and we've spoken with them a few times."

"Your majesty," Dr. Owens said, "what you have taken on is enormous. How are Robert and Elton dealing with this?"

"It's hour to hour, Dr. Owens," Michael said. "There have been a number of repeated blows to deal with, Elton's father being only the latest."

"We're having a school assembly this morning in the upper school to pray for all of you," the school head said.

Michael nodded his gratitude.

Jay returned from the conference room ("It's unbelievably hectic in there, sir, but they're doing well with the calls") and he, Michael, Officer Abbott, and the other security agents walked toward the front gate.

"I feel like Daniel in the lion's den," Michael said, as they approached the large crowd of reporters. "I only hope I fare half as well as he did."

They stopped in front of the reporters.

"I don't have a written statement to hand out," Michael said, with a weak smile. "So, you'll have to take good notes." The reporters could see the strain in the king's face. "The last several days have been difficult for us, but they've been horrendous for the families involved. As you saw, Jason and Jim returned to school this morning. And we hope to establish some normalcy for them again."

"Your majesty," said one reporter, "we hear that Robert Hood is staying with your family at the palace. Is that true? He was spotted on that dancing video."

Michael nodded. "Yes, Robert is there as well as the Jenner children. We asked them to stay with us to provide a haven from this kind of situation we're having to deal with right now," and gestured toward the assembled media.

"How are they doing, sir?"

"They are courageous kids who are going through an experience that most of us will thankfully never know," Michael said. "And I am making a special plea to all of you, and to your fellow journalists, to give these children some peace. I understand the pressures you face in the news business, but I am asking each and all of you to give them some time and space. They desperately need to recover and heal and sticking a microphone in their faces won't help. They have much to work through, which we even as adults would be overwhelmed by."

"Sir, what about your role as an ordained priest of the church? Do you feel any conflict of interest here?"

Michael shook his head. "I feel no conflict of interest. Evil is evil, regardless of where you find it, and it has to be exposed and rooted out. My interest is these children and seeing them heal, and to look at the larger picture of what appears to be decades of abuse."

"Have you talked with the Archbishop of Canterbury about this?"

"I called him Saturday, to determine what steps the church has underway. And he said that a plan was in process. But I have no details on that."

"One more question and then the king must leave," Jay said.

"Sir, do you think the Church of England can survive this scandal?"

Michael didn't answer immediately. "God's church will survive this scandal," he finally said. "And yes, you can note that I said God's church and not the Church of England per se. If we learn that the church itself bears some responsibility here, then there must be profound and fundamental changes, far beyond what I proposed last April. To the extent possible, some kind of restitution will have to be made. Children and families have been horribly victimized by the very

people they should have been able to trust. And we simply can't stand
for it."

Ben Hurst of the *London Record*, who had asked the last
question, caught an implication in Michael's last answer that no one
else did. *He knows more, and he knows this is going to be far worse
than anything we've yet seen.*

From the school, Jay Lanham was dropped off at the palace,
and Michael continued on to City Hall. Traffic had become normal
again, often congested but still moving, unlike the previous week.

Michael had been told that he would occupy the mayor's
office, but he said he preferred to work from a conference room. The
mayor's secretary, Eleanor Whitmire, had found one on the executive
floor and had the room's conference phone line changed to a number
for the king. He sorted through correspondence and then the
department heads arrived for the general staff meeting at 10 a.m.

Each department head provided a status update of important
departmental activities and projects. By agreement made when Myra
Frobisher had called them for scheduling a meeting, individual updates
were limited to three minutes. Serious subjects requiring more
extensive discussion would be held until all updates were made. At

this first meeting, perhaps because the heads were trying to determine what Michael was looking for, no serious subjects were brought up. The Transport for London head said that all operations were back to normal schedules. The Environment head said that the extra trucks from surrounding counties had helped clear all garbage by Sunday evening. The meeting lasted just under an hour.

Michael then began meeting individually with the department heads, starting with Health. Each would last one hour. And his message in each meeting would be the same: "I'm assuming you're in your position because you're fully capable of doing it, and your priority goal is to serve the people of London. I need to hear your problems and your opportunities, and how we might do the work of government more effectively. And I need your help with one thing in particular. Find a time and an appropriate person at the operational level for me to spend some time with your people as they do their job. I'm not talking the administrative area; I'm talking the level of where the work actually gets done."

Over the next two months, Londoners would be startled to hear about and in some cases see the king of Great Britain working with street crews, patching potholes; listening to how mechanics service the huge gear wheels operating Tower Bridge; helping staff do patient intake at a hospital emergency room; walking with inspectors as they checked progress on an environmental cleanup in Battersea; taking fares on the one bus route that still had personal fare takers, the No. 15; spending two hours with inspectors making sure all electrical installations were within code for a concert at Trafalgar Square; riding with police on cruise control and, at one point, watching as police arrested a known drug dealer; talking with residents and inspectors at a public housing community meeting; and more.

For Michael, it was the best part of the job. When he used a card reader to clock a Transport card on the No. 15 bus, the older gentlemen providing the card said, "Blimey, if it isn't the king of England punching my ticket!"

Michael's examples weren't lost on the department heads. As word filtered back of the huge boost to morale and performance the king's visits were making, the heads themselves started their own visits and "ride-alongs."

The church was about 12 miles from Belfast. Ryan Mitchell had arranged for a car to be waiting when Sarah arrived at Belfast City Airport. Local police and Belfast city authorities had been alerted but told that this was strictly a private visit for a funeral and the Queen would be returning to London right after.

The black SUV with tinted windows moved quickly through Belfast and arrived at the church. Sarah waited until the people attending the service had entered the church, a small stone building that had once been a Church of Northern Ireland parish but was now an evangelical congregation.

The service hadn't started when she walked through the door. The security man accompanying moved to the back row, and Sarah walked toward the front. She hadn't thought about where to sit, but when she saw Mandy Flaherty on the front row by herself with the people likely to be the parents and in-laws seated behind her, she walked directly to the front. She saw the six Army men in uniform on the front row opposite.

Pallbearers, she thought.

Mandy looked up, her tear-filled eyes widening, and then she started to struggle to get up. Sarah put her hand on her shoulder and shook her head, motioning to Mandy to stay seated. Everyone else in the pews stood; Sarah smiled and motioned for them to sit. And then she sat next to Mandy, taking her hand.

The minister entered from a side door. He saw the queen sitting with Mandy and bowed his head. He then began the service.

They sang hymns; the minister read passages from the Bible. And then he spoke about Peter Flaherty. The level of detail and emotion in the minister's eulogy told Sarah he had known Peter very well indeed. Mandy leaned over and whispered, "They were best friends from childhood."

At the end of the service, the people stood: Sarah helped Mandy. The pallbearers gathered around the coffin, lifted it, turned, and moved down the aisle toward the door. Mandy and Sarah followed, and then other family members and friends.

They didn't have far to walk. The procession moved to the church cemetery, situated on a hillside facing the sea. The grave had been dug. The pastor said a few words, read a Bible verse, and then pronounced a blessing on all those gathered. The coffin was lowered into the ground, and Mandy dropped a flower atop and a handful of dirt. The security man near Sarah stepped forward and handed her a white rose, which she dropped after Mandy.

As they walked from the cemetery, a man introduced himself to Sarah as Peter's father and said she was welcome at their house for a gathering.

"I would like that," she said.

The Flaherty family lived a short 10 minutes from the church. They talked, they cried, they laughed, they looked at photographs, they shared food. After an hour, Sarah said she needed to return to the airport.

Mandy walked with her to the car.

"Thank you," she said. "I know this must be a disruption to your schedule."

"Nothing's more important than this, Mandy," Sarah said. "I needed to be here."

"Peter was right," Mandy said. "There was a beautiful lady who kissed him on the forehead."

Sarah hugged her. "Will you let us know when the baby's born?" she said.

"I will," Mandy said. "I will."

Once they were airborne, Sarah and the two security men were quiet, saying very little. At one point, she was staring out the window, and then turned to see one of the security officers looking at her.

"Begging your pardon, ma'am," he said. "But that was one of the most beautiful things I've ever seen."

Sarah smiled. "I ache for them," she said. "I ache for the family. They're the stuff that makes this country, and they've given a part of themselves to defend it. That's the really beautiful thing."

Michael returned home to the palace at 4 p.m. that first Monday. He'd intended to go straight to the family loft but was intercepted by Myra Frobisher.

"Sir," she said, "Detective Frees called to say that shortly before noon, Martin Land's body was found by a fishing boat headed down the Thames. When they saw the priest's collar, Scotland Yard was called immediately."

"Was there any evidence of foul play?" Michael said.

Myra shook her head. "Detective Frees thinks it might have been suicide, but they have to do a post-mortem."

"Is Sarah back from Belfast?" Michael said.

"Not yet," Myra said. "The plane is due to land at Luton in about 20 minutes. She stayed later than intended to be with the family after the service and burial."

Michael nodded.

"There's one other thing," Myra said. "A letter arrived in the noon mail delivery. It wasn't marked personal, so I opened it. It's from

Martin Land." And she handed him the letter. "I don't mean to ambush you like this, but it seems extremely important. I did not mention it to Detective Frees."

As Michael took the one-page letter from here, the first thing he noticed was the key taped to it. He read it as they walked toward the library.

He looked up. "Myra, is Joshua here?"

She nodded. "He's in his office."

"I need you to do two things. Ask Joshua to meet me in my office, and then call Detective Frees." He handed her his mobile. "He's No. 12 on my speed dial. Tell him we need to talk with him as soon as possible."

She nodded and went to find Josh.

Forty minutes later, Frees stood in the library, talking with Michael, Josh Gittings, and Myra. Michael had called Jay and asked him to join them. For the third time, Frees was reading the letter from Martin Land to the king. After the first reading, he had called Scotland Yard and fired off a series of instructions. Then he reread the letter twice. It was on the Archbishop of Canterbury's letterhead. Short and to the point, it was dated Saturday evening.

Glynn Young

Your majesty,

It is no secret that I have never been one of your supporters in the struggle over the Church. But with the news of this past week, my conscience has overcome my distaste for your evangelical theology. You are the only one left who can do something.

For at least the last 30 years, and possibly longer, high officials in the Church have engaged in a cover-up of wrongdoing by priests and other church officials. Child molesters have been transferred from parish to parish, the church fully aware yet never dealing with their wrongdoing. Untold hundreds, and likely thousands, of children have been harmed. I myself have helped cover up this terrible sin, while serving for two former archbishops of Canterbury and the current archbishop. All were fully aware of what was happening, as were all of the archbishops in Britain. We thought we were acting in the best interest of the church, to keep the priestly ranks from becoming decimated, but we were not. We set wolves upon the sheep, and upon the lambs.

I can no longer bear my role in all of this. It was a functionary's role, but it was a critical one. Yes, I just followed orders. But I could have refused.

This key is mine for a safety deposit box at the Western Bank in Islington. I've instructed the bank that only I or you have the key, and only I or you can access the contents. In the box you will find a considerable number of copies of parish transfer records. Pay particular attention to the names authorizing all of the transfers for the Rev. Wickham. Note also the transfers for the Rev. Channing Arnold, whose misdeeds have yet to come to light but are worse than most you will hear about. And there are many others beyond those two. There will also be a key and instructions for locating the place I have stored all of the personnel records. These were put in centralized storage at Lambeth Palace, but I moved them Saturday morning for safekeeping. The archbishop has suggested they be destroyed.

I would pray for God to save our church, but I no longer believe it merits saving, and I share blame for that.

The Rev. Martin Land
Chief of Staff

Attachment

"This was written before what happened at St. Thomas," Frees said. "Had Land come forward before this letter, Richard Jenner might still be alive."

He looked at Michael. "We've talked to the bank. No one has attempted to gain access to the box today. The last time it was accessed was Saturday, and that was Martin Land. He apparently added papers to it and took nothing away. So, your majesty, can I prevail upon you to take a ride to Islington? The bank is open until 6 p.m., and they will hold the doors for us. If this isn't convenient, I can get a court order."

Michael stood and nodded to Myra. "Myra, please let Sarah know where I'm going. She was expecting to see me when she returned. Tell her I should be back here in an hour or so. Jay, I need you to start drawing up a plan for how we're going to communicate this, once things start to happen."

"Sir, do you know whose signatures Land is referring to?" asked Jay.

"I'm not certain, but I think so," Michael said.

Driven in a Scotland Yard car with Paula Abbott and other security officers in a palace car behind them, Frees and Michael talked quietly on their way to Islington.

Frees had called ahead to the bank, alerting them to the pending arrival of the king and the need to move quickly and directly to the safety deposit boxes.

The cars stopped in front of the bank, behind a police car that was already waiting, and Frees, Michael, and the agents walked quickly inside. They were greeted by the bank manager, who bowed his head to Michael, and asked them to follow him. They crossed the bank lobby, drawing startled looks of recognition from customers and tellers alike. "It's the king," went the whispers.

In the deposit box room, the bank manager inserted his key into box 331, and Michael did the same. The lock clicked open.

Inside the box was one item, a cardboard box that had originally held letter-size envelopes. Frees lifted the lid, and they saw a thick stack of paper and an envelope for a self-storage facility in Wimbledon.

"We'll need to take this to HQ," Frees said. "I'll call you when we know something."

Michael nodded. He returned home in the palace security car.

At 10 a.m., as Michael had begun his meeting at City Hall, Dr. Owens opened the upper school student assembly at ICS. For typical assemblies, it usually took some time to quiet down the boisterousness and high spirits of the students. For this one, the students had filed quietly into the auditorium. Jason was sitting with Chris in the middle of the seating. He hadn't seen Jane; he was afraid to look for her and thought it was probably no longer even necessary to look for her. All of the upper school teachers were in attendance, standing at the rear of the seats. Owens had asked the students staffing the audio-visual crew to videotape the meeting.

Dr. Owens opened with prayer, then began to speak.

"Since last Wednesday, our school has found itself in the middle of extraordinary events in our country. And there's every indication these events are not over.

"While many young people from all over London and beyond appear to have been affected, two of our own students have been caught up in these events, through no fault of their own. They have been the victims of something that I can only call evil. They have now been freed from that evil, but they will have to overcome it for the rest of their lives. And this was not of their making. It could have happened to any of us here today. But it didn't happen to just any of us; it happened to two young men who are our fellow students, our friends, and members of our family in Christ.

"God will bring good out of this evil, as hard as that may be to believe right now. But he will, because he is a faithful and just God.

"Our prayer is for our two fellow students and their families. Our prayer is for healing. And our prayer is for ourselves, that we may resist evil and overcome it in God's name.

"When these two young men return to ICS, and it is my sincere hope and prayer that they will return, each one of us must welcome them back with compassion, with understanding, with love, and with acceptance. They must know that they have a place here, that they will be accepted and not ridiculed or questioned, that they are one of us and they are one with us, and that we love them.

"As terrible as these events of the last several days have been, much of what has transpired needed to happen. The evil needed to be exposed, in order that it be stopped. It is still being exposed.

"That exposure began because one of our students reached out to a boy who was lonely and withdrawn and pulled him into a prayer group. And the prayer group was open enough so that this young man felt safe to share his deepest, darkest hurts. I want you to know that it demonstrates the truth of scripture – that when two or three are gathered in His name, He is there. And while the road was rocky, it was still a road that the Lord used to bring evil to light.

"And that exposure continued because the other young man, victimized for years, saw the same thing about to happen to his little brother, and took his brother to safety. No greater brotherly love is this.

"And you should know that our king, Michael, has played an enormous role in uncovering this horror. He has provided a haven for our two students, he has worked closely with the police, he has helped our school deal with this, and he continues to help bring this evil to light, even when he knows what the cost to the church will likely be." Owens paused. "Our king has blessed us all.

"This has been a terrible time for all of us, and it will continue to be for some period of time to come. We're going to have a prayer time in our classrooms after this assembly, but if any of you would like to come forward and speak, you have that opportunity now."

Owens wasn't sure if any of the students would step forward, but he hoped at least one might. He was gratified when Jane Barry walked up the steps to the stage microphone.

"I'm Jane Barry, third year upper school." She hesitated, looking around the auditorium, as if gathering strength to proceed.

"I was there last Wednesday when it all started. We had split into our boys and girls prayer groups, and we saw Robert run down the hall and Jason yell at Elton. And Jason ran after Robert but couldn't find him. Jason came back, and he was angry. I'd never seen him angry before, and he was really mad. He told us what had happened to him years ago, like what happened to Robert."

The auditorium had grown profoundly silent. A few of the students had heard the story; most had not.

"He said we didn't know what Robert had gone through, we didn't know what it was like, and it was horrible."

Jane was crying now but continued on.

"I was horrified. I turned my back on Jason. I wanted to run as far away from him as I could get.

"But he took a risk. He took a risk with the people he thought loved him. He thought we would understand. Chris Whitney understood. I didn't. Chris Whitney loved him. I didn't."

Chris looked at Jason, who seemed focused totally on Jane but reached and clutched Chris' hand.

"I turned away from him when he needed me most.

"We can't do that to Robert or Elton. I can't do that to Jason. I hope he forgives me. Jason, I don't even know if you're here. But I'm sorry. I'm ashamed of my behavior. I love you, Jason."

The auditorium was silent, except for the girl crying on the stage. And then a yell was heard.

"Jane!"

Jason had jumped up, and seemingly leaped from seat to seat to get to the aisle. Jane saw him and started running for the stairs from the stage to the seating area. They met at the bottom of the stairs and fell into each other's arms. The auditorium went wild.

While the students cheered, fourth-year student Ivan Mercer made his way to the microphone.

Ivan was a wrestler for the school team and was built like a wrestler. He wasn't known for his academic prowess, classes like English being a struggle and math requiring special tutors just to maintain a barely passing grade. But his friendliness, openness, and sincerity made him universally liked across the school by students and teachers alike.

Ivan stood at the microphone, nodding his head and not saying anything at first, letting the cheering die down. When all was quiet, and Jason and Jane were sitting on the stairs, Jason with his arm around her shoulder and Jane with her head on Jason's shoulder, Ivan kept nodding. For a moment Dr. Owens thought Ivan had forgotten what he wanted to say. And, truth be told, he had. But he recovered with an alternative.

Ivan looked out at the students and raised his fist high.

"Robert Hood rocks!" he shouted, punching the air with each word.

The students looked at him in surprise.

"Robert Hood rocks!" Ivan repeated, and gestured to the auditorium.

And then the students shouted back, "Robert Hood rocks!"

"Elton Jenner rocks!" Ivan shouted.

The students shouted back, "Elton Jenner rocks!"

"Jason Kent-Hughes rocks!" Ivan shouted, his fist still moving up and down.

"Jason Kent-Hughes rocks!" was the response. Students were standing on their seats.

"King Michael rocks!" he shouted.

"King Michael rocks!" they yelled back.

"Robert rocks!" Ivan shouted.

"Robert rocks!"

"Elton rocks!"

"Elton rocks!"

"Jason rocks!" he roared.

"Jason rocks!" they roared back.

Colin Slattery, tears running down his face as he and the other teachers yelled with the students, was amazed to see even Dr. Owens shouting and raising his fist in the air.

"King Michael rocks!"

"King Michael rocks!"

The students began cheering.

Shortly after dinner, Frees called Michael.

"Sir, the coroner says Martin Land drowned," Frees said. "It looks like suicide. Possibly accidental, but most likely suicide. No obvious signs of trauma. My guess would be that he jumped from Lambeth Bridge. The condition of the body suggests he's been in the water about 24 hours, maybe a bit longer. We've confirmed his presence at the worship service at Lambeth Palace until 8 Sunday morning." He paused. "We're withholding his name from the press until the next of kin is notified, and even then, we may not disclose it until we make other moves."

Michael remained quiet. "The tragedies keep multiplying."

"We have a team culling through the transfer records. And there's a pattern with the authorizing names."

"Yes?" Michael said.

"For Channing Arnold, the name that consistently shows up as the authorizing signature for transfer is Sebastian Rowland."

Michael closed his eyes. The Archbishop of Canterbury. The leader of the Church of England. Protecting the predators of children.

"But it's not Rowland who authorized Hugh Wickham's transfers. Well, I take that back. He authorized only the last one, the one that brought Wickham to St. Mark's in London."

"Where was he transferred from?" Michael asked.

"Yorkshire," Frees said. Frees gave Michael the name authorizing the transfers within York, although he didn't have to. Michael knew who it was. "We're still assembling the evidence, but we think we'll have enough to charge both of them with accessory after the fact. We expect to move no later than Wednesday."

"The two highest ranking men in the Church of England," Michael said. He shook his head. "At some point, I have to ask Rowland for his resignation. As titular head of the Church of England, technically he reports to me. Can I do that before you make the arrest?"

"We can wait outside his office for you to finish, and then we'll move in, or I can come in the office with you."

"Thank you, Detective," Michael said. "I think I would like to have you with me. And the other one?"

"Do you need to ask for his resignation first?" Frees said. "We can do it the same way."

"No, Detective-Inspector, just with Rowland," Michael said. "How will you handle the other arrest?

"We'll have to work with local authorities, so it might take a day or so longer than Rowland, but we'll simply show up and arrest him."

Michael was quiet for a long time.

"Sir, are you still there?"

"Yes, I'm sorry, Detective-Inspector," Michael said. "I got distracted. That process should work. Will you bring him to London?"

"Yes. As soon as he's arrested."

"I may ask to see him then."

"We can work that out." Frees paused. "Your majesty, we're still reeling in some of these people, but I want you to know that we've only gotten as far as we did and as quickly as we did because of your cooperation and support. You've done right by these children. Have you heard from Robert's mother?"

"No," said Michael, "there's been nothing. We're prepared to let him stay with us indefinitely. He needs a family that can help see him through some of this."

"Sir, I may have a suggestion," Frees said. "When I come on Wednesday before we move on Rowland, we can talk."

"It's a plan, Detective-Inspector," Michael said.

After he rang off, he sent an email to Eleanor Whitmire at City Hall, asking her to reschedule any meetings set for Wednesday morning.

Dr. Owens gave Jason a copy of the tape to bring home for Robert and the Jenners. Michael, with Hank on his lap, Sarah, Jim and Jason watched it with their four young guests. Robert looked at Jason and smiled, the first smile they'd seen on his face since the dance on Friday. Amanda hugged her brother, and Nicholas high-fived him. Sarah leaned over and kissed Jason on his cheek. And Jim pointed to Hank. "Look!"

Hank had a little fist in the air. "Da!" All of them, including Robert and the Jenners, collapsed in laughter.

Several copies of the tape were made by the school. No one could later account for how it happened, but one of the copies ended up in the hands of a news reporter for ITV (Jay Lanham emphatically denied having anything to do with it). On Tuesday evening, the network played the entire tape on the 6 p.m. news and kept repeating it hourly. All London and most of Britain saw the assembly program, and the British people raised their fists with the students from ICS.

The horror that was the clergy abuse crisis continued to unfold.

Chapter 16: The Mending Begins

The letter Canon Land had left for the archbishop was simple and nowhere near as detailed as that sent to the king. Rowland's letter read, "I'm sorry, Archbishop, I can't do this any longer." The letter had prompted Rowland's frantic search for the records, but so far, even with several staff members working on it, no one knew what Land had done with them.

Almost as bad, no one knew what had happened to Canon Land.

Venneman called Land several times and was always patched through to Rowland. Rowland said that Canon Land was indisposed and was in hospital, with an intestinal ailment. They talked, and Venneman realized how difficult it was going to be to exit the account. The archbishop had too much evidence of his and FBL's involvement.

Venneman's talk with his boss on Monday had not gone well.

"How deep in this are we, Geoff?" Cheryl Pinsky said.

"It's a straightforward account," he said, "no different than any other."

"Have you provided any counsel or advice regarding the clergy abuse issue," she said, "or have you stuck strictly to the activities related to defeating the king's proposals for the church?"

"It's become difficult to keep the two separated, Cheryl," Venneman said. "The news reports have been giving lift to the king's proposals. And I've offered some advice and counsel, yes, but most of my work remains on the parliamentary side." *Which isn't entirely true*, he thought. *It's almost all on the priests, now.*

"I trust you have only given verbal advice and didn't send anything by email?" she said.

"It's been all face-to-face or on the phone," he said. *Another half-truth*, he thought. *No, that's an outright lie.*

"That's something, anyway," she said. "Geoff, this thing is becoming huge. You need to extricate yourself and FBL, by the end of the week at the latest."

"That's the plan," he'd said.

He was walking down Cheapside, headed for St. Mary-le-Bow's café for lunch, when his mobile buzzed. It was Archbishop Rowland. He was almost tempted to let it go to voicemail.

"Yes, Archbishop," he said.

"Did you know that the Scotland Yard detective leading the investigation on the priests has called for an appointment Wednesday?" Rowland said. "He called just a few minutes ago."

"No, Archbishop," Venneman said, "I did not know. I would have needed clairvoyance if it were only a few minutes ago."

"Yes, well, of course," Rowland said. "But he called. I need you here to work through what I should say, what questions he might ask, and how should I generally act. I will also have the archdiocesan attorney here as well."

"Your attorney is likely to tell you to say nothing," Venneman said, "or as close to nothing as you can get."

"I know," said Rowland. "and that's why I need you here as well. If I'm to say as close to nothing as I can, you have to help me translate nothing into credible English."

"All right," Venneman said. "What time?"

"9:30 a.m.," Rowland said. "That's when the attorney will arrive as well."

"All right," Venneman said, "I'll see you then. I'll work up some possible statements and approaches and have them with me."

Sarah sat in her office in the palace. Her office had taken almost no time to be readied, and she had occupied it for several months now. Michael's office was almost finished; it had been in a decrepit condition, indicating that James III had never used it for anything except storage.

The phone rang; the Security Office was calling to say that Tyler Zimmer had arrived, right at 9:30, and they would escort him now.

She didn't know what to expect; she only knew this man from what little interaction there had been when he and her father were business partners in Denver and the luncheon the previous week. And this was the man who was the biological father of her and her two brothers.

There was a tap at the door, and her admin Carrie Waldman showed Zimmer in.

"Hello, Sarah," he said. "Thank you for seeing me."

"Please sit down, Mr. Zimmer," she said. "Would like anything to drink?"

"No, no thank you," he said.

She smiled and waited for him to speak.

"I'm here to apologize," he said, "for what happened last week. It was embarrassing for you and inexcusable for us."

Sarah continued to wait.

"It got everything off on the wrong foot," Zimmer said.

"My understanding," Sarah said, "was that you were as surprised as I was by the arrival of my mother's friends, not to mention what they'd been led to believe. I'm hoping you can tell me that they completely misunderstood something she'd told them."

"I wish I could, Sarah," he said, "but I can't. She offered to help them with the gallery opening and trying to obtain a royal warrant."

"She didn't see what a bad move that was?" Sarah said. "We had just met after eight years and she was promising royal favors to her friends? Can you see where that left me? I was believing that she wanted to find a way to resume our relationship, and instead I find out that we're supposed to find a royal sticker for someone's window."

"I know," he said. "It was awful. I'm so sorry."

"Mr. Zimmer," Sarah said, "does she feel she should apologize? Or does she not understand what she did?"

He was quiet for a moment. "Sarah," he said, "she doesn't think she did anything wrong. Let me explain. There was one thing Seth Hughes could do far better than I've been able to, and that's to cover your mother's lack of social graces. Marie was always like that. She was fun, she was vibrant and colorful, but she could make for some very awkward moments. Seth covered that, and he covered it very effectively. He covered more of her gaffes at parties and meetings than you can imagine. I suspect it was the background she came from, a rather rough-and-tumble family that constantly played one-upmanship and loved to embarrass each other, and especially publicly. I met them after she and Seth separated; we flew to Florida for me to meet them. All I can say is that it was painful, horribly painful. But she seemed to relish it."

Sarah looked away, her face unreadable.

"You probably don't remember how little she had to do with bringing you, Scott, and David up. She liked the idea of motherhood, and she wanted to please Seth, but she always had trouble dealing with the realities of motherhood. Seth was far more influential in your upbringing; I know, because I was there. Do you remember how many times she went to one of your ballet recitals?"

Sarah shook her head; she felt like she was beginning to verge toward tears, and she didn't yet know why.

"Once," Zimmer said. "She went once, and she went because Seth threw a temper tantrum. Seth never missed one, not a single one."

She nodded. "He was always there. He went to David's baseball games, too."

"Do you remember your mother at one of David's games?" Zimmer said.

She shook her head.

"I think one of the reasons I asked to speak to you," Zimmer said, "is that I wanted to be there, too. I wanted to see those recitals and those baseball games, but I couldn't. I wanted to be part of your lives, and it just wasn't possible. I had hoped that there might have been the opportunity to get to know you better, but Marie, intentionally or not, short-circuited that. I would be lying if I said she felt remorseful about what happened. She only felt remorseful about having promised something that she realized was too early to deliver.

"And I need to say this, too, Sarah," he said. "Rightly and wrongly, she is the woman I loved and have always loved. But her behavior last week was abominable. I wish she could see that, but she can't." He smiled. "Part of every life story, I suppose, is a strain of tragedy, no matter how much you love someone."

He looked at his watch. "I'm sorry, I think I've gone past the allotted time."

"It's okay, Mr. Zimmer," Sarah said. "You're helping me understand something. I couldn't understand why David and even Scott felt such antipathy toward her. I think I know now."

Zimmer nodded. "That painting of Michael," he said, pointing to the one on the wall behind Sarah. "It's one of yours?"

She smiled. "Yes, Mike and the boys are a regular subject, and they bear it with great patience."

"It's beautiful," he said. "I was never artistically gifted myself, but there's a long line of artists in our family. My mother was quite an accomplished artist. Everyone thought she was the last generation to paint. She would have been pleased to see a painting like that one, and she'd be pleased to see that it exceeded her own work.

"One last thing," he said. "Marie wants to leave London. She's embarrassed to see her friends, and she thinks everyone will find out what happened. I'll be asking for a transfer back to the States, and I'll likely get it. So, if you think Marie wants to repair the damage with you, I'm afraid she's more concerned about her friends. Perhaps one day she'll come to realize what a profound loss that is." He stood. "It's time for me to go."

"I'll walk with you to Security," she said.

As they walked, she talked about the boys. "We love children," she said, "and we both want to have more."

And then she surprised both him and herself by taking his arm.

They reached the Security checkpoint and exit to Buckingham Road.

"Thank you for that," Zimmer said. "That was very kind. Seth did well." He nodded, and then moved into the checkpoint room and through the exit.

Jane had told her family about the assembly on Monday. Trevor was home late from work on Tuesday, arriving at 7 p.m. His family was in the den, glued to the television.

"Trevor!" Liz said. "Come see. Hurry."

He walked into the room.

"It's the school assembly from yesterday," Jane said. "ITV has a copy of the tape."

Trevor sat next to Liz and watched.

When it was finished, he looked at his family. "It's incredible," he said, smiling. "And that's quite some scene on the stairs with Jason."

Andrew stood up with his fist in the air.

"Trevor Barry rocks!"

Jane stood next to her brother and shouted with him. "Trevor Barry rocks! Trevor Barry rocks!"

Liz stood up and joined in. "Trevor Barry rocks! Trevor Barry rocks!"

Trevor stood and embraced his family.

Afterward, as Trevor was eating his warmed-up dinner, Liz was helping Andrew with homework in his room. Jane joined Trevor at the kitchen table.

"How's my beautiful daughter?" he said.

She laughed. "I need to let my exaggerating father know that his daughter is fine." She touched his hand. "More than fine. Jason and I had a long talk last night."

"I assumed it was him," Trevor said. "I can't think of anyone else you've spent as much time on the phone with as him. And that video suggested something of a reconciliation."

She laughed. "I didn't know how wonderful it would feel to have his arms around me again," she said.

She saw her father's eyebrows go up, and she laughed again. "Dad, if you think you have something to worry about, you don't know Jason. He would never do anything to hurt me, and he takes his faith seriously, with all that implies."

"Well," Trevor said, "you know, beautiful daughter, father worries."

She took Trevor's hand in her own and lifted it, giving it a kiss. "You helped me," she said. "You helped me understand. All I could focus on was the horror he'd gone through. What I couldn't see was the wonderful person who survived it and even overcame it. And I know it changed him, but Dad, he wouldn't be who he is today if it hadn't happened. He'd be someone else, probably just another dopey boy."

Trevor laughed, feeling himself tear up.

"But he's Jason," Jane said. "He's fierce and he's awkward and he's beautiful and he's clumsy and he's got the soul of an artist. He creates. And he's tender." She paused, tears in her eyes. "And he reminds me of you. You took a huge risk telling us what happened to you, and you did it because you loved us and you loved Jason and you wanted us to understand. Dad, in a lot of ways, we were the ones who were broken."

Trevor tried but failed to stop the sob coming from his throat.

After dinner on Tuesday, Michael tapped on Jason's door.

"Can I come in?" he said.

"Sure, Dad," Jason said. "You want to ask about Jane?"

"Well, no," Michael said, "well, yes. Yes and no. I wanted to see how you're doing."

"I'm doing great, Dad," Jason said. "Jane and I talked a long time last night. And I realized something. What we had felt broken, like it couldn't be put back together. And I think that was right, it couldn't be put back together. Because everything had changed. But something better is coming out of it. It's made us closer. Different, but closer. We've learned more about each other. And that's a good thing, I think.

"It is," Michael said. "When we discover we care deeply for someone, I think we tend to consider them perfect. And none of us is perfect, of course. Or we think that this is the person who will make me happy forever. And that's absolutely the wrong reason for pursuing a relationship. It's not about your happiness, no matter what television and the movies say. It's about how God brings together two imperfect people who care for each other, and he spends their lifetime molding them and shaping them together. The point isn't our happiness but how what God has brought together honors Him. It's very hard for us to understand that. What comes from that witness is a blessing. The blessing of love, of companionship, of children, of caring. Happiness can happen, but it's a side-effect. It's not the point."

Michael could tell Jason had been listening intently.

"Sometimes we can see that you and Mom have differences," Jason said. "I know there have been times when you irritate each other."

Michael laughed. "Indeed. Although it's more me doing the irritating than your mother. But that's part of the shaping and the smoothing. We all bring our rough edges into a relationship."

"Jane's really special, Dad," Jason said. "It blows me away that she likes me, that she sees something in me."

"And that, my son," Michael said, standing up, "is true for all of us. I still wonder every day what Sarah sees in me. But I will tell you this. I'm not complete without her. She's become as much a part of me as I am. And that's God's doing, not mine."

The boys were all in bed. Michael and Sarah were sitting on the floor of their bedroom, holding hands, Sarah's head on Michael's shoulder.

"I found myself liking Tyler Zimmer," she said, after explaining what had happened at their meeting. "I even admire his determination to stick with my mother, especially with what he knows are her problems. From one perspective, it looks foolish for him to do that. Most men would probably just walk away. But he feels a commitment that he has to honor."

"It also puts Seth in an entirely new light," Michael said. "He was the one who was there for you and your brothers."

"When you had that big conversation with him in Los Angeles, before we married," she said, "you told him that it was David who might have the most trouble forgiving him, and to go easy with him."

"I think David knew what Seth had done throughout your lives more than you or Scott," Michael said. "And David was the one who felt the closest to Seth. He told me once at school that he knew he had disappointed your father by not going into business, but that he thought Seth would respect him more if he followed what he knew to be right and made a go of it. And when you both came to McLarens for Christmas, you remember when he helped Da birth the foal in the barn?"

She laughed. "I do. I never would have believed that my brainy scholarly brother was down on his knees, his hands and arms inside a horse to pull her baby out."

"He was sticking to Da like glue," Michael said. "He needed some adult male affirmation, and Da gave it to him. Da told me that David had talked about feeling worthless after your father rejected you both. And Da told him that he was God's creation, made in God's image, and because of that he was of immense worth, more than he could ever understand." He smiled. "It was Da who pointed David down the road of faith; Tommy and I just came alongside and gave him a lift."

"I never knew that story," Sarah said. She lifted and kissed Michael's hand. "It's no wonder I feel like your parents are my parents, too, and David's, and even Scott and Barb."

"God never blessed Ma and Da with children of their own," Michael said. "But he gave them a great blessing nonetheless. I upended their lives in a lot of ways, but they loved me like their own. I knew I had their love from the beginning, from that first day I was with them. It's amazing what that can do in the life of a child."

They were quiet for a time.

"How is the tsar of London doing?" Sarah said.

"Well," Michael said, "there have been no disasters the first two days. I've been meeting with department heads and staff. Next week starts my field trips."

"What are field trips?" Sarah said.

"Getting out where the work's done," Michael said. "I've asked the heads to set these up. I don't want to stay in an office. I need to see how people are actually getting London's work done. So far, they've lined up a visit to London Bridge to see gear maintenance for raising and lowering the bridge. And I think I get to help take fares on a No. 15 Routemaster."

Sarah laughed. "I want a photo of that."

"I'm sure we'll see plenty of them," Michael said.

"What will tomorrow bring?" Sarah said. "I mean, literally tomorrow. With the church."

Michael was quiet. "More arrests," he said. "I've cleared my schedule at City Hall in the morning to accompany Detective Frees to Lambeth Palace."

"What happens there?" Sarah said.

"I will ask Sebastian Rowland for his resignation, and regardless of whether he resigns or not, Frees will arrest him," Michael said.

Sarah sat up and looked at Michael.

"Mike," she said. "He's involved?"

"Not as a perpetrator," Michael said, "at least as far as anyone knows now, but as an accessory after the fact. He's transferred abusing priests all over Britain." Michael paused. "Sarah, he's not the only archbishop being arrested tomorrow. There are others. The Crown

Prosecution Service has been alerted and fully briefed. Three of the archbishops are members of the House of Lords. Jay has prepared a communication plan for dealing with the expected media blitz. There will also be a number of arrests of staff at Lambeth Palace."

For a long time, Sarah said nothing. "I didn't know it had gone this far."

"I thought it best to say nothing except to Jay and Joshua," he said. "And Trevor. We've held it very close because of, first, the names involved and the explosion if it leaked too soon, and second, the fact that the investigation is continuing. The records that Canon Land left for us to find are going to shatter the church, Sarah. I thought we were dealing with a church that needed reforming. Instead, we find a church saturated by a monstrous evil. You think you have a handful of abusing priests, and the handful turns out to be hundreds and hundreds, with networks of priests, bishops, and archbishops covering up crimes and even facilitating more abuse. It's a horrible nightmare."

"It seems strange to be sitting here, calmly talking," Sarah said, "when all of this will start to erupt tomorrow."

"It's the quiet before the storm," Michael said. "And its effects will be profound, even more than The Violence."

Chapter 17: The First Wave Crests

Detective Frees arrived at the palace immediately at 8 a.m. For an hour, he and Michael talked in the library.

"I've been informed," Michael said, "that my official office here will be ready for occupancy tomorrow. I'll miss the library, but I think I'm ready for an office."

"It seems to have taken a while," Frees said.

"It's not the fault of the construction and interior design people," Michael said. "When they started working last spring, right after the loft was finished, they discovered significant water damage behind the walls. A pipe had apparently been leaking for years, and because the room was generally unoccupied and used for storage, no one noticed. Or no one reported it, if they saw it. At first, they thought it might be affecting the entire wing, but once they got inside the walls and checked, it turned out to be more contained.

"But once the damage was found, we had to have the Royal Heritage Commission come and inspect. The palace is a protected historic building; they let us get away with the changes for the loft because no major structural changes were required. Once the inspection was done, the inspectors had to draw up a plan. Finally, months later, the approval came, and we could make the needed repairs and finish construction and design."

"It sounds like most of the time was devoted to creating and cutting red tape," Frees said.

Michael nodded. "And the moral of the story is, don't live in a historic building if you can at all avoid it."

"As for our meeting with the archbishop this morning," Frees said, "he believes that this will be an interview about what he does or doesn't know about the abuse cases. And our assessment is that he's already anxious, based on our phone conversation. We've had Lambeth Palace under observation, in case anyone, like the archbishop but not limited to him, attempts to flee. He told us he would have the diocesan lawyer there as well."

"And we should probably expect Mr. Venneman to be there," Michael said.

"Which will actually make things easier," Frees said. "We'll be taking him into custody as well. Officially, it will be the usual 'helping the police with their inquiries' but we have some limited evidence that he's been helping the archbishop cover up certain cases. Canon Land printed copies of several emails from Venneman to the archbishop and included them in that box at the bank. So, if he's there, it will save us the trouble of tracking him down, and we'll bring him to the Yard as well." He consulted his notes. "At the same time, two other archbishops, five bishops, and some 120 priests are being arrested for either the crimes themselves or for being accessories after the fact and covering them up. And I need to tell you, sir, that there are more to come, based on the records we found in Canon Land's storage unit. Likely many more to come. But today will be our largest number of arrests to date and involving well-known names, including the head of St. Simon's Seminary."

"And the seminaries in Cardiff and Glasgow?" Michael said.

"Those arrests will happen tomorrow," Frees said. "You should expect to see a considerable number of arrests at all levels tomorrow and Friday."

"Any estimate of the total number yet?" Michael said.

"My very rough estimate, sir," Frees said, "is about 2,000 priests and likely a third of the church hierarchy."

Michael stared and then looked away, seemingly trying to catch his breath. "The church will not be able to survive those numbers," he said. "We're going to have considerable chaos for a time. There's not even anyone with the needed knowledge to move quickly to consolidate parishes, do the coordination necessary, and try to figure out what we do until we know what we're doing. And I can't do that, one, because of limited knowledge, and two, I'm already committed to the Greater London Authority." He shook his head. "But we have to find someone.

"You may not be aware of this, detective," Michael said, "but for some time, and not as a result of the abuse crisis, I've had a small team working on what a reformed Church of England would look like. We've been stepping up action as much and as quietly as we can. I've said nothing to them about what will be happening, but they'll get a fair idea by this afternoon when the news hits the media."

"All this and London, too," Frees said. "Do you ever sleep?"

Michael smiled. "I do. I have good people to rely upon. And I'm going to need more good people, and very soon. I have a meeting with my attorney, Trevor Barry, as soon as I return to the palace. He's leading my church study team. And then I have to be at City Hall at 12:30."

"Would Mr. Barry be someone to lead the entire effort for the church," Frees said, "or does it have to be an ordained priest?"

Michael was silent, considering what Frees had just said. "That is something I hadn't considered. I've been thinking it has to be someone with ecclesiastical authority or experience. But that suggestion of yours certainly opens up other possibilities. And Trevor

has had to do an enormous amount of research into church history and

ecclesiastical law." He smiled. "He's not a believer, or at least, he's

not one yet. But that is an excellent suggestion, detective."

Frees looked at his watch. "I believe it's time we leave to meet

with the archbishop, sir."

He and Michael traveled together in a Scotland Yard vehicle,

leaving from the Mews instead of the front of the palace. They were

followed by a police car and two palace automobiles. The four cars

wended their way slowly through the morning traffic toward Lambeth

Bridge and the palace.

"My wife's name is Sylvia," Frees said. "She's a doctor. And a

good one."

"General practice or specialty?" Michael said.

"Pediatrician," Frees said. "We've never had children. We'd

been married two years when she got pregnant, and about five months

into the pregnancy she lost the baby. I almost lost her at the same time,

and they had to do a hysterectomy."

"I'm sorry, detective."

Frees nodded. "We thought about adopting from time to time,

but we never did, for whatever reason. Busy with careers, I suppose."

He paused. "Sylvia puts up with a lot from me. Rotten working hours. Calls at all times of the day and night. I tell her I keep doctor's hours."

Michael laughed.

"No word from Mrs. Hood, I take it?" Frees said.

Michael shook his head. "It's as if she's vanished. Mitchell even talked with Mrs. Binch, the next-door neighbor. She said that Mrs. Hood had come home on Sunday, stayed for perhaps two hours, and then a taxi pulled up in front. The driver put three suitcases into the taxi. She gave Mrs. Binch the key to the house and asked her to give it to the landlord. She said she expected Robert to come for his things as some point, and the rent was paid through the end of November. And then she got in the taxi and left. Mitchell also called her firm, and they told him she'd resigned her job. Mitchell even talked with some of your people at the Yard, and they've been doing some informal checks, since she's not an official missing person. She's gone to ground somewhere.

"Last night," Frees said, "Border Control informed us that she left on a flight to Toronto."

"I'd so hoped she'd come back," Michael said.

Frees was quiet. They had reached Lambeth Bridge and were waiting at a traffic light.

"Sylvia and I talked, sir," he said. "We'd like to take the boy in. Robert, I mean. We think we could give him a good home. Sylvia could keep track of research on HIV and AIDS and help him with medicines and therapies. And I've got a lot of contacts with the courts and could probably figure out the foster home or adoption thing to make it happen. We'd have to go through a period of severing Samantha Hood's legal rights, but it's possible. But I don't know what the boy will think."

Michael turned and looked at the policeman. "I don't know what he'll think, either, but my guess is he'll leap at it. Why do you want to do this?"

"Something in the boy got to me, sir," Frees said. "He's a quiet lad, but he had the courage to speak out in his prayer group. It must have been a terrible thing for him to do, but he did it. Had he not, and had your Jason not gone after him that day, the horror would still be going on and no one would be the wiser. And when I've talked to him, it just seems, well, it just seems right. I'd be proud to call him my son." Frees paused. "After all he's been through, including his mother walking out on him, have you noticed his eyes?"

Michael nodded and smiled. "His eyes have hope, in spite of everything." Michael put his hand on the policeman's. "It's a blessing to know you, detective. You honor us all."

"Do you think you might bring it up to him first, sir?" Frees said. "I mean, I think it would make it easier for him than if Sylvia and I just came out and asked him. If you sounded him out, it would give him the opportunity to say no without feeling pressured by us."

"I'll talk to him tonight," Michael said.

They pulled up to Lambeth Palace and stepped out of the car, with the three vehicles behind them. Two uniformed policemen followed Frees and Michael into the palace.

"Have you been here before?" Frees said as they walked.

"Once," Michael said. "During my training, we had a four-day study retreat here. But that was some years ago." He looked at the detective. "And nothing happened, at least that I know of."

They passed the security station, and Michael nodded at the guards. "This is Detective Inspector Roger Frees of Scotland Yard," Michael said. "We have an appointment with the archbishop at 9:30."

"Your majesty, we have Mr. Frees on the visitor list, but I don't see your name," one of the security officers said.

"Is that a problem?" Michael said.

The man shook his head. "No, sir. If you follow this hallway and turn left at the end, you'll reach the archbishop's office."

Reaching the administrative offices, Michael led Frees and the two officers to the Archbishop's secretary's desk.

"We're here to see Archbishop Rowland," Michael said.

The secretary jumped up and bowed her head. "Your majesty, is the Archbishop expecting you as well?"

"No," Michael said, "but it won't matter."

"Perhaps I should announce you to the archbishop, sir," she said.

Michael looked at her desk name plate. "Mrs. Randell, we're fine. There's no need. The surprise will only be momentary." Michael walked to the door and opened it.

The archbishop, seated at his desk, looked at them as they entered. With Rowland was Geoffrey Venneman and the diocesan attorney. Venneman and the attorney rose for the king. Rowland remained seated.

"So," Rowland said. "The king comes at last. With a supporting cast. I'm surprised it took this long. I was expecting the detective here, but not you, your majesty."

Michael opened the folder he was carrying, extracted a single page, and handed it to Rowland.

Rowland glanced at it. "You're asking me to resign my position of Archbishop?".

"Read it more carefully," Michael said. "I'm asking you to resign your position and from the church."

"I refuse," Rowland said. "You will not win. I will not allow you to destroy the Church of England."

"Is that what you see this as?" Michael said. "Winning and losing? This is a game to you?"

"I won't sign this," Rowland said, "no matter how many policemen you have with you."

Michael extracted a page from the folder. "This is a copy of only one of the transfers you authorized for Rev. Channing, the priest arrested Sunday at St. Thomas Church for the rape and torture of underaged boys. There are eight others. Each is signed by you; each includes your handwritten notes."

Rowland stared at it. He looked up at Michael. "Where did you get these confidential records?"

"In the boxes Canon Land directed me to," Michael said. "It was a storage unit, not far from here. There were some 35 boxes of records in all, from all over Britain."

"Those records are stolen property!" Rowland said, almost shouting.

"Those records were in the keeping of Canon Land," Michael said. "He left an explanation of why he had to move them. He said you had suggested that he arrange for their destruction."

"I did no such thing," the archbishop said.

"He taped your conversation, archbishop," Michael said. "In fact, he taped several of your conversations, including all of the ones with Mr. Venneman here, and he left copies in the storage unit. The originals he donated to the British Library, to be made public in two years. They are officially designated as materials from the Church of England historical collection. And, somehow, you authorized the designations with your signature."

"I will fight this outrage," Rowland said. "This is preposterous! All of this is made up."

"Canon Land also signed a statement," Michael said, "giving me, as the head of the Church of England, full control over these records. I turned them over to Scotland Yard. As we speak, two archbishops, four bishops, and an additional 120 priests are being arrested. And that's the total for today. More are coming tomorrow and Friday."

Frees extracted a handheld tape player from his jacket and flipped it on. The conversation was between Land, Rowland, and Venneman, discussing how to contain the damage of the revelations concerning three priests in Suffolk. Frees stopped the tape.

"This means nothing," Rowland said, but both Frees and Michael could see that he was now sweating. "A half-wit defense attorney could make mincemeat of all of this."

Frees extracted a photograph from the folder he was carrying and handed it to Rowland.

"It's from the website," Frees said. "You'll recognize the priest in the photo. It's the Rev. Channing, being assisted by Rev. Wickham. And I'm sure you're at least familiar with the website, since there is a description of it in your handwriting on two of Channing's personnel records."

"So, this is what it is, is it?" Rowland said. "I sign the resignation, this gets destroyed, and the police go away."

"No," said Frees. "This is the deal. You sign the resignation and we arrest you. We don't release the address and password for the website, and your handwritten notes about it, to the news media."

"Make no mistake, Rowland, you're finished," said Michael. "You're being arrested whether or not you sign anything. You've helped destroy children's lives. You've brought dishonor upon God's church, which will not likely survive this disaster. Nor should it, if it allows people like you to flourish. You protected child rapists and torturers when you should have been protecting those children. This isn't a matter of conservative or liberal theology, Rowland. This is a matter of keeping predators away from children."

"Don't sign anything," the attorney said.

Rowland looked at him, and then addressed Michael. "I have your word that you will not release the information about the website?"

"Archbishop!" said the attorney.

"You haven't seen the website, sir," Michael said to the attorney. "Mr. Rowland obviously has. In fact, he has lots of friends starring in it." He looked at Rowland. "You have my word, and the word of Detective-Inspector Frees here." Frees nodded in agreement.

Geoffrey Venneman cleared his throat. "If you'll excuse me, I need to leave for another appointment."

"Ah. Mr. Venneman," Detective Frees said. "I'm afraid you'll need to postpone your appointment, as you are to accompany me to Scotland Yard. Officially, you are helping the police with their inquiries, which will be our statement to the news media." One of the policemen standing near the door nodded at Venneman and led him from the room.

Rowland gave Michael a look of blazing hatred, and then signed the resignation letter. He threw the pen on the desk and handed the paper to Michael. "I'm not the only archbishop involved, you know. You might be more than a little surprised, your majesty, to learn who else is involved."

"I know who's involved, Rowland," Michael said quietly. "He's also being arrested today."

Frees stepped forward. "Sebastian Rowland, I arrest you on the charges of accessory after the fact of child molestation, accessory to forcible sodomy, conspiracy to conceal a crime…"

Michael turned and left.

In the car back to the palace, Michael considered what was going to be happening to the church. Frees had told him that a press conference would be held at Scotland Yard at 11:30, announcing the arrests and the expectation that more were coming.

By 10:15, Michael was in the library, seated with Trevor Barry, Josh Gittings, and Jay Lanham. He explained what had just happened, the other arrests being made, and what would be coming on Thursday and Friday. He could see the shock on the faces of all three men.

"The Archbishop of Canterbury?" Jay said, almost incredulously.

"It's going to rock Parliament and Downing Street," Josh said. "Your majesty, I know the reform proposals are important, but I think we're going to need to consider that Parliament might enact whatever's at hand to try to look responsive to this. And what's at hand are your proposals and variations of them. We need to slow them down, to make sure the best proposals are lifted from the soup, and what new considerations need to be made in light of everything that's happening. I'll talk to Rodgers Clarke. He's been the leading voice for church reform, and he'll be in the best position to calm his colleagues, especially those of my former party affiliation."

"Yes," Michael said, "that's a wise move. We want Parliament to vote reform for the church, but we need the right kind of reform, not some desperate attempt to avoid potential voter wrath."

"Sir," Jay said, "we'll start working on statements and responses. The news media will come here, and some kind of press conference may be required. I'll talk this through with the staff, and get Jonathan working on a statement. He's already been drafting some things you might say, but I don't think we anticipated all of what you've just explained."

"Jay," Michael said, "to the fullest extent possible, I'd like my role in all of this downplayed, and the role of Detective Frees, Scotland Yard, and police agencies all over Britain to be highlighted and commended. They're the ones doing the really hard work."

"Yes," Jay said, as he took notes, "I've got it."

"Trevor," Michael said, "I need you to call the study committee. We will have to revamp everything, and we need them to be part of a larger group. Jay, we'll likely need to say something about this in the statement but keep it general and don't cite any members' names. Trevor, if you think you need to call an emergency meeting of the committee, I leave the decision in your hands."

"Your majesty," said Trevor, "the normal thing to name a replacement for an archbishop and bishop position is that Downing Street draws up a list of recommendations and then meets with the monarch to work out details and the timing of an announcement. These things are usually handled over a period of months, after a church leader gives notice of an intent to retire or his term is ending. What we're dealing with here is rather unprecedented."

"Is that the law or is that standard practice?" Michael said.

"It's historical practice," Trevor said, "but it's been more than a century of being exactly that way."

"Joshua," Michael said, "can you call the PM or the Home Secretary and say I'm aware of the historical practice for naming new archbishops and bishops, but that I need to be directly involved in whom we appoint. We are not in a state of normal, and we're going to have to take whatever steps necessary to save the church. I expect the steps to be drastic, and we're going to have to move quickly. And also, tell him that my preference for Archbishop of Canterbury is Paul Nkane of Nigeria."

He looked at the group collectively. "So, are these our immediate steps?" Michael said. "One, get Rodgers Clarke to slow and likely change the proposals in Parliament. Two, work out a statement and an overall communications plan. Three, contact the study

committee on church reform. And four, talk to the PM about how

we'll find and make appointments."

Heads nodded around the table.

"Your majesty," said Gittings, "should you call Archbishop

Nkane in Nigeria and let him know what's happening? Not offer him

the position yet, but to let him know?"

"He's likely the key to communicating with and holding the

Anglican communion together," Barry said. "At least the conservative

branches, outside of North America and Australia."

"Yes," Michael said, "that's a good suggestion. I'll call him

when we're finished here. Is there anything else that we need to attend

to right now?"

"One thing, your majesty," Trevor said. "How are you bearing

up under all of this?"

"I wish it were all over, Trev," Michael said. "I wish it were

over and done with, instead of being right at the beginning. I'm

bearing up, but I would appreciate prayers from any and all of you."

He looked at his watch. "And now I have to leave to attend to my

tsarist duties at City Hall. I'll call Paul Nkane from the car."

For three days, he had been calling Canon Land's mobile, and finding it went directly to voicemail. He had even called Lambeth Palace and asked to be connected to Land but had been told that Canon Land wasn't available and wouldn't likely be for several days.

He had stopped watching television; he simply couldn't bear the reports piling up of arrested priests and bishops. He could feel the fear building. He had even tried reaching King Michael at the palace. He got as far as Myra Frobisher, who told him she would give the king the message but that he was overwhelmed with doing both London and palace work.

"I know you're on his list of calls to be forwarded immediately," Myra told him, "but he's in so many meetings that it's not possible. I will let him know that you need to talk with him urgently."

And so, he sat, feeling like he was waiting for the inevitable. He had no records to shred or burn, since all records had been centralized in London.

He was staring out of the window when he heard voices outside the office, followed by a knock at the door. A detective and two uniformed officers walked in.

In the courtyard of Lambeth Palace, Michael entered the security car and immediately called Paul Nkane in Lagos. He was surprised at how quickly Nkane got to the phone.

Michael explained what was happening, and he said that there were more revelations coming.

"Archbishop," he said, "I will be calling upon you for help. We're looking at extensive networks of abusers, linked by dioceses, regions, and even three seminaries."

"Your majesty," Nkane said, "may I ask which seminaries?"

"Only one is being announced today, and its head arrested," Michael said, "and that's St. Simon's. The arrests at the seminaries near Cardiff and Glasgow will happen tomorrow."

"Sir," Nkane said, "I do not wish to be the bearer of bad tidings, but Scotland Yard may need to consider a broader investigation."

"Broader?" Michael said.

"Yes," Nkane said. "St. Simon's and Cardiff were feeder seminaries for churches in North America and Australia. Because church attendance was declining in Britain, seminary graduates were often sent to where churches were growing. It started some 20 years ago and hasn't stopped, except more are sent now to parishes in Asia, South America, and a few to Africa. We have generally been able to staff our churches in Africa with men trained at seminaries in Kenya and Nigeria. While you were not a seminary graduate, you yourself were part of that so-called 'sending out' when you went to California."

"Have you heard of things happening in North America or elsewhere?" Michael said.

"There have been rumors, sir," Nkane said. "And I have heard of specific cases in Canada where a few priests were arrested over the years."

"Archbishop," Michael said, "I will inform Scotland Yard. And we may need your help even more than I realized."

Traffic was heavy, and Michael realized that he was about to miss the start of the press conference announcing the arrests. He pulled up the BBC on his mobile. The press conference was about to begin, and it was being televised live.

The press briefing room at Scotland Yard was packed. Frees entered from a door at the side of the room and walked to the podium.

"Good morning. I am Detective-Inspector Roger Frees, and I am the detective in charge of the investigation into the clergy abuse case involving the Church of England.

"This morning, we went to Lambeth Palace and arrested Sebastian Rowland, Archbishop of Canterbury, for his role in covering up and facilitating what we have determined is an extensive network of pedophiles occupying clerical positions at all levels in the Church of England. Also today, two other archbishops were arrested, along with five bishops, the head of St. Simon's Seminary, and approximately 200 priests around Britain. That will bring the total arrested so far to about 300.

"We expect more arrests to occur over the next several days. How many is unknown, as the investigation is continuing. I can say that we consider the investigation to still be in its very early stages.

"We've had broad and deep cooperation from police jurisdictions around the country. We could not have made the progress we have without their involvement and help. And it has meant we have been able to stop the abuse and degradation of children much more quickly than we could have hoped. Our sincere gratitude goes to the police officers and superintendents; we owe them a debt, and we continue to owe them a debt as their efforts are still underway.

"I need to express my thanks to someone else, and that's King Michael. As I stated at our first press briefing, the king had my office involved within minutes of understanding that a child had been abused. But he has done far more, and we would not be where we are in the investigation without his complete and voluntary help. There were witnesses who would speak only to the king, and he made himself available to hear their stories and then have them talk with us. Evidence was placed in his hands, and he immediately turned it over to the investigation. When we had questions about clerical operations, he answered them.

"Without King Michael's timely intervention and support, we likely never would have learned that networks of pedophiles were operating within the Church of England. They were well-disguised and covered up, and they had been covered up and hidden for decades. Records had been kept and hidden, and we were able to locate them only because of King Michael.

"Let me repeat that our investigative efforts are ongoing. Please keep that in mind as this briefing continues. I'll now accept your questions."

Michael's car had finally reached City Hall. The Security officer in the front seat jumped out and opened Michael's door, and Michael made his way to the Embankment entrance. As he exited the elevator and began to walk toward his conference room office, the Security officer at his side, people in the hallways stopped and nodded. Michael noticed a pervasive quiet.

Within minutes, Eleanor Whitmire arrived with mail and papers to be signed. She gave a tight smile and made a slight curtsy, and then spoke.

"We watched the press conference at Scotland Yard, your majesty," she said. "I want to thank you for what you've done." She paused. "My sister's youngest, my nephew, had been abused by the priest at their church. It was covered up. They transferred the priest somewhere else, away from London."

"Ms. Whitmire," Michael said, "I am so very deeply sorry."

"He got into trouble as a teenager," she said. "My sister and brother-in-law struggled with him. They tried counseling, pills, everything." She teared up. "He killed himself when he was 21." She looked away as she composed herself. "If people had had your courage and determination then, he might have been saved. Thank you for helping to bring this to light and stopping it."

She left the room. Michael sat stunned. *How many times we will hear these stories? Hundreds? Thousands?*

Before he did anything else, he sent a text to Detective Frees, relaying what Paul Nkane had told him.

Chapter 18: Once More into the Breach

The media reaction to the disclosures at the press briefing was enormous. When Detective Frees called for questions at the briefing, he at first had pandemonium on his hands, with reporters shouting from all sides. The story had been already receiving extensive media coverage, but the press briefing took the coverage into the stratosphere. News media around the world were reporting the story of the arrest of the Archbishop of Canterbury and the pedophile network uncovered in the Church of England.

The communications office at Buckingham Palace was, for a time, almost under siege. Reporters were asking for information and for interviews with the king. At City Hall, security guards faced the onslaught in the building lobby; two reporters were caught sneaking up the stairs, trying to reach Michael on the executive floor. At 5 p.m., with large crowds gathered around City Hall to catch a glimpse of Michael, Ryan Mitchell at the palace had to supplement the regular guards at City Hall and the police with his security agents, forcing a way through the thick mob of people for the king to reach the waiting car.

The story quickly reverberated across the villages, towns and cities of Britain. It was most intense in England and Wales, but

Scotland and Northern Ireland were close behind. Protests erupted at police stations where arrested priests and bishops were being held; police officers in several towns and cities had trouble maintaining order. Arsons were reported at numerous vicarages; the Bishop of Norfolk arrived home from a luncheon to see a large crowd throwing rocks at his windows.

When several priests were caught attempting to board planes and ferries for Ireland and France, Scotland Yard had to institute identity check procedures, slowing boat and air traffic. Two priests on the arrest list were found hiding in the back of a lorry preparing to leave on the Chunnel train.

To be a Church of England priest had become a dangerous occupation, even for the innocent and those who had nothing to do with the abuse. By the following Sunday, virtually every C of E Church, including London's great cathedrals, stood empty of worshippers. The only exceptions were Southwark Cathedral and the other churches where Michael had preached; their attendance remained normal. While it was coincidental that none of churches where Michael had preached had priests involved in the scandal, people believed that if Michael had preached at a church, then it must be safe.

London's non-denominational and non-C of E churches experienced greater than average attendance.

After the press briefing, when Frees saw Michael's text message, he went immediately to the large conference room where a team of 10 officers were poring over Canon Land's personnel records and the personnel files seized from St. Simon's Seminary.

"We have a new development," he told the group. "Check for any Anglican priest from Britain who may have been transferred or stationed at churches in Canada, the United States, and Australia. I believe we've been setting those aside to focus on domestic cases. We have a credible report that the network may well be international. This will likely be more connected to the St. Simon's files. And the files from the seminary at Cardiff are due here this afternoon. We need to check those for international connections as well."

He returned to his office and was soon meeting with the Yard branch responsible for international police liaisons.

When Michael arrived at the palace at 6, the car had to travel slowly through the large crowd that had gathered. People applauded and cheered as the car moved through and finally entered the gates.

Exiting the car in the palace courtyard at the main arrival portico, he found Josh and Jay waiting for him.

"Meeting time?" Michael said, with a faint smile.

"The PM and Home Secretary are here, sir," said Josh. "They arrived a few minutes ago."

"Right," said Michael, who wanted nothing more than a glass of wine and an easy chair to sit in.

"We tried to get word via your mobile," Jay said, "but the London exchanges have been overwhelmed with phone and text traffic since about 2 p.m. We tried calling City Hall but had the same problem. The news about the church has everyone on their mobiles and landlines."

"Trevor is with them, sir," Gittings said. "It's about the church; Peter wants to move as quickly as they can, both in Parliament and with the archbishop and bishop appointments. But I think he also wants something else."

"Like what?" Michael said, as they ascended the stairs to the state room level.

"He didn't say," Jay said, "but we think he wants you to address the nation. Not tonight, but certainly by tomorrow night. There's been violence in several places, and the police are finding their hands full with demonstrations and protests, not to mention vandalism and personal attacks."

They walked to the White Drawing Room, where the PM and Home Secretary were talking with Trevor Barry.

"Prime Minister, Mr. Hawksworth, it's good to see you both," Michael said.

"Your majesty," Bolting said, he and Thomas Hawksworth both bowing their heads.

At that moment, Brent Epworth arrived with two of the kitchen staff, pushing a drink and snacks cart. "Sir, Mr. Malone in the kitchen thought you and your guests might need some refreshment. There's cheese and fruit, and water, soft drinks, beer and wine. He said to tell you the Chardonnay was particularly good."

Michael grinned. "Bless Mr. Malone. Please tell our palace chef his efforts are greatly appreciated." Epworth poured drinks, handed Michael a glass of the Chardonnay, and left with the two staffers, closing the door behind him.

"This is a treat," Peter Bolting said, sipping his wine.

"This is a most welcome treat," Michael said, spearing a piece of cheese with a skewer. "I haven't eaten since breakfast."

"Your majesty," Bolting said, "we'll get to the point. Josh here told us that he connected with Rodgers Clarke, and everyone agrees to slow walk church reform in Parliament until we get a clearer picture of what's unfolding from Scotland Yard. I fully support that, but I don't want to wait too long before bringing forth some comprehensive reform proposals. Public pressure is going to build fast, and we need to be ready."

"I've thought about that, prime minister," Michael said. "What I suggest we work toward are broad reform policies. And then we can appoint teams or commissions to draft the tactics and the details. Parliament can pass the broad policy changes in a timely manner, addressing public pressure for change, and then we can get into the details to make those policies work. That's going to take time, and we need time to do it right."

"That is an excellent approach," Bolting said. He smiled. "Have you considered a career in Parliament?"

Michael laughed. "No. I have my hands quite full at the moment."

"Who should we work with on the reform policies?" the Home Secretary said.

Michael looked at Josh and then Trevor, and then turned to Hawksworth. "Thomas, Joshua is the obvious point man for parliamentary considerations and plans. For the substance of the reform policies, I would like you to work with Trevor here. He leads my church reform study group, and he's turned himself into something of an expert in ecclesiastical law and church history in the past few months. He's already an expert on monarchial law. Trevor will be my point man for the substance of the proposals, and Joshua will work with you on parliamentary strategy."

If Trevor Barry showed any surprise, his face didn't show it. He did feel his ears warming, and he wondered if they were turning red. It was a huge responsibility the king was putting on his shoulders; it was also a measure of the trust Michael had in him.

"Next," Bolting said, "the appointments. I understand you have someone in mind for Archbishop of Canterbury."

"Yes," Michael said, "I do. Paul Nkane, Archbishop of Nigeria. He is separated from the crisis unfolding right now. He received his seminary training in Kenya. His bishops in Nigeria are all nationals. He's also a brilliant theologian and highly respected, especially among the conservative wing of the Anglican Communion. My church in San Francisco was affiliated with the Archdiocese of Nigeria. He is also fearless and strong-speaking. Most importantly, he is known for his heart for God."

"He sounds just the ticket, sir," the PM said. "The usual process is for Downing Street, meaning my office, to send him the invitation to accept the position. It's also part of the process for you to call him first with the verbal offer. If you like, you can talk with him, and if he agrees, announce his appointment jointly with us, even tomorrow if that's convenient. Then we'll send the written invitation."

"That works for me, prime minister," Michael said, "assuming Paul accepts. If it were me in his position, I'd want to think long and hard about the mess I was stepping into."

"And what of the other positions?" Bolting said.

"We need to wait," Michael said. "From what I know, and from what Detective Frees has told me, Scotland Yard is still determining who's involved. We don't want to appoint a new bishop only to see him arrested the next day. So, while part of me wants to move quickly, to demonstrate that we have the situation in hand, I want to avoid appointing the wrong people. There's an additional consideration. I would like the new Archbishop of Canterbury to be involved; much of that hierarchy will report to him."

"That's eminently sensible, your majesty," Bolting said. "We support that completely. Now, I have one more item to discuss. Would you consider an address to the nation, even as early as tomorrow night? I ask this for several reasons. The people need reassurance. They know the Yard is tackling the pedophile issue, but no one knows at this point what will happen to the church. We still don't know how many arrests may lie ahead."

"This wasn't told to me in confidence," Michael said, "but it needs to be considered that way. Some 300 people have now been arrested; the Yard thinks, looking at the records they have, that the ultimate number may be in the 2,000 to 2,500 range. That's both active priests and people in the church hierarchy. That doesn't include retired priests who may be implicated. We currently have about 9,000 active Anglican clergy, to give some perspective."

For a moment, no one spoke. Even Michael's people hadn't heard the estimated number.

Bolting took a rather large gulp of his wine. "I had no idea. The implications of that are staggering."

Michael nodded. "The number implies that the church may collapse. Most of the hierarchy will likely be implicated. They can't help but be. That's why I want to delay any appointments other than Paul Nkane. We may have a serious shortage of candidates."

"This is all the more reason for a public address from you, your majesty," the PM said. "You may be able to find a way to prepare the public for what's coming. And I might suggest that, right now, you are the only person the public will have reason to trust in this matter."

"All right," Michael said. "I'll do it. Jay, can you make the arrangements with the BBC for tomorrow night, say at 8 p.m.? And is Jonathan still here?"

"Yes, sir," Jay said, "I asked him to stay on for a bit."

"Tell him I will come to his office as soon as we're finished here," Michael said. Jay immediately sent a text to Jonathan via his mobile.

Michael stood, and the rest of the group followed.

"Trevor and Joshua, both of you and I will need to talk tomorrow," Michael said. "I have a pretty full schedule at City Hall, but lunch is free; perhaps we can do a conference call. I also need to call Paul Nkane." He turned to Bolting and smiled, extending his hand. "Mission accomplished prime minister?"

"Yes, sir, and thank you," Bolting said, shaking Michael's hand. "None of us really knew what we were asking when we asked you to accept this job last year, did we?"

"That includes me, prime minister," Michael said. "But God knew, and He will see us through this."

After the PM and the Home Secretary left, and Trevor and Josh headed for the tube and home, Jay walked with Michael to Jonathan Crowe's office.

"I wanted to mention something to you, sir," Jay said. "We haven't told anyone yet, but Alia Mahmoud and I are engaged." Alia was the construction manager who had overseen the remodeling of the royal family's living quarters; she was now tackling renovation of several other royal properties.

Michael stopped, a huge smile on his face. "That is wonderful news! Congratulations!" He hugged Jay. "I can't tell you how pleased I am."

"We're thinking of a winter wedding, likely in January, perhaps right after Twelfth Night," Jay said. "And we were wondering if you might conduct the ceremony?"

"I would be honored, my friend," Michael said. They walked on to talk with Jonathan.

For 15 minutes, the king and Jay sat in Jonathan's office, Michael talking and Jay and Jonathan asking the occasional question. Jonathan was both taping the conversation and furiously taking notes.

When they had finished talking over the substance of the address, Michael posed a question.

"Jonathan," he said, "I know this will likely be inconvenient, but can you work on the address at City Hall tomorrow? I have to be there, and my schedule is mostly full, but if you're actually there, we can talk through questions, practice a bit, and make any changes we need to. You can sit and work in the conference room with me, and I'll ask Eleanor to connect you to a printer."

"Yes, sir," Jonathan said, "I'll go straight there in the morning."

"I'll arrive at 8:30 and meet you in the lobby," Michael said. "Then you can ride with me at 5 back to the palace, and we can make any final changes we need. I hate to eat into your free time, and this plus the address itself tomorrow night will make for rather a long day."

"It's fine, sir," Jonathan said. "This is something vitally important."

"Thank you," Michael said. "I'll see you at 8:30 at City Hall."

That evening, the family, Robert, and the Jenner children sat at the dinner table, Sarah asking Jason and Jim how school had gone. Robert had also started back that day, while the Jenners had remained at the palace.

"Robert?" she said.

He smiled. "It was good, ma'am. Everyone's been super."

Jason's mobile rang. "It's Jane," he said, and dashed to the living room.

"Some of our lives are obviously returning to normal," Sarah said.

"Girls," said Jim, shaking his head.

"Elton," Sarah said, "I'll be accompanying you, Amanda, and Nicholas to the funeral service tomorrow. Your grandparents called and said your mother's been discharged from the hospital. She's doing much better, and your grandparents will be staying with you for a while to help."

"Yes, ma'am," Elton said. "Thank you for having us here."

"And when you return to school," Sarah said, "I suspect you'll find a warm welcome."

"Robert," said Michael, "we have to think about your future."

The boy nodded. "I know, sir. I know I can't stay here forever. But you've all been great."

"Well, you could stay here forever," Michael said, "and we'd be pleased to have you, but another possibility has come up."

Robert looked at him.

"Today, I met with Detective-Inspector Frees," Michael said. "And he raised something with me and asked me to raise it with you."

The boy looked at him expectantly.

"He and his wife have never had children," Michael said. "She's a doctor, by the way, a pediatrician. And they wondered if you might consider being part of their family. I told them I would talk with you. And it's likely something you want to think about. He asked me to talk with you first so that if you decided it wasn't a good idea, then you'd feel free to say no."

Robert looked from Michael to Sarah, and then back at Michael. "I know my mother's not coming back, sir. I think I understand that. Does Mrs. Frees know about, well, about me being HIV positive?"

"Yes, Robert, she does," Michael said.

"And that doesn't scare her?" Robert said.

"It worries her like it would worry any mother," Michael said. "But she's a doctor, Robert, and she knows exactly what it does and doesn't mean. And she'd know how to help you deal with it."

Robert was silent for a moment. "They don't mind what's happened to me, sir, I mean, the things that were done?"

"Robert, Detective-Inspector Frees told me today that he would be proud to call you his son."

Sarah watched Robert with tears in her eyes.

"I'd like to meet with them, sir," Robert said. "I'd want them to be sure."

"I think they'll be thrilled to meet with you, Robert," Michael said. "They're waiting on me to call, in fact. I'll call now, and we'll get something set up."

Richard Jenner was buried on Thursday morning. Shortly before Sarah and the Jenner children left for the service, Michael received a call from Frees. Elton's blood tests had all been negative.

Sarah arrived with the Jenner children to attend the short service at a small nondenominational church near their home and not far from St. Thomas Church.

Edith Jenner had been discharged from the hospital early Wednesday morning. Her parents were staying with her. When she saw her children arrive at the church, she opened her arms, and the three ran to her. She held on to Elton the longest.

After the service, she walked up to Sarah.

"You and the king have blessed my children, your majesty," she said. "I can never thank you enough for what you've done."

Sarah put her arm around her. "Mrs. Jenner, they're wonderful children. You need to be proud of all of them. And they need you now more than they ever have before."

Edith nodded. "I've decided to continue with the business. That's how I met Richard, when he was a salesman and I was a secretary. I know the car business, or the basics of it, and I can learn the rest."

Sarah smiled. "That's great news. And the children want to return to school tomorrow."

She nodded. "They'll be fine. I saw the tape on TV."

Edith stepped forward to curtsy, and Sarah stopped her, and then hugged her. Edith turned and walked back to her children.

On Friday morning, when Edith dropped her children off at ICS, she and they saw the banner stretched across the entrance. "Jenners Rock! Welcome Home!"

She drove to the Lexus dealership. Sales people and staff stood as she came in. She spoke a few words to let them know that the business was going forward, and she would need all of their help and support. And they applauded in both support and relief.

She walked to Richard's office, took off her coat and set her purse on the desk. She looked around for a few moments, and then sat at his desk, and began to look through papers.

Two hours later, she found the combination to the wall safe in a folder. She opened it, and discovered the letters addressed to her and the children.

For a moment she stared at them. She considered destroying them. She finally opened the one addressed to her.

When she'd finished, she looked up and out the window. *So, this is where he came on Saturday night.* And she smiled. What

Richard had never been able to say to her in life he had said in death. But he'd said it.

Edith turned back to the desk and continued to work.

Michael and Jonathan were in the conference room at City Hall. Michael had had back-to-back meetings on his schedule all morning; Jonathan had been working on his laptop. In between meetings, the two discussed specific policy proposals and what elements of the scandal could be included, and what needed to be omitted because of the ongoing investigation. Jonathan also listened in during the discussion Michael had with Josh and Trevor on the phone while eating lunch in the conference room. They talked through the basis for the broad policy reforms that would eventually become parliamentary legislation. Josh told Michael that Bolting had spoken for well over an hour in the House of Commons that morning, explaining and answering questions about what was happening with the scandal, and saying that the king would be addressing the nation.

The broad concepts they discussed included a gradual removal of the church from the national budget, essentially making churches dependent upon non-government resources, especially parishioners; moving away from the episcopal form of church government and toward a more Presbyterian, lay-leader-led form, including at the national level; parish consolidations; consolidation of seminaries from the current seven to two, with the implementation of lay-leader-led boards of overseers; elimination of all national church commissions under the jurisdiction of the archbishops; adding to the number of cathedrals reporting directly to the king; and a sale of all church properties associated with consolidated parishes or what was known as "non-church real estate." All investments of the national church would be scrutinized, and a fund would be created for restitution to victims where possible.

Jonathan would work all of these elements into the draft of Michael's address, keeping the initiatives and changes as broad as possible.

One morning meeting had had to be rescheduled, and Michael used the extra time to call and talk with Paul Nkane, asking him to accept the position of Archbishop of Canterbury. Jonathan, working in the room, heard only Michael's side of the conversation, but he was able to use a lot of what the king was saying for the address.

Paul Nkane accepted, and Michael sent texts to Josh, Jay, and Trevor, asking Josh to let the PM's office know that Nkane's acceptance would be included in the television address.

Right as he rang off with the group at the palace, Eleanor
Whitmire stepped into the room.

"Your majesty, Detective-Inspector Frees is on line 2," she
said.

Michael picked up the phone. "Yes, sir?"

"Your majesty," Frees said, "the arrest was made yesterday
morning, and he was brought to London. We have him in custody here
in the holding cells at the Yard. The official charges are accessory
after the fact and conspiracy. There are some 10 or so counts for each
charge right now, and I expect more will be added later."

"Is it possible for me to see him?" Michael said.

"Yes, sir," Frees said. "I don't know what your schedule is, but
tomorrow morning would likely be a good time, possibly about 8:30.
We can arrange something else if that's not convenient."

Michael glanced at his calendar. "No, Detective-Inspector, I
think that will work fine. I'll come to the Yard."

"I'll be waiting, sir," Frees said. "And sir?"

"Yes?"

"Sylvia and I are looking forward to lunch on Saturday."

"So is Robert," Michael said. "And so are we."

Right before Michael and Jonathan left at 5, Jonathan printed two copies of the revised draft. In the car, Michael read and made comments and a few revisions, and Jonathan followed along with his copy of the text.

As they reached Westminster Bridge, Jonathan heard Michael sigh.

"I think we've got it, Jonathan," Michael said. "I know I've worked you to the bone today, but I think we're there. It's everything I want to say and everything I can say."

"When we get to the palace, sir," Jonathan said, "I'll make these changes and print the new version. Do you want to use a teleprompter or speak from the text?"

"Let's go with the text approach," Michael said. "We've gone through it so many times that I'm close to having memorized it. I'll likely speak from the text."

"Afterward, I'll be in the communications office with Jay," Jonathan said. "I'll be editing the transcript and working from the final text version, for posting on the website. Jay feels it's important to have it public as soon as possible, so that there is an official text."

They had reached the point where The Mall meets Constitution Hill, and palace security guards were removing barriers to allow the king's car to move through the gates.

"I can't thank you enough for your work," Michael said. "I almost feel as if you've crawled inside my head."

"It's my job, sir," said Jonathan. "And history is happening here. It's a lot of work, yes, but it's an honor to work with you on this."

Michael had yet to occupy his new office, but Jay, working with Brent Epworth, decided to use it for Michael's address. The BBC film crew had arrived at 3 p.m. to set up equipment, check lighting, and do sound checks. Jay subbed for Michael as the model. A monitoring station was set up in the office next to the king's, and this is where Jay, Jonathan, and Josh would stand with the BBC producer and various technicians to watch the address.

Epworth, working with Davey Malone in the kitchen, had a food buffet station set up nearby for both Michael's staff and the BBC crew. Katie Shields, Jay's deputy communications officer responsible for online content, was in the communications office with two other staffers, finalizing the post for the king's website and preparing for the simultaneous posting on the primary social media sites.

As soon as Michael finished his address, a new section on the site would go live, and include the text of the address, a summary of the major policy proposals, background on Paul Nkane, and short biographies of the 12 people serving on the king's church study team, including Trevor Barry. The communications staff had already filmed a video of Trevor talking about the team's work to date, and what would be happening going forward. At Michael's request, Katie had also added a comment section, for visitors to post their comments and suggestions. Jay had spent a considerable part of the day making initial media contacts and preparing background materials for the media.

Michael had a quiet dinner with Sarah, the children, and Robert. Joan Plunkett had joined them, and she was addressing the hunger needs of one Prince Henry. Jason and Robert both knew that Michael would shortly be making one of the most important speeches he had ever made and would likely ever make, and both kept giving him what they thought were covert looks. Michael could feel the tension and concern radiating from Sarah.

"It's okay," Michael said to Jason and Robert. "It's a speech. An important one, I admit. But you don't have to keep looking at me like I've just sprouted a third eye."

The two boys laughed.

"And, my beautiful wife," Michael said, "I'm concerned, too, and a wee bit nervous, so you can relax."

"They're just worried," Jim said, spearing a forkful of salad.

"Should I feel hurt that you don't seemed to be concerned a bit, Young Jim?" Michael said.

"Nah," Jim said. "You'll do great. You always do great. You can't cook, but everything else is great."

Michael laughed.

"It's true," Jim said. "Remember what you did to the omelet the first night we lived in the new loft in San Francisco? It was burned so black you threw the pan out with the omelet, so nobody would know."

At that, the laughter became general, with even Ms. Plunkett laughing so hard she got the hiccups.

"Is that why the frying pan was always the odd man out in your cooking pot set?" Sarah said.

"I don't remember," Michael said. "I plead amnesia."

"Well," said Jim, "I don't plead amnesia. And I remember you went and got us Chinese takeout."

"I think it's time for me to get ready for my talk," Michael said. "I hope the British listeners are more sympathetic. Obviously, this crowd cuts no slack."

Sarah walked with him to his office.

"My husband, God has put you in this place to do his work," she said. "And when you honor God, you honor your family and your country."

He smiled at her, and she kissed him. And then she returned to the family loft to watch the broadcast with the boys and Mrs. Plunkett.

The BBC staff had moved expertly to set up the recording equipment in Michael's office. They also had assistance from Myra Frobisher, who was threatening death to anyone who messed up the new furnishings.

Michael came in and was seated at the desk. Behind him was a credenza with family pictures; on the wall was a painting Sarah had done of the three boys seated, with Jason holding Hank and Jim standing with his arm on Jason's shoulder. It was so realistic that it looked almost like a photograph.

A young woman came and dabbed Michael's nose and face with a very light powder. The cameraman checked and said the powder had removed the glare on his face.

"We're set," the cameraman said.

"Three minutes to broadcast," the news producer said. "I'll be next door, watching from the monitor."

Only three people were left in the room: the cameraman, the lighting man, and Michael.

The countdown was beginning.

"Five, four, three, two, one, we're live, go," the producer said, over a microphone from the room next door.

Michael began to speak.

"Good evening. Prime Minister Bolting has asked me, as head of the Church of England, to talk with you tonight about both the scandal that has engulfed our church and what we're doing about it, as well as the outlook for the church longer term.

"The last 10 days have been very hard. The revelations about child abuse have rocked us all. More than 250 priests, five bishops, and three archbishops have been arrested, and the police investigation is still in its early stages. I need to emphasize that. The investigation has just begun. We should expect to see more arrests, across a larger geography, and more revelations. The horror is not over.

"It's a horror with many dimensions. Unable to face disclosure, two priests of the church have committed suicide. Others have been arrested, trying to flee responsibility. The Archbishop of Canterbury is in police custody, charged with collusion and cover-up. People I knew, or thought I knew, people I considered friends, are now charged with terrible crimes, accused themselves of harming children or aiding and abetting priests who harmed children.

"It is a dark night in the history of our church."

In the loft, Jason was the first to notice that Michael wasn't reading a text. "He's just speaking it, like he's memorized it. It's like when he opened Parliament." Sarah shushed him.

"As terrible as all of that is," Michael said, "it pales to nothing in comparison to what countless children and their families have suffered – and suffered for decades. Innocent children have been victimized by the very people they should have been able to trust. For some of these children, the abuse was short-lived and fleeting. For many, it went on for years. And just last Sunday, one father killed himself in a worship service, crazed by the mistaken belief he had allowed his child to be victimized. The horror that I feel, that we all feel, is still nothing compared to the horror and pain these children and their families have experienced.

"Many of these children are now adults. It is both a great tragedy and an outrage that the abuse was allowed to continue for decades. It should have been stopped when it happened. And it could have been stopped. But it wasn't, and the institution we know as the Church of England, its leaders, and its seminaries bear responsibility for that. While nothing we could do can erase what happened to these children, we must make restitution, wherever, whenever, and however possible. We are still working on details of what that might look like, and we will have an announcement within a few weeks.

"Parliament will shortly begin consideration of proposals for fundamental changes in the policies and structure of the Church of England. We don't know what the final laws will look like once enacted, but we know in substance what they will be.

"We will see an eventual reduction of government subsidies for the church, ending in complete financial separation.

"We will likely see the consolidation of parishes, and a significant one.

"We will see major changes in how parish churches are governed, including the active participation by lay leaders.

"We will see significant changes in the staffing of seminaries, and a consolidation of seminaries.

"We will see changes in the offices of bishop and archbishop.

"And we can expect to see a national board of lay leaders working with the archbishop of Canterbury to administer the church and help lead the Anglican communion.

"Every aspect of the church will experience profound change. That our church, a church of which I am an ordained priest, allowed child molesters to operate as freely as they did is unconscionable. And yet it is but one example of how our church has effectively abandoned its responsibilities for shepherding the flock entrusted to it by God.

"I want to emphasize that the Church is England is not by itself God's church. God's church is far larger. And I would ask God's church to pray for the children and their families, and for those who are now adults. And to pray for the future of the Church of England, because right now, God alone knows that future, or even if the Church of England has a future, which is very much open to question.

"Archbishop Paul Nkane of Lagos has graciously agreed to become the next Archbishop of Canterbury. I can't tell you how much of a personal sacrifice this is for anyone to accept the position at this time in the church's history. But he did, and I am personally thankful.

It will be his duty to help lead the Church of England through its transformation.

"He will be assisted by a team of 12 people who have accepted my invitation to examine the abuse scandal, to make recommendations for addressing it, and to do so quickly. And I've asked them to prayerfully consider the future of the Church of England, and what changes need to be made if the Church of England is to continue as a denomination of God's larger church. That team will report to me, and it will be chaired by Trevor Barry, an attorney and expert in how monarchial, parliamentary, and ecclesiastical law operate and intersect.

"I have assured Archbishop Nkane that he will have full freedom, and my full support, to make whatever changes are needed, within the policy changes to be established by Parliament. That includes staff, operations, commissions, properties, and policies. Our hope is that the Church of England will return to the only true base it has, and that is the teaching of God's Word and the shepherding of God's flock.

"For the vast majority of Britons who do not attend church of any kind, I believe this is your issue as well. What kind of Church of England eventually emerges will say much about who we are as a people and a nation. And I ask for your prayers, too.

"It is my hope that we will see a new Church of England, a reformed and reborn Church of England, one that teaches God's word, tends to his flock, and protects his children.

"Thank you."

Chapter 19: "I had to save the church!"

At 8:30 a.m. Friday, Michael arrived at Scotland Yard, accompanied by Paula Abbott from palace Security. Eleanor Whitmire at City Hall had been informed he wouldn't be in until 10:30. Frees was waiting for them at the entrance.

Michael still hadn't gotten used to the stir and reaction his presence could cause. As they walked through the lobby to the elevator bank, Michael's presence nearly stopped everyone. People bowed or curtsied. Many nodded, smiling.

Waiting for an elevator, Frees looked back at the people in the lobby, most of them being Scotland Yard officers arriving for work.

"Do you feel like you're always on parade?" Frees said.

"A bit," said Michael. "But it comes with the job. As long as it doesn't go to my head, it's OK."

Once on the elevator, they descended two floors to the holding cell section.

"What's happened to Mr. Venneman?" Michael said.

Frees chuckled. "He was scared to death he would be charged Wednesday. We interviewed him for six hours, he had a lawyer in, but he was fairly cooperative. We'd obtained a court warrant and seized a laptop he had at home as well as his work computer. It made for quite a scene at FBL; his boss was shouting about police brutality, but one of the officers said he heard her tell someone to fire Venneman immediately. My guess is that he may have to testify, but we will not likely charge him. But we will let him worry a bit." He laughed. "It's not his real name, 'Geoffrey Venneman,' that is. He amplified it a bit to make it sound more posh and upper class. His real name is Geoff Venn."

Exiting the elevator, they followed Frees down a hallway.

"He's with his attorney in a conference room that's part of the cell block, sir," Frees said. "They know you're coming. Ms. Abbott, we'll have to walk through the cells here to the other end where the conference room is, so don't be thrown by the comments. We have both white-collar and violent criminal types housed individually in these cells."

She nodded.

They entered the cell block, and the catcalls and lewd comments started immediately at the sight of the female security officer. And then they stopped just as suddenly when the inmates recognized the king. The inmates stood as Michael passed, surprising him and Frees. He gave each a short nod of his head and a slight smile.

Frees looked at one inmate, with a questioning look on his face. "Him we stand for," the inmate said. They followed the duty officer to the conference room.

"I suppose I must recognize the fact that these are my people as well," Michael said.

The duty officer opened the door to the conference room.

Philip Johnston, Archbishop of York, was sitting at the table. He was wearing the regulation orange jumpsuit and he was handcuffed. His attorney stood nearby.

Michael was struck by how old and frail the archbishop looked.

"Even in these circumstances, it's good to see you again, Father Michael," the archbishop said. "And I suppose I did it again, didn't I, calling you Father Michael. A habit I cannot seem to break. We always had the option to use 'father' instead of 'reverend,' and it always seemed to fit you better, as young as you were. And still are."

Michael looked around at the others. "If it's possible, I'd like to talk to the archbishop alone. Can we do that?"

Frees looked at Officer Abbott and the duty officer, who both nodded.

"I must insist that I remain with my client," the attorney said.

"John," the archbishop said, "you can stand outside for a few minutes. I seriously doubt the king is wired to record our conversation. And since I will plead guilty, it's not an issue even if he is."

"Archbishop!" the attorney reprimanded.

"Step outside, John," Johnston said. "The king and I go back too far for there to be any secrets between us."

They all filed out and Frees quietly closed the door. Michael sat at the table.

"So," the archbishop said. "Here we are." He paused. "As I would have expected, you have played a heroic role in all of this. They allowed us to watch the BBC broadcast last night. For those few moments, I forgot who I was and what I have done. All I could see was you taking charge and offering hope. The British people would likely elect you dictator-for-life if you asked them for that right now."

"You inspired me when I was a student," Michael said. "I heard you speak at that missions' conference, and you inspired me so much that I spent my summer in Malawi, and even wanted to do full-time mission service there."

Johnston acknowledged Michael's words with a slight tilt of his head.

"You were my sponsor for ordination," Michael said. "I wanted no one else."

Johnston kept looking at him, not speaking.

"You spoke for me when Parliament met to discuss offering me and Sarah the throne," Michael said.

"I would speak the same today," the Archbishop said.

"You supported me when I spoke for reformation."

"And I would do so again, Father Michael," Johnston said. He smiled. "I said it again."

"You crowned me king."

"It was the best moment of my entire ministry," Johnston said.

"And you've shuffled child molesters around virtually every parish in York," Michael said, "wrecking the lives of countless children and families. And for what?"

"We needed priests. I had to save the church," Johnston said.

"You had to save the church?" Michael said, shouting as he stood up. "How dare you sit there and say that! How dare you! Who named you savior of the church? God already has a savior, Archbishop. His name is Jesus Christ! Do you add idolatry to your list of crimes?"

Frees and the others in the hallway could hear Michael's words plainly through the door. The duty officer considered opening the door. Frees, recognizing what he was thinking, shook his head. "It's all right," Frees said.

"Yes, Father Michael, I suppose I must add idolatry to my list of crimes," Johnston said. "With that unerring instinct of yours, which you have demonstrated for as long as I have known you, you've nailed it precisely. I put myself in the place of Jesus Christ. And I brought down disaster upon the church and upon myself."

"So why? Can you tell me why?" Michael said, sitting down.

Johnston paused before answering. "I listened to my own rationalizing. We were short on priests, desperately short. And then we began finding that among those we did have there were a number of problems. We sent them to psychiatric counselors and to centers to cure addictions. And they would seem to be cured. But they weren't. They would seem healed for a time but then problems would start happening again. Their treatment never lasted. And we needed priests."

"Problems?" Michael said. "Archbishop, let's be precise. They were not problems. They were children. And these men were child rapists and torturers."

Johnston looked down at the table.

"How could you rationalize this?" Michael said. "Archbishop, I've had two young men staying with us at the palace. They're 16 years old. Their abuse has gone on for years. Archbishop, one of them was not only raped and abused repeatedly for years, he was tortured because the priest in question happened to be a sadist and practiced what he called his special little punishments. Do you want to hear the details? Would you like to hear what he did when he tied the boy down? Would you like to have been at St. Thomas Church when the boy's father, crazed with guilt for not protecting his son, blew his brains out in the worship service?"

"No, Father Michael," Johnston said.

"And the other boy, Archbishop, is HIV positive," Michael said. "He's 16 years old and he's HIV positive. By the way, he's the one whose chief abuser was Hugh Wickham. Does the name sound familiar? The one you shuffled among seven different parishes in York over a 12-year period before Rowland finally took him into London? This boy was raped, and sometimes gang raped, by ordained priests of the church you were so desperate to save."

Johnston didn't reply.

Michael felt spent. "So, can you tell me how this started? Where did this begin? How did you fall into this?"

Johnston looked up. "It was 30 years ago. I was a new priest, even if I was older than the norm for a new priest. I'd come to England for my theology training, and it was something unusual then to see a Nigerian priest in the Church of England. I was supposed to have been assigned to a parish in London, one where many African nationalities were living, to serve in a kind of mission outreach. But with no explanation, I was suddenly sent to a small parish in Yorkshire." He paused as he seemed to search his memory. "St. Timothy's, in western York."

He looked down at his handcuffed hands as he continued. "The Archbishop had suddenly removed the priest from the parish. He'd been there a little more than a year. I was not told why, but I replaced him. I learned later it was because legal action had started in his previous parish over a child being molested. But he was literally taken away in the middle of the night and brought to a sexual addiction center for treatment. I didn't know that until later."

"So, I arrived in this parish, and I was clearly out of place, the tall black Nigerian with his African accent among all the farmers and townspeople of a village in York. It was a very conservative place, and I was greeted with not a little suspicion.

"On the Thursday before my first worship service, we had practice. The choir would practice, the priest would practice, the altar boys would practice, and so on. We would run through the service, although it was mostly for the choir to rehearse. And we'd finished, and everyone dispersed to go home. Except for one altar boy. I didn't realize he had followed me back to the office. He must have been 11 or 12. I don't recall his name. He was a handsome child, with those high cheekbones that promised he would be a handsome man." Johnston's voice broke. "An almost irresistible target for a pedophile."

After a moment, he continued. "I only realized he was behind me when he closed the door. I turned, and he was undressing. And I asked him what he was doing. And he told me that he was serving God, that Father Frawley always had him come to the office after practice to serve God."

Michael couldn't contain his tears.

"I told him that was over," Johnston said. "I had him dress and go home. I called my bishop and asked him what to do. And he told me to do nothing. He said that this was being taken care of, and that there should be no lasting damage to the boy. When I protested, I was told to be obedient to my vow and to my superiors. And that's what I ultimately decided to do."

"You followed orders," Michael said.

"As you say, Father Michael, I followed orders," Johnston said. "Over time, as I rose in the hierarchy, I continued to follow orders. This was not a common thing to happen, but it was also not uncommon. And then one day I was signing those orders and giving those orders myself. I don't really know how many priests were involved, ultimately. Over a 30-year period, perhaps 50 or 60 out of 500 or so. But, clearly, too many. I know you will tell me that one was too many. But you do it enough, you rationalize it enough, and you end with what we've ended up with."

"So, you had 50 or 60 to deal with over the years," Michael said, "and the Bishop of Durham had his 50 or 60, and Exeter, and Manchester, and Norfolk, not to mention four or five bishops in London, plus every other diocese in the country. And those 50 or 60 became 400 or 500, they became more than 2,000, and a pestilence turned into a plague. That's how many priests are expected to be arrested, Archbishop. Two thousand. And we're not including retired priests, and that doesn't include the pedophiles sent from St. Simon's and Cardiff to Canada, to the United States, and to Australia. This is what your rationalizing has led to."

Johnston looked at Michael but said nothing.

"What happened to Frawley?" Michael asked.

"He spent more time in treatment and addiction centers than in parishes," Johnston said. "Much later, he was diagnosed with Alzheimer's Disease. He is still alive, in a hospital in York, but his mind is completely gone."

"Do you ever wonder what happened to the boy?" Michael said. "The altar boy?"

"I will be honest with you, Father Michael. I do not."

"He would be what, now?" Michael said. "Forty-one or forty-two?"

Johnston nodded.

"So, Archbishop," Michael said, "what has that boy with the high cheekbones had to live with his entire life, assuming he's still alive? Guilt? Shame? Nightmares? Did he have to have counseling for years? Does he sit around wondering if he could ever truly feel like a man? Does he hate God? All he was asked to do by that child rapist was to serve God, right? That's what Frawley called it, is that right?"

Johnston had been staring at the table. He looked up and faced Michael directly. "There's another thing I need to confess, Father Michael."

"What more can you say?" Michael said. "Do I want to hear this?"

"Perhaps not," Johnston said, "but I need to tell you. For years I've worked closely with Sebastian and Canon Land on all of this. Even after the conflict when you spoke at the Bishops Conference last spring, we worked together. The only thing that changed was that Canon Land became my primary contact at Lambeth Palace." He cleared his throat. "Several times during these past few weeks, he asked me to contact you to see if I could learn any information that might help Sebastian and the rest of us."

"We talked, what, three times?" Michael said. "Did you learn anything helpful?"

Johnston shook his head. "Only by inference of implication. Land asked to see if I could somehow influence you to in turn influence Scotland Yard, and I told him no, that he didn't understand our relationship and that if I did that you would realize what I was doing immediately. But I did try to find out what you knew."

For a time, Michael said nothing. "You were the only one left in the church hierarchy," he said finally, "that I thought I could trust. You're telling me now that I was wrong. But even then, I didn't tell you much."

"You didn't," Johnston said. "Michael, I'm sorry."

Michael stood, tears on his cheeks. "I loved you. I was proud to have you as my sponsor and mentor. I wanted no one else to crown me king." He paused, his hand on the doorknob. "The worst part of this is that I still love you. I will pray for you, Archbishop, and I will pray that God forgives me my anger. And I'm angry especially because I still care for you. I wish I could hate you. It would make all of this easier to bear somehow."

Michael opened the door and left.

Johnston stared at the open doorway.

From Scotland Yard, Officer Abbott accompanied Michael to City Hall. He had two department heads left to talk with, and those would be finished by 2 p.m. The discussions had gone well; everyone was trying to be helpful and at the same time walked a bit on eggshells; Michael had the power to dismiss without cause, if need be. But so far, he had not encountered any reason or cause at all.

What he had found was a recurring theme about the commissions. The heads of the departments never directly criticized the commissions, but they might as well have done so. The commissions had been set up to placate simmering issues, unhappy constituents, a polyglot of reasons, and they all operated outside the regular departmental activities and budget. And it had been the commissions that had been at the center of the dispute that led to the city shutdown.

Michael saw the solution: eliminate the commissions as separate entities and fold their work into the appropriate departments. He could get away with it without political repercussions as the emergency executive. He would meet with the commission heads next week, and then he would announce the move. He would also consider something of a homily or sermon to accompany the announcement – explain why the commissions were bad ideas.

Finished at 2 p.m., Michael left to return to the palace. In his new office, which Myra Frobisher had made sure was left in perfect order after the broadcast, he spent a good hour in a conference call with Father John Stevens and Paul Finley in San Francisco. Father John was the head pastor of St. Anselm's in San Francisco, and the priest Michael had served under during his two years as assistant pastor. He had conducted Michael and Sarah's wedding service. Paul Finley had been the chair of the church's elder board when Michael came to St. Anselm's, and he was continuing to serve in that capacity. Paul was a real estate developer who had sold Michael the loft condominium near the church that had been home for him and Jim and then Sarah and Jason.

Hearing their voices felt like a balm on his soul. "I can't tell you how good it is to hear you," Michael said.

"You've had your hands full, Michael," said Father John. "The Archbishops of Canterbury and York arrested along with, what is it now, 200 priests?"

"It's 250," Michael said. "And five bishops."

"Do you think this is the end of it?" Paul asked.

"The police are still treating this as an open investigation," Michael said. "Detective-Inspector Frees says we're only at the beginning. The number could go much higher, perhaps involving a fourth of the active priests in Britain."

"A fourth?" said Father John. "That would put it at 2,000, perhaps a bit higher." He was quiet as the reality sunk in. "You're talking a very different church on the other side of this. Michael, this is a heavy burden for you to carry."

"Well, Father John," Michael said, "it helps to know that it's really God who's carrying the burden. But there have been times in the past 10 or so days when it's been very hard." He paused for a moment. "I'm calling to ask for your help. We've formed a team to look at all of this and figure out what needs to be done. Not just about the recent events, although that's certainly a major focus, but also about the church's future. And I'd like both of you to help if you can. What that means is spending a full week here in London, and then undertaking various assignments. What I think would be particularly valuable for us to get hold of is how the governance system works, with a strong lay leadership and also a strong priest or minister."

"But it's really more to learn what's inside your heads and your hearts. I'll cover all of your expenses, of course, including the air fare for you and Emma and Eileen. I know you were just here in May for the coronation, but we would love to see all of you again, and you could stay with us here at the palace. If you need to think about it, you can get back to me, and you won't hurt my feelings if you can't. But we truly need your perspectives, and I think you could add a lot to what we're trying to do."

"What exactly is that, Michael?" asked Paul.

"Create a new Church of England," Michael said. "That's as simple as I know how to say it. The old church is dead, Father John. I had originally been thinking in terms of a new reformation, but I think we're well beyond that. This scandal is like a stake to the heart. We're still seeing the quivering, but the stake is in."

At first, all he heard in response was silence.

"I thought both of you had a considerable amount to offer," Michael said, continuing. "Father John, you somehow managed to lead an inner-city church to begin to grow again. And Paul, to me you represent the kind of active lay leader that I think we desperately need here in Britain. Strong teams of lay leaders would help provide accountability for the priests and bishops, assuming we even have bishops when this is all over. I think what I may be talking about here is a presbyterian model for an episcopal church, which flies right in the face of half a millennium of Church of England history. But the episcopal model seems to have brought the church to a disastrous dead end, and then it played a kind of co-dependent role in decades of child abuse. So, spiritual growth and accountability are two of the goals I'm setting before this group."

"Who have you asked to lead it, Michael?" Father John asked.

"I announced last night that Paul Nkane, Archbishop of Lagos, will be the new Archbishop of Canterbury," Michael said. "He's a little uncomfortable with my ideas for strong lay boards, but he understands why I think they're so important. And while he knows I probably won't compromise on this, he also understands that I will listen. So, this won't be a slam dunk for Father Michael's crazy ideas; there'll be lots of discussion and debate. I've also told Paul that he has my full support in restoring the supremacy of Scripture and whatever restructuring of the administration is needed. I believe he intends to rid Lambeth Palace of whatever vestiges of Sebastian Rowland and so-called liberal theology may be left.

"But leading the reform panel, my study team or think tank, is an attorney named Trevor Barry. He's been a consultant for me on monarchial law and parliamentary law, and he's spent the last few months turning himself into an expert on ecclesiastical law and history as well. I should tell you that he is not a believer, although he is married to a Christian. We're working on him, of course, and I know it sounds odd to have a non-believer leading an effort like this one, but I've come to have an enormous trust in him. It sounds odd, but I keep hearing God tell me that this is the man he wants in this position. I'm hopeful that, one day, God will explain why, but for now, this is sufficient."

"Michael," Father John finally said, "sign me up. I'll rearrange whatever I need to rearrange."

"Me, too, Michael," said Paul Finley. "And we're honored that you've asked us to participate. When do you want us to come?"

The reaction to Michael's speech was swift, and it was overwhelmingly positive and supportive. The opposition within the church hierarchy to Michael's reform proposals collapsed with the arrest of Sebastian Rowland, and it remained mute, fully grasping that the future of the Church of England was in grave doubt and that it would not be the Rowland faction trying to save it.

The news media, even the most liberal, showed the king solid support.

As *The Times* pointed out in a front-page editorial the day after the broadcast, "King Michael accepted the Church of England's responsibility for the child abuse scandal, said restitution would be made to the fullest extent possible, and raised the possibility of dissolution. We can't imagine any other public figure today accepting that kind of responsibility. And more than that was what he didn't say

– that he and his family gave shelter to two of the abuse victims, and that he played an instrumental role in bringing this evil to light.

"We are awed and humbled by our young king. May God bless him."

An opinion poll taken by *The Guardian* over the weekend showed support for the king at an astonishing 96 percent.

But even more shocking was what happened in the churches.

The first Sunday after the broadcast, most of the churches stood virtually empty. The Sunday after that, following an appeal by Michael via an interview with *The Guardian*, churches were packed. At packed, standing-room-only worship services across Britain, even in churches with no priests where services were led by lay volunteers, men and boys of a variety of ages began to come forward, to say what had happened to them at the hands of priests. More than 12,000 men made statements. More than 800 priests would be arrested as a result, bringing the total at that time close to 1,400. And the investigation would continue.

A week after that, the first arrests would be reported in North America and Australia.

Roger and Sylvia Frees arrived at the palace on Saturday at noon. Michael had told them they would be eating with the family in the loft, and that Saturdays were mandatory dress casual. And to underscore the point, Michael told them that he and Sarah would be in blue jeans.

Sarah and Jason had fixed serve-yourself chili and sandwiches, while Robert and Jim set the table. Michael was ordered away from the kitchen and placed in charge of chasing Hank around the loft.

Ryan Mitchell, the palace's security chief, brought the policeman and his wife to the loft

Sylvia Frees was about 40, Michael saw, about the same age as her husband. She was slender and had dark hair. Something about her reeked of doctor – Michael expected to see her whip out a white coat at any moment. As they ate and talked, he could see her eyes keep finding Robert, evoking a smile each time.

"It's such a lovely day," Sarah said, "why don't we walk in the gardens? Hank loves to run in the grass." They soon found themselves in the gardens and grassy areas so well maintained by Mr. Albright, with Jason and Jim running with a football thrown between them and Robert walking along the gravel walks with Roger and Sylvia.

At one point, Frees peeled away from his wife while Robert and Sylvia continued to walk and talk together. He strolled over to Michael and Sarah.

"Your gardeners have really done a fine job here," Frees said.

"Mr. Albright's just started," Michael said. "When we arrived last December, he took us on a tour of essentially what was the garden structure at the time, what with winter and all. He had barely been able to keep what was here, with all of the financial problems the royals were having at the time. So, we had him start drawing up a master plan, and my Ma helped some with that. He started phase one this spring. Phase two next spring will be the big one, with some major gardens being put in. And phase three the following year."

"It's a shame it has to be behind the gate, so to speak," Frees said. "Many people would love to see it. You might even charge admission."

Michael looked at him thoughtfully. "That's an idea, Detective-Inspector. We're considering opening the palace for summer tours again, to help pay for maintenance and upkeep. A tour of the garden could be part of that." Sarah could see wheels beginning to turn in Michael's mind.

"So, how are Robert and Sylvia getting on?" she asked.

Frees nodded and smiled. "I think this is going to work out."

A few minutes later, Robert and Sylvia walked up to them.

"Your majesties," Sylvia said, "this has been a lovely time. We've been talking, and Robert's going to come stay with us."

Robert nodded. "I don't know how to thank you, sir, I mean for taking me in and taking care of me." He paused. "We're going to go get the rest of my clothes and things at the old place, and then we're going home."

"That's wonderful, Robert," Michael said. He looked at the three of them. "This has been the very best part of all of this. And it's been God's blessing that we've gotten to be part of it." He suddenly looked around, and saw Hank running toward Jason and Jim. "And pardon me just a moment while I catch the little rascal." Michael dashed after Hank.

The team appointed to study the C of E convened on November 5. They were assisted by Michael's legal and accounting firms, which had started working on legal issues and an accounting of the church's assets the Monday after Michael's address on the BBC.

The first two days of meetings were focused on the child abuse scandal and possible mechanisms for restitution. The next three days were focused on the future of the Church of England. Father John made an in-depth presentation on how inner-city churches could grow, and Paul Finley spoke on the role of a strong lay board in guiding the church. Eileen Stevens and Emma Finley got to play tourist with Sarah, who cleared her schedule for the week.

On that Friday, Archbishop Nkane announced the proposal for restitution, which included the sale of numerous church properties and the proceeds devoted to payments to victims and their families. Michael and Sarah supplemented the fund with a one-billion-pound donation and insisted that it be anonymous.

Two weeks later, Nkane announced the first in a series of changes for the church. All of the existing 15 C of E commissions, including the Commission on Diversity in Church Life and the Commission on Israeli Aggression in the Mideast, were disbanded immediately. Four departments were closed, including the Office of Social Justice. The Administrative Offices on Great Smythe Street, where Michael had received his assignment for St. Anselm's Parish in San Francisco, were closed, with some functions moved to Lambeth Palace and others discontinued, with the property itself put up for sale, the proceeds of which were to support the restitution fund. It's location in the City of London brought intense investment interest.

On December 1, Archbishop Nkane and Trevor Barry announced the initial findings of the study team, which would be implemented beginning in January. The broad array of recommendations ranged from a return to the old-style Book of Common Prayer for church liturgy to the appointment of lay elder boards for every church parish. Training programs were to be implemented for lay leadership. The power of the bishops and archbishops over individual parishes was to be sharply curtailed, and each parish priest would report to the church's board of lay elders.

A new denominational structure was to be created, with major church decisions made in an assembly of both clergy and lay leaders, and with lay leaders being in the majority. The bishops would report to the Archbishop of Canterbury, who would in turn report to the new assembly, which would be led by a board of lay leaders and presided over by the king. Several seminaries were to be closed, including St. Simon's, with training of men for the priesthood to be concentrated in three locations – London, Edinburgh and Birmingham. Seminary properties were also to be put up for sale. Almost 1,000 parish churches were to close, with some buildings mothballed for possible future expansion and others sold outright.

Chapter 20: Dancing Prophet

In mid-December, the third- and fourth-year classes at ICS had their annual Christmas formal. Usually held at a hotel, the event this year would be at Buckingham Palace, courtesy of one third-year, upper school student with a solid connection to King Michael and Queen Sarah.

Wearing his tuxedo, the first time since the coronation ball in May, Jason rode in a palace security car to Jane Barry's house. Beside him was the corsage he had for her. He had conspired with Jane's mother Liz to figure out the best kind (wrist) and the best color for her dress (a bluish-green formal that matched her eyes). He had also bought a small bouquet for Liz, and a single, long-stemmed red rose for Jane.

When the doorbell rang, Jane, in the last throes of the panic of getting ready in her room, stared wildly at her mother. "Mother, he's early!" she said in a wail.

Liz smiled, two pins in her mouth as she helped put the last touches on Jane's hair. "Keep still. We're almost done. He's not early; he's on time. And I don't think he'll leave without you." Liz was in a new formal dress herself; she and Trevor had volunteered to be chaperones.

Trevor, in a tuxedo but not yet wearing the jacket, answered the door.

"Hi, Mr. Barry," Jason said. "I've come for Jane."

Trevor smiled and shook his hand as Jason balanced the collection of flowers. "I believe she's almost ready, which, when you're older, you'll come to recognize as meaning that liftoff is anywhere from 10 to 30 minutes away." Jason grinned.

In his tuxedo, and with his wavy, longish hair, Jason looked all grown up. Trevor smiled to himself. *You blink your eyes and these children have become adults.*

Liz walked into the living room. "Hello, Jason. She's got just a few minutes and she'll be down. You look wonderful in that tux."

He blushed. "Thank you, Mrs. Barry. You look really hot yourself." He handed her the small bouquet. "This is a small thanks for helping me with the corsage."

"Oh, Jason, they're lovely," said Liz. "Let me find a vase. Thank you so much." And she went toward the kitchen, blushing (and simultaneously pleased and embarrassed) at being called hot by a teenaged boy but knowing that "the boy with the rough edges" had meant it as an honest compliment.

"As you Americans like to say, Jason," Trevor said, grinning, "I believe that was a home run." *Although I'm not sure if it was the flowers or the compliment that knocked it out of the stadium.*

"She's nice, you know?" Jason said. "I mean, well, you know she's nice, but she really went out of her way to help me with the corsage."

"You're right," Trevor said. "She's nice." *And you're right, she's hot.*

Liz came back in with the flowers in a vase and placed them on the fireplace mantle.

"That's lovely, Jason, thank you," she said and squeezed his arm.

And then Jason looked up the stairs. Jane was coming down, smiling shyly. To her father, she looked like a grown and beautiful woman, and he felt his heart simultaneously soaring and breaking.

Her blue-green dress was formal length with small shoulder straps. The color highlighted the color of her eyes. Her hair was put up, and Liz had managed to dress it with small, discreet flowers. The dress fit fairly closely to her body, not too closely to be suggestive but close enough to say that this was a very attractive young woman. Jane and Liz spent weeks looking for the dress.

Trevor looked at Jason watching his daughter. The boy positively glowed. And with sudden but absolute certainty, Trevor was startled to realize that this young man, this American with the rough edges, would one day be his son-in-law and the father of his grandchildren. *And it's good. She'll be safe in his hands. I can trust him to take care of her.*

Then he looked at Jane, and he saw the same glow as she looked at Jason.

Jason turned to Trevor with a smile that lit up his face. "Have you ever seen anyone so beautiful?" he asked.

Trevor nodded. "Yes. I married her."

Jason turned to Jane. "You look beautiful. I've got the best-looking girl at the dance." And the girl blushed. Liz handed her the flower for Jason's lapel.

Liz had been watching Trevor and Jason's reactions to Jane, and saw that these two men, one young and one middle aged, had bonded in an extraordinary way. And then blushing with the warmth of Trevor's words, she stood on her toes and kissed him.

Jason grinned at Trevor. "I think it was your turn to hit the home run." And Trevor laughed.

The cars were lined up for the security check at the palace, each driver and license plate checked against the pre-arranged list. With four security agents working the cars, the line moved unexpectedly quickly. Some of the young people had driven; others were being dropped off by parents at the interior courtyard entrance.

As the students entered the palace, they first checked their coats, and then were directed down the long hallway toward the stairs or elevator. The palace was decorated for Christmas. The official dining hall on the first floor had been turned into a buffet supper room, with the ballroom next door.

Dr. Owens and his wife Martha stood next to Michael and Sarah, greeting the students as they approached. The band was already playing.

Robert Hood walked up with his date, Amanda Jenner, both of them attending their first dance. Robert smiled and shook Michael's hand, and Sarah hugged him.

Michael looked at his wife. She looked spectacular. Sarah's hair was up, and he could see the gentle slope of her neck, and he was having great trouble resisting a touch. The dress was a golden, almost yellow, silk and wool blend with silk shoulder straps and a plunging back. Around her neck she wore a simple pearl on gold chain, the one he had given her for their first Christmas together when they were still students. *She's dazzling*, he thought.

Michael was in a tuxedo. He and Sarah had debated, and then decided to wear the platinum crowns of their coronation and the ones used for all state and formal occasions. And the students loved it, the crowns adding to the allure and splendor of an event at Buckingham Palace.

Elton Jenner arrived, introduced his date, and walked on. It was the first time he had been allowed to attend a dance, his mother smiling when he had asked and received her permission. Sarah caught Michael's eye and squeezed his hand.

Then came Jason and Jane.

Michael watched them as the Owens greeted them, and he was struck by the complementary thought to that which had struck Trevor Barry earlier. *This young woman will be our daughter-in-law*.

"Your majesty," Jane said, as she curtsied.

Michael took her hand and kissed it. "You're beautiful, Jane. And I'm speaking of both the young woman and her spirit."

"Hi, Dad," Jason said, grinning.

"And then there's this rascal," Michael said, laughing, pulling Jason to him to hug him.

Jane was greeting Sarah as Jason looked at his father and arched his eyebrows with a smile in Sarah's direction.

"Yes, son," said Michael, "I know. She's hot."

Sarah heard him. "Mike, behave."

It was crowded and festive. The students moved back and forth from the dining room to the ballroom. Chaperones were here, there and everywhere, but managed to keep themselves in the background. Dr. Owens was particularly pleased with how well behaved the students were.

At one point, Michael led Sarah to the dance floor, and Michael at first suggested a jitterbug, which Sarah declined. "A waltz, Michael, if you please," she said. Ivan Mercer led the applause afterward. "Didn't I tell you King Michael rocks?" he yelled. And the students roared back, "King Michael rocks!"

At about 10, still early in the evening and with Sarah talking to some of the chaperones in the dining hall, Michael slipped away and went to the small dining room down the hall and around the corner from the main events. A fire was going in the fireplace, and he pulled a chair in front of it. He thought back to the events of September and October and the tumult of change that was following for the church, and the stability created for London, and he said a small prayer of thanks for what God had seen them through.

"Oh, I'm sorry, your majesty. I was looking for the WC and I think I took a wrong turn," said Trevor Barry, who then wondered if he had just committed a major faux pas by mentioning the bathroom in the presence of the king.

"It's good to see you, my trusted counselor," Michael said, and Trevor shook the king's hand. "You did take a wrong turn for the WC, but if you go through the door there across from us, you'll find another one on the left. There are all kinds of surprises tucked away around here."

When Trevor returned, Michael was standing by the fire, and smiled at him.

"I have to tell you, Trevor, that we love Jane," Michael said. "She's a delightful girl."

"And Jason, sir, seems like a part of our family," Trevor said.

Michael laughed. "Don't take this the wrong way, but our Jason spends so much time at your house that Sarah and I refer to you as the in-laws." Trevor laughed with him. "And I'll call you Trevor if you'll call me Michael." Seeing the surprised look on Trevor's face, Michael gestured with his hand. "I know it's not the official thing you're supposed to do, but sometimes it's a relief to be called just by my name. So, you have an official dispensation from the king of Great Britain to call him Michael." He paused, and then spoke. "Could I interest you in a glass of wine? You won't hurt my feelings if you say no."

"A glass of wine would be great, Michael," Trevor said.

"Follow me," and he walked Trevor back to the kitchen, which was calmer than earlier but still busy.

"Mr. Malone," Michael called.

"Yes, your majesty?" The palace's executive chef stuck his head out of the pantry door.

"Do you think you might rustle up a couple of glasses of wine?" He looked at Trevor. "Red or white?"

"White, if you have it."

"Mr. Malone, do we have some of that California Chardonnay you served the other night?"

"Yes, sir, we do." And in short order the chef brought the two full glasses to Michael and Trevor.

Michael and Trevor wandered back to the small dining room and sat in front of the fireplace.

"Did Jason tell me that you're an enthusiastic cyclist?"

Trevor laughed. "Well, I'm not in the same league as an Olympic gold medalist, Michael, but it is my sport. Andrew was interested for a while, but as he's gotten older he's been veering more to football. So, you can often find me solo on some of the biking trails and lanes in western and northern London, and occasionally I take a few days off for a cycling vacation."

"Why haven't we talked about this before?" Michael said. "And where do you go?"

"Generally, all over," Trevor said. "I've done Cornwall and Wales, and the Oxford area. I'm thinking about going to Norfolk in the spring for a weekend. Liz sometimes comes along but generally stays at the hotel or B-and-B and does some shopping or just sleeps in. And once or twice I've stayed with my parents in Yorkshire and biked around my old stomping grounds."

Something stirred in Michael's memory. *Yorkshire*. But he couldn't connect it.

"Where in Yorkshire?" Michael said.

"It's a small town in the west, about 40 or so miles from Leeds. From my parents' house, I can bike almost to the Pennines."

"Jason says your family is Evangelical Presbyterian. Were you raised in that church?"

Michael saw a shadow cross Trevor's face.

"No, actually I was raised C of E," Trevor said, "but I left in my early teens, no offense intended."

"None taken," Michael said.

"I joined Liz's church when we were married," Trevor said. "She was raised Evangelical Presbyterian, and I had become kind of a nothing in religion."

"When you were in the C of E, would you have known or met Philip Johnston? It's an odd question, I suppose, given that he's in prison now, and seven months ago he was the Archbishop of York and put this crown on my head. But he told me he started his pastoral career in western Yorkshire. I think the parish was called St. Timothy's? Do you know it?"

Trevor stared at Michael, not answering.

"I'm sorry, is something wrong?" Michael asked.

"St. Timothy's was my parish." He hesitated. "I met Philip Johnston only once, his first week there. I stopped going to church about that time. Not because of him, but, well, I just stopped."

Then it hit Michael. *Western Yorkshire…St. Timothy's…the altar boy with the high cheekbones. Father God, this is unbelievable.*

Trevor saw the look of understanding on Michael's face. *He knows.*

The two men stared at each other.

"Trevor," said Michael, "the etiquette book says I should say something polite and shallow right now and steer the conversation into safer waters. But were you an altar boy at St. Timothy's?"

Trevor stared, and then nodded. "Did Jane say something about this?"

Michael shook his head. "No, she didn't. Nor did Jason, if he knew." And Michael explained his last conversation with the Archbishop of York at the police station in October.

Trevor sipped his wine. "I told the family. I told them when the scandal was happening, and Jane was struggling with how to respond to Jason."

"Your wife didn't know?" Michael said.

Trevor shook his head.

"I asked the Archbishop if he knew what had happened to you, or if he wondered about you," Michael said. "But he didn't know."

"Do you know what happened with Rev. Frawley?" Trevor asked, his eyes clouding.

"The Archbishop said that some years back he was diagnosed with Alzheimer's," Michael said. "And while he's still alive, his mind is completely gone."

Trevor looked down at the wine glass in his hand. "I wish my own memories were wiped away." He hesitated. "Liz and the kids have been unbelievably supportive. But there are times I still feel broken. It's amazing. This was more than 30 years ago, and I can still feel broken." He looked at Michael. "I never talked about this with anyone else. I don't know why I'm talking about it with the king of Britain. I don't mean to put you in a bad spot."

"You're not putting me in a bad spot," Michael said. "But I think I know why, Trevor. Just like your missing the turn for the WC and coming in here tonight. And I just happened to be sitting here by the fire, thanking God for what he's brought us through. In October, I told Father John and Paul Finley that I had a non-believer leading my church reform team, and that I knew he was the best man for the job because God had told me he was. What I didn't know was why.

"Now I know why. Who better to lead the effort than someone who lived it, who knew first-hand exactly what it was? As hard as I know it must be for you, I think we were supposed to have this conversation. I'm honored that you would talk with me about it." He smiled. "The man who helped raise that delightful young woman must be special indeed."

Trevor smiled. "Thank you, Michael."

"So," Michael said, "I was wondering. Might you be open to have another cyclist come along on one of your rides?"

"You?" Trevor said.

Michael nodded. "I need to get back on my bike on a regular basis. I use a stationary training bike here in the palace and occasionally get out, but it's rare. And it's always better if you can cycle with a friend."

"The weather is supposed to fairly mild tomorrow," Trevor said, "and I was going to get in a good ride. You'd be more than welcome if you're free, but I'm not quite in your league."

"I am free," Michael said, "and I'm not in my league any more, either. A major surgery in San Francisco last year changed a lot of that. It may be more a question of if I'm in your league. And I'll likely have to drag a security officer along with us. What time?"

"Can you meet me at my house at 10?" Trevor said. "There's a pub along the way where we could get something to eat. Do you need directions to our house?"

"I think 10 will work fine," Michael said. "And I don't need directions. Every one of our drivers and security officers knows exactly where you live, because Jason's had them memorize the route."

Trevor laughed. And then he smiled. "Thank you, Michael."

As Michael smiled back, Sarah and Liz walked into the room.

"I was looking for my husband," Sarah said, "and when Liz told me her husband was a cyclist, I knew if I found her husband I'd likely find mine. So, tell me, were you two talking bikes when we walked in here?"

Michael and Trevor both burst into laughter.

"That answered my question," she said. "Gentlemen, it's time to return to the dance."

Back in the loft, the party over (and a great success), Sarah was still in her dress, sitting on Michael's lap in the overstuffed chair in the living area, her arms around his neck. Her shoes were off, as were Michael's, and he had undone his tie.

"I finally get to touch your neck," he said, as he traced his fingers across her back. "I could barely resist touching you when we were standing in the reception line."

"You'd have scandalized Dr. Owens and half the student body if you had," Sarah said.

He nuzzled the side of her face and hair. "You look fabulous. This dress is unbelievable. I wonder how the zipper works."

"We are waiting up for our son, to see how his evening went," Sarah said.

"There's always someone ready to kill the party," Michael said, with an exaggerated sigh.

A few minutes later, Jason came through the loft's main door. He walked over to them and kissed Sarah on her cheek and Michael on his head. He plopped on the floor.

"You guys really know how to throw a party," he said, starting to take off his shoes. "It was a total blast."

"Did Jane have a good time?" Sarah said.

He looked at them both, and then answered her. "She had a great time. I'm going to marry her one day, Mom." Seeing the surprised look on Sarah's face but not on Michael's, he nodded to his father and said, "Dad knows."

Sarah looked at Michael. "You do?"

"When they came through the reception line," Michael said, "something told me this was our future daughter-in-law."

Jason was staring, almost open-mouthed. "I know this sounds weird, but the first time I saw Jane in the library, it was like I knew as soon as I saw her. I knew she was the one created for me, and I was created for her."

"Oh, my," said Sarah. "This is serious. I think I've heard this before."

Michael smiled. "It's what I thought, son, when I first saw your mother here in our class in Edinburgh. Almost word for word. And while it took about a year longer than I would have liked, it turned out to be a pretty good result."

"Well, then," Jason said, grinning, "everything's cool."

After Jason had gone to bed, Sarah, still sitting in Michael's lap, had her head leaning against her husband's. She stroked his cheek.

"It didn't sound like Jason was making that up, Mike," she said.

"Sounded pretty authentic to me," Michael said.

"But they're still a bit young to be making major decisions," Sarah said.

"So, I suppose, my Sarah, we'll just have to have faith and see what happens."

"Mike?"

"Yes, my own self?"

"I'd like to show you how that zipper works."

"It's a plan."

"But first, I need to tell you something else," she said. "There's a reason I didn't want to jitterbug."

"Yes, my love?"

"I'm pregnant. I'm at eight weeks."

Michael was speechless.

"One other thing, Mike. The doctor's fairly certain it's twins."

The End

Acknowledgements

The heart of *Dancing Prophet* was written in 2007. It was my response to the arrest of a man in my St. Louis suburb of Kirkwood. His name was Michael Devlin; he was charge with scores of counts for the kidnapping and abuse of two boys, one of whom had disappeared several years before. Devlin lived in an apartment complex about 1 ½ miles from my house, on the route I biked several times each week.

I can't explain my reaction, but writing a story seemed to help. The story has nothing to do with Devlin, his victims, or my suburb, but it helped me make sense of what had happened.

Most of the manuscript for *Dancing Prophet* was written before the latest round of scandals engulfing the clergy and hierarchy of the Roman Catholic Church. This story was not meant to be prophetic. I can say two things. First, most of this was written long before a U.S. cardinal resigned, and an 887-page Pennsylvania grand jury report was published. Second, my story is mild compared to the reality.

On a trip to England in 2017, I spent a considerable amount of time in the area known as the Temple, Lincoln's Inn Fields, and the Royal Courts of Justice – the heart of the legal profession in Britain. If you want to know where the character of Trevor Barry came from, walking those streets, seeing courtrooms, discovering Horace Rumpole-like pubs, and peering in windows at sale prices for wigs and gowns might explain it.

Several people played an important role in the publication of this book.

The tour staff at Buckingham Palace and Windsor Castle are some of the most knowledgeable people you can find. I hate to ask questions (ask my wife; it's like asking for directions), but the tour guides, ticket sellers, and room guards always had interesting things to say.

Mark Sutherland at Dunrobin Publishing always manages to find the time to read a manuscript and always comes back with something encouraging to say. Carrie Sutherland and Jodi Richardson served as proofreaders and the first two readers after Mark. Ryan Stiles came up with a smashing cover design; he designed the one for *Dancing King* as well.

And I have reading friends who've been with me from the beginning: Susan Cannon, Jim Tobin, Megan Willome, Randy Mayfield, Diana Trautwein, J of India (he knows who he is), Sandra Heska King, Martha Orlando, Susan Jones, Luke Davis, Charity Singleton Craig, Doug Spurling, Lane Arnold, Susan Kirkpatrick, Cindee Re, and so many more. They've offered encouragement and support.

Readers include my children – Travis and Stephanie with my three grandsons, and Andrew with his two Boston terriers. And they include my wife, Janet, who's always been there. Without her love and support, there would be no books.

About the Author

Glynn Young is the author of *Dancing Priest*, *A Light Shining*, and *Dancing King*, the first three books in the Dancing Priest series, and the non-fiction book *Poetry at Work*. He is an award-winning speechwriter and public relations executive and was named a Fellow of the Public Relations Society of America in 2005 and a member of the St. Louis Media Hall of Fame in 2009.

A native of New Orleans, Glynn received a B.A. degree in Journalism from Louisiana State University in Baton Rouge and a Masters in Liberal Arts degree from Washington University in St. Louis.

He is a contributing editor to the online poetry journal Tweetspeak Poetry (www.tweetspeakpoetry.com) and blogs at Faith, Fiction, Friends (faithfictionfriends.blogspot.com) and his professional blog (glynnyoung.com). You can find more information about the Dancing Priest series at dancingpriest.com.

Glynn and his wife Janet live in suburban St. Louis. They have two adult sons, Travis and Andrew; a daughter-in-law, Stephanie; and three grandsons, Cameron, Caden, and Jacob.

www.ingramcontent.com/pod-product-compliance
Lightning Source LLC
Chambersburg PA
CBHW030748030726
47497CB00001B/193